DUNOON

10 SEP
2 2 NO
19 JUN 2014   17 APR 201
1 2 JUL 2014
7 FEB 2012

KV-579-238

VULTURE'S
LAIR

By

HALLUR HALLSSON

Argyll and Bute

34115 00523729 8

All rights reserved. No reproduction of any part of this
publication is permitted without the prior written
permission of the publisher:

English Publication 2012
Copyright © Hallur Hallsson 2012

Bretwalda Books
Unit 8, Fir Tree Close, Epsom, Surrey KT17 3LD
www.BretwaldaBooks.com

To receive an e-catalogue of our complete range of books
send an email to info@BretwaldaBooks.com

ISBN 978-1-907791-22-2

Printed and bound in Great Britain by
CPI Group (UK) Ltd, Croydon, CR0 4YY

Bretwalda Books Ltd

The closed mind paves the way to serfdom,
where Nay is Hell's estate and the Devil
its landlord.

All that has happened, can happen, and
all that can happen, happens in the eternal
stream of time.

A nation's struggle for survival at the
farthest reaches of the sea will last
throughout the ages.

ARGYLL AND BUTE LIBRARY SERVICE	
34115005237298	
Bertrams	17/07/2012
	£9.99

Heavily armed guards rush in formation from their armoured vehicles. The wail of a siren echoes off the highrises and blue flashing lights attract curious passers-by to the scene. The bright lights of TV cameras and camera flashbulbs amplify the tension. Sólman Smithson jumps out of a black limousine and runs in the direction of the European Fisheries Bureau in the Berlaymont Building, which extends outward from its core in four directions and reaches thirteen storeys to the sky.

Dressed in his neat blue suit and carrying a briefcase, Sólman regards the scene with distaste. "Bloody mess. These people do nothing but cause problems," he growls angrily.

In the lobby he finds broken windows and a truck. Someone has driven the huge rig through the door, smashed up the entrance and dumped fish on the floor. A rank smell emanates from the putrid pollock scattered all over. The scene is deafening. Someone curses vigorously in terse Icelandic. A deep, powerful voice fills the room with an old Icelandic hit from the Cod Wars:

Though the cod is none too bright,
it's none too fond of Kom'zars'.

A roar of laughter follows.

Sólman spins round as he recognizes the voice. "Krummi!" he exclaims. "All we need now is for old Helgi to arrive to really stir things up."

A giant of a man stands on top of the wrecked truck. He is wearing a pair of old jeans, wellington boots and an old, chunky jumper. A great black beard cascades down to his chest while a battered old cap is perched on top of a mass of unruly black hair. As Sólman watches, the giant Icelandic fisherman stoops to pick up a pollock and hurls it at a gaping bureaucrat, catching the man a blow on the face.

Sólman shakes his head in disbelief. Krummi had lost a bone in his middle finger and was afterward nicknamed "Krummi Nine-and-a-Half" back in the Westmann Islands. Now the powerful giant is at it again, troublemaking and demonstrating; this time in Brussels. Ever since the incident at the Selvogur fishing ground all those years ago, Krummi has been blacklisted by the police throughout Europe. It is a wonder that the Fish Fight Club that Krummi set up has not been Black listed by the authorities.

There are six men throwing putrid pollock at the armed guards, which is naturally an uneven match. Shouts and curses ring throughout the lobby. The Icelandic fishermen led by Krummi are putting up something of a fight. This isn't the first time that men from Iceland have caused trouble in Brussels but this time they have little chance against the superior numbers of police. One by one they are handcuffed.

Finally Krummi is the only one left standing. He is up on the stairway landing, besieged by six guards. The giant Islander grins; his white teeth flashing in his pitch-black beard, eagle eyes sparkle with pride and prowess, thick black hair curls down his neck. He flings a particularly big pollock at the guards.

"Take that as a present from the men of the Fish Fight Club", he shouts. Three of the guards fall flat into the slimy fish offal. It's a sight to see them drop, their arms and legs flapping. More guards join in, making it nine assaulting Krummi on the landing. They pummel the Islander, who staggers but laughs thunderously. There's a gleam in his eye, the pride of an undaunted man against a superior force.

He jumps from the landing and slides across the slippery floor. The deep voice resounds throughout the lobby. "Are you having trouble keeping your feet, boys?" he says, roaring with laughter. Four of them lie in the offal, looking fairly shamefaced. The rest attack from two sides but Krummi defends himself agilely, striking them heavily with a pollock.

Krummi gives another monstrous laugh and puts down the fish. He takes a sheet of paper from his pocket and starts reading a declaration: "The Icelandic fishermen of the Fish Fight Club demand that control of the Icelandic fishing grounds be handed over to the Icelandic people…"

An abrupt whistle cleaves the air and bright flashes light up the lobby. The Westmann Giant covers his face with his hands when the intense light of the flash bomb cuts into his eyes and at once a net is cast over him, knocking him flat. A group of guards jump on him and manhandle him to the floor. A moment later Krummi is in handcuffs.

They've subdued the strongman.

Sólman goes over to his old friend as he lies there in the offal with four black-clad security guards, powerful as oxen, on top of him.

"Isn't that enough of this nonsense, Krummi?" asks Sólman, in an attempt to calm the powerful Islander. "Tossing around rotten pollock?"

"There is something rotten in the state of Brussels," replies the giant with a scowl.

"Why not cod?" asks Sólman.

"Icelandic hands haven't gutted cod in many a year. You should come out to the Islands and see how things are first-hand," replies Krummi. They've lifted the giant to his feet and Krummi towers over all of them, despite being bowed by the cuffs.

"Icelanders want to fish," growls Krummi, grinning despite a rapidly spreading black eye.

Sólman is at a loss for an answer.

"Subsidies devour people's pride and turn them into pitiful lazybones," says Krummi as they lead him away. "But not us in the Fish Fight Club. We still stand proud."

Sólman watches Krummi being marched away, then he grabs his holph and calls Mangi Steffensen, the Governor of Iceland. The Governor appears on the screen and Sólman projects him in hologram to his side. Steffensen is sitting in his opulent office in Reykjavík. Sólman stands amid the broken glass and rotten fish in the Berlaymont.

"Krummi's been busy here with his mischief and devilry. Smashed up what he could here in Brussels, beat a man or two with a putrid pollock," says Sólman morosely.

"God dammit. The Raven's at it again," replies Steffensen, clearly taken aback. They look each other in the eye: Sólman grave, angry, and accusatory and Steffensen defensive, sitting in his chair in Reykjavík.

The Governor stands up, finding it uncomfortable to have to look up at the Brussels bureaucrat. They face each other.

"The stench here is disgusting," says Sólman, scowling.

"It's rotten," replies Steffensen with a grimace, his nostrils distended. He covers his nose and hurriedly turns off the smell facility on the holph. Sólman turns the holph to show him the lobby, the heavily damaged truck, the twisted steel, broken glass and rotten fish. Steffensen glances over the area and has trouble suppressing a grin. Krummi is a damned troublemaker, but you have to hand it to him. What a mess!

"They're not pleased here in Brussels. They hadn't the slightest idea that Krummi was in town," says Sólman, waving someone away.

"I'll have it looked into, but that devil must have sailed from the Westmann Islands to slip into Brussels unnoticed," says Steffensen, who clearly wants to end the conversation as soon as possible.

"A report has to be filed on the security breach," says Sólman gruffly.

"I'll put the State Security Director on it," replies the Governor, turning away. The conversation is uncomfortable, so Steffensen reduces Sólman to one-quarter size; the bureaucrat from Brussels is less threatening at a smaller scale.

"The report has to be filed within a week," insists Sólman.

Governor Steffensen looks round and calls to someone out of view "Get me the State Security Director, and get him at once." He turns back to Sólman with a serious expression on his face. "Don't worry. We will sort things out at this end. You will get your report on time."

Sólman Smithson ends the call, then steps carefully through the glass fragments out onto the sidewalk. He pushes through the crowd that has gathered outside the doors of the Berlaymont and heads for his own office at the Peripheries Bureau. He's aggrieved that he's had to attend to this, but there was no avoiding it since the surveillance of vehicles is part of his department. He had protested that the project been assigned to the Peripheries. "It doesn't belong here," he had said but been overruled.

The never-ending Icelandic demonstrations are making things difficult. The situation is intolerable. The constant uproar and protests are giving Euro-Icelanders a bad name in Europe, particularly in Brussels.

A man in a black suit watches Sólman leave. He discreetly talks into his e-notebook and glances at the workmen already starting to clear up the rotten fish. Then he melts away into the crowd as if he had never been there.

In his office in Reykjavík, Governor Steffensen leans back in his chair and curses softly. "Bloody Sólman never did have a sense of humour," he mutters. The holph on his desk winks and he stabs the button to summon up an image of the State Security Director for Iceland. "Hello, Jón," he says wearily. "Heard the news from Brussels?"

The jovial face of Jón H. Matthíasson drifts into view as the holph gets into focus. "Watching it on the holoTV now, my dear Governor," says the grinning Matthíasson who is usually simply called Highpoint as have all the heads of security in Iceland since Iceland joined the European Union. "Krummi sure knows how to make a mess. Serves those stuck up snobs in Brussels right, if you ask me."

"Well, I didn't ask you," snaps Steffensen. "I've already had that prig Sólman Smithson on to me demanding a report on how Krummi got out of Iceland without anyone noticing."

"My team of watchers lost him in the fish market at Heimaey out on the Westmann Islands last week," says Highpoint turning away from the holoTV to look at Steffensen. "My guess is he hopped on to a fishing boat and got out that way. Probably went to Scotland. You know his Fish Fight Club has some members there?"

"Yes, I know," says Steffensen. "But your guess won't be good enough for Brussels, nor for Berlin. Check out which boats have been out of the Westmanns recently and which have put into Scotland. And check Ireland as well. You never know. I am afraid I am going to need answers for those Eurocrats who run our lives nowadays."

Highpoint nods, then turns back to the holoTV and chuckles as he flicks off the holph at his end.

Steffensen pulls his keyboard towards him and starts doing a Report Form as the basis of his report on Krummi to Sólman. He's never really got hold of this new technology. He has been Governor of Iceland for a decade and is getting fed up with the thankless task. Thank goodness retirement is not far off.

When he was a boy there was no such thing as a Governor of a member state of the EU at all. The position had been developed by the European Union in the wake of the Euro Crisis. The first Governor had been in Greece, and the second in Italy. At first they had been manoeuvred into positions as Prime Minister of their respective countries by the European Commission. Everyone had said the appointments of these unelected Eurocrats was to be just temporary to sort out the Euro crisis, then elections would be held. Of course, the elections had been put off again and again. Then the positions had been converted into those of Governors appointed by what was then the EU Commission. Of course the Commission paid attention to the views of those involved, but those tiresome elections had been done away with.

Things had been really bad in Europe during the Euro Crisis. As a sign of how crazy Europe had become, someone pointed out that the President of the European Central Bank was Italian and the Pope German. It simply couldn't get any crazier.

Governor Steffensen snorts. And now here he is stuck between the Devil and the deep blue sea. The Icelanders think all he does is pass on orders from Brussels and Berlin, while the Eurocrats think all he does is pass on moans from Iceland. He sighs. Perhaps he ought to join Krummi's Fish Fight Club. At least life would be simple then.

He resumes going through the files.

Next morning Sólman Smithson is on the train to Berlin for important meetings with the Financial kom'zariat regarding subsidies paid to the peripheral countries. He has bought today's copy of the *Bild* newspaper to catch up on the latest events in the capital city. It always helps to make some polite small talk with the Berlin Eurocrats before a meeting begins. The first headline to pop up on Sólman's e-reader makes for uncomfortable reading. "The Stench Comes from Berlaymont" screams the page. Naturally it reports everything in the worst possible terms. The offal and rank odour are considered symbolic of the collapse of European fisheries. Sólman goes through the headlines. He projects a story, listens to the soft computer-voice and once again watches Krummi in the Berlaymont. "Humiliated by Icelandic fisherman". The headlines are negative and depressing. Sólman scowls. That won't help the latest bid for funding for Reykjavík. He does not want to go through these depressing news stories on Iceland, so he projects a story on the war in Kazikistnam. "Bloody mess," runs the headline.

This is not a good start to the day. Sólman stares out the window at the landscape as it dashes by in the early morning sunlight.

Sólman hasn't visited the Westmann Islands since going to study in Copenhagen after graduating from Bifröst University. As a teenager he worked in the Westmann Islands for two summers processing capelin and helping out around the fishing ports. After moving to Brussels, Sólman had adopted the surname Smithson. He thought it appropriate to stick to the good old tradition so he kept the meaning of his father's name, but he changed the spelling from Smiðsson to Smithson as the latter is better understood in Europe.

Sólman Smithson has quite a sound. People always look up and at him when his name is announced at conferences: Sólman Smithson. All eyes focus on him. It's a pleasant feeling, and at such moments he always stands up slowly and calmly, looks deliberately over the conference room and bows. He is the chairman of the Euro-Icelandic Friends' Society in Brussels, the expatriate society of Euro-Icelanders. People trust him.

The Icelandic problem is on everyone's lips. Demonstrations and clashes are getting on the nerves of the locals in Brussels, since they impart a dismal hue to the life of the city. Those damn top drawer Eurocrats in the gleaming capital city don't have our problems, sulks Sólman. They made sure that all the problematic issues have been left behind in Brussels: the peripheries, fisheries, and agriculture are in the Berlaymont, which was once the pride of the old European Union. The European Parliament is still in Brussels, and it is as ineffective as always, but there is talk of moving it to Berlin in order to enhance its honour and respect. The discussions have been dragging on for nearly two decades.

There was no such foot-dragging over implementing the Komizar system, recalls Sólman. The old European Union had moved from representative democracy – so popular in the 20th century – to participatory democracy in the 2020s. To Sólman's neat bureaucratic mind it had been a splendid move. Much better than having to deal with all those tiresome referendums when people kept voting the wrong way – or with those cursed MEPs who kept saying the wrong thing. Sólman knows his history. He recalls reading about some British Member of the European Parliament who had kept banging on about the EU being undemocratic. Fool.

Under Demcowill the EU had stopped holding snapshot referendums and instead engaged in long, meaningful conversations with specialist organisations that could be relied upon to have in depth knowledge of a subject. It was far more productive for the Eurocrats to have these meaningful talks that produced sensible policy options. Of course the specialist organisations needed money to work with, so the EU funded them.

It was Demcowill that had produced the concept for the advancement of the Komizar system. The former Commissioners of the EU were given enhanced powers and prestige to become Komizars of the Great European State. All very sensible, reflected

Sólman. Now, there were powerful Komizars heading each department of the government, people able to implement policies that were right for the Great European State. The departments then implemented the policies and the specialist organisations reported back on how effective or otherwise the policies were being.

A shadow passes over Sólman's face as he recalls Krummi. There is always minority of people who oppose and create havoc: want to determine how things are run. What nonsense. Demcowill produces the best policies. People should be grateful instead of arguing.

The Idea of Europe is living proof of the "little engine that could." The achievement surpasses everyone's brightest hopes. When a fragile seed was sown with the signing of the treaty for the European Steel and Coal Community in Paris and a few years later the Treaty of Rome, Europe was still licking its wounds from the battles of World War II. Someone back home insists that the Treaty of Rome was signed on a blank piece of paper. That's just crazy talk, goes to show how far those nut-heads are willing to go in their negative gibberish: who would sign a blank piece of paper? Anyway, since then most European countries have joined what was the EEC, then the EU and now the GES. Sólman's native Iceland approved the New Covenant early this century. Only the Swiss remain outside the United States of Europe, but that will be remedied – in time.

Europe's sun as a world power shines brightly. It is of great importance that Komizar Trinxon stand proud among the great world leaders of China, America, India and Russia. The might of Europe as a world power, with its population of close to a billion people, compensates for its declining standard of living. Europe's share of gross world production has shrunk from more than a third, when the first oil crisis came knocking, to a tenth in the world of super states.

In 1974 Europe's share of gross world production was 36%; in 2010 it had shrunk to 25%, and to 15% in 2020. The trend had been considered inevitable by almost everyone. The goal is to increase Europe's share of world production by 2% each decade. The humiliation of the 20th century is a long forgotten nightmare.

Sólman's train pulls into Berlin, the capital of the Great European State. He collects his papers and makes his way to the special taxi rank reserved for men and women on state business. The taxi whisks him through the city on the special road lanes reserved for official vehicles. He peers past the huge traffic jams where the ordinary citizens sit and fume at the great Beethoven Hall. Unquestionably the great building is the pride of Europe and the most modern construction, where the First Komizar, Rikard Ditlev Trinxon, rules. The White House in Washington resembles an Ikea-shop in comparison to the grand hall opposite the Brandenburg Gate.

Europe has certainly reclaimed its old seat in the world, muses Sólman. The next Olympic Games and football World Cup will be held in Berlin. Great expectation prevails among the citizens of the continent, since Europe is sending a team to the Olympics for the first time; it's a go for gold. European medal winners will give Europe its own new heroes. The idea of a European national soccer team has been bandied about. No European nation has won a World Cup title in decades, and insult was added to injury when the United States of America won the final in the last World Cup, men's and women's teams. Disgraceful, Sólman thinks. It will be an impressive sight when 140,000 spectators rise from their seats and shout:

"Europe... Europe... Europe!"

It will be echoed in every home.

The people's shouts of encouragement will resonate across the entire continent. Sólman climbs out of his taxi and enters the hall for his meeting. How he wishes he could get a job in Berlin to enjoy the great city and all the opportunities it has to offer.

2

Krummi lies on his back on the hard bed in the cells of the Brussels police station. He stares at the ceiling and muses on the coincidence of meeting Sólman at the Fish Fight protest. Of course, he knew Sólman lived and worked in Brussels, but even so. Odd to see him at the protest.

Krummi's mind drifts back to the Westmann Islands, those wild islands off the south coast of Iceland where he was born. He was born Hrafn Illugason, the son of captain Illugi Elliðason, a successful fisherman known throughout Iceland. But within a month of his birth he was being called Krummi, the Raven, for the glossy black hair that covered his head from birth. Krummi is powerfully built, like his father; he started going to sea when he was 12 years old and by 15 was already considered a first-class fisherman. Krummi is quite a bit older than Sólman. They parted ways when Sólman went south to Europe, by which time Krummi had already been going to sea for over a decade. He was much better suited to fishing than to going to school. Of young Krummi it was said that he was always at sea, and when he wasn't, he was flirting with the girls:

My name is Cold Krummi, I come from the Isles,
the ladies are charmed by my wonderful wiles.

Krummi croons this bit of the ditty about Cold Krummi in his prison cell in Brussels. His grandfather had taught him the poem, which had once been popular in Iceland although its subject had been Einsi from the Isles. He grins, his white teeth flashing in his black beard. Krummi's mind drifts back 40 years to the incident at Klettsvík Bay when he had saved Sólman's life. It had been a glorious day in the Westmann Islands, over twenty degrees and perfectly still. He had set out from Friðarhöfn; Peace Harbour over to Bjarnarey Island. He was fifteen years old, big, imposing, and precocious. That's why he was allowed to go to sea alone, even though some grumbled and gave him a hard time about it.

Krummi felt as if he had the world at his feet, being young and a successful fisherman.

The image is vivid in his mind, it is as if he's in the boat all those years ago.

He is going to hunt puffins on Bjarnarey, as generation after generation of Islanders have done. He has entered the harbour mouth. The crag Heimaklettur rises straight up from the sea, eddying with bird life and looking amicably down on the boy's black head of hair. Heimaey Island snuggles up comfortably to its cliffs, assured that everything is safe and sound protected by such pillars. Klettsvík Bay lies ahead of him and Ystiklettur Crag, swarming with birds. Up on Danskhaus Peak a hopping raven croaks, flapping its wings as if wanting to say something important. Krummi smiles at his namesake. Out near Klettsnef Bluff he spies killer whales playing in the sunshine. He spots someone labouring away at the old Keiko pen, floating on the waters of the sea off the shoreline. Puffins throw themselves off Ystiklettur Crag and a guillemot peeks out over the edge of the cliff.

On Ystiklettur, on Ystiklettur
the elf-wife's living,
once she came to me, once she came to me,
courteous, warm, and giving.
The wave, the wave, the wave blue and cold,
out at the crag sings songs of old.

As he recites the old ditty, Krummi's eyes wander to the hunting hut on the cliff, where, or so the story goes, Rún's dog met its destiny. The dog had started barking in the night, then gone suddenly silent. The next Rún knew the dog was thrown into the hut by unseen hands, stone-dead. Ystiklettur is known to be haunted. Krummi watches a gannet take flight and dive into the bay for sand eels.

"Greetings, Queen of the Atlantic", calls Krummi happily, but his raven namesake raises a ruckus up on Danskhaus, as if wanting to draw his attention to the bay.

Krummi notices that the boy at the pen is little Sólman Smiðsson, a boy younger than himself but at the same school. Sólman is also watching the gannet, and he and Krummi wave at each other. Krummi looks east toward Bjarnarey. He is eagerly looking forward to his stay on the island. The croaking from Danskhaus suddenly becomes a screech, causing Krummi to look up at his namesake, which has taken to the air and now flies screeching toward the pen. Little Sólman is nowhere to be seen. Krummi looks around for him but isn't really worried as it is no big deal to fall in the sea. He is surprised at the ruckus by the raven, which flies again and again over the pen. Krummi heads toward the pen, scanning for signs of Sólman. He sees the boy bob up but there seems to be something wrong.

Then he hears the boy's desperate cry.

And he knows it is serious.

Krummi phones the emergency services number. An agent at the control board in Reykjavík appears on the screen of his vidphone.

"What's your emergency?" asks the young woman in a controlled voice.

"I'm at Keiko Bay in the Westmann Islands," he says resolutely.

"A boy has fallen into the sea. Something's dragging him down. Send help immediately," he adds.

In Reykjavík it is always useless to mention Klettsvík by its proper name, since it is identified with the killer whale Keiko, who was transported there from Hollywood in 1998 after starring in the movie *Free Willy*.

"Where are you?" asks the girl.

"I'm on my way into the bay," he says.

"Your message will be forwarded to the police and rescue teams in the Islands," she responds, and immediately begins to send out the call. She hangs up.

Krummi pushes the throttle wide open but feels as if a huge amount of time passes before the little boat reaches the pen. There is no sign of little Sólman anywhere. He sails alongside the pen, peering down into the green depths that reveal nothing, until air bubbles suddenly appear on the surface and Sólman's terrified, staring eyes appear to him from out of the deep. He is obviously caught in something that is pulling him down.

Krummi takes a knife from its sheath and dives in after Sólman. He swims down and down but it seems that the sea is determined to hold on to its booty, as Sólman sinks steadily deeper into the depths. Finally Krummi reaches him, Sólman's life is slipping from him, his eyes distant and lifeless. A tangled mess of netting has wound itself around both of Sólman's ankles. Krummi cuts at the net but it is incredible how the mess has entangled the boy. Krummi flexes his muscles and throws in all his strength but feels as if his lungs are about to burst.

The damn net won't come loose.

Sólman appears lifeless and Krummi has to swim away from him to the surface in order to take a breath. He gulps oxygen greedily into his aching lungs when he finally breaks the surface. In the distance he sees the flashing lights of the rescue boat, but knows they will be too late. He dives down again toward Sólman, swims down, down, down but feels it is taking an eternity to reach him. Finally he gets down to Sólman. Then again he hacks desperately at the net. Sólman's lifeless body stares with glazed eyes out into the depths but finally, finally Krummi manages to saw through the net. He feels Sólman's small body emerge from its shackles. Krummi wraps his arms around Sólman and swims with him to the surface with all the powers of his life and soul. Finally at long last they break the surface. Krummi shoves him up onto the pen's dock and begins CPR.

"Solli!" he shouts, blowing air into Sólman's lungs and compressing his chest.

Sólman does not respond but Krummi keeps on, on and on blowing life into him.

"Come on, come back!" he shouts determinedly.

Out of the corner of his eye he sees the croaking raven strutting on the dock. The lifeboat is just laying up at the dock when seawater spouts directly into Krummi's face.

Sólman starts coughing violently and Krummi slumps forward, exhausted.

Three rescuers have reached them. Both Krummi and Sólman are taken off to the Westmann Islands hospital.

The media heralds the incident at Klettsvík as one of the greatest rescues in the history of Iceland. A fifteen-year-old teenager had dived twice to a depth of nineteen meters and freed a boy from the grip of a thick ghost net. They compare the rescue to the achievement of the giant Islander who had swum through the Atlantic's freezing waves when Hellisey fishing boat sank back in the 20th century. Krummi had always thought the comparison rather overdone. Guðlaugur Friðthórsson had swum for 6 hours through freezing water then walked for 2km before reaching a farmhouse and collapsing over the doorstep. His body temperature had been down below 34C. Friðthórsson had survived as if he were a superhuman, all Krummi had done was dive deep.

Krummi comes back to the present. He has been worked over by the security guards in the Berlaymont and his entire body aches, although he had been careful not to resist too much when they assaulted him. He had never intended to get into a fight, but first and last to make his actions a symbolic protest of the humiliation of Iceland and Icelandic fishermen. He will continue to hold that torch high while there is any vigour in him.

That is what he has promised his wife Bríet and himself

"Now I'm thinking of home," he croons, smiling.

Krummi's life had taken an unexpected direction when love came knocking. Bríet was twenty when he first saw her, he had been several years older. He knew immediately that he wanted to spend his life with her. His friends had teased him, but they'd probably never known love. He, who'd been the favourite of the Island's girls, never looked at another woman again. Everything changed when he met his love on the south side of the Free Church one Culture Night when he was young and foolish. It could just as well have been yesterday.

Krummi smiles broadly and recounts some lines by Tómas Guðmundsson.

Still it burns inside my mind
more than any other man might find,
how it was you stirred my heart.

The memory is as vivid as if it were happening now.

It is as though time stops outside the Free Church. Bríet Leósdóttir is with her girlfriends: a tall, blonde queen, beaming with pride, while the Islander is out of his element in Reykjavík. He and a few friends walk together in a small group down Fríkirkjuvegur Street. He has been staring up at the churchtower, lost in his own thoughts, when he runs into Bríet. Their eyes meet. He blushes like a beetroot when she smiles at him mischievously.

"You sure are confident," she says with a smile.

He apologizes but it comes out clumsily, since he is, truth to tell, a timid little bungler before this queen. He stammers some sort of nonsense and doesn't know what else to do. Her mischievous smile disappears and is replaced by a mysterious one, then to one overflowing with curiosity and finally mysterious friendliness.

He tries to say something intelligent.

"I was looking at the stars. They're shining so brightly," he stammers trying to act intelligent but failing miserably, or so he thinks.

Krummi smiles to himself in his prison cell.

In spite of it all, he hadn't messed things up that momentous

August night when love opened up his heart. They had walked along Tjörnin Pond with their friends, but before he knew it the two of them were strolling alone southward down Laufásvegur Road. The stars in the Reykjavík night sky had shone even brighter than at autumn equinox, when he hauled in fish far out on the Selvogur fishing ground. She had moved out to the Islands when she finished her literature degree at the University. They have two sons, grown taller than him now.

He has enjoyed fishing even though things have become so constricted for Icelandic fishermen. He is a successful hunter by nature, whether he is fishing out at sea around the Islands or going after foxes or reindeer up on the heaths. A week before sailing abroad he had killed a bull reindeer from a distance of 850 meters at Eyjabakki. Krummi is in fantastic shape for a man well into his fifties. He has eagle eyes and is an excellent marksman; multiple Icelandic champion in shooting with rifle and pistol.

"How time has flown," he says out loud to the empty cell as he taps energy points to release tension within.

And how fickle life is.

The fisherman Krummi is in a prison cell in Brussels while little Sólman is one of the highest placed Euro-Icelandic bureaucrats.

During a break in his meeting in Berlin, Sólman finds himself alone at the coffee machine. He gets a milky cappucino and sits down. Meeting Krummi after all these years, has stirred things up in his mind. He too reflects on his ordeal at Klettsvík. He had stumbled and fallen into the sea. The goddamn tangled mess of netting had wrapped around both of his feet and there was nothing he could do about it. He did, however, recall seeing Krummi from the depths as the net dragged him down. Then everything had gone black, pitch-black. He had woken up in the hospital a week later. They said he was a lucky son-of-a-gun to regain his health; the rescue was declared a miracle. Krummi had come to visit him in the hospital but the rest of that summer had been surreal. Everything was as if in a fog. The terror was always nearby, everywhere, no matter where he went. It wasn't something that he could point to, however. It just was.

Sólman shakes his head, it's as if he's reliving that dreadful summer.

He had felt abandoned while in hospital. How he had missed father who had been busy in Reykjavík those fateful days. Father had phoned and explained that a political crisis was taking up all his time, the future of the country was at stake. Sólman would have to understand. However, father stressed that he had done well being able to survive that terrible ordeal. That had made Sólman proud. He was very proud of his father who was constantly in the media, people always asking what was best for the country.

His parents had divorced when he was only five years old. He had remained with mother in the Westmann Islands. Father had moved to Reykjavík with his new fiancée and Daisy, the Labrador dog. Sólman had felt guilty, blaming himself for his parent's divorce since he had all too often been reluctant to finish his dinner and too lazy to run errands when told to do so. Everything had changed when father moved to Reykjavík the day after he had refused to go to the supermarket to buy milk for Dad's coffee. Sólman had run out of the house, breaking the big living room window with a stone, as he had been so frustrated with his parents' fierce quarrelling. He had run to the seashore and hidden behind a stone for the entire day. The police had found him as darkness had set in.

The next day father was gone. Mother became depressed, constantly scolding him and blaming father for their misfortune. She would take all kind of pills which she claimed made her life tolerable. Sólman would have done anything to get father back. He would dream of their happiness, as Dad and Mom held his hands walking down to the harbour, all of them smiling as people waved to them. But then there were the nightmares when some dark faceless figures chased him in circles around the house. He would run, faster and still faster until he'd wake up crying, all alone in the darkness.

ARGYLL AND BUTE COUNCIL
LIBRARY SERVICE

He had loved it when allowed to visit father in Reykjavík. He would make sure to do anything that father required of him, particularly making sure that there was enough milk in the refrigerator. He took great care to be nice to his infant half-brother, especially when father was around. However, father was constantly complaining about the stupidity and short-sightedness of his political adversaries who were to blame for the country's demise. Father would say that the senseless resistance and constant bickering about Europe was holding the country back and making people want to leave.

Sólman always dreaded going back to mother in the Westmann Islands, but father insisted that mother needed him. She would be all alone if it wasn't for him. Father had stressed that he needed to be a good and obedient son: mother relied on him. Sólman would nod, although with a sadness in his heart. He was intent on being a good son, having failed his parents with such drastic consequences. If only he had gone to the supermarket instead of breaking the window.

Sólman shakes his head, there is solemness in his eyes. Memories come flooding.

He had married a girl named Gitte during his studies in Copenhagen but they had divorced just over a decade ago. One day she took her things and left without even so much as a goodbye. He went to Copenhagen to try to change her mind, but she wouldn't budge. She said she had no desire whatsoever to live in Brussels. He had suggested he put in for a transfer to Copenhagen but she slammed the door on him. Gitte was granted custody of their daughter Daniella, after which she pretty much disappeared from his life. He had repeatedly tried to reach her but it was no use. She had accused him of not being there for her during a vulnerable phase of her life.

Yet he hadn't walked out on them.

It was Gitte who ran off. Young Daniella had run into bad company. He had often gone to Copenhagen and tried to get her out of Christiania. She had sunk ever deeper, without him being able to prevent it. "You weren't there for me," she'd shouted over and over. "You failed me, Dad... you betrayed me."

Even today Sólman would wake in a cold sweat with her accusatory face staring at him. Her shrill voice and deep despair cuts his heart. He'd been called out of a meeting to answer a phone call from Gitte, who was overcome with grief. Daniella had been found in a filthy room in a dilapidated shack in that damned Christiania slum. She'd been dead for three days, a horrendous sight. They'd found syringes in the toilet.

Sólman runs his fingers through his hair, drenched in sweat.

He leans back in his chair.

I ought to have skipped those endless meetings and tedious, useless cocktail parties with lethargic bureaucrats who blather on and on about subsidies here and quotas there, he thinks sadly.

Sólman looks down at the agenda for the coming sessions of his many meetings. He is a bureau chief in the European Peripheries Bureau in Brussels. He is deeply devoted to Iceland and the economic situation there is causing him concern.

There are now 260,000 Euro-Icelanders back home, with the population decreasing. Unemployment is endemic and the state is notorious for its dodgy practices at milking the fishing grounds of the European subsidy system. But despite all the subsidies, its people are moving away. It is said that the Euro-Icelanders simply do not want to live in darkness and cold far from the city lights of Europe. The number of Europeans of Icelandic descent on the European mainland has increased enormously. In Scandinavia their number approaches one hundred thousand. Twelve thousand are thought to be in Berlin and Brussels, a huge number in Britain, and well over twenty thousand in sunny Spain. Businessmen have flocked overseas in search of opportunities as well as academics. The best and the brightest are simply gone.

Sólman has always tried to put the Icelandic subsidy applications at the top of the pile, since, in all honesty, there is a squabble for every single euro. It is no easy matter to show preference to his homeland, since controls have been tightened due to embarrassing scandals in the system. He himself has had a taste of scandals.

Anyway, it is hoped that the new naval base in Hvalfjörður will create between three and four thousand jobs, which will come in handy. Berlin places great emphasis on strengthening the European Fleet in the North. In Iceland, the inhabitants have generally welcomed the building of a naval base in Hvalfjörður, although there have been some demonstrations on Austurvöllur Square. Endless, these Icelandic demonstrations. They argue about everything up there in the high north.

The Westmann Islanders had gone ballistic when Berlin issued an edict proclaiming all fishing grounds officially European Territorial Waters. There were angry demonstrations in towns by the coast, but all was fairly quiet in Reykjavík. The people by the sea still refer to the Icelandic fishing grounds in defiance of the official version. Of course, they should accept the new term: the European Territorial Waters, as it is within the Great European State. Sólman can't help but shake his head in disbelief at his countrymen's constant obstinacy and resistance.

The discovery of mankind's greatest oil reserves in over half a century have focused attention on Greenland, where drilling operations have been invaluable to Europe. Sólman ties his hopes for Iceland's economic future to three oil refineries being built in the Westfjords. Annoyingly the refineries will have to be smaller than had been planned to cater to the demands of environmental NGOs. Oh well, that is the way Demcowill works. Europe stands fast to its commitment to the environment in accordance with the provisions of the Constitution of the Great European State. It is what helps the GES have such influence in the international community.

His mind turns to the ongoing disputes over Greenland which is still not a state in the Great European State. The Greenlanders want to sell their oil to the US in an exclusive deal. What nonsense. Some even say they want to be part of America, but that is out of the question. Sólman is confident that history is on Europe's side in this matter. Of course, arguments for why this largest island in the world should be part of America are poor. Europe's claim is built on solid, international legal grounds: the Icelanders' settlements in Greenland more than a thousand years ago but beyond all else Danish colonization of it since the Middle Ages.

Ooops, he's got to be careful not to use that 'c' word.

Anyway, disputes over the polar regions have become increasingly sensitive. A Demcowill Conference on the issue some time ago clearly demonstrated that it was in the interests of the Greenlanders to join the Great European State. If the Greenlanders were properly educated they would see that the Demcowill view was correct. "As it always is," adds Sólman out loud. His outburst quite surprises him, he can't help a little smile.

The government in Washington appears ever more aggressive. People compare the government of Joanne X. Longria with the notorious Bush government, that invaded Iraq despite Europe's protests. Of course the British took part in the invasion, but Europe got its revenge by denying the infamous Tony Blair the office of the first president of the old European Union.

Some say that Washington is turning eager eyes to Canada, the more Europe grows and strengthens. Europe needs to strengthen ties with Canada to hold the Americans back and their gluttonous eyes away from Greenland. It is perfectly clear to Sólman that the idea of Canada joining the United States of America is a response to the growth and advancement of Europe. The power ratios are very much in favour of Europe, since its population is almost a billion as opposed to some 350 million in the West. There are two superpowers: Europe and China. Russia is finding its feet again and India keeps rising. Isolationism has once again taken over America.

Relations between Iceland and America are next to nothing. Iceland's embassy in Washington is history. Political relations with Washington are in the hands of Berlin. Flights to America are routed through London. It has been decades since Keflavík Airport was the transfer centre for flights across the Atlantic Ocean.

Icelandic people are officially called Euro-Icelanders. Sólman feels it self-evident and incredibly natural to say: "Good morning. My name is Sólman Smithson, European."

This, however, is like poison in the blood of many. Two decades ago a directive had been issued to the effect that the inhabitants of the continent were to associate themselves with Europe rather than a nationality. However, a temporary exemption was granted, since the directive had been widely ignored. People could still call themselves Euro-Icelanders, Euro-English, and so on. The British took the opportunity and harped on about Margaret Thatcher's nonsense, saying that she hadn't grabbed socialism by the throat in order for it to sneak in through the back door. Thatcher's age-old nonsense has delayed the process and actually caused serious damage.

Bickering and complaining are constantly found in Iceland, and yes, in Norway where people are continually whining, but the exodus from North-Norway has its roots in oil depletion. It is absurd to blame Europe for the Norwegians' wasting away. Sólman finds his countrymen unruly and recalcitrant.

The matter is incredibly simple. Iceland is a European nation. It is natural to name oneself after one's continent like the Americans do.

Jóhn Jóhnson, European. Sólman likes the comma, which many have put into their name.

The Euro-Icelanders' obstinacy has raised more than one eyebrow in Europe. Yet some have pointed out that the Euro-Icelanders are endlessly grumpy and forever contentious. They blame the New Covenant for all of its disasters instead of turning a critical eye on themselves. Up north at the Arctic Sea, the struggle has been particularly ruthless, difficult, and violent. Someone compared the disputes over Europe with the debates about membership of NATO and the US military base when the Althingi, the house of parliament, was stoned and brother fought brother at the beginning of the Cold War. Politics in Iceland have always been extreme, downright crazy.

Iceland has the reputation of being politically chaotic.

At the European Cultural Bureau, it is hoped that a new generation will adopt new habits, with European history and culture being taught in the schools, even in the kindergartens. Sólman is convinced that his people will see the light, even if it doesn't happen while he is above ground.

A shame what a difficult time old Iceland is experiencing.

A bell rings. Sólman gets up, throws away his coffee cup and returns to the meeting for yet another detailed discussion about the subsidies to be paid to island sheep farmers.

3

The fight against terrorism never ends and the precarious situation in world affairs means that suspicious looking people are monitored carefully. It just stands to reason, like that incident in the Berlaymont so clearly illustrates. Sólman has to agree with high ranking fellow bureaucrats on the issue. Society simply has to be knowledgeable about movements of gutless, immoral individuals who go about killing people, bombing society's institutions and crushing trucks into buildings. It is unfortunate that every single person has to be scrutinized, but those who have honest intentions have nothing to fear. There is a lot on Sólman's mind at that meeting in the underground conference room in Berlin.

Terrorists and criminals will have nowhere to run.

In Brussels work is being done on developing a system to fight crime that is to be implemented in European cities. It is called Pre-Crime. The system is based on genetics, combined with the genius and the magic of the holph-technology. The recent discovery of the Tylovector — the human violence gene — has made Pre-Crime possible. It roots out criminals in much the same way as alcoholics and junkies are rooted out with DNA-mapping. By sensing Tylovectors in the blood of violent offenders, authorities can predict major crimes.

Pre-Crime's brilliance is for all to see, as a brutal attack and murder was prevented in Heysel Park in Brussels. A convicted murderer and notorious rapist attacked a teenage girl. Scanners picked up the rapist's vector beam which confirmed the intent of a future crime. The area was lit in an instant. A hologram of a black-uniformed guard stood over the scum, who was pointing a knife at the girl's throat as she lay there with her clothes ripped off, scared out of her mind.

"Throw down your knife," thundered the commanding voice.

Although the hol' was only a projection, not real, the recreant was terrified, threw down the knife and ran off as fast as his feet could go. The police apprehended the wag close to Heysel Stadium, since the system provides for rapid response. He was convicted of rape and attempted murder. The Tylovectors in the villain's blood confirmed that the girl would not only have been raped but that she would have been killed in the amoral criminal's brutal attack — if Pre-Crime had not been utilized.

Pre-Crime had prevented a rape and murder.

Sólman admits that he felt proud when the media covered the girl's rescue in detail and praised the new technology.

Crimes in Heysel Park have decreased dramatically, though there are one or two "blind spots" still to be covered. Monitoring of criminals and terrorists has been strengthened indescribably. Both are said to justify the existence of Pre-Crime. The system is under constant development. Besides Heysel, there are trials in two remote places: Iceland and Cyprus. Transmitters are implanted in people in trial areas. Scanners measure men's Tylovectors as the transmitters send signals to hol'-operation-centres. A black-clad holographic security guard is instantly at the scene of event to stop violent offenders. Shortly afterward, the police appear and take away the lout. A broad consensus prevails concerning Pre-Crime. The goal is for the system to be in operation throughout Europe before the end of the century.

With Pre-Crime, hopes are pinned on a society without crime; the perfect society where evil is driven out once and for all. It will be virtually impossible for bad people to commit evil deeds. Expectations run particularly high in this regard in the war on terror; against the worst of the very worst.

Pre-Crime is bad news for terrorists and criminals, they state categorically. It's emphasized that the system increases the safety and security of the Great European State and, in the bargain, ensures transparency and openness for the good of the people. The system serves law abiding citizens who have absolutely nothing to worry about.

Pre-Crime is a phenomenally powerful system for surveillance. Simple and effective and the good news keep coming.

The media reported recently that Pre-Crime prevented a man from killing his wife and her lover. The husband had forgotten his glasses when going to work, so he returned to get them. He discovered the pair in a tryst in the bedroom. It was a huge shock to him.

"Sylvia, how can you do this to me?" he exclaimed, completely stunned, as she poked at the cover, and her naked lover jumped out of bed with his trousers at his heels. The cuckold grabbed scissors from the night-stand and looked derangedly at his wife's lover.

"Arnaud... I... I beg you..." she stammered.

However, the amount of Tylovectors in his blood crossed the danger limit. The transmitter sent signal to hol'-operation-centre which immediately acted as horrendous crime of passion would be committed unless something was done. A black-clad hol' thus appeared at the foot of the bed.

"Put down the scissors, put them down," thundered the commanding voice.

The man was utterly terrified and dropped the scissors on the floor. The lover dashed out of the room and down the stairs. The wife, out of her mind with fear, ran screaming into the bathroom and locked the door.

The husband fell to his knees and burst into tears. Shortly afterwards, the wailing of police-cruiser sirens penetrated the room. A police officer burst in through the bedroom window and as the rhythmic footsteps of armed police officers sounded on the stairs, the hol' vanished. The cuckold lay cowering on the floor, overcome with grief.

Pre-Crime had prevented a crime of passion in a suburb of

Brussels. Political and social-reform groups hope that Pre-Crime will finally help prevent domestic violence, one of the greatest evils of Western civilization.

A violence-free society is around the corner.

Krummi's terrorist act may have been prevented if the system had been activated in the Berlaymont area, although it must be said, that there is more to it. In fact, the incident should have been avoided. Sólman fears it may reflect badly on him at the Peripheries Bureau. Every vehicle on every road, no matter how trivial, is to be tracked every half a second to within a yard, as it emits every 'heartbeat' to the system in Berlaymont. The system was one of the great benefits of the Galileo Satellite Project that the old European Union had developed with the Chinese. It had been sold to the public as a better form of satnav, with a side benefit of making it possible to make road pricing automatic. The police had quickly moved in to use the system to track all vehicles, claiming it was to catch criminals. That had not been the case with Krummi's truck, so there will be a special investigation into how the giant was able to disconnect his truck from the system.

It is, however, classified information, top secret, that the system is able to identify humans on board, but that is the responsibility of Surveillance on the Twelfth Floor of the Peripheries Bureau. Every Icelander in Brussels is under special scrutiny of Surveillance; that is also classified information as well: top, top secret. Sólman is not anxious whatsoever about the failure to track the truck, since it's not the first one and will not be the last, but there were others who failed as well. Surveillance should have identified and monitored Krummi in Brussels. He is confident it is not his fault.

However, the whole affair is unpleasant. "The link to home is constantly becoming more of a nuisance," Sólman curses.

The simple truth is that the system simply has to be able to know, or all is in vain.

"I must ask you to take off your hat as you are deemed suspicious.

You can't be identified in the security camera," a hologram of a black-uniformed security guard told a startled young man outside the Supreme Court in Iceland.

He looked at the hol' in amazement, dumbfounded.

"Right now... for real," the hol' repeated, scowling. The man was still speechless, and clearly frightened. "These are the rules," the hol' added hastily.

As the young man nervously took off his hat and guiltily looked into the camera, the hol' stated within a split second: "Gunnar Jónsson, you are never to wear a hat in a way that hides your identity." Then the hol' vanished into thin air, case closed. The system takes great care not to harass people more than necessary. That evening a fine of 100 euros was removed from Gunnar Jónsson's bank account by the State Justice System.

Back in the cold country there is the so-called neighbour watch: people are encouraged to report suspicious activities of their neighbours. Posters to that effect have been put up at public transport stations. It's been successfully done in Scandinavia for over a hundred years, so it's proper to do it in Iceland, Sólman totally agrees.

A father of three children blew the horn of his brand new grand vehicle. His wife and children came out running and proudly jumped into the shining blue vehicle. In nearby houses, curious eyes watched the family drive away as curtains were lifted.

Two weeks later officials in uniform knocked at the family's door. "Good morning, we are from the Inland Revenue Office," said an officer in brown uniform.

"Can I be of assistance?" replied the father of three.

"Are you the owner of that thing?" asked the officer pointing at the vehicle.

"Yes," replied the startled owner.

"We need to go through your papers to check your income and expenditures. Your neighbours have reported your brand new expensive vehicle and wonder if you can afford it. We need to check how your standard of living compares with your income," said the officer quite firmly.

The man was clearly shaken as he should be: tax evasion is a serious felony.

It has to be admitted that people are increasingly monitored. That much Sólman can confirm, due to last winter's frightening incident. He can still feel the sweat on his forehead.

He had been in Heysel Park walking home after a good night out. He had emptied his beer and thrown the can on the grass, looking around guiltily as he knew that he was breaking the law. Then out of nowhere, the intense glare of floodlights blinded him as a black hol' suddenly appeared, standing opposite him, thundering in a commanding voice: "Pick up the can and bin it!"

The hol' had stared coldly into Sólman's frightened eyes. He had realized that he was looking a hologram in the eye, and knew there was no way to escape. The hol' had pointed at the empty beer can. Sólman had violated the laws of good behaviour in public places.

"Absolutely inexcusable," Sólman had stammered.

He had apologized but he was so alarmed that he had wet his pants, to his shame. Sólman had broken down but the pitch-black hol' showed no sympathy. Sólman had felt a stinging chest pain as he picked up the beer can and threw it into the bin. The hol' had vanished immediately and the lights gone out. Sólman had received a fine of 100 euros, automaticallywithdrawn from his bank account later that day.

Sólman has learnt that the incident was a mistake, which will be eradicated. Mistakes are to be expected and he's confident that mistakes will be dealt with. He hopes to get repayment of the fine.

Although this may seem excessive, Sólman finds criticism on Pre-Crime too often way out of line. Dissident voices tend to make him quite angry, like *The Sunday Telegraph's* claim that the powerful European Intelligence Agency, EIA, is gaining a powerful tool which basically regulates and controls the whole European population. What nonsense, as always, the media focuses on negatives. Sólman supports Komizar Trinxon's courageous criticism of the media.

"Pre-Crime will revolutionize society for the better," Trinxon had emphasized in a speech in London and stated further: "There will always be those who undermine the hard work and honest intentions of the Council. I will not shirk responsibility because I sincerely believe in the good work we are doing in the service of the Great European nation. I say to critics: mankind is on the threshold of impeccable society; elimination of terrorism, crime and domestic violence."

Despite Trinxon's assurances, there has been some grumbling that the development of the system is engulfed in secrecy and that the director of the Secret Service, Mr Slobodan Pašiĉevic, is becoming too powerful. He's scarcely known to the public, his mystifying background being a perpetual puzzle. "Can You Trust Him?" *The Spectator* had asked in a headline below a picture of the director of the Secret Service as the Agency is referred to among Europeans.

Trinxon had been firm in his response. "The slander about Mr Pašiĉevic is typical for the irresponsible media, a shameful character assassination attempt. You will not succeed in your ceaseless negativity and demoralising bullshit. You must stop this backstabbing. Perhaps it's time to issue a directive that outlaws this kind of journalistic filth. There is no doubt in my mind that it's constitutional and, if contested, would be ratified by the European Court of Justice," Trinxon had exclaimed angrily at a press conference in Belgrade, pointing fingers at some members of the media.

However, the media keeps at it. "Big Brother isn't just watching you; always, everywhere. Big Brother also wants to have a talk with you, scold you and discipline you," was written in an editorial in *The Times*.

Sólman thinks that the media is way out of line in its constant negativity. The fanatics clearly do not understand the good intentions of Komizar Trinxon. They deliberately mislead people.

The media have created Euromyths to mock the bureaucracy. They neglect to inform, which is despicable. The media should stick to the facts declared by the government, not myths or jokes. It's sad that Eurosceptics are still to be found, and it's shameful how they distort things.

Sólman would be the first to admit that everything is not perfect in the Great European State, but even the fiercest critics must admit that much has been achieved. "So much has been gained in this Current Age," Sólman says out loud to himself. He's quite startled when he finds fellow bureaucrats looking at him, some even grinning and pointing at him.

A thin man of medium height with stinging eyes, high chins with a tidy moustache above his straight lips, stares out of the great picture window that fills an entire wall of his office on the 20th floor of the Headquarters of the European Intelligence Agency. Chief Director Slobodan Paśiĉevic's hair is slicked back, his face troubled as he turns abruptly to face his underling.

"So what you're telling me is, that Pre-Crime has serious faults. Is that right?" He walks to his desk, his cold eyes bore into those of bureau chief Anke Müller who stops reading at once.

"Well, not quite," she replies nervously. She's always uneasy in the presence of the Chief Director, then she adds hesitantly. "It's a success, but..."

"But what," the Director hisses.

The woman tries to regain her calm. "There have been a few awkward mistakes in trial areas," she says in a subdued voice. "There's been some ruckus in Iceland because of a man who was thought to be hiding his face. Pre-Crime misinterpreted his intentions, yet he received a fine." Anke Müller looks up. "You know how touchy things are in Iceland right now. This sort of thing just gives the troublemakers an excuse to accuse us of being heavy handed."

Paśiĉevic's nods in annnoyance but then tries to find something positive to say as he opens his e-notebook. "I know but the 'neighbour watch' has gone quite well. Remember that incident three months ago when neighbours reported a tax evader in Reykjavík to the Inland Revenue. His expensive brand new automobile evoked suspicion and people acted upon it. The guy was caught cheating red handed. That made people happy."

"True, very true," Anke Müller hurriedly replies. But 'neighbour watch' is not what Anke Müller has in mind, so she adds nervously: "There was an incident in Heysel Park. It was thought to be an attempted mugging but it turned out to be a bureaucrat who threw his can on the grass instead of into a bin. He was so terrified that he wet his pants. We really don't want to go after such minor cases but mistakes are made and there seems to be no turning back to correct things."

"Wet his pants. Who's the coward?" Paśiĉevic interrupts grinning.

"He's a department chief in the Peripheries Bureau, official of Icelandic origin by the name of Smithson."

"No matter," Paśiĉevic replies, tidying his moustache.

"Oh, er," says Müller. "Then there was the Fish Fight protest in Brussels. Pre-Crime should have detected that but did not."

"Those Icelander's are a constant nuisance, constantly jumping at their own shadows," the Director replies.

"Yes, Chief Director," Anka Müller says as formally as possible. "My point is that Pre-Crime has not been working properly in its trial areas. It has arrested innocent people because they felt guilty about minor misdemeanants, but people committing serious crime have slipped through our net as their Tylovectors go undetected, probably because they are psychopaths. The mistakes are causing unease. We recommend that the trial areas be discontinued until further work has been carried out on the system."

Paśiĉevic slams Müller's notebook as he leans over her and slowly whispers to her anguished face. "I'm really disappointed in your incompetence. You simply have to do better, Miss Müller. I expect better results next time you report to me." He turns and the woman leaves in panic.

The Director walks to the window. "Bloody fools constantly

messing things up," he mutters angrily, looking over the River Spree that flows on through the city as it has done for centuries.

4

Eighteen months after the incident in Berlaymont, Krummi and Sólman meet at a café on the Rue de la Montagne in Brussels. The Islander has just been released from prison and has been instructed to clear out of the city by midnight. Before leaving he had suggested a meeting with Sólman. The neat Eurocrat was not sure if he should go but he owed the big fisherman his life so he had felt compelled to agree. Sólman is late due to a tedious meeting at administration.

"I never told you about the raven on Danskhaus?" asks Krummi roguishly as Sólman takes a seat.

"The raven at Danskhaus?" echoes Sólman with a look of surprise.

"When you fell off the dock, a raven screeched horribly and took off from Danskhaus. It's what made me look around for you. The Danskhaus – the Dane's head – was functioning after all," says Krummi.

"You don't say," replies Sólman hesitantly.

"It's not unlike the folk-tale from Herjólfur Valley, when a raven saved a farmer's daughter from death in a landslide that wiped out all other life on the farm. The farmer had charged those in need a fee for sips of water, but the daughter had secretly given thirsty people water to drink and was richly rewarded," says Krummi with a broad smile.

"I guess I'm not completely hopeless, then, if a croaking raven sees fit to come to my rescue," replies Sólman with a smile.

They both laugh.

"You don't smell like fish guts anymore," says Sólman grinning.

"Now listen," says Krummi tapping the table with his fat finger, "we're caught in a vicious circle in this damn European net. It's choking us."

"Aren't you being a bit overdramatic?" asks Sólman.

Krummi grins, his white teeth flashing in his pitch-black beard as he looks Sólman in the eyes. "It's about to get much more dramatic," he goes on. "The bloody politicians should have put their feet down like our great medieval chieftain and one of Europe's greatest ever poet, Snorri Sturluson; the author of Heimskringla and Edda Poems; the man who preserved Nordic heritage as Iceland became one of Europe's great cultural centres of the time. His compatriots quailed and submitted to King Haakon in Norway in that turbulent 12th century and Gissur had Snorri killed.

"Now our damn politicians have submitted to Europe, and everything has gone to the Devil. People have streamed south to Europe. It was six hundred years of starvation and misery under foreign rule and now it's compensation, subsidies, and shut the hell up – with best wishes from Europe."

Sólman smiles. Krummi certainly has style. He is right, however, about the emigrations. "There is another side to this," he counters. "Iceland's decline has caused the best analysts in Brussels and Berlin a great deal of head-scratching. It's certainly not a simple matter, by no means a simple matter. It is however absurd to blame Iceland's failure on the Great European State. It seems that the country's decline comes from within. Some say that disunion splinters the nation, with people arguing and bickering endlessly. Others point to wind, rain, darkness, and terrible cold combined with the all pervading stench of fish offal. Who wants to live on such an isolated lump of rock?"

Through the years, Sólman has avoided arguments about the Icelandic problem, since the debate tends to be farcical. Moreover, he has seen the careers of some of his European colleagues go down the drain after making comments to which the higher bureaucracy in Berlin has objected. There is no denying the endless movement of people to Europe. Each year thousands board planes and never return. They say that Europe has sucked up the cream of the national crop; that Iceland's best have gone abroad.

Krummi grunts. "We at least agree that the 21st century Viking of the Atlantic is only purring."

"Oh, indeed," replies Sólman. At a conference in Finland, which he attended, a finger was pointed at lack of opportunities in Iceland after the great crash at the beginning of the century. Suddenly the opportunities were abroad; in London, Berlin, Copenhagen, Stockholm and Oslo. "Someone compared the 20th century movement of people from the countryside to Reykjavík with the exodus to Europe in the 21st century," Sólman adds.

"That figures," replies Krummi.

"In fact," Sólman continues, "we discussed this at a meeting of the Peripheries Committee several months ago. Someone from north Iceland delivered an angry lecture about what he called the evils of the Great European State; typical nationalist bullshit. The man poured his anger out over the audience and in that way wrecked his own argument. The audience members simply shook their heads, as always when nationalist idiots flap their arms, blaming everything and everyone, instead of themselves. We get the same nonsense from Britain and Norway.

"Then toward the end the guy finally made some sense. There had been prosperous fishing towns on Iceland's coast in the early 20th century, but then Reykjavík's population expanded at the countryside's expense. The population got sucked southward and blown into Reykjavík as if through a giant harvester. The same process has just moved on as the inhabitants of Iceland have packed their things and moved to Europe."

Krummi replies philosophically. "People moved away from the candlelight of the countryside to the electric lights of Reykjavík and from there to the neon lights of major European cities. We need to stop gaping at Europe. We have to change things; make our own decisions. Independence is the way out of this rotten hole that we find ourselves in."

"Is there a way back?" Sólman asks sceptically.

"Now they are trying to do away with the Icelander," growls Krummi. "The island out upon the farthest reaches of the sea isn't fashionable enough for your fellow Eurocrats. National pride has been labelled evil ethnic politics. Icelanders are told that they have to follow the call of the times and become Europeans. There is endless prattle about how the Icelander should think of himself as a European: the new man, you see, because that's how it is supposed be in Europe. As if being an Icelander isn't enough. Unbelievable bullshitters." Krummi's expression has turned quite emotional.

Sólman is surprised by Krummi's outburst. It's true what they say about his countrymen, he thinks: always angry. However he feels he's beginning to see things from a different prospective. At that conference in Finland, an expert from New Zealand had stated that the course of events in Iceland had always been evident due to laws of physics: quantum mechanics. The European magnet was too powerful for Iceland to be able to hold its own: study physics, study quantum mechanics, the expert had said.

Sólman hadn't thought much about it at the time. He looks out the window, then turns quickly to Krummi. It's as if a light is being lit before him, as Sólman says zealously: "The magnet, here's the magnet itself in the flesh. Simple physics! Of course just simple physics, simple quantum physics." His statement takes even him by surprise.

"What nonsense is this? Magnet, quantum physics. Have you lost your mind?" asks Krummi crustily.

Sólman smiles apologetically but he feels the blood coursing through him. It is a good feeling, he thinks, and something that he hasn't felt for years. Well, in fact it's quite new to him and he's become very enthusiastic. "Brussels is the magnet in the flesh that sucked up the Icelanders' self-confidence and sovereignty. Two powers collided, the stronger of them won. It could not have gone otherwise. Iceland's decline was inevitable because the European magnet is so overwhelming that everything is pulled southward."

Krummi looks at Sólman in disbelief, he's never seen this side of Sólman. "But it wasn't inevitable, not at all," Krummi says calmly and continues: "Let's not forget the sea. We lost control over the fish. When we were kids out on the Westmann Islands we had control over our own fishing grounds, but our politicians sold them out to Brussels. Before we knew it, everyone was living on bloody subsidies, lazy and fat. Then came God damned quota-hopping and European fishing vessels all over the sea. We were shoved away from the table. I don't know why our forefathers fought the Cod Wars against the British lion back in the 20th century, only to hand the fishing grounds over to some arrogant komizars. We drove the Brits out of our waters, all right, only to relinquish them back to greedy and greasy Komizars."

Sólman can't argue about the fish.

Krummi continues his sermon: "My grandad was in the coast guard back in the good old days. He was on board the gunboat *Odinn* when it was rammed by the British frigate *Scylla*. He used to tell the story over and over when I was a kid. Though the cod is none too bright, it's none too fond of Brits." Krummi roars with laughter. "Our great 20th century Nobel laurette Halldór Laxness said that if the Icelandic villages became German, next would come castles with German overlords and mercenaries armed with lances. What is the lot of the nation that wrote famous books? People would be forced to become the servants of a puppet state. A fat servant is not a great man, but freedom lives in the heart of a slave with a bloody back. Remember Jón Hreggviðsson who killed that Danish hangman, but he got away with it." Krummi laughs heartily, his white teeth flashing in his pitch black beard. "Laxness understood the soul of the Icelandic nation. Iceland is burning! The europhiles would sacrifice our national freedom to the service of political convenience." The giant towers over Sólman who looks away as he sips his beer.

They fall silent for a while, as if there is much to contemplate. It's Krummi who breaks the silence. "It's bloody amazing how things can get messed up," he says, suddenly melancholic.

"True indeed," replies Sólman, scowling.

"Like the television we have to watch these days," Krummi says with a sarcastic look.

Sólman smiles. "Oh come on. Even you must know that the *European State Television* has been well received since it was launched barely a decade ago."

Krummi looks sceptical, but Sólman is not put off. "Well, people are reasonably content with it and *Euro-News*. The station is going to cover the upcoming Olympics in grand style."

"Watching is not the same as being there," remarks Krummi.

"True," agrees Sólman. "It would be nice to go to the Olympics."

"No point," growls Krummi and then knits his brows. "They've issued... what do they call it? Oh, yes, an edict. People may only discuss sport, not politics; no banners or demonstrations." But then he grins. "Perhaps I should drive a really powerful truck to Berlin, make a stylish entrance!" He laughs heartily but there is no laughter in Sólman's mind.

Krummi looks out the window. "Bugger," he says, glancing at Sólman. Krummi scowls and stands up. "It's best to get going. They're on the lookout for me."

Sólman notices two men with wide-brimmed hats standing on the other side of the street. Krummi towers over Sólman as he puts on his coat. "They told me to go to Hell. I'd better push off back up north to the outermost sea like Sæmundur the Wise."

Sólman grins at Krummi's reference to the 10th century Icelandic scholar and sorcerer who supposedly crossed the Atlantic on the back of the Devil in the form of a seal. It is said that Sæmundur lost his shadow after tricking the Devil to grab it instead of his soul.

Krummi grins back. "You can be sure I'll knock the god-damn seal on the head with my prayer book," he says as he walks out on to the boulevard this sunny day.

Sólman knits his brow pensively and scratches his head. He tries to recall the legend of Sæmundur the Wise and how a prayer book fitted in. Oh yes, he hid a prayer book out of sight and then tricked the Devil into doing his bidding. Did Krummi mean he would trick the Great European State into doing his bidding? Sólman watches the giant fisherman stride off down the street, the two men trailing in his wake.

He's baffled, again he scratches his head. Has Krummi lost his shadow?

5

That evening Sólman lets himself into his apartment in the European district. He picks up his memory chip that contains all his papers of the Euro-Icelandic Friends' Society. "I'm a European," he says aloud to himself in his apartment in the European district that evening. "I'm a genuine European citizen," he reiterates. "You can be a Euro-Icelander and a European. No contradiction. Krummi is wrong. We can have the best of both worlds." Deep inside, Sólman feels a compelling desire to seek answers to Iceland's problems.

Sólman has never before considered Iceland's destiny so deeply. It is as if a blindfold has been removed from his eyes. Of course the generation that took the momentous decision to join the EU hadn't foreseen its isolating effects; the exodus or the loss of talent. Independence, however, is not the answer. Krummi is a romantic fool. The answers to Iceland's problems are to be found in Brussels and Berlin. They just have to be found.

Sólman looks out the window at the brave new world of Europe. He knows with certainty that the decline of Iceland had been inevitable; that the boom years of the 20th century had just been a momentary fantasy. Iceland could never have maintained its freedom and prosperity among the European, American, Asian and Russian super-giant super-solutions. Iceland had to choose a team: Europe, naturally.

There is simply no room for a small country in the world of super-states.

Sólman shakes his head. He is convinced that he is right. He goes to the kitchen to cook supper.

6

Copenhagen shudders under an overcast sky one morning in March. Sleet lashes the city driven by a cold northwesterly wind, the temperature just above freezing. The winter has been hard on everyone, yet another cold bitter winter.

A sombre looking man walks hastily over Vesterbro Bridge, his brow knitted in thought. He wears a tweed overcoat, its worn and frayed velvet collar pulled up to his chin. Helgi Thorláksson is returning from a stormy meeting of the board of the Royal Antiquaries Club. Despite its prestigious position, the Club is under threat. There once was a time when it enjoyed the undivided respect of everyone engaged in Nordic literature research, being under the wing and favour of kings and queens, emperors and barons who had made grand donations to the Club, which had enjoyed prosperity, but at the same time slowly and quietly acquired enemies.

Now, the villains have taken over the Antiquaries Club by abject, amoral, deceitful means as the great Hans Christian Bentsen is on his deathbed. "Those villains would never have dared do anything if Bentsen was fully active," mutters Helgi angry and bitter.

Under the direction of Bentsen, the Antiquaries Club's influence had reached its highest peak, research on old Icelandic books being the most splendid feather in its hat. The Club's research has shed new and unexpected light on the Icelanders' origin. Bentsen had wanted Helgi to become Club Secretary, which in practice means director of all the club's activities; for Helgi to continue his work. But in closed back rooms, powerful professors scheme to undo Bentsen's intentions. They want to abandon proper research into the Nordic past and instead write papers on how Scandinavia has always been a true and integrated part of greater Europe. Helgi had pointed out that they wanted to change direction only so that they could get their hands on the fat research funds available from Berlin, and go to the plush academic conferences in Nice, Barcelona and Athens – all of them funded by Berlin for professors who do what they are told. In response the professors had pointed repeatedly at Helgi Thorláksson's past, even called him a terrorist.

"By this they intend to wipe out the Icelandic heritage. The bastards intend to leave studies of Nordic literature for dead," mutters Helgi, shivering from the bitter cold. "It does not fit the Great European State and its false history of a united culture and history." Helgi is a stocky man, a bit taller than average, with salt-and-pepper hair and long sideburns, his eyes contemplative. Everyone calls him "the professor" though he holds no such position.

He is from the Westfjords, raised at an old parish farm, Hrafnseyri, birthplace of Jón Sigurðsson who led Iceland's struggle for independence in the 19th century. The farm stands high in a grassy hollow with a sweeping view of the deep fjord, girded by sheer Westfjord cliff walls and wide open to the choppy sea; beyond are the shores of Greenland. In his youth Helgi had spent long hours up on the majestic cliff top above the farm with a book in hand with Dynjandi in the distance, the most majestic waterfall in Iceland. From the peak, the waterfall can be heard in calm weather speaking with elves and hidden people.

As he hurries through the rain-sodden streets of Copenhagen, Helgi reflects on the assault that had come after he had published his paper on the name of Iceland in the prestigious journal of the Antiquaries Club. In the course of the centuries the old meaning of the name "Iceland" had been lost and replaced with ice and icebergs; the prefix "ice" taken literally. It is entirely wrong to associate "Ísland" – as it is spelled among natives – with icebergs and glaciers. No-one would associate Ísleifur with ice, yet the prefix "ís" is in the name, and is of course indicative of a god. "Ís" originates from the ancient god "Es," and the pagan gods Æsir. Helgi had linked his theory to ancient Sanskrit literature from India that tells of a white island in the north where gods and saints dwell.

Iceland is the sacred island — the island of the gods, according to ancient belief.

"The story has survived deep in the consciousness of the nation and the intelligentsia can't bear to think of this," mutters Helgi. He has the habit of talking to himself and passers-by look at him askance.

Helgi had first come up with the idea years earlier when he had packed his bags and gone to the great city of Calcutta at the mouth of the Ganges in order to sip from the well of Indian culture. He discerned a relationship between the ancient Vedas of India and Iceland's Eddic poetry and formulated a hypothesis concerning Iceland's name, but at the time there had been no hard evidence.

Then unexpected verification had come recently with the discovery of an old stone tablet on the banks of the Brahmaputra River describing a tribe that had set out in search of the island of the gods. Using genetic samples, a relationship between the ancient world beyond the great mountains and the inhabitants of the island on the outermost sea had been demonstrated. Helgi had published his work which had started the witch hunt. The intelligentsia does not like the idea that Iceland has links to the very roots of civilization. It wants Iceland to have links only to Europe.

And now at a fateful meeting earlier that morning the opponents of the new theory had taken over the Club and had made clear their aim to oust Helgi. They had all been there, all those Berlin lackeys eager to get their snouts into the trough of Berlin funding. There had been more of them than there should have been. More people voted than were entitled to vote. It had been a stitch up, an illegal meeting. There had been several people that Helgi had never seen at a Club meeting before. He remembers one man, dressed in a black suit, who had seemed to be taking minutes on his e-notebook.

The rain trickles down Helgi's neck. He knows that his maligners will show no mercy. "They steal everything they get their hands on," he mutters as he steps into a café on Islands Brygge. He is bitterly frustrated about the brutal conclusion of the meeting. The Antiquaries Club has been his mainstay. Although his wages are neither high nor generous, his partnership with Bentsen has been like a cornerstone ever since he made his way to Copenhagen all those years ago. He had come to Denmark in a daze of depression. Bentsen had taken him under his wings.

Helgi whispers an ancient Veda.

You are what your deep, driving desire is.
As your desire is, so is your will.
As your will is, so is your deed.
As your deed is, so is your destiny.

Deep, deep, deep, very deep in the Icelandic national identity is knowledge of the great history; the great inheritance and the great journey of the generations in search of the land of the gods. It is the great quest for the island at the outermost sea where the gods were to be seated at the high table. An island in the north connects two worlds: the old and the new. It holds the deepest yearning for a better world. Never in the history of mankind, until the settlement of Iceland, had tens of thousands set out into the unknown across the wide sea with the stars as their guide. The magnet that pulled so strongly had been the deepest consciousness of the people beyond the great mountains that had set out on a journey and come to the ocean on the west coast of Europe.

This people knew its destiny.

With the deepest consciousness and determined will the people had boarded their longships and cargo boats and sailed the ocean toward the island of the gods across the sea. There had never been any examples of a people setting out into the open mouth of the Fenris Wolf, who had bitten off his shackles and chains. The settlement of Iceland is one of the miracles of history. The Icelanders are a part of a nation that travelled from east to west; they travelled farthest west of all and in a small, ancient chest was preserved the ancient heritage that was later recorded on calfskin in their ancient language. The people on the distant island in the northern seas preserved the history of the Nordic peoples and the ancient Vedic wisdom appears in the Eddic poems. Icelandic Viking poets were welcome guests at the royal courts of kingdoms.

Helgi orders a coffee. His mind goes back to the old days when he was young and the pretty Guðrún Sigurvinsdóttir was the love of his life. He remembers an old poem, a favourite of Guðrún's.

Have faith in this world
Nobleness of highest splendour:
God in Universe,
God within you.

Helgi remembers a lecture that he and his beloved Guðrún had attended back when life smiled at them. It was a brilliant self-made computer scientist who claimed that *Bible's* story of the creation of the world is actually man's creation of the word. The word is, therefore man is. Homo sapiens is the creator of the world of words. In the beginning there was the word and the word is with God and the word is God. The word is God's home. The word is humanity's sacred sanctuary.

"I will hand you the keys to heaven." Guðrún had reminded Helgi of Christ's prophesy and added: "The spoken word is Peter's keys. The ancient Icelandic language is one of Peter's keys which thousands of years ago were brought from beyond the great mountains."

The solution to the Bible's great puzzle is to be found in the Icelandic language which has been spoken for thousands of years, the young lecturer had said. His words had made powerful impact on Helgi and Guðrún. One of Peter's key is the Icelandic language that the forefathers spoke during the Age of Settlements over a thousand years ago and beyond. The language that the forefathers had brought with them in a casket from beyond the great mountains was preserved by an isolated nation at the farthest reaches of the sea; a nation that dug itself farther and farther into the ground, searching for shelter from the piercing cold of the Little Ice Age. The key to unlock the Bible's mysteries lies in the transparent

Icelandic language.

"The human mind is Heaven's residence where the world of words was created. This creation is deep, deep within man where the river of life-energy flows forth," Guðrún had said.

"From where does life's energy come from?" Helgi had asked with a sigh.

How he misses Guðrún. He feels as if life's puzzles were an open book to him if she were with him.

Life can be so cruel.

Helgi stares morosely into his coffee and realises it has gone cold without having been tasted. He comes to a decision. He is going to Brussels to meet an old friend in the hope of unwinding the events of that morning. He is not optimistic but still intends to try. He flicks on his holph and dials a Brussels number.

7

Sólman puts the meat on the kitchen island and cuts the fillet in half. He stuffs the steak and wraps it with butcher's twine. The doorbell rings. Sólman is expecting a visitor, he goes to the door and opens it. Helgi Thorláksson smiles amicably and shakes Sólman's hand firmly. "We haven't seen each other in a long time, friend," Helgi says.

"True, very true. Too long," agrees Sólman. "Is it fourteen years?"

Helgi is not sure. "Way too long ago," he says smiling. Their friendship has a long history, however. Helgi is slightly older. They had met in Copenhagen, when Sólman was studying European Law and Helgi was completing his Nordic Studies. Sólman had gone to Brussels and Helgi stayed in Copenhagen.

"You've come just at the right time. I was just putting the steak in the pan." Sólman invites his friend into the apartment. "Would you like some whisky?"

"I'd accept a Scotch whisky; no-one refuses a twelve-year-old Laphroaig," replies Helgi when he spies the bottle in a cabinet. Sólman smiles. His contacts in the Berlaymont had ensured him the good bottle. The whisky industry had suffered badly after the abrupt temperature drop in the northern hemisphere, but after a Demcowill health conference had taken place on whisky's severe health risks, an edict had gone out on strict rationing. Whisky is hard to get these days. Sólman pours them drinks.

The kitchen is part of the living room. Helgi sits at the kitchen-island as Sólman starts flambéing the steak and then puts it in the oven. He takes a bottle of red wine from a rack and curses himself silently for having forgotten to open it an hour ago. He uncorks the bottle with a pop; Cos d'Estournel, a dry, cherry-red Bordeaux with mild acidity and a strong after-taste. Decent wine, he thinks.

Sólman is quite satisfied with his apartment in the European District. It is nearly a hundred square meters, on the twelfth floor, with an excellent view and nice balcony. He spends many hours there alone, reading for pleasure. That is when he feels best. Life in Europe is easy compared to back home, and everything relatively close by. It's uplifting to visit the sunny Mediterranean as the stinging North Sea cold slinks ever more steadily over Brussels.

"Morgunblaðið was given a moratorium last week," says Sólman as he chops vegetables and adds: "These have been difficult times for the newspaper; it's said never to have managed the leap into this century."

"Yes, a sad chapter in the story of once a proud paper and breastwork of democratic powers," Helgi replies, looking into his glass. "It took a hard stance against the Soviet Empire; Stalin's gulags. It was often buffeted by the winds, but told the truth and nothing but the truth," he adds.

"Whatever the case, dinner's ready," Sólman says cheerfully.

They sit down at the table.

"I heard that Krummi is free again," says Helgi changing the subject. "His Fish Fight protest at the Berlaymont were all over the news in Denmark. They were quite dramatic. But I did think that the court's treatment of the Westmann Giant seemed harsh," says Helgi as Sólman pours him wine.

"The Icelandic demonstrations get on people's nerves. It's no simple matter, being a Euro-Icelander," replies Sólman. "The Friendship Society issued a statement condemning the madness at Berlaymont and urging respect for law and order. Continuous demonstrations create a negative image of Iceland and its people. I wanted to soften the language of the statement, but others on the board wanted to go further and recommend harsher penalties for the villains. We reached a compromise but we had to condemn the actions of Krummi and his companions – they really did go too far." Sólman chooses his words carefully.

"I've never met Krummi even though we served our sentences at the same time," says Helgi. He pauses, obviously in a reflective mood. "Your Friendship Society has issued another statement about Krummi. It's still not very friendly," he adds.

"Hooliganism is intolerable, of course, and we have to keep in with Berlin. But give us some credit, we did make it clear that the situation at home is difficult. Everything is done to get things going again, the subsidies are at maximum, but it's like water off a duck's back. There's no end to the exodus to Europe. People are fleeing the darkness and grumbling," says Sólman.

"If only the matter were so simple," says Helgi in his deliberate manner.

"It's hard to read the signs these days," agrees Sólman. "Iceland made the right choice when it joined the European Union. We were faced with a difficult choice. The situation was bad but the trouble is that things have just got worse. The economic decline back home is depressing."

"That's a new tone from you," exclaims Helgi in surprise. Their friendship is a bit unusual, considering their completely different attitudes toward political issues. "Not that there's much point in being an independent or a sceptic these days," continues Helgi morosely as he cuts at his steak. The issues back home in Copenhagen are making him quite aggressive. "The Komizars rule Europe now. Everyone bows to Berlin." Helgi snorts. "Decisions are taken at meetings in Berlin. Referenda and elections have become part of the past, done away with as the public kept voting against the elite."

Sólman finally manages to get a word in as Helgi puts a juicy morsel into his mouth. "The Great European State is and has been a controversial subject in poor old Iceland, I will allow you that," declares Sólman. "But not everyone feels as you do. You forget how bad things had got. The Althingi had stopped being an effective parliament and fallen into disarray as squabbles and petty disputes took the place of effective government. No wonder it was stripped of real power and is now only symbolic.

"In any case, not all that much really changed under the new arrangement. Iceland is a state in the Great European State instead of a republic within the European Union. Six of one, half a dozen of the other, if you ask me." Sólman pauses. "You detect a new tone, you say. I will admit that at times I miss the old Republic, with all of its merits and flaws. However, that was the old days. I was only a boy when Iceland joined the Union."

Helgi sniffs. "Well, maybe you've got a point," he allows. "But what about recent events? What about Krummi?"

Sólman smiles. "Oh yes, Krummi. I suppose there will always be a Krummi, but I am just one man, and one man can't change things. I am a faithful servant of the European state. That is my job. I have to be careful what I say and do. In spite of it all, I live and work in Brussels. I don't want to lose my job."

"But don't you ever ask questions," demands Helgi.

"I met the Westmann Giant yesterday," says Sólman, and starts outlining their conversation in the cafe on the Rue de la Montagne.

Helgi listens thoughtfully, nodding in agreement. "Krummi is right," he says. "Independence will give Iceland back her soul, her courage and her future."

8

Time has passed quickly, the evening has being going as well as could be expected. Sólman had been slightly worried about having Helgi over, because despite their friendship the European question has always been like a long, nearby shadow. Sólman had felt sympathy for the solitary man during their years in Copenhagen. The students in the dormitory had looked up to Helgi and were, of course, familiar with his tragedy. Sólman had asked Helgi twice about the riots and the death of his beloved Guðrún, but Helgi had avoided answering.

"The memory is too painful," Helgi had replied, looking into Sólman's eyes. Sólman could sense his friend's grief, but all of the students in Copenhagen were amazed at Helgi's stoic calm and serenity in the light of the tragedy. Although Helgi was a loner, the students sought out his friendship. Sólman had always known Helgi's attitude toward Europe, but that had not changed their friendship. And of course, Helgi had known that Sólman had always been a firm supporter of Europe.

There had been a great deal of turbulence in issues affecting the nation at the start of the 21st century. They discuss the events leading up to Iceland's entrance into the European Union. Helgi recites a poem by Matthías Johannessen:

Oh, you who break the shell
of this new day, take
them in your arms, lift them
onto the wagon-worn
cart-horse of history
so that we can bring them
from beneath the sharp-edged moon

of time,
the sorrows of time are heavy
as lead,
so that we can bring them
away from the cutting gleam
of the nation's history
to beneath the sun-pale sky
and home.

There's a short way to go
and soon day will dawn
anew.

Helgi feels that he can hear the weary horses and the heavy purl of time in this magnificent poem. It was composed when Europe's shadow was cast over everything in Iceland. The one who broke the shell embraced discontented, wayward drifters who had been consecrated to death. The expanses, however, were still on the Pass of Hope's side; the poet's hope for a bright new day. "Naturally, the poet grimaced and pulled his jacket tighter in the piercing cold," says Helgi after a while.

Sólman clears away the meal and pours them whisky. "I disagree about Iceland finding salvation in independence. We need Europe as a backbone, we can't survive alone out there on the periphery," he says. "Look. Our united Europe is much larger and stronger than the USA. Absolutely amazing. The Great European State extends from Reykjavík in the west to Kiev in the east; from the Barents Sea in the north to the Mediterranean in the south. Europe is massive." He warms to his theme, feeling the excitement of the dawning new age. Europe had emerged from the shadows of post World War II; had reclaimed what America and the Soviet empire had taken after the defeat of Hitler. For the better, in fact.

Helgi grunts and speaks more gravely than before. "But Sólman, old friend, this vision of a superstate blinds you to the facts that we are between continents." Helgi continues reciting the poets, this time

Thórarinn Eldjárn:

That we on the smallest continent
occupy Hliðskjálf,
but know nothing of
this world or another.

Near-sighted Eurocans
on the mid-Atlantic ridge
with no focused vision
of Eumericana.

From Hliðskjálf; the throne of Óðin, the world's smallest continent lost its vision when the new semi-god came knocking on the door. The bard Tómas Guðmundsson composed:

And if someone should long for some other land,
let him go there himself, on the tiller his hand.
For the aim is one — nor east nor west across the wave —
we shall keep for ourselves the land our Lord gave.

Helgi abruptly slaps his knee as if enough is enough. He needs to calm down, not let the disappointments of Copenhagen get the better of him. "You're really a culinary genius, dear friend," he says smiling to defuse the tension that's building. "Thanks for a delightful supper."

"You're welcome, my friend," replies Sólman. "When you're living in Brussels you can't avoid living and breathing Belgian cuisine. Although a lot here in Brussels has declined, the cuisine is still celebrated."

"The same can't be said for Copenhagen, even though Danish sausages and Tuborg Grøn are always good," replies Helgi with a smile.

They rise from their seats.

9

The two friends stand out on the balcony in the rain, whisky glasses in hand, and regard the European District. Sólman finds it an impressive spectacle and he points out the sights to his visitor from the north. The Berlaymont houses the offices of the Peripheries, Fisheries, and Agriculture Bureaus. The building is quite old, built in the early days of the European adventure. Not far away are the offices of the Ministry of Defence of the western region, in the palace of Charlemagne, King of the Franks, who, by his major conquests laid the foundation for the western European state more than a thousand years ago. And of course there is Europe's unclean child: the European Parliament.

Sólman recalls that annoyance and suspicion regarding Berlin occasionally appear in Britain. London had been furious when headquarters of the western defences were located in Brussels but Berlin just shrugged its shoulders, Rome and Paris looked the other way. Opposition in the UK has more or less fallen silent. The sun of the British Empire has set long ago and British politicians have become lightweights after numerous failed attempts for repatriating powers to Britain. The Peripheries Bureau is considered important for maintaining the unity of the great state and nurturing areas that are struggling, not least in the northern regions where land meets the outermost sea.

"The European fathers acted in good faith," says Sólman as he points at the historical buildings.

"No doubt they started off with good intentions but they made serious errors. The authorities are remote, untouchable, and incomprehensible to ordinary people," Helgi replies quite calmly, looking toward the Berlaymont as he continues. "The new class of Komizars does not have its mandate from the people for the people;

the bureaucrats are out of touch with people's lives. Hanging on the outside is the European Parliament with nameless MEPs who profit from it and double-profit. The system does not account to anyone, and auditors have their hands over their eyes so no one stops the euros that disappear into the pockets of the indolent. No one has control over anything; everyone looks away as the auditors deny responsibility for the waste. But above all, Europe's founding fathers forgot to take into account the nature of power. They overlooked the inevitable craving of a multinational organisation for hegemony, a craving that sucks up everything and sweeps everything that is deemed discomforting into a giant dungeon." Helgi turns to Sólman. "That's how it is with the Icelandic nation, serving its cruel sentence in a giant dungeon."

To Helgi it has always been incomprehensible that Europe's founding fathers should have set out on their journey without reckoning with history. They appeared to have learned little from the legacy of medieval times, the colonial age, not to mention the wars of the 20th century. This is even more bizarre considering that they stood on the ruins of Europe after World War II. In their zealous desire for peace, the guilt-ridden fathers overlooked minding the guardians of democracy to ensure that the Euro-train would not jump the tracks, which of course it did, as throughout the ages. How ironic. They had started out in Rome by signing blank pieces of paper, which basically became standard practice as the bureaucracy swelled and puffed up.

"Let's face it," Helgi continues, "Europe has never come to terms with its 20th century flirtation with authoritarianism, totalitarianism, hegemony or bureaucracy. Nazis ruled in Berlin, fascists in Rome and Madrid, communists in Moscow and a cocktail of all of these across the continent. The French kissed the Nazi boot. They tiptoed along until they were overwhelmed by the Hun's tanks."

Sólman looks at his old friend, who has a lot on his mind. The heaviness in Helgi's words reminds him most of speeches in the old days in Reykjavík. Helgi talks passionately. "In the world of big solutions, mankind got stuck in swampy tracts. Everything became huge; huge companies, huge corrupt banks and huge states. Politicians love affair with big bankers sealed the fate of democracy; people who handle other people's money form the new Nomenklatura. Individual freedom got lost in your Demcowill. Everyone is so confused that nobody knows what to do, and therefore no one needs to stamp the receipt, because truth does not exist; it is relative in the world of Demcowill. History is cyclical; the world spins in circles again, again, again and again. It's yet another year, and yet again we have the people downtrodden by big government to the glory of the state: the Greater European State." Helgi again looks at the spectacular view of the great buildings.

"I don't know whether history is cyclical, but it certainly rhymes," Sólman says philosophically. He, however, finds some truth in Helgi's comments but points out that the Icelandic nation had been obliged to choose sides after the collapse of the banks at the start of the century. "The Icelandic banks became way too big. It was madness," says Sólman, making quotation marks with his fingers for the word "big". "And then they collapsed like houses of cards. Europe was our best option," he adds lifting his whisky glass. "Cheers."

Helgi grins as his friend lifts his glass, salutes and replies sarcastically. "The sun sank into the ocean and with it courage and boldness. Sharks picked up the scent of blood. When the sun rose, the nation had lost its way. The nation that broke into prosperity in the 20th century, with individual freedom as its guiding star, was completely lost at the dawn of the 21st century. The ideology of collectivism became the motto of the day; statism, socialism, supervision and surveillance. Freedom and individual rights gave way before the undefined interests of the ever-moving herd.

"The nation protested the meltdown caused by a few corrupt bankers, bribed by depraved businessmen; flames burned to the rhythmic banging of pots and pans. The individual was driven into exile. The great collapse was a spiritual shipwreck to the nation," Helgi has become quite cynical as he recites a poem.

Then hatred surged, like waves at sea,
and they cursed tyrannic plutocracy.
Finally the crowd went on the attack,
gallows raised for that bloodthirsty pack.

Sólman laughs heartily at Helgi's eloquent and brilliant rhetoric. "This reminds me of times gone," he says laughing heartily.

Helgi's eyes sparkle in the cold Brussels night. "And then there is Krummi and men like him," he says and again salutes. "Iceland's farmers and fishermen have always been slow to anger, but they had had enough when raising sheep had become just a hobby and all of the country's pigs and chickens had been killed. Instead of eating mutton and downing Icelandic skyr, the Icelander drank diluted European skimmed milk, devoured Danish bacon, scoffed down German sausages and gorged on Polish chicken breasts."

Helgi reflects on the first big demonstration after EU membership. It was a few summers after the nation had commenced on its great migration to the Euroland that the farmers shook their fists and stamped their feet to the barking of dogs on the square in front of the Althingi Building. They poured out milk and turned out sheep and cows. People were shocked by the farmers' actions, since the sheep and cows destroyed the flowerbeds. The residents of Reykjavík's elite had long since forgotten that they were descendants of farmers; let alone poets and kings.

The leader of the farmers had come from a remote valley in the Eastfjords that had been known first and foremost for monsters and hauntings back in the dim and distant past. Kormákur from Dagshús had brought along a lice-covered dog that howled endlessly and rolled impetuously, it being no easy matter to bite the lice from its fur.

"You can take it from me, freedom is worth more than the height of the ceiling on the farm. I'm afraid they've forgotten that here in Reykjavík," Kormákur had said to his dog. "No one here owns his own land, since everything is on credit with interest, compound interest and compound compound interest — with interest on top of that. He who owns his own land is free. It's better to scamper off than to accept their freedom."

However, the stench was so rank that the city people didn't dare come close to the farmer and his dog. The foster-brothers were taken aside, washed and deloused. The farmer shook his head over this treatment by the representatives of kindness in Reykjavík, but the dog stopped howling. After the delousing the farmers lost their leader, since the beast had stopped fawning at its master.

Kormákur set off on a journey throughout the world in search of his own Dagshús.

"Blood follows the track," Kormákur said to his dog in parting.

Helgi smiles to Sólman as he concludes his sermon. "Since Kormákur, farmers haven't been seen protesting in the capital. The rednecks evaporated like dew before the sun, and the chief hobby of the new rustic is to practice gentleman-farming in the countryside with subsidies and subsidized subsidies from smiling, all-embracing bureaucrats while the auditors look in the other direction.

Oh, wonder!
How many fair creatures are here!
How beautiful mankind is!
Oh, courageous new world
wherein such folk dwell.

Sólman smiles faintly as Helgi recites the classic work on the brave, new world. "Now we have Krummi. The struggle of a nation at the farthest reaches of the sea for its survival will last throughout the ages. All that has happened, can happen, and all that can happen, happens — in the eternal stream of time," concludes Helgi.

62

★ 10 ★

"Oh, very esoteric," says Sólman.

Sólman leans over the rail and looks down at the parking lot, where two men are fighting like dogs. "Endless nonsense in these people," he comments distractedly.

"It's a peculiar human bent to fight," agrees Helgi, "and governments use that as an excuse to oppress – which always seems to come as an eternal surprise. Europe has become a superpower. Has it made the Europeans free and happy? No. The Great European State is good at monitoring its own citizens, my friend. It can't be denied that the bureaucrats understand the art of looking over people's shoulders."

"That may be true, but human rights are guaranteed in the European Constitution, human rights are engraved in it as if in stone," says Sólman determinedly.

"Is that so?" asks Helgi doubtfully.

Sólman hesitates as he looks at his friend.

"Human rights... engraved in stone," reaffirms Sólman.

"Hopefully you're right but I don't share your conviction," replies Helgi, looking deeply into his friend's eyes. "Although Armstrong stood alone on the moon, mankind was with him in spirit. One man held the torch aloft and the masses were inspired. One man broadened mankind's knowledge."

Sólman shakes his head. "Armstrong on the moon. What does that matter?"

Helgi fully understands Sólman's puzzled expression, since he hasn't made his point particularly well, but one voice can change destiny. "Europe doddered like a frightened mouse around Adolf Hitler; the world preferred to shut its eyes and dance the polka and jive until Winston Churchill inspired and emboldened millions to stand up against the black threat. Freedom drove off the evil monsters. Although justice won, the task is eternal.

"Evil is always at work. It beguiles people into supporting its cause by donning ever-changing new clothes until the Hun throws off its disguise and draws its sword, and then there is a need once more to face evil. An uncountable number of Western thinkers and artists praised Joseph Stalin, who took hammer and sickle in hand and waved the red flag of communism in the name of equality. Stalin lined up innocent men and women in front of execution squads or beat them to death in the Gulags.

"Still, they waved the Stalinist flag with pens in hand and proclaimed the arrival of the Soviet Empire. We must never lose sight of the freedom of the individual nor let down our guard over democracy which they have run away from under the pretence of Demcowill. What rubbish. There is danger at the door when the state sticks its hands down the shirts of its citizens because the Devil himself with horns and a tail is said to be plotting treachery against the state. If the Devil is to be chased off, they claim it's imperative to stick their hands down people's shirts to beat him. Which comes first, the chicken or the egg? The state or the Devil — which is the greater enemy? Freedom and democracy are treasures that may never become glittery trinkets on a display shelf. Unfortunately, the demagogues of all ages have tricked people into following them with illusions. The statists never allow themselves any rest. They are constantly at work." Helgi pours himself a glass of water and recites a poem:

Still the statists are afoot.
None of them says it,
they just long for it.
None of them says a whit,
they simply strive for it:
United States of Europe.
Bigger than Big Brother to the west
though the people say "Nay, nein, non".

"Democracy was like a small blossom with a quivering tear among the violent men formulating their treacherous plots," says Helgi, who then recites some lines from the old national anthem, which had not been sung since the Republic was dissolved.

For you one day is as a thousand years
and a thousand years a day, no more.

Sólman hasn't heard the national anthem in years. He had completely forgotten the words of the song. For a moment, Sólman wonders about his own guilt. Is he a living symbol of Orwellian dualism? Sólman has admitted to two opposing viewpoints. He has always been aware of the lie, yet has been a devoted servant of unchecked power. With dualism, he has erased the truth and enjoys lounging on downy couches in Brussels. He has closed his eyes to the destiny of his own nation. He is part of authority, part of the illusion.

He has mocked the truth through docility toward the ruling powers. He has told lies and pushed discomfort aside.

Falsehood always precedes the truth.

What had Orwell written on the facade of the Ministry of Truth?

War is peace
Freedom is slavery
Ignorance is power

Falsehood always comes first.

Sólman fingers a euro in his pocket and imagines Winston Smith handling the coin with its slogans of war, peace, freedom, dependency, and ignorance along with an portrait of Big Brother. Sólman says not a word. A lie on a white surface. None of them says it, they just want it to be: The Great European State. Then he shakes his head angrily. That damn Helgi twisting reality to his own romantic version of the past. Human rights were written into the European Constitution, damn it, and that was all there was to it.

"The Republic was doomed," exclaims Sólman. "Europe was the future, it is the future."

"We ran into bumpy ground and lost control," replies Helgi.

The two friends look over the handrail at the men fighting below; the police have arrived to intervene.

Helgi pauses a moment then seems to gather himself together and smiles ruefully. "I am sorry, old friend. I did not come here to moan at you about old politics. And after you cooked such a great steak and managed to find this wonderful whisky as well.

"I just get fed up with it all, you see. When the idea was proposed that the nation try adopting the euro on political grounds, without membership in the EU, the bureaucrats from Brussels emerged from their mouse-holes and said nay, nej and nein. Iceland did not enjoy the same friendship as other small European states. The bureaucrats in Brussels spoke like politicians, having received promotions at the start of the Current Age. The First Komizar had sauntered around with the leaders of the G8 like any other elected leader. No one said anything, it just happened. The bureaucrats of all nations nodded their heads blissfully over the growth and development of the bureaucracy."

"Well, when you put it like that," Sólman smiles. "I suppose dear old Iceland was basically forced into the old European Union."

They both fall silent. Then Helgi pushes his whisky glass to one side. "Anyway, I have business with you," he says carefully.

"Oh?" exclaims Sólman.

"I'm being pushed out of the Antiquaries Club. But more to the point, Iceland has been cast out," says Helgi.

This news surprises Sólman. He knew of Bentsen's illness, but everyone had hoped that Helgi would take up the torch.

"How could this happen?" he asks.

Helgi describes the bullying of the Professor's Party, as he calls it. "The key meeting where I was practically sacked and the Club changed direction was convened illegally. I tried to point all this out, but they just over ruled me. I've never seen so much spite," says Helgi. "They would never have attacked Bentsen. They followed the scent of blood like wolves pursuing their prey. I'm afraid that

Icelandic studies will be stuck in a cubbyhole. Fanatical archaeologists have taken over the club in company with modern literary thieves. And people want to suppress the theory of the naming of Iceland, since it is taboo that ancient wisdom has something to do with the history of Iceland's settlement. They are not interested in the truth, only in getting their hands on the lucrative funds from Berlin – but that cash come with strings attached."

Sólman raises an eyebrow. He had never had much faith in this new idea about the settlement of Iceland. However, he has a sincere interest in helping his friend.

"What do you want me to do?" he asks.

"You could use your influence," says Helgi.

"You know that my department does not deal with cultural issues, but I will of course do my best, I will do my very best," replies Sólman a bit sceptically, clearing his throat. "Despite the problems, Icelandic voices can be heard in the corridors here in Brussels. We have influence."

"You know that I have few places to turn to," replies Helgi sadly.

"That's crazy, guys," Krummi shouts from the new *Elliði* as he sails up next to the European trawler, the *Zeus*. They are to the west of the Westmann Islands. Krummi watches as the crew members of the *Zeus* throw dead fish back into the sea; it's not just a few undersized or damaged fish. It's basket after basket of prime cod.

There is a tone of desperation in the voice of José Clayey, the captain of *Zeus*, as he shouts back to Krummi: "I can't put a sign on the nets saying: 'No cod today, please.' I hate discarding fish but this is Europa..." He says something else, but the freshening wind whips his words away.

"This bloody discard rule is brutal rape," shouts Krummi across the grey waters but the captain just shrugs his shoulders. Discarding is the action that fishermen carry out as they catch fish in their nets, after reaching their quota as defined by Brussels. Fishing vessels in the North Atlantic throw away up to half of what they catch to stay within their quotas. The problem is that in a mixed fishery where many different fish live together, fishermen can't control the species that they catch. Fishing for one species often means catching another, and if fishermen are not allowed to land them, the only option is to throw them overboard. It's estimated that discards in the Atlantic are about 50% of the total catch.

After Berlin pronounced Icelandic fishing grounds as European Territorial Waters, there is no stopping the European fleet. "They really don't give a shit nor have the slightest intention of responsible fishing," Krummi curses, but deep within he knows that he's fighting a losing battle.

As his own boat rises and falls on the swell, Krummi does a quick calculation. There are tons of fish going back dead into the sea from the *Zeus*. Thousands of people could have been fed with these fish. But the law from Brussels says that the fish can't be landed; the excess catch must be discarded. These are fish for which the *Zeus* no longer has any quota; they filled their cod quota. Up to a million tonnes of edible fish are being thrown away every year. It's enough to supply the chip shops of Britain for over a decade. The crazy irony is that the quota system is meant to conserve fish stocks, particularly cod. Krummi has organised his Fish Fight campaign against the madness. He puts the blame on the system, rather than the fishermen who throw away the fish.

The *Zeus* is fishing for plaice, pollock and haddock; a few dozen tons of these species have indeed been caught and are now packed in ice. But they can't stop catching cod, which then has to be discarded. It's the Greenland cod that unexpectedly migrated to Icelandic fishing banks early this spring. It's not the first time that the Greenland cod pops up in Icelandic waters, and will not be the last.

"This is immoral!" shouts Krummi and adds: "If this is conservation, then I'm the Mad Hatter. It seems obvious to me you can't conserve fish by throwing a million tonnes of them back in the sea, dead."

José Manuel Cleyey nods in agreement, but what can he do? He's only captain. "If we could only land all the fish we catch, we could go to sea for half as many days, use half the fuel and no fish would be wasted. It's madness!" he shouts back.

Krummi shakes his head as he turns the *Elliði* away, back to the Islands. It's the system that is at fault; a system that rapes nature. Krummi certainly had tried his best when he cut the trawler's lines in the old days and threw pollock in Brussels. He's done with protests. He's been doing all he can with his fish fights.

Now he has other plans.

11

The strong southeasterly wind and rain appear to have no effect on a man standing next to the memorial to the students who died in the conflict on Austurvöllur Square in Reykjavík. The memorial is a short distance from the statue of Sæmundur the Wise riding on the seal; modest, as if placed on sacred ground like Jan Palach's cross on Wenceslas Square in Prague. The eternal flame casts a pale light on the rain-drenched face of Helgi Thorláksson, who stares vacantly at the ground. This is his first visit to the old country since being released from prison all those years ago. The memory is painful. It is his first visit home since Guðrún's death, despite numerous invitations over the years for him to return.

He has had to admit defeat in Copenhagen. The professors have taken over the Antiquaries Club; shown him to the door — actually kicked him out into the blackest darkness. It hurts. Meeting Sólman had wakened a strong desire in him to return home. It had taken Helgi completely by surprise, but in all honesty his trip home has little to do with Sólman. He knows deep inside that Sólman can do little even though he is perfectly willing to help and has encouraged him vigorously.

At least as far as Helgi has understood.

A fresh gust of wind lashes rain into his face. He hunches his shoulders and hurries off. He walks toward the National Centre for Cultural Heritage on Hverfisgata Street. Helgi had considered applying for a job there, but then thought better of it. No point. Better known as the Culture House, the Centre is still one of the most venerable building in the country. A poor nation had built the grand building around its books. It had long housed the National Library but had become dilapidated until it was rebuilt around the nation's culture. It is now divided into the Iceland Room on the one hand and the Europe Hall on the other. The European Cultural Institute has expressed an interest in infusing new life into its activities and strengthening ties across the ocean. The administration wants to give the building a new name: Europe House. Wave upon wave of demonstrations have followed, so the Komizar for Culture in Berlin hesitated. However, the idea will soon be re-proposed; of that Helgi is sure. The manuscript exhibition has been moved to the East Room on the second floor, while the Greenland exhibition takes up the rest of the space.

After dining with Sólman, Helgi had flown to Copenhagen, but Iceland pulled hard enough to bring him back to his old homeland. Now he's going to meet the Westmann Giant who had taken on the dragon in Brussels with putrid pollock for a weapon.

First, though, Helgi is on his way to the Culture House to meet an old classmate, Leifur Eiríksson. They had worked together in opposing the major state, but Leifur had been overseas when the fighting broke out on Austurvöllur Square, all those years ago. Now he is a professor at the Nordic Institute. Helgi leaves the rain-drenched memorial and plods through the dripping streets to reach the Institute. He passes several students in the lobby.

Leifur comes out to meet him and his handshake is firm.

"I was starting to think that I would never see you again," says Leifur, who is always called "the Red" though his name might have led to him being called "the Lucky" like his namesake who discovered America. The reasons are obvious: a full head of red hair and an obvious connection to the terrifying warrior who settled in Greenland more than a thousand years ago. His nickname had been a constant topic of conversation in the old days. Many people wanted to name him "the Unlucky" due to his bad luck with women. It hasn't been an easy matter being called Leifur Eiríksson, even though it sounds good.

Their careers have been different and completely contrary to what was predicted for them when they were students. Fame had been predicted for Helgi, while Leifur was expected to become a desk clerk.

How the world can be capricious.

Leifur is the country's most renowned scholar, ever since he solved the puzzle of the authorship of *Njál's Saga*. He had managed, through unexpected revelations, to prove that the chieftain Snorri Sturluson really had written the saga. The eternal dispute over the authorship of *Njál's Saga* is now a thing of the past. Helgi, on the other hand, had become an outsider, meeting only closed doors after the tragedy on Austurvöllur Square. He had gathered the crumbs that fell from the table in Copenhagen. They had been comrades in the fight against the abolishment of the Republic.

"The Republic was a brief consolation," says Helgi as they walk past the flag and coat of arms of Europe.

"The Nomenklatura misled the nation. The nation would have done better to be on its guard against the blarney about European glory," replies Leifur.

They go up the stairs past the Greenland Exhibition in the library into the side room where the manuscripts are on display. The old map of Iceland's settlement hangs on the wall. Lines show the routes of the settlers from Norway and the British Isles to Iceland and on to America.

"The settlement of Iceland during the 8th and 9th centuries is one of the great achievements of mankind; the greatest mass exodus across the sea that history up to that point is able to tell. They set out across the churning sea rather than endure the injustice of their overlords at home. It is remarkable that the people who created some of the greatest literature of the Middle Ages should so disastrously forget the lessons of its history," says Leifur.

They stand before the manuscripts of the Kingsbook edition of Eddic poems and Flateyjarbók, which are on display in the Culture House in honour of the recent visit of the Komizar of Culture. During her visit she had tried to calm the waves that rose following the proposal to rename the building Europe House.

Leifur looks hard at Helgi and changes the subject. "Some of my contacts say that you are thinking of leading the opposition to the Great European State."

"The idea has come up," admits Helgi.

"And what is your reply?" asks Leifur.

"It depends on the premises of the fight." Helgi's expression is ironical and it is clear that he does not want to reveal his cards.

"You speak in riddles, my friend," says Leifur.

"If, like the Westmann Giant in Brussels, people go sliding around quoting the old heroes with grins on their faces, then everything is possible. I do not mean to propose violence or vandalism as weapons, but instead the old books and Icelandic verse. I must admit that so much has changed since we were young. So few ravens are to be found today. I'm not sure that I understand these new Ice-Europeans who think only about compensation and subsidies. The Icelander is angry because ... just because he's angry," replies Helgi.

He recites old verse:

If only the louse is Icelandic
it's an honour to be bitten.

Leifur laughs heartily. "Our countrymen have always been extremely angry and it's not easy for the nation to put things right again. It's long been easy to mislead an Icelander. It must be admitted, however, that Demcowill is a clever word, a good trick," admits Leifur ruefully.

They walk into the Jón Sigurðsson Exhibition Room. Icelanders always refer to Jón as their president although the title is associated with his presidency at the Icelandic Literature Society in Copenhagen. His heroic performance in 1851 when the Danes tried to annex Iceland lives in folklore up to this day.

"Jon Sigurðsson did not resort to idle talk, pretence, or illusion, no boasting or bombast. To be and not to seem — that was the man," says Leifur. "When we were children we all learned how he has declared 'I protest' at Althingi. And the rest of the men at Althingi joined in shouting 'We all protest', even when the Danish troops came with fixed bayonets."

"No glib talker or demagogue," adds Helgi. "And his action worked. His leadership bore fruit on the thousandth years anniversary of the Icelandic settlement in 1874 when the Danish king paid his first visit to his colony upon the farthest reaches of the sea and brought the islanders their constitution. Jón Sigurðsson stopped the Danes from annexing Iceland and thus laying the foundations of sovereignty. They punished him by keeping him away from the event."

"Was it inevitable?" exclaims Leifur, suddenly angry.

"What?" asks Helgi in surprise at his red-haired friend's outburst.

"Abandoning the Republic? They managed to keep the Commonwealth alive for four centuries, but the Republic just a century," says Leifur.

Helgi looks at Leifur, but then says emphatically: "The zeitgeist of super-solutions confused the nation, but of course it was difficult to paddle against the stream. Of course it was difficult to resist Europe's encroachments. Of course the national ship ran into breakers. Europe tightened the screws and refused to grant the nation shelter."

"The message from Brussels was clear: we swallow you," says Leifur.

"The ogress stole Búkolla," adds Helgi recalling the old Icelandic story of a lost cow rescued from ogresses by a small child. "Moo, moo, my Búkolla — moo now, wherever you are."

"The nation hasn't even started looking for Búkolla, never mind rescuing her," concludes Leifur.

12

"Surtur was just a taste of things to come when he stuck out his head at Surtsey," says Leifur satirically. The volcanic island of Surtsey had formed in an eruption in November 1963. The crew of a fishing boat was the first to see it, and then the world watched in amazement. The old prophecy in the poem *Völuspá* was coming true. Surtur came to the country with fire. "Remember the legend. Surtur was the evil dragon breathing fire. It was stretching its claws toward the country at the farthest reaches of the sea." Leifur looks at Helgi and they cannot help but smile. They both loved playing games with references to the old sagas and old gods.

"The European dragon seemed harmless at first, but then it fattened, thriving well. Its spectre spread throughout the continent. It coiled itself up south of the Westmann Islands and awaited its opportunity," says Helgi, before quoting the ancient pagan prophecy in the book *Völuspá:*

> *From the south fares Surtur*
> *with bane of branches,*
> *shone from his sword*
> *the battle-god's sun.*
> *Cliffs quake,*
> *ogress reels,*
> *the dead tread Hel's road*
> *and heaven is rent.*

In the old pagan tales, the evil warrior Surtur came from the south, breathing fire and embers that reflected off the weapons of the gods as they prepared their defence, but their doom could not be avoided, nor could the undoomed come to Hel. At Ragnarök, the Twilight of the Gods, mankind and the gods perished in a terrible battle against the giants and the forces of evil. The sky was rent and the earth sank into the sea, the sun darkened and the clear stars vanished from the sky. It was a terrible vision of the end of the world, and Surtur had started it all off.

Leifur looks at Helgi, who gazes out the window at Arnarhóll Hill where the statue of Ingólfur Arnarson stands, recalling his arrival as the first Norse settler in Iceland. "Despite Ragnarök, everything wasn't finished," Leifur says thoughtfully. "The pagans said that the eddying green Earth rose from the sea and humanfolk settled in Gimli. Was the hall in Gimli, despite all else, simply the Republic that lasted for 100 years? I wonder."

Helgi smiles and Leifur pours coffee into their cups.

"But when everything seemed to be going as well as could be in Gimli, a shadow drew over the sky." Leifur recites the last verse of *Völuspá*.

The dismal dragon
Niðhöggur comes flying,
the flashing viper
from Niðafjöll;
bears on his wings,
—flies over field—
bodies of men.
Now she will sink.

There is a grave undercurrent to Leifur's words as he recites the final stanza, since the outcome of the final battle is not yet determined. The seeress had seen the great, flying dragon, Niðhögg from the Niðafjöll Mountains. "You're preparing for battle with the dragon from Niðafjöll," says Leifur, who has stood up to leave, to go teach a class. "And dragons are an unforgiving enemy. The outcome is precarious," he adds. "You will have to watch yourself."

They part on the steps of the Culture House. Helgi wraps himself in his tattered old overcoat, winds a scarf around his neck, puts on his hat and walks down Hverfisgata Street. Neither Helgi nor Leifur pay any attention to a man in a black suit with an e-notebook in hand, watching the passers-by.

The old International House is on Helgi's left, Arnarhóll Hill on his right. There are some drifters in heated conversation by the statue of Ingólfur Arnarson which a poor nation had raised to celebrate its sovereignty in 1918. In the distance is the concert hall Harpa, to which so many hopes had been pinned. Gaps have formed in the old glass wall. When emigrations started occurring, attendance declined sharply at the Icelandic Symphony's performances. People said that since the elite had left the country there was no one left to applaud, so the symphony was disbanded, losses and long-winded talk having set their mark on its management. Rock and roll had taken its toll and marked the building; the concert hall, once the pride of the nation, had seen better days, although it was hoped that better times were ahead due to a handsome grant from Berlin. The Europe Bureau now had its offices in the former Central Bank. European warships are anchored in the Strait, warplanes fly over Mt. Esja.

The Ministry Offices are now on Helgi's left, as well as the statue of the Danish king Christian IX, whereas the statue of the Icelandic patriot Hannes Hafstein had been taken away for mysterious repairs that have lasted several years. Hannes Hafstein had become Iceland's first minister back in 1904. The Governor has been based in the Ministry Offices ever since the country became a state in the United States of Europe. Helgi plods on through the bleak streets.

Standing at the window of his plush offices within the Ministry Offices, Governor Mangi Steffensen watches the hunched figure move off through the rain. Helgi's sudden arrival had been reported to him, of course, but he is still surprised to see him. "There goes trouble," Steffensen mutters under his breath as the man passes out of sight. Then he glances up at the sky. "Will this cursed Icelandic rain ever stop?"

Governor Steffensen turns from the grey scene outside and leafs impatiently through a stack of files. All of this paperwork gets on his nerves, but that is not his concern now. No, that is not what is worrying him. For the hundredth time he fingers the latest order from Berlin – the demand for increased surveillance of Hrafn "Krummi" Illugason. Of course, thinks Steffensen, the Westmann Giant is unpredictable and up for anything. And he did go too far with that Fish Fight in the Berlaymont. But even so, the locals won't like it. Krummi has a lot of support. Berlin places extreme emphasis on suspected terrorists being kept in check with the Olympic year coming up.

Steffensen holds the directive and hammers the paper crossly with his fist, referring as it does to national security. However, he has to admit that the giant had cunningly sailed under cover of night with his rotten pollock to Brussels, where the foul stench was downright unbearable.

"Control the giant," he snorts to himself. "That is easier said than done."

Steffensen has an appointment to meet the regional government in the Ministry Offices in half an hour. He has been Governor for ten years, but has to admit that he finds it a thankless task. It is no easy matter to govern Iceland, where all the complaining could kill anyone, since the people bear no respect for authority and have little understanding of the nation's problems. No one has been able to come up with a practical solution to halt the exodus south to the major European cities any more than the exodus to Reykjavík from the farms in the 20th century could have been halted.

Yet people still argue constantly and tear their hair.

Then there are those who want to break from Europe and establish an independent fantasy state in the spirit of the past. Their voices find a certain amount of popular support. The nation is in no way prepared to stand on its own two feet. Some even say they should re-adopt the old, tattered króna?

Steffensen shakes his head; their foolishness is ridiculous.

He is cautious by nature, perhaps too hesitant. He knows deep down that new times are looming. He feels stuck, like a louse between two nails: the nation and the federal government in Berlin. Only last night he had voiced his thoughts at an after dinner speech to businessmen in Reykjavík.

"What I have been needing in particular is initiative in innovative thinking and other talents useful for forging paths for advancement. I have seen little, no doubt too little, for major changes. I have been conservative, no doubt too conservative, but I hope that I have not done too much direct damage during my term, although I have obviously done indirect damage by not doing what might have been demanded of me."

Mangi Steffensen smiles to himself, recalling the banqueters' bewildered looks when he had spoken so openly. People had looked at each other and shaken their heads. He had felt annoyed because he knew that the bureaucrat golden boys in Berlin looked down on him as an Icelandic yokel, while the locals thought of him as a lackey of Berlin. He had endured fierce criticism from all directions, and so his support has dried up and the bastards in Berlin are now going to sacrifice him. He is sure of it. His usefulness is over. The bureaucratic gang that holds firmly to the reins of power no doubt has its eye on new candidates.

"Maybe they won't manage it," he says out loud.

The nation adores this Krummi and now Helgi Thorláksson is back in Iceland. Maybe it is simply best for those ruffians to take the reins. Steffensen had gone so far as to hint at this in his speech. "I would be perfectly thrilled if ultimate authority were placed in the hands of people who have the abilities that I lack for strengthening the nation and forging new paths of advancement."

The bureaucrats in Berlin had been furious, had gone completely ballistic, having understood the gibe. He knows the obstacles are impossible to surmount, but he felt he had to make the statement. Steffensen laughs out loud, but it is a laughter devoid of joy.

The saying "louse between two nails" had spread like wildfire throughout the country.

Steffensen has nothing to lose. He is going to fight for his political life to the last drop of blood. Political opponents sometimes have to pay the price of underestimation. He slams the clenched fist of his right hand onto the punching bag hanging from the ceiling, following it with a left hook. He had been a decent boxer in his youth and still knows how to deliver a punch.

"We will see who gets the political funeral. Perhaps I'll be sending flowers to Berlin before flowers are laid on my coffin," he says, slamming his fist into the punch bag.

He is indignant at being nicknamed the "Regent" by Krummi and his friends. It was the old name for the Governor in Iceland back when Denmark ruled the island. He knows he should not let the name irritate him, but still. A near namesake of his had been the last to take orders from the king in Copenhagen, which is an unfortunate coincidence. It gives his enemies the opportunity to practice the Icelanders' national sport of bickering and backbiting. A new ditty had spread like wildfire:

> *Let's hate this hound*
> *that leaves us bound*
> *with its nasty Euro-sound.*

Mangi Steffensen frowns, feeling the day to be grey and grim. He needs to appoint an observer to a fifteen-man European negotiation committee concerned with the migrant cod from Greenland. Talks are scheduled to commence next week. Brussels has demanded that the cod be defined as straddling stock. Trawlers from Europe are already hoovering up the fish. Even the Russians could come if they paid a fee to Brussels. The Icelandic fishermen are completely furious, absolutely out of their minds with rage at having to see the cod go to European quota-hoppers who fish Icelandic waters dry. Krummi was stirring things up, Steffensen was sure of it. It would have been better if the big Greenland cod had never swum over the boundary line.

"Why the hell is the cod roaming between countries," mutters Mangi with a frown. The rules have always been clear; straddling stocks belong to Brussels. He finds the issue of the Greenland cod to be a difficult matter that crystallizes the dilemma concerning straddling stocks. People had turned a deaf ear to straddling stocks back in the old days, claiming there had been so few of them. Then the straddling stocks had boomed thirty years ago. That was when Krummi had startled the nation awake when he cut the Basque nets. And now, once again, straddling stock is on the table and Krummi again stirring things up with his Fish fight bullshit.

"It would teach Berlin a lesson if I appointed Krummi to be our observer", mutters Steffensen as he slams the punching bag and laughs ferociously.

13

It had all been so different back when Steffensen had witnessed Iceland joining   Europe, he was then still young and a firm supporter of the cause. The First Komizar, Helmut Bardenfleth, had made an unexpected trip to Iceland. A thick fog had settled over Reykjavík that cold morning, but the air was still. Military parades took place in Bardenfleth's presence, a German cruiser lay in the outer harbour, beside French and Danish frigates. The MPs at Althingi had been rather upset about this, although they held their peace as they reported for the session. On the Althingi's agenda was the Bill on the Dissolution of the Icelandic Republic. The Great European State was due to be founded at a ceremonial meeting in Berlin. The Bill had been delayed in the Icelandic parliament due to opposition, which upset Europe, since it was considered entirely out of place for a tiny state in the Arctic Sea not to be part of the Great European State. Steffensen recalls how all arguments inclined toward strengthening Europe in the new world of super-states; the continent had to be able to meet the challenges of Current Age.

Steffensen reaches into his desk and pulls out a rather battered and old fashioned e-book. He calls up his diary entry for the day. "Today a European regiment carried out military exercises in Reykjavík. Troops came ashore at dawn and the soldiers marched through the centre of town. This neither stirred up nor frightened the MPs. When we assembled for the session we found it inappropriate rather than an annoyance."

The Icelanders had finally been granted an opportunity to familiarise themselves with the terms for joining the European Union that Bardenfleth intended for them. Berlin considered Iceland to be legally part of the European state, and that therefore the fundamental laws of the European state should apply in Iceland. The country was to be a state within a federation of European states. Legislative authority was to be in the hands of the Komizar's Council and the European Parliament in Brussels.

In other words, Iceland was to be a part of the new Great European State for all eternity.

The Nation Party had objected to the European Parliament having complete authority to intervene in all of Iceland's affairs. They argued that only the nation itself could relinquish such a right, not a simple majority of the assembly. There should be a referendum first. They argued that every promise made concerning Iceland's position in the new Europe had been broken. The bill on Iceland's position had been debated in recent months without any conclusion being reached. Bardenfleth's visit to Iceland had been unexpected and some people found it aggressive, not least due to the presence of troops in Reykjavík.

A ditty was composed about the soldiers that proved popular in bars and cafés:

Those boys there can handle guns
most of them are Euro-sons
their fathers rule as Kom'zars.
They're supposed to keep us all in check
so we don't protest, smash, and wreck.

Bardenfleth had been first to speak, delivering an impassioned speech about the importance of the case for Europe. The Althingi had to conclude this matter at its session that day, before the ceremony in Berlin; did the Icelandic MPs wish to have the postponement of the ceremony in Berlin in a few weeks time on their consciences? Postponement of the establishment of the Great European State?

Bardenfleth had hammered his fists on the table. The matter had been under discussion for too long in parliament, without any conclusion, he argued and lamented that the MPs had failed to complete their task. This was to be blamed on the well-known

Icelandic slovenliness. By that he meant the gibberish concerning parliamentary procedure.

Bardenfleth wanted to postpone the session until the autumn. With a postponement, he would win two things by procedural sleight of hand: the Great European State would be established with Iceland being present in Berlin and the Althingi could formally conclude the dissolution of the Republic that winter. Everyone would be satisfied.

"I propose that the Althingi immediately adjourn this session," Bardenfleth had said. Several parliamentarians sprang up from their seats, declaring it absurd to adjourn the session without reaching a conclusion, since the Althingi could never repeal the agreement in the autumn.

Steffensen had described the atmosphere in the room in his diary: "Things started becoming unruly in the assembly room. Everyone was shouting each other down. Some shook their fists and climbed up on the tables. The leader of the Nation Party was like a lunar eclipse." He smiles to himself.

Then a young man wearing a student's graduation cap had stepped up to the audience rostrum, followed by twelve students, all wearing white caps.

"May I ask for a hearing," the young man had said in a strong voice.

That had been the first time Steffensen had seen Helgi Thorláksson. He had heard of the young literary prodigy, of course, and his exciting new ideas about the old sagas, but he had never expected the youngster to be as charismatic as he was on the podium that day. The entire assembly room had looked up toward the young people who stood erect on the rostrum.

The president refused to hear Helgi and declared the assembly adjourned. Then Helgi Thorláksson called out in a loud voice over the room: "Then I protest this procedure." It was Jón Sigurðsson all over again. There was uproar.

Komizar Bardenfleth and the president of the Althingi had stood up from their seats and started walking toward the door. "I hope that the MPs have heard that we've adjourned the meeting," said Bardenfleth loudly red-faced with anger, the president at his back.

But young Helgi was unmoved, and persistent: "I protest in the name of the people and will appeal the disregard for the law that we have witnessed here."

Bardenfleth strode to the door with the president at his heels.

"We all protest," said the students at the rostrum in one voice, and a number of MPs joined in the protests but Bardenfleth and most of the MPs strode through the back door of Althingi, out into the thick sombre fog where soldiers under arms ensured their safety. This was taken as a sign that the politicians were incapable of performing their duties. The nation was leaderless in everything except what bowed to European rule. It was as if people broke down; the nation's self-confidence was shattered. But stepping forth on the Althingi's rostrum was a young man with a clear view.

When the students and those few MPs, who backed them, walked out onto Austurvöllur Square through the antique door of the Althingi, the fog had lifted and the sun shone brightly. Those MPs refused to attend the reception for Bardenfleth and his supporters, as they raised glasses of champagne to the new Great European State that the Althingi would formally put its stamp on that winter. Troops marched along the streets of Reykjavík and at the outermost harbour warships awaited orders.

Steffensen could see the events of that far off day as if they had happened only yesterday. And now here was Helgi Thorláksson's walking the streets of Reykjavík once again.

Of course, the idea of Iceland being able to continue as an independent state had been ridiculous. A nation whose entire population could fit on one of the big avenues of any major European city: absurd, absurd, absolutely absurd, said the spirit of the times – and Steffensen had agreed. In the evening Bardenfleth had flown out of the country, his job done.

Steffensen had been all on the side of joining Europe, but he had not been alone in thinking that Bardenfleth's conduct had been unacceptable. And Bardenfleth had to pay a high price for his actions, since he had been replaced as the highest European bureaucrat. He was later appointed Governor of that troubled district in the Balkans. Someone, maybe it had been Helgi, had said this was just a con. Bardenfleth had been punished to appease the Icelanders and fool them into thinking Europe cared about Icelandic feelings. Once the fuss had died down nothing would have changed.

In the days that followed Helgi Thorláksson had been unstoppable. He had led demonstrations, appeared on television, swamped the newspapers with statements and appeals. Then he had published what he called "The Address of a Patriot to the Icelandic Nation" and emphasized that "we ourselves must create the rules of the game. We have a good platform on which to stand."

However it all ended so tragically that winter with the bloodshed on the streets when Parliament finally passed vote on Iceland becoming member state of The United States of Europe. Beethoven's the *Ode to Joy* became the anthem of Iceland.

"Magnificent music, magnificent," says Steffensen quietly after humming part of a movement of Beethoven's masterpiece. He had become Governor of Iceland, and now had a whole decade behind him in that office. "How time has flown," he says to himself. Was his time up?

"I don't think so," he mutters as he delivers a hard right hook to the punching bag. "Absolute bother and eternal trouble," says the Governor as he leafs through the pile of files. Finally he finds what he is looking for.

The ever-croaking Krummi.

"We need to go above and beyond," he says quietly. "If we are going to keep that swine Pašičevic in Berlin happy. "Get the State Security Director in here," he calls to his secretary.

Helgi walks over Lækjartorg Square west of Austurstræti Street and turns into Café Europe on Pósthússtræti Street. The statue of the gang of four, who promoted Iceland joining Europe, faces him on Austurvöllur Square, although it is more or less covered with messy graffiti. Gone is good old President Jón's statue. The Althingi Building is on the south side of the Square.

The flag of Europe flaps on its pole.

The number of MPs in the Althingi had been reduced to thirteen when the Republic was dissolved. The Althingi's position is very different to what it was during the Republican period. Legislative functions are a thing of the past. In order to increase the assembly's respect, its president holds public receptions in the Althingi building. The only job Althingi has is to puts stamps of approval on European directives and regulations, as well as overseeing the MPs' seats in the European Parliament. Three Euro-Icelandic MPs at a time attend the European Parliament. They share the seats, basically one year at a time, although the rules are complicated. Their lifestyle gets on people's nerves, particularly the tendency to place relatives in high and well-paid positions, not to mention the ridiculous entertainment expenses and private drivers in black limousines.

Helgi sips his coffee.

He is waiting to meet the Westmann Giant for the first time. Krummi Nine-and-a-half is late.

Helgi looks over at Austurvöllur Square and feels a knot in his stomach as the memory floods his mind. He had been so young back then.

It is as if it were yesterday.

14

It is six months after the tumultuous meeting at the Althingi. The students are demonstrating on the Square of Sæmundur the Wise in front of the University of Iceland. There is great anger and zealousness, Europe intends to dissolve the Republic and the Althingi is prepared to rubber stamp the deed later that day.

"Dissolution of the Republic is a betrayal to the nation," Helgi declares in a thunderous voice at Sæmundur's Square. He is the acclaimed leader of the student opposition to the renunciation of the Republic. The twelve students at the core of the opposition form a line behind him on the podium. Guðrún is behind Helgi at the lectern. His eloquence and passion has caught the nation's attention. Some people hate him, others idolise him.

"They intend to do away with the Icelandic nationality. We reject this," he thunders in a deep voice that resounds throughout the square.

"Long live Iceland... long live the Republic!" the students shout.

"We are eternally Icelandic," thunders Helgi, and a wave of joy spreads through the crowd gathered on the square.

"We are proud Icelanders. Our ancestors put out to sea from Norway rather than tolerate injustice; they wrote Sagas that will live for eternity; they withstood the Little Ice Age and decrepitude; they protested against Danish tyranny; they gained home rule; they cast off the chains of poverty; they established the Republic. Never, never, never will the Republic be dissolved. The Icelanders are one man, one soul. They put their feet down against the Danes two hundred years ago. Now let's stand up for Iceland. Let us all protest! Our message today is clear. We put our feet down. We stand up for Iceland. We are one. We are Icelanders. We all protest!"

Seldom has an Icelander stirred a crowd as does Helgi

Thorláksson on that chilly December day so long ago. "We protest, we protest... the Republic lives... the Icelandic Republic forever!" chants the crowd again and again.

Opposition to the dissolution of the Republic has caught the government completely by surprise. People fiercely oppose the dissolution of the Republic. The student protests at the Althingi in the spring have had deep impact, and in the autumn the opposition solidified when the students embarked upon an open struggle against the agreement with Berlin. The police estimate that sixteen thousand people attend the meeting on Sæmundur Square in front of the University of Iceland, but the students claim that many more are there. The leaders stand at the westernmost end of Sæmundur Square, on the stairs up to the old university main building. People are literally everywhere; several stand on the statue of Sæmundur on the seal and wave the Icelandic flag, and everywhere banners wave: All for Iceland... the Republic lives.

The twelve students have taken their places on the podium hand in hand, waving to the people, who chant: The Icelandic Republic forever... forever... forever... Iceland forever!

The heavy murmur of the crowd can be heard all the way to Austurvöllur Square, where a large crowd of policemen, heavily armed, have formed an array surrounding the Althingi building, the government having considered it fitting to have robust contingency plans, since along with the meeting on Sæmundur Square, the unions are demonstrating at Lækjartorg Square.

The Althingi is debating a bill submitted by the government of Unionists and Crats on the dissolution of the Republic and confirmation of entry into Europe. Laws have been amended and the government has declared that a referendum is no longer required, but rather a simple parliamentary majority in order to ratify Iceland's membership in the Great European State. The bill proposed by the government of the Unionists and the Crats had been under discussion the day before, but the session was postponed when the youngsters gathered on Austurvöllur Square. The demonstrators and the police had clashed; fourteen of the Althingi Building's windowpanes were broken.

Few could have predicted the size of the crowd now.

Someone holding a bullhorn climbs to the top of the statue of Sæmundur on the seal: "Let's march to Austurvöllur...to Austurvöllur... to Austurvöllur!" shouts the student.

Helgi reminds the students that they have only planned to protest on Sæmundur Square. The voice on the statue of Sæmundur takes little notice. "Let's march to Austurvöllur!" The guy is pulled down from the statue but the crowd takes up the challenge and before long the people's voices resound louder and louder: "To Austurvöllur... to Austurvöllur... to Austurvöllur!"

People begin streaming from the square in the direction of downtown.

"Now it's going to get crazy!" shouts Helgi to Guðrún. The noise is deafening; the students are impassioned. Helgi and Guðrún embrace each other.

"I have a bad feeling about going to Austurvöllur," shouts Helgi in Guðrún's ear. Something is whispering to him, but she shakes her head with a determined expression.

"My love, of course we will go. We will not let this outrage go unprotested. We will not let that be said of us."

They look deep into each other's eyes and exchange a passionate kiss, although those nearby look at them curiously and most smile indulgently. Guðrún has a strong sense of justice and has urged Helgi on in his opposition to the dissolution of the Republic. Guðrún pulls him down from the podium. They join the crowd as it surges north down Tjarnargata Street. Before long they are on Austurvöllur Square.

Helgi has never witnessed anything like it. The throng covers all of the square and the surrounding streets. They are to the north of the old Cathedral. Many people hold bullhorns and shout slogans against the government; everywhere banners covered with slogans protesting the dissolution of the Republic and the Great European State wave in the wind.

The government's response is sudden and violent. Policemen armed with tear gas form a barrier to the Althingi building. In addition, a huge reserve force lurks in side streets. The reserves are members of the Red Guards, the youth branch of the Crats and Unionists.

Several hundred people apart from the Guards are inside and behind the Althingi building. The leaders of the Crats and Unionists have urged their supporters to gather at the Althingi building and oppose what they are already calling "the mob's violence". The workers are also pouring into Austurvöllur. Thus two parties have stormed Austurvöllur; students and workers. The two parties now face the assembled forces of the police and Red Guards.

It is estimated that over sixty thousand people have gathered at Austurvöllur Square in front of Althingi.

The people begin raising an uproar when news spreads that the parliamentary session has been adjourned after a hurried vote. The Althingi has dissolved the Republic and ratified Iceland's membership in the Great European State. Inside the Althingi debate had been cut off without warning and a vote by roll call driven through. A narrow majority had voted to dissolve the Republic.

Stones begin to rain over the Althingi building, shattering most of its windows. Fragments of glass are thrown far into the assembly chamber, even to the chairs of the assembly president, secretaries, and ministers. Clods of dirt and rock rain over MPs. The president of Althingi is hit by a piece of lava rock and a glass shard slashes his eyebrow. The president's face is covered in blood; the ministers sink terrified into their seats.

Outside the wave of unrest amplifies.

"Betrayal of Iceland... treason... traitors!" shouts the crowd.

Things get out of hand when some MPs try to sneak out of the parliament building. Punch ups break out. Word spreads on the square that Nation Party MPs have been handcuffed and placed under arrest. The rage increases steadily. The abolished Secretary of State is seen sneaking into a car under the protection of Red

Guards, hunching down on all fours and ordering the driver to get out of there as quickly as possible. A teenage girl rushes up to the Minister and slaps him so hard that it knocks him down.

"You've betrayed the nation," she says in a calm voice as a group of Red Guards jump on her.

The minister shrinks back to his car, staring with terrified eyes at the crowd.

"Poor man. You'll remember your whole life that a woman beat you," shouts the crowd.

The police, with a gang of Red Guards behind them, bursts forth waving their clubs, but the crowd drives them back. Then the grey-uniformed tear-gas squad rushes out of the Althingi Building and shoots tear gas, driving the crowd back and causing numerous protesters to fall and become injured in the crush. It is a major assault as countless gas cylinders are shot into the crowd, causing the clouds of gas to darken the sky and block out the sun.

"Gas…gas…gas!" resound the bullhorns. It's total chaos at the square.

Gas canisters explode. People try to flee. Helgi has trouble seeing what is going on. He moistens a handkerchief in the dew and pats his eyes. Out of the corner of his eye he sees a police officer run up to Guðrún as she lies on the lawn. The officer strikes her heavily with his club and presses a taser to her throat. She jerks and grabs her head. The man strikes her again and presses his taser once more to her throat. Helgi hears himself shout as he rushes to her. The officer strikes Guðrún yet again with his club, pressing the taser against her head as Helgi crashes to the ground from a blow to the neck. He has no idea where the blow comes from, but is bloodied and dizzy. He sees Guðrún lying on the ground.

"Guðrún!" he shouts, staggering to his feet.

When he finally reaches her, Helgi stares at Guðrún's glazed eyes. He holds her lifeless body in his arms, her head covered in blood.

"Guðrún, Guðrún, Guðrún!" he cries desperately, his pain resounding across the square. Several people stare at him, as he kneels with the lifeless body in his arms. Her broken eyes stare unresponsive into the void.

Guðrún is dead.

Then Helgi sees the officer with the taser and throws himself on the man with all his strength, striking him in the face so hard that blood gushes from his nose. Wild with rage, he strikes the man again and again until he feels a splitting pain when someone kicks him in the gut, and then in the face as four or five uniformed men throw themselves on him, fists flying. Helgi feels the world spin and the handcuffs close around his wrists.

Everything goes black.

15

Helgi comes to. A light shines in his eyes and a voice comes from beyond the brightness. Helgi grabs his head and opens his eyes. He sees a man older than himself, clearly well into his thirties. The man draws nearer to the hard bench where Helgi lies and extends his hand.

"My name is Einar."

They shake hands. Helgi looks around at the bare walls of a room barely big enough to stand in.

"They beat me to a pulp and threw me into this cell," says Einar. "I find that bloody harsh, for throwing back one rock that landed next to me. Icelanders have always thrown rocks, never with any penalties. It was mainly the heroes of the Middle Ages who had reason to complain after getting hit in the head with rocks. Some of them never stood on their feet again, being stone-cold dead, but that's another story. That was when we learned to throw stones. The nation hadn't forgotten that excellent art when it started playing handball. That was the start of our love affair with the beautiful sport of team handball. As far as I know no one got hit in the head with a rock at Austurvöllur — at least not thrown by me. My last name's Jónsson."

"I'm... oh, bugger," stammers Helgi, again grabbing his head. His headache is killing him. It's as if a dull knife saws and saws at his belly and chest.

"I'm pretty sure that your name isn't 'O. Bugger.'" Einar laughs heartily.

"Helgi Thorláksson," comes the reply, in a weak voice.

"That was an ugly, screwed-up mess on Austurvöllur, absolutely awful. I'm told two people were killed by police violence, twelve were taken to the hospital, some injured seriously. A boy lost an eye when a tear-gas canister hit him in the face. It sort of made up for it, though, when they managed to beat the crap out of the thug who killed the girl," says Einar earnestly.

Helgi is still covering his face with his hands and his piercing cry of anguish echoes in the cell. His grief is overwhelming. This isn't a nightmare.

"Guðrún, my love," he moans.

"Did you know her?" asks Einar in a low voice.

"Guðrún." He lies face down and buries his face in his hands.

Einar is clearly quite startled.

The cell door opens and two uniformed police officers order Helgi to follow them. They walk down a corridor and into a room with mirrors on two walls. In the room are two men who introduce themselves. Thóra Sveinsen, Duty Officer, and Steinn Hall, the defendant's attorney.

"Defendant?" repeats Helgi in surprise.

"Yes," replies Steinn, who informs Helgi that he is charged with breaking the arm and ribs of a police officer, knocking out four of his teeth, breaking his nose and causing facial wounds requiring numerous stitches.

"I want to extend you my sympathy. What happened to Guðrún was horrendous," says the attorney Steinn.

"The cause of her death was cerebral haemorrhage," says the duty officer, before continuing without further ado. "You face serious charges. It is a grave matter to attack and seriously injure a police officer performing his official duties."

"He killed my girlfriend in cold blood," Helgi replies heavily.

"The young woman was hysterical and attacked the man performing his official duties. He was defending the Althingi and himself," reiterates the female officer.

"Lies, damn lies. The devil attacked her as she lay on the ground from the tear-gas attack and the chaos. The attack was brutal. She had no chance to defend herself," shouts Helgi.

"The police officer was defending himself from attack. An investigation has been made into the matter. The taser did not kill her. She died of cerebral haemorrhage," says the officer, politely but determinedly.

"You lie!" shouts Helgi, rising from his seat. "You lie! He struck her with his stick and drove his taser into Guðrún's neck, time and again he drove the taser into her neck and struck her repeatedly with his stick. I saw him do it." A police officer steps forward and pushes his hand firmly on Helgi's shoulder, forcing him to sink back into his seat.

Steinn turns to the officer. "My client's testimony contradicts the perfunctory conclusions of the prosecutor's investigation. We need to go over the details of the case. It matters a great deal to the reason for the attack on the police officer."

"Attack. The god-damn bastard murdered Guðrún." There is deep despair and sadness in Helgi's voice. "The bloody system is going to cover up the murder. He killed Guðrún." Helgi's voice breaks and he collapses onto the table.

"The incident requires investigation. I smell a rat," insists Steinn.

The police officer eyes Steinn coldly. "She received a blow to the head when she fell to the ground, the investigation has concluded. She was only tased once. It did not lead to her death. She died from the cerebral haemorrhage. I repeat, the police officer did not kill her," Thóra's voice becomes more determined. She stands up and walks out of the cell. The attorney glances hesitantly at Helgi, but then follows the female officer out the door.

Helgi's face is covered in bruises, his eyes are black, his nose crooked and he has an unbearable pain in the lower part of his chest. Yet he takes no notice of the pain; it just seems very far away.

His heart bleeds for Guðrún's death.

16

A six-year prison sentence is demanded for the pummelling of the Guard. He is still in custody, the trial exhausting, the persecution relentless. Day after day Helgi is brought to the trial by the same two officers. He is disillusioned, truth to tell. They had banned him from attending Guðrún's funeral. His attorney Steinn Hall seems to be no good, putting up meagre resistance. The trial is in the smallest courtroom in Reykjavík's courthouse, so few are able to attend. Security is tight, police officers seem to be everywhere.

Helgi and Einar are still sharing a cell.

Einar thumbs through the media. "They say that sentence will be passed on you next week," he says.

Helgi doesn't answer: he is lost in a world of melancholia. Einar is to be set free that afternoon, free of all charges. His trial is finished and the release of him and ten others is to be viewed as the government extending a reconciliatory hand. Helgi Thorláksson, on the other hand, has to answer for his disgraceful attack, declare the authorities.

The nation is in turmoil after the events on Austurvöllur Square. The special prosecutor Sigga Friðþjófs issues a report on the deaths of the students. The young man is said to have been trampled to death as the mob retreated when the police were forced to use tear gas defending Demcowill. The young woman is alleged to have attacked a Guard who had defended himself. Neither taser shot nor punches are said to be the cause of her death, but rather a cerebral haemorrhage due to some congenital defect, states the prosecutor referring to an autopsy report.

"A bare faced lie and cover-up," curses Helgi who has denied access to the autopsy report.

The prosecutor calls the attack on the police officer unprovoked, brutal, and savage. A young man who has placed his weight on the scales of the European cause and the defence of Althingi, has suffered severe injuries. It will take him a long time to recover.

"Lies and hypocrisy," says Helgi bitterly.

Einar looks up as he is thumbing through the newspapers. "A deranged mob attack the Althingi," says Einar, laughing. "Deranged mob. The press buys the official version. It was the Police and the Red Guards who were blood-red with rage," he adds.

"Oath of Fidelity to the European Ideal." Einar laughs loudly when he reads the headline of *The Press*.

"What about the dead; where is the respect due them? What about the injured: the boy who lost his eye? Will he be compensated?" he asks, continuing to flip through the paper.

"Iceland has become one big lie," says Helgi in a sad voice.

"In *The Post* they say that the other dead student climbed up on Sæmundur on the seal and urged people to march to Austurvöllur, but was pulled down from the statue," continues Einar. "Bizarre," he says thoughtfully. The philosophy student had been found dead by the south entrance of Hotel Borg nearby. "There are suggestions that he was beaten to death and his body tossed from a window of the Borg," Einar says with an astonished look.

Helgi had paid the philosophy student little heed on Sæmundur Square that fateful day when he encouraged people to march to Austurvöllur. He recalls dimly having seen the student pulled down from the statue, but hadn't felt anything about it. No one had paid it any attention, since everyone had turned their attention to the podium.

Einar breaks the silence and looks up from the newspaper. "Nothing but bloody lies," he shouts. "The Prosecutor claims in *The Press* that the student was crushed to death beneath the fleeing crowd. This is all one grand web of conspiracy and lies."

Helgi looks up but says nothing. He is in no mood to discuss the events of recent days. His grief has made him numb and apathetic. He has no interest in life without Guðrún; sees no future, just a night of blackness.

The silence is interrupted by an astonished cry.

"Here it says that President Jón Sigurðsson looked away from his pedestal," shouts Einar loudly. "A miracle, claims *The Post*," he adds, overcome with awe. "The statue of Jón Sigurðsson turned 65 degrees. The freedom fighter now looks up at the old school, where the National Assembly took place two hundred years ago. Now *The Post* is doing some reporting! If this isn't a message from the Almighty and the champion of freedom about a poor cause, then I don't know what can be called a clear message," he adds, laughing contentedly.

Helgi makes no reply.

The door to the cell is opened. Two guards stand in the doorway.

"You're free to go, Einar," says one of the guards.

Einar goes over at Helgi and holds out his hand. "Good luck to you, mate," he says.

Helgi looks up and shakes Einar's outstretched hand. "Goodbye," he replies, his expression downcast.

The trial is drawing to a conclusion. Helgi senses that the whole system is against him, that the sentence is a forgone conclusion, decided behind locked doors in secret back-rooms. He feels as if Judge Karl Bergdal has a grudge against him. In prison during his interrogation Helgi demanded time and again to see Guðrún's autopsy report, but to no avail. Steinn Hall, his lawyer, has been of little help.

Helgi takes the matter up at the trial in Reykjavík's Criminal Court. He addresses the court in a calm voice. "I ask the court to grant me access to Guðrún Sigurvinsdóttir's autopsy report. We lived together in the dormitory. I, as her closest cohabitant, have the right to view the report."

For a moment, the courtroom is completely silent. Judge Karl slowly stands up from his seat as if he's buying time while considering the request. "This court does not have the power to grant you the request," he proclaims and adds. "Guðrún Sigurvinsdóttir's cause of death has no relevance to this case." Then Judge Karl turns to the prosecutor Sigga Friðþjófs who seems to be taken aback by Helgi's request.

"This request is for the prosecutor to decide," the judge concludes.

The prosecutor stands up from her seat. "That is not quite the case, your honour," she says throwing a poisonous glance at the attorney, Steinn, and then at Helgi. "The request is to be addressed to the Directorate of Health. You should direct your request to the Directorate," she says, adding: "Though I have the report, I'm not allowed to hand it over due to confidentiality."

The prosecutor's response comes as a surprise to Helgi who turns to Judge Karl. "This is news to me. I repeatedly asked the police and the prosecution for the autopsy report but was refused time and again. Now the prosecutor tells me to turn to the Directorate of Health. It's obvious they're playing games. The transparency they so much boast about is non-existent. And besides, I strongly protest that Guðrún's death has nothing to do with this trial. Guðrún's death has everything to do with this trial. She was attacked by a thug, it was brutal provocation."

Judge Karl interrupts him quite abruptly. "It is I who am in charge of this trial and I have made my ruling. There is nothing more to say. You can turn to the Directorate of Health for the autopsy report." It's obvious that the judge is annoyed by Helgi's unexpected request. He brings the gavel forcefully down. "It's late afternoon. This trial is adjourned for the week." Judge Karl stands up and disappears into his chambers.

There is a hiss of surprise in the courtroom. People voice their displeasure as Helgi is lead out of the courtroom by police officers.

Despite expecting little success, Helgi decides to take the matter up with the Directorate of Health. He receives permission to visit the offices of the Directorate in the company of two police officers. There he is informed that the autopsy report is with the Laboratory of Pathology. The lab is quite close by.

Helgi knocks at the doors of the Laboratory of Pathology. He states his request; he's there to get Guðrún Sigurvinsdóttir's autopsy report. The woman at reception hesitates for a moment as she looks at Helgi and then at the uniformed police officers. She then makes a call announcing Helgi's arrival. Shortly afterward a man in a white coat arrives in reception: a small man, not more than five foot four, with blonde slicked-back hair, squinty eyes behind round metal glasses and a mouth that forms a thin straight line under a thin nose, probably in his early forties. It is almost as if the man has no face. I'll be damned, Helgi thinks to himself.

The man takes off his glasses. "My name is Doctor Róbert Hanson. What can I do for you?" he asks in a low passive voice.

Helgi presents himself. "I'm here to get access to Guðrún Sigurvinsdóttir's autopsy report," he says quite firmly.

The doctor looks at the police officers and then turns to Helgi. "Come to my office," he says and before turning to the officers. "You'll wait outside. I'll let you know if I need your assistance."

They hesitate and look at each other and then at the doctor. "We are not to let the prisoner out of our sight," says the taller of the two.

"Follow me," Doctor Róbert says without looking further at the officers.

The three of them follow the doctor upstairs to a corridor on the second floor, and from there to an office with a Chief Physician sign on the door. Róbert invites Helgi into the office, pauses for a moment and then addresses the officers: "You may also enter." The police officers give each other an indulgent smile.

That's a funny little man, Helgi thinks, getting a nasty feeling about him. However, Helgi smiles politely to the doctor who offers the officers a seat by the door and invites Helgi to his office table. He then sits by the large, grand table. He looks for a while at Helgi and then asks in a passive tone: "You want information on Guðrún Sigurvinsdóttir?"

"Yes, I'm here for the autopsy report," Helgi replies as calmly as possible.

Doctor Róbert asks a clerk to bring him Guðrún's autopsy report. He then turns to Helgi and says. "This will only take a moment. The clerk will bring the report in a minute."

"Excellent," Helgi answers, satisfied with how things are progressing. His hopes of getting the report have certainly been raised. He gives the doctor a friendly look.

Doctor Róbert takes off his rounded glasses and cleans them. He puts them up again, slowly and carefully, as if not wanting to miss out on anything. "I will read aloud the findings from the autopsy report so that you'll have necessary information," he declares slowly, emphasizing each and every word.

Helgi is taken aback. "What do you mean, read the report aloud to me? I want the autopsy report handed to me so that I can present the findings at my trial," he says sharply, and adds sarcastically: "I expect you've heard about the trial."

"That's not the way the system works. And yes, I know all about your violent past, but by law, I'm not allowed to hand the autopsy report over to you," the doctor replies emphasizing the last words as he yet again takes off his glasses.

"What do you mean?" There is surprise and obvious anxiety in Helgi's voice. He has difficulty comprehending the doctor's comments.

"You're a thug who has broken the law," says Doctor Róbert. His voice is becoming quite strained, as the tension intensifies, and he adds: "By Icelandic law the report is confidential."

"I was closest to Guðrún, we shared lives, we were going to be married," exclaims Helgi, frustrated and annoyed, disregarding the comment about his character. As he speaks, a clerk enters the office, bringing Guðrún's autopsy report. The police officers are now standing.

"Of your relationship with the deceased I have no doubt," Doctor Róbert states, as he stands up, and walks toward the clerk, who hands him a file. He flicks through the papers, then looks coldly at Helgi and adds: "However, you misunderstand the law. Confidentiality is between the patient and his doctor."

Helgi is petrified, he simply doesn't know what's hitting him. "Confidentiality between patient and doctor?" he stutters. "I want the report," he then exclaims in a thunderous voice. The officers step forward.

"The report is confidential," the doctor says abruptly.

"Confidential?" Helgi repeats again, more and more confused. "I'm her family. We were to be married," he adds.

"That may be the case, but patient and doctor are the only ones to have access to medical documents," Doctor Róbert says now in a low, almost whispering voice.

"Patient?" Helgi exclaims in surprise, completely confused. "The patient is dead, Guðrún is dead, how is she supposed to read through the files?" he shouts.

"Privacy is important. The patient is the only one to have access to a medical document, besides his doctor of course. The same goes for an autopsy report. The dead is the only one allowed access, except his physician, of course. Confidentiality has to be protected," the doctor says, pointing a finger at Helgi, before putting on his glasses, and taking a step forward. "Your fame doesn't buy you any privileges in this matter. I'm just an ordinary fellow, quite content being just a plain ordinary fellow," the doctor says, before adding in a whispering voice: "Do you want me to read extracts from the autopsy report?"

Helgi looks down at the little man. He can hardly believe his own ears. He takes a step forward and stretches his arm toward the file in the doctor's hand. "I want the autopsy report," he shouts in despair, but then feels the officers' heavy arms on his shoulders. They force him into the seat.

"Do you want me to read from these files?" the doctor whispers into Helgi's ears as he leans forward.

Helgi looks at the police officers, and then at the doctor as he covers his face with the palms of his hands. "I will not grant you the satisfaction!" he shouts, standing up and hurrying out of the office with the two officers at his heels.

"Please yourself and mind your manners, you ruffian! It was fortunate that I asked the officers into my office," Helgi hears the doctor shout from his office.

The following week Helgi's sentence is passed at the Criminal

Court of Reykjavík. He is sentenced to four years in prison for advocating riots and what the Court calls "...molesting a police officer who was defending the Althingi – the cradle of Demcowill."

17

Helgi is all alone in the cell, now that Einar is long gone. He buries his face in his hands and repeatedly goes over events at Austurvöllur. They all seem to be in a haze, a black mist. He blames himself. What bloody stupid foolishness to wind up in this nightmare. Where has all this nonsense led him? He's responsible for Guðrún's death; he claps his hands to his forehead and closes his eyes.

Guðrún is dead.

There is nothing he can do to bring her back to life. He had prated on the podium and worked the crowd into a frenzy. He hadn't known how to keep his damned mouth shut, has never known how to keep his damned mouth shut. He had taken her to Austurvöllur. He had lost her in the confusion and suffocating haze of smoke. It was absolutely inexcusable. She had trusted him.

"Guðrún!" he shouts in his cell, but no one hears his anguished cry. "Guðrún!" he shouts, but his voice is hoarse and weak.

He slumps over the table.

Goddess was the word that came to mind when he first met Guðrún. Her image is so vivid in his mind, as if it happened yesterday. He pictures her every detail.

He was at Thingvellir with fellow students when he first saw her. She was scribbling something on a sheet of paper on the bridge over the river Öxará. It is as if Thingvellir had turned into a setting for a play about a goddess captivating her audience. He had stopped, feeling compelled to stare at her on the bridge. He had fallen behind his companions as they walked down Almannagjá Ravine.

Thingvellir that memorable day come to live.

Guðrún was down by Drowning Pond as his companions walked

by, blabbering about nothing. He strolled behind and watched her out of the corner of his eye, like a shy boy. She was drawing and scribbling something, but it was her full head of jet-black hair that captured his attention. It felt to him as if her beauty lighted up Thingvellir; the cradle of world's first National Parliament. He did not dare talk to her, but strolled along after his companions down to the plain.

Months passed, an entire summer and then came the autumn. Helgi constantly thought of Guðrún, but she seemed to have vanished.

Then he attended a class on the female heroes of the Icelandic sagas. There she was, sitting near the front. She was so imposing and indescribably elegant that he forgot time and place. The professor's voice dissolved into meaninglessness and the students turned to stone as he beheld the goddess on her throne. The lecture sort of dissolved into thin air, but he couldn't care less, though it later bit him in the exam. After the class he went to the café.

She sat there alone, peering at a book.

He was taken completely aback and turned to go, but cursed himself for his cowardice. He took courage and walked up to her table. She was Guðrún — a woman on God's path.

"Are you studying Icelandic literature?" he had asked, tentatively.

"No," she had replied smiling. "I am studying law and working on a paper about women and the injustice of some of our old laws. The fate of women at Thingvellir was often a story of savagery and violence," she said. He was captivated by her sparkling humanity and eloquence when she told him the tragic story of women who had no advocates. He had listened to her fascinated, absolutely captivated.

"Did you know Iceland executed women for adultery as late as 1762," she had asked and continued. "Women were led out onto the cliff-spur and stuffed into bags that were pulled over their heads. A rope was tied around their waists and they were forced to stand a long time on the edge of the crag, because executions were not just punishment; they were warning markers as well. They were pushed off and held underwater with staves until dead."

He tried to add something clever to the discussion and explain how the Drowning Pond had been deeper than now, more like a small lake than a pool, with a heavy spur of rock that had been blown up when a bridge was built over the Öxará River. The vandalism had been the clumsy deed of men who hadn't known better.

"We know of eighteen women who were drowned in Drowning Pond. Justice during their day was based on prejudice. Of course little has changed." She had told him about the sentences and open violence against women.

"The first woman to suffer the savage fate was named Thórdís, from Sólheimar in Skagafjörður. She was convicted of bearing false witness and swearing an oath on the Holy Book that she was a virgin, when in fact she was with child. At first she refused to name the father, but after slaps in the face and the curses of the authorities, she turned her terrified eyes to her brother-in-law. The judges declared it out of the question that such an honourable farmer could have seduced her with magic so they drowned her."

"Her crime was her humanity," he had said, but the words sounded coarse and somehow tangled. He felt like Tanglefoot in the comic books.

She had laughed cheerfully with a gleam in her eyes. Rays of happiness had filled the room and they had become inseparable.

Their route had laid through the isolated Westfjords, Helgi's childhood home.

Spring had passed in a gentle mood, the sun's rays gilding Iceland's largest bay: the Breiðafjörður. A snow bunting had sung at the foot of a field and a southerly breeze burst into laughter beneath the wings of a snipe. High over the Westfjord peaks an eagle had spread its wings and scrutinized the land with swift eyes. They had been at Rauðisandur – Red Sand – one of the country's most beautiful area, surrounded by steely cliffs. Where the land meets the sea, the red-gold shell sand shines with a lucid brightness, causing even the famous Snæfellsjökull Glacier on the other side of the fjord to fill with envy. In Bæjarós Estuary curious eyes had watched the lovers; seals closed their eyes and rolled over in the warm sand.

Guðrún and Helgi's happiness had been clear for everyone to see.

They had woken in the middle of the night, quivering with wondrous joy, risen and fallen in deep pleasure as they had made love beneath the glorious song of the golden plover. Nature had resounded with their love; the songs of the migrant birds and the watchful eyes on the seashore. It had been as if Red Sand had opened its arms to the glory of its creator on this bright summer day. They had saddled their horses, mounted and rode south to the isolated Seven Rivers Farm – Sjöundá. He had been startled when her horse's hooves had made a smack as it had stumbled in the stony river, but Guðrún had laughed with contented laughter.

Their happiness had seemed eternal.

The fates of women were of constant interest to Guðrún.

"Back in 1801," she had told Helgi, "the year that the British fleet under Admiral Nelson bombarded the royal city of Copenhagen to punish the Danes for having submitted to the pan-European domination of French dictator Napoleon Bonaparte, a pitch-black váfugl had cast its shadow over the countryside here where the seven rivers run to the sea."

"Váfugl?" Helgi had interrupted.

"You know, the vulture. The bird of doom and death," she had replied.

Helgi had looked blank so she had told him the story Gunnar Gunnarsson the poet had written about the tragedy at Seven Rivers Farm. A woman had walked erect into a courtroom, her expression full of pride, looking at her judges with just a hint of a frown. A black homespun sweater with trimming of velvet had fallen closely against her beautifully shaped bosom and plump body; her cravat carefully knotted and pinned with slender pins, her skirt uncreased at the hem. No man had been untouched by the presence of the woman, who had opposed the authorities in the courtroom. Proudly she had asked them what they wanted of her. The gleam in her eyes had been powerful; determination had shone snow-white as a light blush spread over her dark, downy skin. She had stood undaunted before the authorities.

"Ok," Helgi had interrupted. "She was a brave woman. But who was she?"

Her name was Steinunn, and she had lived at Seven Rivers Farm with her husband Jón but had been led astray when a new neighbour named Bjarni had arrived with his sickly wife. Bjarni had lusted after the healthy, beautiful Steinunn and decided to seduce her. So Steinka, as she was called, had let herself be persuaded by a load of stories about how the grass was greener on the other side.

Bjarni had gone to her in the barn and wrapped around her a wondrously fair scarf that he claimed had been woven in the faraway land of Lombardy. She had never set eyes on such a treasure. She had blushed and adjusted her skirt. She had then laid the scarf in a small coffer, locked it and hid the key away from her husband's piercing eyes.

Bjarni had praised the distant lands of Italy, Spain and elsewhere in Europe where the sun shone and happiness was said to dwell. Beyond the cliffs, far from the cottage, were halls so tall and bright that all of Red Sand would fit in them. He had promised to raise his sail and take her over the sea; promised her happiness, far from the cold and hardships of the outermost sea. This was something different than the drudgery with Jón, who had picked his nose and hardly ever emerged from the sheep shed. Jón had grumbled about the velvet that she had bought for her skirt; accused her of being wasteful and ostentatious.

"Gunnarsson likened the arrival of this evil man to a pitch-black vulture perched at Seven Rivers Farm," Guðrún had said. There had been such compassion in her eyes when she had told him the story as they had stood at the ruins of the farm.

Helgi had nodded. "So Steinka had fallen for Bjarni and they began a passionate affair? She had given herself into the power of the black vulture."

"Exactly," Guðrún had confirmed.

The darkness had laid like a black veil over the tenant farm at the seven rivers; even the brightness of Red Sand did not dare cross the threshold. By dawn two people were dead, butchered. Bjarni had murdered his wife and Steinka's husband. She was accused of being an accessory to the murders.

"Happiness can not be conquered," Steinka said at the trial.

"Depression conquers," she could have added.

The pitch-black vulture had locked its claws into its prey.

Steinka paid a high price.

After the judges demeaned her and struck her in the face, they had locked her in a dungeon attached to the courtroom. A flash of fear had appeared in her eyes: foreboding, though carefully hidden, abstract but immoderate. Steinka was sentenced to be beheaded, her head to be fixed to a pole at the place of execution, where her body was to be buried. This did not happen, because Steinka died of hardship in the nation's prison at the foot of Arnarhóll in Reykjavik where there were said to be sixteen hardened criminals. Steinka, all alone among the worst of the worst, preferred to leave this world, which can be so cruel to its most vulnerable.

"They disgraced her, broke her, and defeated her," Guðrún had declared. "She never killed anyone. But the judges said she had led Bjarni on and that was enough. There was no relief from the anger, violence, and cruelty of the scowling male authorities," Guðrún had said as she walked among the farm ruins. "Her corpse was tossed like a sack of mouldy grain onto the side of the road at Skólavörðuholt. Passers-by stoned the cairn," she had added, fragile and sad.

"Was that the Steinka Cairn?" he had asked.

"Yes, Steinka was buried for over a hundred years beneath cold stone, as a reminder and warning to women: 'advarsel' and 'skrækkelse' in the language of the Danish masters. It wasn't until they were digging trenches and spewing poison gas in European battlegrounds at World War I, that they deemed it alright for Steinka to be given rest in consecrated ground," Guðrún had replied.

Rauðisandur and the tragedy at Seven Rivers Farm was behind them.

They had lain in the deep grass on the peak above the old farm at Hrafnseyri, Helgi's home. A southerly breeze had stroked their faces incredibly gently, and in the distance the hidden people had held longwinded conversations in the great waterfall, the snow-covered heath above them. He had stroked her jet-black hair and looked deeply, very deeply into her dark brown eyes and felt her passionate heartbeat where she had built their love a nest. Helgi had picked a blade of grass from her hair and embraced Guðrún.

He is brought back to the present as a blast of wind hammers a sheet of rain into the windows of Café Europe. He peers out down the rain lashed Pósthússtræti Street. Several figures hurry past, their heads bowed against the weather, but none of them are big enough to be the famous Westmann Giant. Helgi looks at his watch. Where's Krummi?

18

Krummi is hurrying toward Café Europe and his meeting with Helgi. He knows he is late, but he has spotted a damn plain clothes policeman on his tail and wants to get rid of him first. Krummi turns a corner, then sprints for a bus. He hops on at the last minute, watching the hapless policeman stop in exasperation. He rides the bus for two stops, then gets off and looks about. Nobody following him. Good.

A blast of salt-laden wind blows up from the harbour and his mind goes back to the days when he was the hunter, not the hunted as he clipped the tails of the Spanish trawlers.

"We'll let the bastard have it!" cries Krummi from the bridge, grinning, his white teeth flashing in his black beard.

"We're with you!" replies deckhand Gaui Karlsson, at the wheel.

The ship cuts through the waves at full speed with spray flying from the bows; the engines roar like a lion, resounding across the entire sea. *The Elliði VE* is the most magnificent ship in the Westmann Islands fleet, a successful fishing vessel that cleaves the waves with such power that no other Icelandic fishing vessel can reach such speeds. But Krummi and his men aren't catching fish this time. They are going to cut the nets of the Basques, who have their hands in the bottomless cod on the Selvogur fishing ground.

The marine environment around Iceland has changed so drastically that migrant species have become an acrid nightmare. Iceland has been given a red card and everything is decided in Brussels. Icelandic fishermen have to sit and watch as goddamn foreigners fish mackerel, herring, redfish and blue whiting, even though the fish are in Icelandic waters most of the time. Iceland has given up a 800 thousand square-kilometre area of sea to Brussels.

The straddling stocks swim just beyond the limits of Icelandic waters, prompting Brussels to shout: "Aha... aha... aha, European straddling stock, so everyone owns it and we decide; aha... aha... aha... ahahaha!"

Krummi shakes his head in disbelief. "Almost eight times the size of Iceland where the pirates follow the smell of blood!" he shouts, lowering his binoculars.

"What's that you say?" asks Gaui with a startled look, staring at his skipper.

Krummi laughs to himself, lost in his thoughts. More than anything else, the bloody quota-hoppers get on the nerves of the terse sea-hero who knows how to put things into words. Just as the sun sets in the sea, so had the Basques sailed in a sunny mood out beyond the horizon with the gutted fish and a sod-you sign.

"The bastards snuck into our fish the back way, like thieves in the night," growls Krummi. He glances at his deckhand, but Gaui is ignoring him as he stares with alert eyes at the foaming waves of the high sea.

"What the hell were all the Cod Wars for?" Krummi shouts at Gaui.

The man looks at his captain. They smile mischievously.

Krummi is going to let his deeds do the talking, not sit on his backside and curse the world's injustice. Something has to be done to awaken vigour and passion in his people, as in the Cod Wars of the previous century. He is going to take a stand. He is going to do it for Icelandic fishermen. He is going to do it for Iceland. He is going to do it for Bríet and the boys. They have talked it over time and again. Bríet agrees with him. He does little without checking first with Bríet.

They have been inspired by the passion and eloquence of Helgi the student leader and support the Republic's struggle against the European dominance. The fighting on Austurvöllur Square has shocked the nation and the people are extremely alarmed at the death of the students. He feels it impossible to let the workers and students fight alone and serve prison sentences. Everyone has to pull hard on Iceland's oars. The world has to know that the Icelandic populace is shaking its fists and will never accept being a tenant farm of Europe, which treads upon the nation's fishing grounds in dirty shoes.

"Hard astern!" shouts Krummi. "Össi, are you ready with the clippers?"

"Everything ready, Captain," cries Össi Guðmundsson, at the stern. Krummi laughs fiercely; the bugger absolutely deserves it, and more. Those bastards are out there on the fishing ground just a few days after the tragedy on Austurvöllur Square. Brussels has no decency.

News that a fleet of fishing vessels from the Pyrenees is scooping up fish southwest of the Westmann Islands has provoked intense anger and indignation. The fleet is called "The Hoover", having fished out fishing grounds all over the world. Now it is in Icelandic waters. The coastguard is supposed to be monitoring the situation. "Monitoring it!" huffs people but the coastguards are nowhere to be seen. The ordinary populace, which still lives in bare-bones fishing villages around the country, is in a frenzy of rage. Icelandic fishermen are defenceless. It was bad before, but now has got worse.

Krummi knows that the Basques have cast their nets into the sea. He has gotten word of twelve trawlers with an EU frigate to protect them. He is going to cut the bastards' nets, since the coastguard with its mouse heart stirs neither hide nor hair. There is a cold southeasterly wind and heavy waves, but for an experienced Icelandic seamen like Krummi that is simply an advantage.

A sudden burst of sunlight shines on Krummi's masculine face and his black hair blows in the wind as he looks with his eagle eyes at the sea through the wide-open window on the bridge of the Elliði. In the distance the Westmann Islands rise from the sea and above them the majestic Eyjafjallajökull. The crew is in high spirits, because the Westmann Giant's voice echoes strongly, making every rafter sing as the ship ploughs through the waves.

Proud sails my galley on the sea so wide,
storm and wave it can safely abide.
You have all our love,
we you all adore,
soon our Iceland will come into our view.
Iceland, proud Iceland ...

Krummi orders hard astern and the *Elliði* shoves its way into the group of trawlers. It is like a fox in a henhouse, with cackling hens flying everywhere. The Spanish frigate *Armada Español*, flying the gilded European flag, pursues the *Elliði*, but Krummi couldn't care less. He makes ready to clip trawling lines, turning now hard to starboard, and clipping the Bilbao bastards from behind. One set of nets is cut, then another. The other trawlers are pulling in their nets now, but Krummi races on. He gets behind a third and feels the cutters snag the net. Then the tension is gone and the nets are sent down into the depths. This enrages the Spanish and the captain on the *Armada* cleaves the waves and steams straight for the *Elliði*. Krummi watches as the frigate approaches, expecting a hail from the naval captain or even a shot across his bows.

Instead the frigate makes straight for the *Elliði* at 34 knots. Spray flies from its bows as it plunges into a great, grey wave. Krummi is puzzled. Why does the Spaniard not hail him and tell him to prepare to be boarded. Krummi has his documentation ready and back home Bríet has a statement ready to give to the press.

"Shit. The bastard is going to ram us," shouts Össi.

Krummi stares in horror as the frigate makes a 30-degree turn to starboard. He slams his fishing boats engine into full power and feels as the propeller bites. The boat begins to move forward, but it is too late. The three-thousand ton frigate with its thirty-thousand horsepower engines steams at full speed into the five-hundred ton fishing vessel. Össi and two other sailors are at the stern winch, where the clipper is paid out. The cold, green seawater engulfs the stern as well as the men. Krummi staggers as the *Elliði* is thrown on to its side. He grabs the wheel for support, but his boots lose their grip and slithers across the deck to crash into the cabin wall.

The *Elliði* is on it side and green waters surge over its bulwarks as the boat is pushed aside by the frigate. Krummi feels his ship spinning crazily sideways, but the starboard engine is still revving and slowly claws the boat away from the frigate's deadly bows. Krummi manages to get to his feet as the boat rights itself. He tears open the cabin door and stares aft to where his crew had been. The deck is awash and pieces of broken fishing gear roll about.

"Are you OK," calls Krummi.

"Don't worry about us," shouts Össi, drenched and bloodied, when Krummi appears. Össi salutes and Krummi knows that he can trust his men. He looks up at the towering sides of the Spanish frigate. A row of expressionless faces peer down at him.

"Bastards", shouts Krummi. Then he looks toward the enemy ship's bows and sees that they have been crumpled and buckled. A large hole in the bows is letting in water. "Hah," shouts Krummi. "They came off worse." He looks around and sees the trawlers ahead of them have their trawls out. "We'll get our revenge yet," he snarls. They get the starboard engine running, and on one screw clip the trawl from behind another Basque trawler. Only a few minutes have gone by since the frigate crashed into the *Elliði's* side.

Össi shouts a warning to Krummi. The captain of the Armada must be furious. He has again punched the frigate's engines from zero to over thirty knots, and is driving his ship hard despite the hole in his bows. He comes crashing at full speed, waves frothing at the bows. The frigate crashes again into the *Elliði* and pushes it 70 degrees to starboard, causing it to turn completely on its side. The frigate lies with its prow on top of the *Elliði*, driving into it at full power. The *Elliði's* bow is up and the ships are hooked together. All of the *Elliði's* engines have stopped and the electricity is knocked out.

On the bridge, deckhand Gaui, hanging onto the wheel, shouts: "We're capsizing. She's capsizing!"

"No!" shouts Krummi. "She won't capsize!"

Slowly but surely the *Elliði* rights itself and turns in the mouth of the frigate. The two ships grasp each other on the heavy ocean waves. It is a miracle that the *Elliði* remains afloat. The *Armada* slips off the Icelandic ship and its gaping prow crunches beneath the waves.

They manage only to restart the starboard engine on the *Elliði* and Krummi heads back toward the Westmann Islands, though slowly. As he goes he watches the frigate wallowing in the waves. The ship is down by the bows. Krummi grins and calls out to his crew "That Spanish bastard is taking on water. The captain won't be able to get up much speed with that hole in his bows. Let's go home. We've done enough for one day." Then his smile freezes. A tugboat roars out from behind the frigate and heads straight for the *Elliði*. The size of the bow wave shows the boat is moving fast.

"Looks like, this bastard wants to finish us," says Örn.

Krummi laughs hilariously, as he sees the *Armada* so damaged that it is forced to withdraw. Its prow is gone and the sea reaches up to its front gun port.

"We've clipped The Hoover's wings!" shouts Krummi out on deck. The boys have never seen the Westmann Giant in such a mood.

"The invincible fleet is defeated!" shouts Gaui from the wheel, but is alarmed when he looks to larboard.

The tugboat is rapidly approaching the *Elliði*.

"Monster to larboard!" yells Gaui.

"I need a miracle, lads!" shouts Krummi into the engine room. "You need to restart the larboard engine, otherwise we'll be swimming with the cod!"

The call echoes throughout the engine room.

The faces of the men in the engine room are beaded with sweat; their sleeves are rolled up their arms. They try to restart the larboard engine, which moans and sputters back into silence.

The monster boat approaches rapidly. Krummi can see the men on board now, their faces are twisted with anger but the wind whips away whatever they are shouting.

"Damn it," moans Gaui, turning the wheel.

"Wrench, boys!" shouts the chief engineer, Rúnar Kárason.

He grabs the wrench and leaps onto the engine. His hand motions are steady and confident.

"Restart!" he cries.

They restart the engine, which still sputters wretchedly but then begins to spin faster, faster and faster. Finally the *Elliði's* lion heart resounds again over the entire Selvogur fishing ground. The Spanish tugboat is less than 400 meters away and is closing the distance to the *Elliði* rapidly.

The *Elliði's* engines are stretched to the limit and the noise from them is deafening. The ship plunges into the waves and sea pours over the pilothouse. The men on the bridge stand to their knees in seawater, the bridge's windows being open, but the *Elliði* is gaining speed. Despite that, the enemy draws nearer. Every eye on the *Elliði* is fixed on the enemy. One of the men on the tugboat brandishes a rifle over his head. "They wouldn't dare", thinks Krummi. But suddenly he is not so certain. He turns to look ahead toward the Westmann Islands and suddenly his face lights up when he sees the Westmann Islands fishing fleet ahead of him, steaming west toward the *Elliði*.

"They're blowing their horns, boys!" shouts Krummi, pointing at the fleet as it sails to meet them. The good old Icelandic flag flaps on its pole on every ship but behind the *Elliði* can be seen the tugboat's blue flag with its golden stars. Krummi looks back along the *Elliði*. The ship's stern is a wreck. The steel had folded as if it were linen. The davit is wrenched around 90 degrees off the *Elliði*. The *Armada* had dragged the davit with it when it ran off the *Elliði*. It was a great stroke of luck that it had split apart.

The crew at the stern was damned lucky to escape with their lives, thinks Krummi quite shocked at the Spaniard's vehemence.

The tugboat is now about 100 meters away but the *Elliði* churns faster, faster, and faster toward the oncoming fishing fleet. Still, the distance between the ships closes in a frenzied game of cat-and-mouse on the ocean waves. The *Elliði* trembles from prow to stern and the sea washes over the ship every time that it plunges into the waves. In the distance the wounded frigate can be seen limping downcast on its slow journey southward.

"It's running away with its tail between its legs!" shouts Gaui, laughing uproariously.

"You've done your duty, mate," replies Krummi, before calling down into the engine room. "Boys, can you give me a little extra power; just a tiny bit of extra power? We need two to three miles more."

Chief Engineer Rúnar is drenched in sweat over the engine.

"Doing our, doing our, doing our best," sings the engineer repeating a popular tune, his wrench aloft.

"Look at those beauties," Krummi says with a smile as the *Elliði* creeps forward just a touch faster. The distance between the vessels slowly but surely increases. Twenty minutes later the *Elliði* sails in among the Westmann Islands fleet. Every horn is blown. The dreadful tugboat has turned back. In the distance the frigate sails away, its prow submerged and its stern aloft, its screws barely managing to touch the sea. It looks to them as if the golden stars have been taken down from the pole.

Gaui suddenly sticks his head out of the cabin. "Here, you want to listen to this," he puts the radio through the boat's loudspeaker and the air is filled with ceaseless cursing in Spanish. "I don't understand what they are saying," laughs Gaui, "but they don't sound very happy."

19

The fleet with the battered *Elliði* at its head steams back to land. Fishermen in the fleet have radioed ahead with news of Krummi's battle. People have started gathering at Cape Stórhöfði to celebrate the return of the *Elliði*. Álsey Island is now to larboard, Surtsey to stern and starboard. They can hear horns blowing on land and there are blinking car lights as far as the eye can see. News of the events on the Selvogur fishing ground have obviously reached home. In the distance three helicopters can be seen over Landeyjarsandur Estuary.

"The Spanish would have done better keeping away from the lair. The *Armada* had the same fate as the headless bird hunter on Álsey Island," says Krummi as he looks toward the island southwest of Heimaey.

"That old tale," laughs Gaui. "My dad swore his grandad was there when the bird hunter abseiled down those cliffs. Says that there was no scream or shout or any sound at all – just a little jerk on the line. And then when they hauled him up, his head was missing."

They sail past Suðurey and up to Heimaey – the main Westmann Island. It is obvious that everyone, anyone who possibly can, has come out to welcome them. Krummi has never seen anything like it; people waving and blowing horns. The Islanders are retrieving their men from the Spanish fleet, just as the old gods rescued the beautiful god Baldr from the malevolent Hel. The damage to Krummi's ship clearly provokes great interest and astonishment.

They enter the harbour at Ystiklettur Crag. Three helicopters bearing the blue stars of the coastguard appear over Heimaklettur Crag.

"They haven't come to join the celebration," says Krummi with a grin, pointing to the sky.

"I'll bet they want to give us an escort," replies Gaui, frowning.

They dock at Básasker Pier. Everywhere they look people are celebrating and waving, the sun in their faces. When Krummi emerges from the bridge of *Elliði* a wave of joy courses through the throng. All of the Westmann Islanders, who still endure despite the setbacks of the years, have assembled down at the harbour.

"The people are warm, despite the cold!" shouts Gaui in Krummi's ear.

Flashing blue lights slowly make their way down Heiðarvegur Street. Someone shouts that four police vehicles are on their way.

"The heavily armed Viking Squad has come to pay homage to you, Krummi!" comes a shout from the crowd. "Let the bastards try!" shouts another. "They want to grant you the Order of the Falcon, like the skippers during the Cod War with the Brits!" yells a third.

This is met with loud laughter.

The police cruisers can come no further than the Spit. Out jump two-dozen black-uniformed men, fully armed. They run in two columns in the direction of Elliðaey. A few locals step into the troopers' path, thinking to block them.

Krummi jumps up onto the back of a lorry. "Let them through," he cries in a strong, commanding voice.

The riot squad hesitates, but the locals step aside.

"We always welcome visitors," thunders Krummi. Those gathered burst into raucous laughter and start stamping their feet and clapping their hands.

"Krummi... Krummi... Krummi," chants the crowd in rhythm.

The squad has stopped. The policemen hesitate and some finger their guns nervously.

Krummi jumps down from the platform and extends his hands.

"People have their different ways," he says in a loud voice, grinning. Krummi walks straight over to the black-uniformed fighters. "Your colleagues put their lives at risk against the superior strength of the British fleet during the Cod Wars. They took on the frigates of Her Majesty with smiles on their lips, and won," he says.

People start humming their own version of a tune that was immensely popular during the Cod Wars. Instead of the gunboat heroes taking the might of the English Navy, it's Krummi who takes on the Spanish Armada. The people sing louder and louder:

Although Spanish battleships are firm in their might,
Krummi truly gives them a fright.
And bitter to Europe is the salt drink,
as the Armada fancies it Elliði can sink.

The heavily armed police officers hesitate in front of the defiant Islanders.

"Yet, things are different now. You shackle your own kin for shooing off foreigners from our livelihood," says Krummi, who now towers over the squad leader and stares coldly into his eyes.

Krummi extends his hands as a sign that they can handcuff him. "These two hands will do, I believe, because the responsibility is entirely mine," he says.

"I am only following orders," says the officer. "I have to arrest all your crew."

"And do you remember the royal executioner in the novel Iceland's Bell?" Krummi's white teeth flash in his black beard. "He was only following orders, but he came to a sticky end."

"Didn't a dog piss on his grave?" asks Gaui with pretend innocence.

The policeman's face goes suddenly hard. The handcuffs snap shut.

They lead the Westmann Giant and his men to a police cruiser.

The people watch as if paralysed, until someone starts chanting, followed by the entire crowd, their chant echoing off Heimaklettur Peak: "Krummi... Krummi... Krummi... Iceland... Iceland... Iceland!" The people repeat again and again.

Krummi stops and salutes his people, surrounded by the fully-armed squadron. The giant holds up his hands, his handcuffs reflecting the silvery camera flashes and lights of the television cameras.

"Krummi... Krummi... we stand with you... we stand with you... all as one... all as one!" chants the crowd.

A squad member pushes the giant ahead of him. A great wave of anger passes through the throng but the Westmann Giant grins and turns around, towering over the man. The squadron leader orders the officer to stand aside.

"Let's keep calm," he tells Krummi. "Otherwise the entire situation will get out of hand."

"You can rest assured of that," replies the giant. "I don't want any nonsense and certainly no ruckus. Settle down your men, otherwise they'll end up in the harbour. That would be too bad," he adds in a calm voice.

They walk to the police vehicle and Krummi turns to the people.

"Long live Iceland... long live the Westmann Islands!" he shouts, and the crowd echoes him.

"Long live the Islands... long live the Islands... long live Iceland... long live Iceland!" chants the crowd in one voice. Heimaklettur amplifies their chant, making Heimaey seem to quake, as in the volcanic eruption of old.

Krummi and his men step into the cars and wave to the people.

The policemen slam the door shut behind them and the line of cruisers drives off into the gathering dusk. Shortly afterward a low din can be heard from near Ofanleiti House. The helicopters take off and vanish from the Islanders' view behind Heimaklettur.

Krummi becomes a national hero overnight for the fight on the Selvogur fishing ground. Great anger and resentment spreads quickly when news gets round of the arrest of Krummi and his men. Eighty thousand people gather at Lækjartorg Square to protest European violence. The masses do not fit on the square, so large numbers stand at the Ministry Offices while the rest snake southward down Lækjargata Street and up Bankastræti Street.

Leifur Eiríksson stands on the statue of Hannes Hafstein, offering him a good view of the throng, which extends as far as the eye can see. He has never seen anything like it. He is right in front of the Ministry Office which the Danes had built as prison at the foot of Arnarhóll during colonial times: it's where Steinka had died of hardship amongst the most hardened criminals of the time.

Leifur had come to the country earlier that day and therefore missed the terrible events on Austurvöllur Square that had paralysed the nation. He'd been in Copenhagen when he had received news of the tragedy and death of Guðrún, and of the *Elliði's* exploits on the Selvogur fishing ground.

When he'd heard of the people's protests, nothing else would do but to join in and let his voice be heard. "Independent Iceland, independent Iceland, independent Iceland!" he shouts as loud as his vocal cords permit, and those nearby join in with him until the people's demands echo over the square and throughout the buildings. John Lennon's Peace Column lights up the sky over nearby Viðey Island. The "tower of light" rises four kilometres up and dances in the overcast clouds. It's as if the great musician's spirit is with the people. "Imagine... yes imagine all the people living for today," Leifur hums the maestro's tune.

"Independent Iceland, independent Iceland, independent Iceland!" Thousands upon thousands of Icelanders raise their voices and find an outlet for their pent-up pain, anger, and disappointment. The throng's chants are extremely inspirational, absolutely extraordinarily awesome and unparalleled; such unanimity. Those gathered demand that Krummi the Westmann Giant be released from prison immediately and that the actions of the Spanish frigate be condemned.

"Let's cut the government's nets," shouts someone, and the crowd laughs.

"We demand an independent investigation into the violence on Austurvöllur," Leifur shouts until he grows hoarse and the crowd echoes him. "Independent investigation... independent investigation!" the crowd roars.

After the meeting youngsters march to the European Fisheries Agency and stone the building, breaking all of its window panes.

The youths climb into the garden, making it particularly difficult for the police to constrain the crowd. It isn't little pebbles that people cast: many stones find their way in through the windows; the fencing is shattered, flowers trampled and trees destroyed. After a huge commotion the demonstration finally breaks up.

The Icelandic Minister of Fisheries, Eik Thorman, is summoned to Brussels to meet with the Komizar of Fisheries and apologize for the clipping of the trawls of the European trawlers, which he stresses had been operating under European law. He laments the damage to the Fisheries Agency building and promises that Iceland will shoulder the costs of all damages.

Even this humiliation is not enough to satisfy the EU Komizars. What about the troublesome giant fisherman? He has to be taught a lesson. Thoman returns to Iceland with his orders. Krummi is locked up for two years and his ship is confiscated, then sold to pay compensation to the Basques for damages and their lost nets.

This trip to Brussels is the minister's final official act. Shortly afterward the new Governor is installed, coincidental to Iceland becoming a state in the United States of Europe. The Icelandic Republic has been dissolved just over a century after its foundation at Thingvellir.

Krummi shakes his head as he turns away from the bus stop and darts down a narrow alley. For twenty minutes he walks quickly, but aimlessly around the city, stopping every now and then to make sure nobody is following him. Once he sits on a bench for five minutes and watches to see if anyone else stopped as well. But nobody does. A man in a black suit walks slowly by flicking through an e-notebook, but he does not seem to pay Krummi any attention and Krummi ignores him. Krummi knows he will be late for his meeting with Helgi, but better to be late than to have a policeman eavesdropping on what they have to say to each other.

✦ **20** ✦

Helgi's eyes turn to Austurvöllur. It is terribly cold and windy; few people are out and about. The flag of the Great European State, blue with gold stars, flaps wildly over the Althingi Building. The crown of Christian IX has been removed from the building and replaced with the coat of arms of Europe. Austurvöllur is empty and there's still no sign of Hrafn.

Helgi looks at the clock.

He has waited for over half an hour for the Westmann Giant.

Helgi is surprised that Krummi hasn't shown up. He has been looking forward to meeting him, the most renowned man in Iceland. Hrafn had been just as eager that they meet.

His keenness was obvious in his expressions on the holph.

Helgi had beheld the giant in all his might when he projected him in full-size. Krummi is not just a giant; a giant can be colossal in many ways. Helgi had looked up in amazement at Krummi out on the deck of the new *Elliði* with screaming seagulls flying along the boat as they hauled in fish from the sea. The new *Elliði* has a crew of only three although it almost performs like the old one.

"I absolutely refuse to meet you unless you call me Krummi," Hrafn had said, laughing monstrously, overwhelming the seagull cries; a powerful stench of offal blended with a fragrant scent of the sea had wafted to Helgi's nostrils.

He had looked up at the giant.

"Krummi Nine-and-a-Half," Helgi had replied playfully.

"That's the long-line," Krummi had replied, laughing raucously. "Down at Peace Harbour, a bunch of kids were rolling over a shed, but unaware of a girl under it. I saw the impending danger, threw myself forward and managed to push her out of the way, but the shed crashed on my middle finger. That hurt, I can tell you: the

Raven's croak could be heard throughout the Islands, but the girl escaped with a mighty scare and a bloody knee so she was as good as new, but I became known as Nine-and-a-Half," he had added, as he put forward the stump, grinning with his white teeth flashing in his pitch-black beard.

They had agreed to meet at Café Europe.

Helgi looks up in surprise as noisy chatter comes from a table nearby.

Several glamorous-looking youngsters have recently entered the café. They laugh a lot, slap the table a lot. Their noise carries throughout the restaurant and the group does nothing to hide their wanton topics. Helgi vaguely recognises one of them, a muscular guy with short-clipped hair and pursed lips. Helgi can't quite place the loud young man, then remembers him from a TV news report on the hedonistic lifestyle of Reykjavík's extravagant young things, called Bimzi. It is a world that is alien to Helgi.

"How do I become as fit as you?" a tanned, blonde guy asks Bimzi, stroking his gelled hair. "I've been trying to bulk up by doing extra exercises, but now it's come time to scrape off the excess fat and start getting thrilling and filling the containers. What do you recommend to get as grooved as a squealer at Little Hraun prison?"

Helgi shakes his head in confusion. He does not understand this new youth slang.

"For a start, don't call some steroid-head selling ephedrine tablets," replies Bimzi. "They don't do a damn thing if your diet's messed up. You don't need to worry, since you're in aikido, but you need to pump iron if you want to get rid of that fat asap. Everyone thinks that the weights bulk you up but doesn't delete fat. It's bullshit, pure bullshit. Few things delete fat like proper lifting."

The other youngsters take stock of the words of the leader.

"Which do you find hotter, a g-string or lace boxers, you know what I mean," says a blonde girl smiling seductively at the hero.

He gives her a wild look, leans toward her and puts his hand on her thigh. "Both ridiculously sexy," he says, before adding, with a loud laugh: "I'm a Diesel man, even though a lot of people find Levis more macho. I don't give a shit which I'm in, since the only problem is the tightness because my ass is like a truck; normal pants barely fit."

They all laugh.

A boy sitting slightly off to the side speaks up, directing his words at Bimzi, whose lips are still pursed.

"This life seems to revolve around being in shape and shagging girls one after another, lying in tanning booths to look cool and tough, choosing friends based on their appearance. You people who mix sex, drugs, and rock and roll with working your asses off on weight benches, eyes frenzied. What can be said about you sex, steroids, and tanning-booth types? This all seems to revolve around appearance, not content."

The slight is obvious and the group falls silent, but Bimzi doesn't let it bother him.

"Sure, it's a pathetic life, I admit it. It's pathetic to have only famous friends and drive a Benz. It's pathetic to see City spank United. It's pathetic to have a thirty-centimetre dick and jerk 270. I wish I were a dumbass so I could sit in a café with a ciggie and a book of poetry." He looks coldly into the eyes of his companion, who blinks and looks away. The leader has spoken.

A dark-haired, serious-looking boy speaks up, allowing a touch of depression to slink up the table leg.

"I hate my job: everyone there's an idiot. I've been offered a new job but the ditzy bird says I've got to be on call for three months," he says.

"Damn, man, you just need to get fired. Take your chicken dick out and wave it in the bird's face. You'll definitely get a bulletproof boot in the gut," replies the leader.

"If that doesn't work then catch her on tape. Get her all worked up and shout obscenities. If she shouts back, you'll have the recording and can use it against her, just like that," adds a tablemate.

The group laughs and slaps the table again wildly. The noise fills the room and nearby patrons glance at them annoyingly.

"Doddi's got his hands full with forty-year-old dames. I went ballistic when he gave mom the eye after divorcing dad," says a guy at the end of the table, slightly hesitantly.

"That's not a problem. Mom's dating a black Yank and the noise from her room is making me crazy. I'm not into some black dropping bombs on my old lady," replies one of his friends, with a ring in his nose, all worked up.

There's more laughter, gab, more beer ordered.

A strong-looking, rather short girl with hefty shoulders and arms starts describing her problems in a rather rueful tone. "I bulk up like a man so I get these muscle-wings and look like a trucker lesbo," she complains. "I've tried just burning calories but it hardly makes any difference. I've got a great body except for this problem. Before I bulk up my form's perfect, god-dammit."

"It's just in your head. Guys make much more testosterone than you," says the leader as he purses his lips before resuming. "I've often heard girls say that. If you pare yourself down properly you shouldn't have muscles like a man. The fact is that the more muscle mass you have, the easier it is to pare down. If you do a lot of reps, you don't bulk up so much. Pay attention to your diet, lift weights three times a week, and burn calories the other three days."

Suddenly a cool bird is conjured up out of the holph; the hol' leans up against the girl with the sturdy shoulders, which, however makes no difference, since she is only an image. The girl starts chatting with Bimzi. She is lying at home on the sofa, dressed scantily. He reduces the bird to quarter size, making her seem to lie on the table. He's describing a party at which the famous Golgi Geirsson had shown up.

"Marz played for Golgi. I gave the band some steroids so they got tighter, screamed at the group and got Henró to take the drumsticks. It's just like he was born with drumsticks up his ass, such rhythm, wiped Zommy Bee's ass for sure," says Bimzi, bursting out in laughter.

"I wish I could have been there but had to be with the gang at a family reunion," says the girl with a frown, as if she's unhappy about having missed the party, but then she smiles her prettiest smile at Bimzi.

"The sound was really awesome and Golgi great," continues Bimzi. "Fúsi really surprised me on guitar, great solo. The band absolutely rocked. Golgi backed me up on keys, ripped his tanktop. We hammered the sound, dudes. Never better."

The girl is obviously annoyed because she's suddenly in a loud argument, most likely with her siblings or parents. "Get the hell out of here," she shouts, and her quarter-size image disappears into thin air without the girl with the stocky shoulders paying the least attention.

Bimzi shrugs.

Helgi has had enough. He has better things to do than listen to a bunch of young fools waste their lives. He stands up to leave when the door flies open, a rush of cold air and rain sweeping into the café to blast the youngsters and mess up Bimzi's carefully gelled hair. And then the doorway is blocked by the Westmann Giant, soaking wet. Krummi smiles, shakes himself and walks over to the table.

Helgi smiles back, his face brightening. He finds himself smitten by Krummi's brilliant energy and joy of life. The man's primal power and self-made pride brighten the room.

Even if such a man were in chains and the Komizar's executioner were knotting up his straps, he would grin through his teeth, in the Devil's name. Onward, in the Devil's name, thinks Helgi, smiling.

The patrons look at the Westmann Giant and start whispering about him. Everywhere in the room people are whispering, except the young people, who seem fenced off in their own world. Krummi's handshake is firm.

You folk who inherit need!
At the springs of life, abundant indeed,
thirsty and poor, you pay for great sin,
in deeds, little nation, you must begin
to erase your need, your emptiness fill —

all that is needed for this is will.

"Einar Benediktsson knew how to inspire the nation to great deeds, knew how to motivate people, unlike the doldrums these days, when one's every step is monitored," says Krummi, glancing out the window toward the surveillance cameras on the old Reykjavík Apothecary.

"You're an inspiration to the people," replies Helgi.

"It's a tall order to wake a nation that guzzles beer while waiting for the next message from Brussels," says Krummi, signalling the waiter. "One beer," he says with a grin, glancing quickly at Helgi and then at the kids, who laugh contentedly in their own world, chattering about ephedrine, testosterone, and body groomers.

"It's time to scrape those damn golden stars off the Althingi. We have work to do. We need to put our fists down, like the truck drivers who refused on Komizar's orders to sit on their haunches up on the heaths with coffee mugs in hand. When they handcuffed the men at Red Lake, a string snapped in the nation. It's your job and mine to get the harp to sound again." The giant's eyes sparkle and his white teeth flash in his black beard.

"Oh, everyone has completely forgotten me," replies Helgi. He feels melancholy setting in; it has increased as the years have passed.

"Completely forgotten. Far from it," says Krummi determinedly. "The nation will never forget your fiery speech at Sæmundur Square. You opened people's eyes. You awakened people to knowledge about the Icelandic nationality and the Republic. A cock crowed as soon as the Althingi rejected the Icelandic nation. Indolent MPs approved the betrayal barefacedly, but the Apostle Peter knew how to feel shame. The nation gathered at Austurvöllur. We all protested, all, all, all as one! It was a courageous nation that protested the golden euro on the blue field in exchange for lame subsidies that deprive people of their self-respect. You are the reason that I clipped the net from the back of the Basques."

"Blood was shed for nothing on Austurvöllur," replies Helgi sadly.

"It's up to us to show that Guðrún and the student died in the service of a living cause," replies Krummi slowly and heavily. "The dedication of the memorial on Sæmundur Square kindles a flame in the heart of the nation. This flame becomes a bonfire when they trample it into the mud."

Helgi had always regretted not having attended the memorial dedication. The memory had been painful but he had got the clear message that he was not wanted. In hindsight, he should have faced his adversaries. "You, I, and the people hold the torch aloft in memory of a hero," says Helgi, looking deeply into Krummi's eyes.

Then he smiles and sings an old, lewd 19th century song mocking the Danes, but which he turns against the Europeans:

Blessed Vikings of ice,
Eur-opportunity knocks!
They're squirming with worms
and look so much like cocks.

They both laugh heartily, causing the young folk to look up and smile faintly at the men's noise.

"The cocks of Copenhagen have moved to Brussels," says Helgi, laughing loudly and feeling better. Spending time in Krummi's company is doing him good. His mood is lighter and he enjoys the Westmann Giant's mischievousness. "The Danish Nellemann, rest his soul, wanted to buy the souls of Icelandic students for Danish silver in the king's city of Copenhagen back in the 19th century. Of course there were some who wanted to sell the country for fat jobs," Helgi adds, getting all worked up. "The nation was so disgraced by cold and hardship that it dug itself down into the ground where no one could witness its shame, and on top of that bowed so deeply that its nose touched the ground and handed over its saga heritage to the delight of the king and the glory of Copenhagen. President Jón Sigurðsson hammered pride, courage, virility, and last but not least knowledge into a nation that had forgotten to stand upright. President Jón risked everything for Iceland; office and advancement, and didn't give a whit for the meat-kettles of the king and nobility in Christiansborg Palace. The young poets dedicated verses to the man who rose up from his time period," says Helgi before reciting a poem.

To say thanks, all admit is right
the guardian, ward
of freedom's radiant light
that history names
Iceland's shield and sword.

Krummi nods in approval. "Bizarre to argue that the Icelandic nationality was dead and buried and that European would take its place. The nation sailed the sea to freedom but got caught in the nets of pencil chewers," says the Westmann Giant.

Helgi looks out the window. Outside people run as fast as they can out of the soaking rain, their umbrellas getting caught by the strong wind. Some dash drenched into cafés, others into cars, slamming the doors behind them. Helgi knows that he has made up his mind, and there will be no turning back. He plans to add his weight to the scale for recovering the soul of the Icelandic nation; recovering the Icelander from the monstrous hands of the European bureaucrat. In the Kremlin, attempts were made to invent the new man. They called him a Homo soveticus; so perfect that he was said to be free from all lust and greed. Yet the new soveticus was more interested in dissipation and vodka so the dream became a nightmare.

Now it is Homo europus who spreads over the European continent like fire. In the land of fire and ice, Homo europus is content with his euro subsidies and dispenses Ritalin to frayed farmers who eat Spanish chickens and worn-out sailors who watch their European peers sail away with the catch beyond the furthest horizon. In the dreamland no one suffers, because former sheep farmers and hungover sailors live on subsidies. Awaited is the day when they go on pension or to the grave, moving that problem out of the picture.

"You and I," says Helgi, his expression serious as he looks at Krummi. "We'll offer the soul of the Icelandic nation, but a powerful leader is needed to lead the great march to freedom. Our time has passed, but the future is for the young people."

Krummi nods in agreement.

He is fully aware that the nation needs more incredible magic than what old terrorists can conjure out of their hats. That's why they are sitting at a café. Gutlessness and wheeziness characterize contemporary political dissident powers. The indolent think only of their profit and beneficiaries of subsidies, complain about the subsidies being too low. The black night of the soul of the Icelandic nation is as the blackest fog on the moors, appearing as if it will never let up.

Krummi looks over at the young people. "Ephedrine, testosterone, and body grooming. Is that everything?" he asks mockingly.

"All that's needed is to light a spark in people's hearts," says Helgi.

"God knows I've tried, but I lack all political insight," replies Krummi.

"And I'm better off bending over dusty old books," says Helgi.

"You were the great leader of our youth. No one has stepped forward with such power or inspiration," says Krummi determinedly.

"The spark in my heart was extinguished with Guðrún's death," says Helgi, looking deeply into his coffee cup, as if wishing to read the future. He then looks resolutely at Krummi, having long since made up his mind. "The closest associate of the Komizar for External Relations in Berlin is a young Icelandic woman; sparklingly talented, passionate, and a poet. Her name is Júlía Ingólfsdóttir. I've heard a lot of very good things about her and she's had an outstanding career. A Danish friend of mine watched her work wonders on a conference in Reykjavík. She absolutely enchanted the room. So impressed was the Komizar that he got her to join his team in Berlin. The world is at her feet, and she personally is said to support the restoration of the Republic. Despite her young age, she has already made a name for herself among the leading Icelandic poets. The one who writes poetry as she does, loves freedom and her country."

Helgi recites Júlía's confession of love for a storm:

I love you, love you, eternal strife,
my blood churning, I offer the song of my life.
To you, storm so free, raging with speed
with boldness and joy my heart pays you heed.

Krummi is able to appreciate his colleague's delivery of the poem about the storm, which rages over the grassy ground. "I have heard of Júlía," he replies. "But I had never thought of getting her involved. Maybe it's because she'd gone to work in Berlin, but it is a genius idea. With Júlía on board, we'll be able to revive Iceland's good fortune," he thunders, causing the café patrons to look again at the giant.

Some shake their heads; people who found it ridiculous for him to throw rotten pollock in Brussels. It had been a disgrace to the Icelandic nation; bad for the image of the country and its people. "Go back to the Islands," shouts a voice from the far side of the café.

Others encourage the Westmann Giant. "When are you going to Brussels next?" comes another shout.

"We're coming with you!" shout the kids.

Bimzi challenges Krummi to an arm-wrestling match but the giant spurs Júlía's poetic steed about Snorri Sturluson:

Oft times in Thorri
when dusk starts to fall,
I recall father Snorri,
who composed Háttatal

With Skúli he once shared board,
wrote poems of his Norwegian lord,
and of his kinsman, Hákon the king,

who morosely deprived us freedom.

"I want out! I want out now!
I want out," the hero did say,
and out steered his prow
to Iceland that very day.

Later to doom he was lost,
for the king he inevitably crossed.
And Borgarfjörður's slopes of frost
weep along with its hills.

The people in the room laugh loudly.

They start applauding Krummi, who bows respectfully. He grins, his white teeth flashing in his black beard. People stand up, some whistle.

"Such genius, such inspiration! Iceland's glaciers will rise from the sea," says Krummi to the people, cheerfully. He feels as if something great is happening, something that can make a difference.

Then Krummi looks out the window, still grinning. Two people can be seen beneath umbrellas striding purposefully toward Café Europe.

Krummi turns quickly to Helgi.

"Police," he says quietly. "I thought they'd already flayed me. What more do they want?" Krummi has stood up and makes ready to leave. "You and I and Júlía: let's join hands. We'll outsmart the Devil," he says with a gleam in his eyes.

"We'll do our sacred duty, as will hopefully all well-wishing men and women. If the Icelandic nationality survives another thousand years, then hopefully people will say: 'This was their finest hour,'" replies Helgi loud and clear.

They say goodbye, there being no time for long speeches. Krummi walks out onto the street. The sun has broken forth from the clouds.

Helgi knits his brow and shakes his head; has the Giant lost his shadow?

The swishing of clothing, footsteps and people's voices are heard further down the corridor. The two policemen walk briskly into the room, look around carefully, then leave quickly. Helgi watches them and recalls an old saga.

Day has dawned
cock feathers rattle,
time for bondsmen
to labour and toil.

His mind wanders to the Thormóður Kolbrúnarskáld's encouragement of the household servants, as Iceland's freedom fighter — Iceland's honour, sword and shield — cited when he instilled courage in the Icelanders in the mid-19th century. It would be necessary to inspire passion, as had happened when the nation started its quest for its own rights and independence two centuries ago.

Helgi pulls on his coat. "Day has dawned," Helgi says clear and loud. People at the café look at him curiously and someone asks in a firm voice. "Aren't you the guy who led the rebellion on Austurvöllur?"

Helgi smiles companionably. Krummi is right: despite everything, he isn't totally forgotten and buried in Copenhagen.

"The time has come to do some work," he says with a smile, wrapping his scarf tightly around his neck and putting on his hat. He is going to untie the knot that is thought to have been tied so tight for so long; tight enough, some think, to last for eternity.

"We're with you," says the people, who stand up and salute: "Cool, super cool," someone shouts. Helgi walks cheerfully out into the rays of the sun lighting up Austurvöllur.

He checks on his shadow.

21

It is a clear, cool autumn day — the time thirteen-zero-zero. Sólman Smithson, who has thrust his chin down to his chest to protect his face from the cold, damp wind, turns hastily in through the glass door of the Berlaymont, yet is not quick enough to prevent a gust of sandy dust from blowing into the lobby along with him. On the wall hangs a huge facial portrait of the First Komizar. Rikhard D. Trinxon has black hair, and a large black moustache: he could be called handsome, though the lines in his face are very deeply grooved. The portrait dominates the lobby. Sólman doesn't pay much attention to it but heads for the stairs, since the elevator is out of order.

He has arrived at the offices of the Peripheries Bureau.

On the way in he passes Nedum Tillotson, a small man with dark stubble, precise and diligent. On his knees is a very old, folded newspaper and he holds a Dictaphone close to his mouth. Tillotson looks up; a hostile gleam reflects from his glasses in the direction of Sólman, who barely knows the man. Tillotson works in the Archives Department and seldom discusses his work. Sólman walks past Tillotson into the corridor, which has two rows of cubicles on each side. A constant rustling and murmuring come from the corridor. Even if his life depended on it, Sólman could not name all of the employees who work for him in the department. Sólman takes pride in his job though most of the work is tedious, but sometimes, however, they are given challenging and complicated projects that demand all his talents. Then he truly enjoys himself, since he needs no direction beyond the principles of Ensós and guesswork on what is required of him.

The offices of the Peripheries Bureau fill three storeys in the Berlaymont.

Sólman walks along the seemingly endless corridor past office after office. His is a position of some responsibility, but despite his title he has far too many superiors. There is of course Komizar Leif Sörenbøim, and under him the director and general managers of each division. Sólman's department is responsible for the fringe areas and development of the virtual and pseudo-sciences. According to the organizational chart, he reports to the manager Mauro Spignioli, but communications go through two supervisory agents: the Euro-Turk Nazdar Hamill Özalilz and the Euro-Romanian Nicolai Meninescu. Communications are formal and polite; Sólman has nothing to complain about. He meets with Spignioli twice a year but has never met the director, Andraii Janúkólowski; has only caught glimpses of him. He's only seen Sörenbøim in the media. This is fine with him, but he has to admit that relations can be difficult. Accusations that he has given Iceland preferential treatment have strained his relations with some of the bureaucrats. He feels as if an unexplained irritation among the employees of the Peripheries Bureau has been spreading during the last few years. It is difficult to ascertain the significance of the problem, but of course the increasingly more intractable cases get on his nerves.

Sólman has taken up the issue of the Antiquaries Club for Helgi, but with little result. People have merely shaken their heads and say that Berlin is not interested in changing the decision. He still hasn't worked up the courage to call Helgi.

Sólman is lost in thought when Nazdar suddenly emerges from one of the offices and steps in front of him. The Turk lays a hand on his chest and smiles apologetically but amicably.

"You are requested to attend a meeting on the Twelfth Floor. I've been asked to accompany you," the Turk says calmly. He speaks with the odd toneless European bureaucratic accent, which is calmly and quietly working its way in among the bureaucracy.

Sólman is surprised, because Security is on the Twelfth Floor. "Twelfth Floor," he echoes, obviously quite shocked.

Nazdar shrugs apologetically. Relations have always been good between them, although they haven't shared many laughs.

"What do they want from a bloke like me," asks Sólman, forcing a wry smile, but feels that Nazdar is not amused. There is something being left unsaid, although they can't have anything on him as he hasn't done anything. Well, not since that old business about the Icelandic goodwill grants and he was hoping that they were long-forgotten. He had received a reprimand about that at the time, but the issue was then dropped. They can't possibly be digging that up. Nothing else worth mentioning comes to mind, they can't possible be inquiring about the incident in Heysel Park, nor Krummi's truck. Anyway, that would not pose a problem.

They need to go down to the multi-storey car park to take the lift up to the Twelfth floor. It is a special elevator that never breaks down, and provides the only access to the Security Bureau. They say that the arrangement ensures the independence of the bureaus of the Peripheries, Agriculture and Fisheries. Two guards with their arms crossed on their chests appear as the lift opens. Sólman steps out but is surprised when Nazdar remains behind.

"You're not coming?" asks Sólman in astonishment, finding that his voice trembles.

"No, but I'm sure I'll see you soon," replies Nazdar, in a sad tone.

They walk down the corridor, Sólman in the middle. The guards lead him into a windowless room with mirrors on two walls. There is a table in the middle of the room and three chairs. Two on one side and the other opposite them.

"Have a seat," one of the guards says dryly. Sólman feels relieved, since there is no sign of threat in their voices, although they can hardly be termed friendly. But then he isn't looking for friendship. He sits down and the guards walk out without saying another word.

Sólman has to wait for forty-five minutes before two men walk authoritatively into the room and sit down opposite him. He recognizes one of them, a Euro-Norwegian slightly younger than him; he is fairly sure that the man is from Oslo and is called Olav, but cannot remember his surname. Sólman has seen Olav several times around the place, but they have never socialized. Still, Sólman can't help but feel some antipathy toward the man. There is something in his attitude, something ... bitter. Sólman does not recognise the other man, but guesses that he is a Euro-German.

"I am Rudolf Kessler and this is Olav Seiferdal," says the Euro-German slowly, before adding: "I am from the European Security Headquarters in Berlin, Seiferdal is our chief of surveillance here in Brussels." He clears his throat, his face expressionless, but the Euro-Norwegian taps his fingers rapidly on the table. The Euro-German looks with a scowl at the fingers of his colleague, who glances back at him apologetically and clenches his hands in his lap.

The Euro-German looks at Sólman.

"You attended a meeting with an Icelandic terrorist at the Café Rue de la Montagne," he says abruptly.

The statement takes Sólman completely by surprise. This he has not expected. They are inquiring about his get together with Krummi in Brussels. It is absurd to call it a meeting at the café, because they simply drank a couple of beers.

"We were just recalling old times," Sólman replies while scolding himself for meeting Krummi in a public place. He should not have met Krummi at that café. Stupid fool, Sólman thinks. Surveillance is even more advanced than he realises.

"You sat together for two hours at the back of the café," says Kessler staunchly.

"At the back of the café. Not at all. We sat there because there was a table free," sighs Sólman. "We're childhood friends from the Westmann Islands, old friends and colleagues." Sólman pushes against the back of his chair as if he is trying to get as far away from the men as possible.

"What did you discuss?" insists Kessler, leaning across the table as if he is challenging the Euro-Icelander; telling the ruffian that he is caught in the net.

"We discussed the situation at home, the shortage of fish. Cod had hardly been seen in the Islands for many years until just recently, just pollack or saithe. They blame the foreign fishermen, the quota-hoppers. The Basques buy Icelandic boats, man them and sail away with the catch. The quotas come with the boats. And then there are the straddling stocks. I feel it my duty to meet with people from back home, being chairman of the Euro-Ice Friends' Society in Brussels," says Sólman feeling slightly more confident.

Seiferdal's look is tangibly hostile. "Why did your bureau fail to monitor the rig?" he asks snappishly.

Seiferdal only mentions the truck and is careful not to mention the humans on board, Sólman senses. The bastard obviously doesn't realize that Sólman knows their dirty little secret. Sólman finds this comforting so he decides to go into details on the software problems. "We've been having backup problems. 'Dirt' gets into the system when mathematical functions come up, due to incorrect coding and implementation. There was a defect that we traced back to vague system requirements. Part of the problem, believe it or not, relates to a lack of understanding how humans interact with computers and coordination. The Ceobeol code simply would not comply, so we had to upgrade the support software." Sólman feels he's getting ahead in this interrogation. He looks into Seiferdal's angry eyes and adds. "The department is getting on top of the problem, next month we..."

Seiferdal slams the table and shouts: "Stop bullshitting, you filthy Icelander! This sluggishness is unacceptable: the truck should have been monitored."

"I agree, but then we were supposed to monitor only the truck: someone else should have known that the Westmann Giant was in town. It was not my responsibility," Sólman replies calmly.

Seiferdal interrupts him, obviously annoyed since he gets the gibe. "Your relationship with Krummi is unacceptable."

"He saved my life when I was a boy," Sólman replies confidently. This Euro-Norwegian is causing him no problems.

Then the Euro-German stands up and walks behind Sólman. "What about the Olympics?" Kessler says abruptly.

"What about them?" asks Sólman in surprise. Where is the man heading? He does feel slightly relieved, however, because to his recollection they had never mentioned the Olympic Games in their conversation at the café.

"What about them?" exclaims Kessler grumpily. "You discussed the Olympics."

They look at him suspiciously and then at one another.

"You must believe me." Sólman feels the sweat beading on his forehead as the doubt creeps in. He tries to remain calm although he now recalls mentioning the Olympics at the café. But it is all rather vague, he's confused. "All I said was that it would be fun to attend the Olympics in Berlin," says Sólman hurriedly.

"Oh?" says Kessler.

"I said that I was planning to go to Berlin, but Hrafn showed no interest," replies Sólman.

"Hrafn mentioned bringing a truck to Berlin, making a stylish entrance. I ask you: are terrorist acts being organized for Berlin? Where will these acts take place?" Seiferdal looks triumphantly at his boss as he concludes his questions.

Sólman is lost for words, confused as he desperately tries to recollect his conversation with Krummi.

"You've just admitted to discussing the Olympics with Hrafn Illugason. You said it! First you denied it," Seiferdal screeches.

"Krummi was only joking," Sólman tries to explain.

"So you think terrorism is a joke?" Seiferdal slams the table.

"No, sir... I... I'm not suggesting..." stammers Sólman.

Kessler sits down and stares icily at Sólman who feels the situation is getting really awkward. This is much worse than the gibberish three years ago about the grants as this involves state security. He feels the sweat on the palm of his hands, all over his body. He never should have gone to that damn café with Krummi.

"We didn't say a thing about protests, let alone terrorism. I just expressed my interest in going to Berlin. No protests," Sólman reiterates, leaning forward on the table to stress his words but he feels devastatingly helpless.

Kessler abruptly, leans forward across the table so that his face is close to Sólman's. "What part does Helgi Thorláksson play in your plans?" he asks.

Sólman jerks back as if he's been punched. "Helgi Thorláksson... the Professor," he moans.

"Yes, the Professor who has never been entrusted with an official position. Is he connected to the terrorist plans?" Kessler stares deep into Sólman's eyes.

"Helgi is an old schoolmate. I invited him to dinner and we enjoyed an excellent evening together, just recalling old times. We never mentioned the Olympics." Sólman tries to speak slowly, emphasizing every word.

Seiferdal leans forward, laying heavy emphasis on his words. "Helgi suggested that opposition would be justified and that it is time to take action."

"Action?" exclaims Sólman. "Action? Absurd. How do you know what we were talking about?" Sólman feels the anger well up within him, as well as dry out on his lips. Make no mistake, they are inquiring about the safety of the state.

Kessler stands up abruptly and looks at Seiferdal. They walk out without saying a word. Sólman remains behind on his cold chair.

He feels horrendous.

Time passes by without anyone entering the room. Sólman feels the tiredness coming over him; he leans his head on the table and falls asleep.

He jumps up when the door is pushed open, its noise echoing throughout the room. He is sleepy and stiff. A long time has passed.

The same two men sit down opposite Sólman again.

Kessler speaks first and asks whether Sólman wishes to change his testimony.

"Change my testimony, no, not at all," answers Sólman.

"You are fully aware of the gravity of the case. This pertains to the security of the state. You are required to disclose information if you have any knowledge of terrorist activities. You know that," says Kessler with a frown.

"Yes, of course I know the security laws. But I assure you. I have broken no law. I do not believe for a second that Krummi is planning terrorism," replies Sólman. He immediately realises the contradiction. Krummi has just committed an act of terrorism, according to its strict definition, although many people in Europe and in Iceland look upon it as an act of protest.

"We are going to release you," Kessler says slowly but forcefully, looking almost amicably at the Ice-European. "You are obligated to let us know if you have any news of terrorist acts. The events in Brussels have had their effect on people. We must ensure the utmost security." Kessler's voice is almost friendly.

"Of course," answers Sólman hurriedly.

"If there are any Icelandic demonstrations or acts of vandalism in connection with the Olympic Games then you could be in bad shape. You know that, don't you?" Sólman feels chills go down his spine and sweat yet again break out on his forehead. Kessler's voice is authoritative and threatening. "You are free to go," he adds.

Sólman nods, sad and gloomy. He hurries out of the room and almost runs to get into the lift that will take him down to the underground car park.

After he has gone Kessler turns to Seiferdal. "What do you think?"

The Euro-Norwegian shrugs. "I think he was scared of us. He told the truth. He doesn't know anything. But I'll lay good money that the big fisherman is up to something, and that the saga scholar is in on it."

Kessler nods. "Yes. I agree. Anyway, write up the report and include this interview in it."

"Sure," replies Seiferdal. He glances at his watch. "I'll get it done in the morning then send you a copy."

"Better make it two copies," says Kessler. "But only indent for one. I have my reasons," he adds when Seiferdal gives him an odd look.

Kessler can't imagine why the Vulture is interested in this minor bureaucrat and his meeting with the big fisherman, but if the Vulture wants a copy of the report then Kessler is not going to argue.

22

The young woman goes to the window and light falls on her brilliantly beautiful face as she looks out over Kurfürstendamm. Dark clouds are drifting over Berlin from the west, it will rain soon. Júlía Ingólfsdóttir is just over thirty, born in the Thingholt area of Reykjavík shortly after the dissolution of the Republic. She has deep roots in Icelandic rural culture. Every summer in her childhood she had helped out in all the work with her grandfather and grandmother at the farm Skúlaskeið at the foot of the Eyjafjöll Mountains beneath the great volcano. On her speedy steed her mood is lightest as the fells come flying and she feels as if she dashes through her entire life in a single sprint. She has had the greatest career of any Icelander in Berlin.

She is expected to reach the highest rank in the civil service in Berlin.

She is the personal assistant of Erich Devereaux, the Komizar of State. Júlía is a cosmopolitan; she read French literature at the Sorbonne and speaks all the major languages of the continent fluently. She had directed a theatre group in Iceland, become nationally renowned for her sparkling intelligence and poetic eloquence. Her reputation has travelled so widely from the farthest reaches of the sea that Berlin has called on her to work alongside the sparklingly brilliant Devereaux. The Komizar himself has deep roots in old Europe; his parents were French and German. He is from Elsaß-Lothringen, or Alsace-Lorraine, the province that was a bone of contention between France and Germany for so long when the tanks carved deep scars in the countryside. The young Devereaux is like a fresh breeze in Berlin, unlike the older Komizars. Actually, it was Devereaux who had invited Júlía to work with him.

There is a knock on her door and Júlía signals her secretary to open the door. Her visitor is a bureaucrat from Brussels, and Icelander named Sólman Smithson who says he has a delicate matter to discuss. The man enters, a neat little man in a blue suit. Yet another hard-working bureaucrat, thinks Júlía. She waves the secretary to leave them and invites Sólman to sit down.

"So, what is the trouble?" asks Júlía.

Sólman explains about Kessler and Seiferdal, his interrogation on the Twelfth Floor and about his innocent old friendship with Krummi and Helgi. "I will admit that I am rather alarmed. I have nothing to hide, of course, but you know how the Security System can twist innocent facts to appear suspicious. I am concerned that my position as head of the Euro-Ice Friends Society may have attracted unwelcome attention. Conditions in Iceland are a bit jumpy right now. It is in our interests as good Euro-Icelanders to smooth things over. I was wondering if you could assure the powers that be of my good intentions. This is, of course, a lengthy process. Slowly and steadily the authorities have been becoming more aggressive," says Sólman as he sits in Júlía's elegant office and gazes out over the throng on the Ku'damm.

Júlía senses Sólman's nervousness. It does not bode well that Kessler was involved in a small, tiny matter like this. Trinxon's personal security man had no business being there. What's he up to? What's Trinxon up to? She decides to confide in Sólman. "There's no denying that I distrust Trinxon's secretiveness. I suspect Trinxon of having formed his own intelligence clique," says Júlía.

Her words come like a bolt from the blue. Sólman hasn't suspected Komizar Trinxon of involvement in the interrogation on the Twelfth Floor.

"Of course I know nothing about any clique. They were hard to deal with but I actually have little to complain about. They were polite, though I admit that I felt they knew uncomfortably much about my private life. Although it's understandable that the Security Bureau concerns itself with Icelandic terrorists. Krummi is of course a tricky customer, as was demonstrated in Brussels and on the Selvogur fishing ground. And the conflicts on Austurvöllur Square were horrific events, but so long ago" says Sólman.

Júlía nods supportively. "Don't worry, it is not just you. Trinxon's bullying of opponents is not limited to Iceland. In many places he's like a grey cat, uncontrollable, truth to tell." Sólman's concern does not surprise her, but she feels he's letting himself be cowed too much; tiptoeing, preferring not to upset anyone. However, Trinxon's authoritativeness is of great concern to her, his secret clique is out of control, and its methods questionable, to say the least. However, she is not going to discuss the Komizars' disputes any further. Devereaux has challenged the First Komizar; asked him directly whether he organizes illegal operations.

"Absurd," Trinxon had replied with a look of astonishment.

Júlía looks at Sólman but then continues. "It was to be expected that views were divided on the dissolution of the Republic. But it is not right to bring up these old disputes all over again. Helgi Thorláksson is without doubt one of the most important Nordic scholars in Europe and Krummi's actions have once again made him a national hero back home. We must face the fact that the European Fisheries agenda has more or less wiped out Icelandic fishing. That, of course, is a great shame, and it has drained the Icelanders of dynamism and strength." Júlía is focused and determined.

"That is certainly correct. Seafaring is no longer a way of life back home. I am a Westmann Islander, an old friend of Krummi. He actually saved my life when we were young," Sólman hurriedly answers.

He admires Júlía's youth and beauty, but chooses to change the subject. "I'm going to Reykjavík at the end of March," he says. "A conference on the rejuvenation of the peripheries," he adds distractedly. He sits hunched, rubs his forehead with his left hand and looks out the window. It had started pouring rain, obscuring the view of even the next building over.

Júlía looks at Sólman. He looks awful. The interrogation on the Twelfth Floor has clearly taken a lot out of him.

She quotes an ancient proverb that seems appropriate for the moment:

To his friend
a man shall be friend,
To both him and his friend.
But let no man be friend
to a friend,
of his foe.

Sólman looks at her and smiles. He knows that his days in Brussels are limited. The interrogation is a direct signal of Berlin's mistrust in him. It may be time to take a new direction in life. He has nothing to lose. He feels it deep within himself; is he hearing a cawing from Klettsvík? "A man's reputation never dies," he replies.

Júlía smiles indulgently. She understands what Sólman means. He stands up from his chair and says goodbye. Despite it all, he feels better as he takes the plush lift back down to street level.

He steps out into the rain-sodden streets of Berlin and heads toward the shelter of his hotel. Suddenly he stops, oblivious to the rain and the people who almost bump into him. A smile spreads across his face. "What the hell," he mutters. "You only live once." He stands still while thoughts race through his mind. After a while he walks off slowly. His life will never be the same again.

Júlía stands at the window and watches the raindrops trickle down the glass.

She recalls the time when Erich Devereaux came to Iceland for a conference on the new Europe; it was claimed that the 20th century had been America's but the 21st century belongs to good old Europe, which has risen from the ashes and is now the most powerful state in the world, with close to a billion inhabitants although its share in global production has shrunk to a tenth. The conference had been a continuous boasting about the Great European State, causing even Devereaux to shift in his seat with boredom. A Danish economist had claimed that statistics showed that the continental states had benefited from the Great European State; the experiment had succeeded, though the small states had no political clout. Worst of all though, was the constant decline in the standard of living, not least in some isolated territories, but that would have happened even if Europe had not merged into a super-state.

"Iceland is the best known example of deterioration," he had said, as matter-of-factly as taking a drink of water. "However, research has shown that the Euro-Icelanders are doing quite well on the continent, actually simply wonderfully," the Dane had said before quoting an old tune:

Look on the bright side.
The world,
it could be worse.

The old colonial pride had been too much for Júlía. She had torn her carefully prepared lecture to pieces in front of a full house and delivered what the press had called her "sermon of fire".

"Here we are and can do no more," she had begun her speech. "We can do nothing other than admit that Europe has failed its littlest brother. From no nation has Europe demanded so much, even so disgracefully much. Iceland was forced to give up its resources, even though they were the foundation for the Icelandic identity and economy. With one stroke of its pen, Europe gained almost a million square kilometres of land and sea; I repeat, as much as a million square kilometres. Do you think that the Swedes and Finns would have ventured to step across the threshold if Europe had demanded their forests of them; just like that, demanded Swedish and Finnish forests? They said that Brussels control over the fishing stocks was just a formality, that it made no difference. It was a lie. Everyone knew that it was a lie.

"They lied without blinking an eye.

"They knew better, because the same had happened in the British and Irish fishing industry. British fishermen had no voice after their bitter defeat in the Cod Wars, so they were sacrificed. The fate of British and Irish fishermen should have been a warning sign. Of course, Europe should not have been playing with fire when it appropriated for itself the nation just beneath the Arctic Circle." She had spoken emphatically; her voice had been sharp, but was devoid of any anger or bitterness.

She had continued: "The nation that sailed the choppy sea and was pounded by heavy breakers swallowed the lies because it had become frightened and lonely in the winter storms at the farthest reaches of the sea. It bowed its head to the foreign power. Vultures took flight, desirous of prey. They held secret councils in dark, smoky back rooms, their eyes shot sparks of greed and they marked out the fishing grounds. The nation lived through the siege. It undermined its confidence. The power went to Brussels and then to Berlin. The nation at the farthest reaches of the sea became isolated in the darkness and lost its best people, by the tens of thousands, south to Europe."

Júlía had held the undivided attention of the room; Devereaux paid special attention. She had surprised everyone by asking foreign conference delegates about Umeå. Even some of the Euro-Swedes had never heard of Umeå.

What's that? asked someone the audience.

No one in the room had come to the Swedish town of Umeå. Swedes merely shake their heads when the name comes up, because in their opinion, it's way up north in no-man's land. "Few people go there, very few," she had said emphatically.

"Umeå is further south than Iceland," she had added. A murmur ran through the room as people exchanged glances getting her point.

Her thunderous speech had touched strings and evoked mixed reactions from the delegates. Devereaux had come to speak to her afterward and praised her speech. Júlía knew that his words had great weight, since it was predicted that he would have the office of European President, although it was just the European Nomenklatura that elected the president; a small group within the indolent upper class. Still, he was not the typical Eurocrat. She bore deep respect for the man, being of a completely different make than the unlikable, unpopular Trinxon.

The conference had been in January. The weather had been bad:

gales, snow, and bitter cold. "We need new vision, we need your voice," Devereaux had said to Júlía. "I will be in touch, but I admit that I will be happiest the moment that the aircraft lifts off up out of the Reykjavík darkness. I understand your situation better here, up north below the Arctic Circle. Thanks to you."

Now Júlía is in Berlin.

Time flies like a leaf in the wind.

★ 23 ★

The day after her meeting with Sólman, Júlía leaves her office and walks down the corridor to the office of the Komizar of State in Berlin, at Werderscher Markt. The building has a colourful history. The Nazis tore down the medieval palace and in its place raised the Central Bank of the Third Reich, which later housed the headquarters of the Communist Party of Soviet Germany; even Stalin would have been proud of that construction. Upon the collapse of the Berlin Wall, the German Foreign Ministry was moved to Werderscher Markt, which received a face lift. With the establishment of the Great European State, the Komizar for External Relations had been given an office there with his bureaucrats, and they had closed down the old answering machine.

She enters the ante-chamber where a pair of secretaries look up and smile at her. Without bothering to knock, Júlía opens the heavy oak door that gives entrance to the large office of Erich Devereaux, Komizar of State. He's working with some graphs on the 3-D screen, throws them up one by one. He waves Júlía to a chair as he compares statistics. She looks at the man for whom she works and recalls his background.

Erich Devereaux had been brought up in Strasbourg, the medieval city named after the German word for "street." The city is the largest in Alsace-Lorraine, or Elsaß-Lothringen; the province that has suffered for centuries; the province where warring armies brought fire to the civilian populace, which desired only to cultivate the earth in peace and engage in trading on the banks of the Rhine.

Eventually Devereaux finishes with his graphs, turns off the 3-D screen and looks at Júlía. "So Trinxon is at it again, eh?" says Devereaux. "What is it this time?"

Júlía outlines her visit from Sólman. "Under Trinxon Europe has started behaving like a paranoid empire," concludes Júlía.

"I'm worried about Trinxon and the democratic decline among the bureaucrats. The man is getting more and more pushy. Arrogance spins its web in the shadow beneath the Komizar's table," says Devereaux with a thoughtful look.

"Trinxon is a threat to the people," replies Júlía.

"True," agrees Devereaux. "But then men like this big fisherman and his saga-reading professor friend can stir things up and give Trinxon an excuse for what he does." He pauses. "You know that the Komizar threatens me endlessly. I have my hands full constraining the man. He is flying solo more and more. And now I hear he is plotting with Zlato Zarkowsky," says Devereaux. Komizar Zarkowsky is in charge of Europe's military affairs.

"That proposal for the naval base in Hvalfjörður came from Trinxon and Zarkowsky, without the matter being discussed with me or the other Komizars. I argued fiercely when I heard about it, but those Siamese-twin Komizars claimed the authority to be in charge of the matter and told me I would do nicely to keep my mouth shut. Without support from other Komizars there was nothing I could do. And they all seem frightened of Trinxon.

"Now Trinxon and Zarkowsky have increased the size of the European military in Kazikistnam. Again none of the Komizars will back me up. You'd think Trinxon had a hold on them."

"Maybe his spies have found some secrets and he is blackmailing them," suggests Júlía.

"Maybe," says Devereaux. "I would believe any dirty secret of a couple of them, but not most. Anyway, I had a meeting with Trinxon yesterday. He suggested I should go for the Presidency. It's just a trick to get rid of me. The President is a puppet. He wants me out, but I am too popular to be sacked. This Komizar system is obsolete. To be honest, it has never had the right to exist. But it has proven to be absolutely impossible to reform it. The bureaucracy is bulging, as in the long-departed Soviet Union, which ended with fossilized KGB spies not to mention Stasi's East-Germany. God protect us from such a fate," says Devereaux.

"Then the Wall fell and the evil empire went up in smoke. Look on the bright side," says Júlía with a wry smile.

They both laugh.

"Now I have a surprise for you," says Júlía with a grin. "The big fisherman and his saga-reading professor friend have asked to see me. You don't need to be a professor to guess their reasons."

"What will you do?" asks Devereaux.

"You know that full well," replies Júlía with a determined expression.

"I would do the same," he answers.

She reminds him of the comment about new vision for the solutions to the Icelandic problem.

Devereaux smiles. "Absolutely right," he says, and continues: "If I can assist Iceland in any way, I would like to, and you know that too. This matter should be close to my heart, being from Strasbourg. Unfortunately I am extremely disadvantaged for the time being here in the bureaucracy, but never say never."

★ 24 ★

Olav Seiferdal buttons the top button of his royal-blue shirt that reaches up to mid-neck; the collar is w-shaped in front. He puts on a grey striped suit coat that he had bought for a ridiculously high price in Paris three weeks ago, looks in the mirror contentedly, runs his hand through his hair. He quickly runs over the orders given him by Kessler just before he left. He is used to getting peculiar assignments, that is what being in the Security Bureau is all about, but even so it all seems a bit odd. And Seiferdal had got the strong impression that Kessler had been a bit jumpy. Too much emphasis on secrecy. It was as if even the Security Bureau was not supposed to know what he was up to.

Seiferdal is the only passenger on the private jet of the European Security Bureau, which has just landed at Reykjavík Airport. He looks out the window and takes his coat off its hook. Seiferdal frowns as he steps out of the jet. It is as usual: Icelandic wind, sleet, bitter cold and darkness. What a dump!

He bows his head, uses his briefcase as a shield against the horizontal rain and jogs out into the darkness in the direction of his hotel. He loses his footing on an icy patch next to the fence and falls flat into a muddy puddle. The briefcase opens and documents fall into the puddle.

"Satans djævle Island," he curses, thoroughly drenched, his knees and hands bloody.

He gets up, luckily managing to gather the wet documents and shoves his way with a curse in through the hotel's back entrance. Two uniformed officers from the State Security Bureau try to hide their smiles when Seiferdal appears like a thundercloud. It is the division chief, Hrönn Halldórsdóttir, and Officer Thorleifur Sigurðsson. Olav curses silently. Trust the damn Security Director

156

to send these two to irritate him.

"Welcome to Iceland," they say as formally as they can, but Seiferdal gives them the evil eye. He can tell that they're amused by his condition.

Bloody Icelanders, full of envy, he thinks.

Seiferdal checks himself into the hotel and asks for a bandage. He goes up to his room. The soreness in his knee is intense as he cleans out his wounds. Then he hops into the shower. He curses as he recalls that he has no change of clothes. He calls the lobby but there are no clothes to be had there. He would have to buy a new suit in town. "Satan's Reykjavík." He curses vigorously as he slips into his wet, torn trousers, his wet shirt and dirty overcoat.

Things get no better when he opens his briefcase, because all of his papers are drenched. "Damn this God-forsaken rocky island!" shouts Seiferdal.

Hrönn and Thorleifur wait patiently in the lobby.

It is an angry man who comes down in the lift to join them. Just a short time ago he had landed in a private jet. He had felt like a count, but everything had gone wrong. It is as though dark storm clouds hang over the Euro-Norwegian Seiferdal, whom few people like, since he is difficult to work with. People have to go above and beyond.

They nod at Seiferdal.

"I need to buy clothes," says Seiferdal sullenly.

"No problem," they reply sympathetically, but the Euro-Norwegian frowns, feeling little sympathy from these bloody Icelanders. What do they call their spite? Quite right: thórðargleði, as they rejoice over people's mishaps.

After buying clothes they go to the office of the Security Directorate on Skúlagata. He asks them to stop the car close to the door and doesn't beat around the bush, but instead rushes straight in out of the rain.

"They can park the jalopy themselves," he mutters as he pushes open the door to the Security Director's office.

Seiferdal is not expecting to get much help from Jón H.

Matthíasson, State Security Director of Iceland, or Highpoint as he is known. In Seiferdal's view the man is an inexperienced idiot. Everytime he deals with Matthíasson, Seiferdal ends up in a rage of exasperation. He is not disappointed.

"Welcome to Iceland," smiles Highpoint as he ushers Seiferdal into his office. The Icelander's eyes flick over the Euro-Norwegian's muddy clothes in a bag. "How can we poor northern islanders help you?"

"I have been sent here in great haste," snaps Seiferdal. "To find out how you are getting on tracking the movements and plans of the big fisherman Hrafn Illugason. And because we have received reports about Helgi Thorláksson returning to Reykjavík for the first time in thirty years."

Highpoint nods. "Yes. This is not considered good news."

"Not good," exclaims Seiferdal. "It's bloody disastrous. Information suggests that Krummi the croaking raven has plans for doing his worst at the Olympics in Berlin. They aren't going to have the putrid Icelandic smell over their heads in Berlin. And no one knows what the miserable professor is up to." He glares at the fool Matthíasson.

Highpoint sighs. "I am afraid that virtually no new information exists about Krummi and Helgi, yet the rumour is going around that the two are up to something with the leaders of the Nation Party – you know that small political party that wants independence from the Great European State. They have won a few seats on local town councils, and a couple in the recent Althingi by-elections but nothing much. So far as we can tell they are planning an election campaign, nothing illegal in that."

Seiferdal sneers. "It is suspected at the highest levels in Berlin that this dissident political organization you are talking about is developing trained anti-European squads. Is a republican terrorist army being raised? This question had been asked in all earnestness by First Komizar Trinxon himself. And I am in Reykjavík to find out."

That much was true, but there was a lot that Seiferdal was under strict orders not to tell Matthíasson.

It had raised eyebrows in Berlin when a relatively low-placed bureaucrat in the Peripheries Bureau had knocked on the door of the First Komizar and demanded an office for a special Komizar of Icelandic affairs in Berlin. The Security Bureau had looked into the little man Smithson and found that he had links to the terrorists Krummi and Helgi. And since Kessler and Seiferdal had interviewed him on the subject they had been called in. These Icelanders are insane and unpredictable. Seiferdal always gets in a bad mood when Icelandic issues come up, since it's never certain which way things will go. He curses his luck at being dragged into this latest mess. He did not really like the fact that Kessler had given him precise orders not to tell Highpoint about some of things that he would be doing while in Iceland. He did not mind doing illegal things, all part of the job, but he did prefer to have clearance from the local station chief in case things went wrong.

"We need to know what they're up to," shouts Seiferdal sullenly, wishing that he could add, "you idiots," but he resists. He has a strong feeling that the Security Director has no real interest in keeping watch on the rogues. "I need two policemen full time on the job. You know who," says Seiferdal.

"You know that we're short-staffed and can't spare officers to wash Europe's dirty laundry," replies Highpoint. "Besides which, your boss in Berlin is crazy and paranoid. There aren't any terrorist acts in the pipeline, much less a republican army in the spirit of those old Irish religious extremists. There have never been any grounds for armed struggle in Iceland. It is just a pair of idiotic romantics and a small political party of no account."

Seiferdal smiles sarcastically. "No terrorist acts! What do you call the incident in Brussels with the fish? What do you call the violence at Austurvöllur Square or the madness on the Selvogur fishing ground?"

Jón H. Matthíasson says nothing. Austurvöllur and Selvogur were years ago.

"You have no choice," snaps Seiferdal. "I want Smiley and Díella. It wouldn't look good, if Berlin needed to grab you by the scruff of your neck." Seiferdal's voice is ice-cold and his glance piercing. "I have a directive instructing you to give me those two officers. From here on they answer to the European Security Bureau."

Highpoint remains silent. He opens the envelope and reads the directive. He looks sadly out of his window at the Strait. Trinxon is undoubtedly behind this, they have done their homework, and besides, he has to play along or things could be very difficult for him. He has asked around about this Seiferdal from Surveillance. Nobody likes him, this toady of the Berlin authorities.

And he would want Smiley and Díella, since they're known for fawning and kissing up to the European bureaucracy. Thord Thorson and Díella Stensen had done a job for the EIA chief Paśićevic some months ago, and Matthíasson strongly suspect it had involved illegal surveillance of some Icelandic businessmen. The issue had been swept under the carpet and the files conveniently lost. Highpoint had heard that the trio had set the evidence on fire in a barrel under cover of night at Thingvellir of all places. He had not asked any further questions. It does not pay to ask too many questions about Paśićevic.

Strange, the pair of them, Highpoint thinks. Both have changed their names to adapt to European tradition.

"All right," sighs Highpoint. "I suppose I have no options." He gets up and opens the door to call to his secretary. "Ragnar, go and get Thord Thorson and Díella Stensen will you?" He turns back to Seiferdal. "They will be here in a moment."

Highpoint wonders if he should tell this loathsome Berlin toady that Júlía Ingólfsdóttir is unexpectedly back in Reykjavík. He decides not. Let the bastard find out for himself. If he can.

Seiferdal's face lights up as Thord, known in the force as Smiley, walks into the office along with the ever sombre Díella. There is as always a big smile on Smiley's face and a joke on his lips, though they say that Smiley's smile never reaches his eyes, just as they say that a smile has never appeared on Díella melancholic face.

Smiley immediately cracks a joke about the Icelander who always sneaks quietly past pharmacies so as not to wake up the sleeping pills. Seiferdal laughs his heart out but Díella is as always sombre. Highpoint is in no laughing mood at this lame joke. As the trio leave the room Smiley cracks another one about the policeman who catches a thief and as he is about to handcuff the crook, the wind blows the policeman's hat off. 'Shall I get it?' the thief asks cunningly. 'You think I'm stupid? You wait here while I fetch it,' the Icelandic policeman replies scornfully. Smiley laughs his heart out. "The scornful Icelandic policeman ..." he repeats sniggering.

Highpoint is relieved as their voices fade away. He's fully aware that law and order are no obstacle for the three of them, but what can he do?

25

Helgi smiles and Krummi grins when they set eyes on Júlía beneath the overhanging shelter where she awaits them. They round the corner. She waves to them. They are meeting for the third time, planning their tactics over the next months. They are going to a meeting with the leadership of the Nation Party.

Truth to tell, there is a great deal of apathy and insipidity among the Nation Party. It is as though the party members have forgotten the meaning of the party's name. Listlessness and apathy have lain like a nightmare over all the party's work for many years. It is as if the nation is sleeping a deep, sound sleep and completely lacks the courage to gain a foothold in this world of super-states. Quite a few people in recent weeks have spoken to Helgi and Krummi, urging them to raise the opposition against Berlin.

They had smiled amicably but kept their cards to themselves.

It is clear to Krummi that putrid pollock is not the answer, although it has its uses. He had experienced that on the Selvogur fishing ground and in Brussels. It requires clear political vision to waken the nation; encourage it to great deeds and strengthen its valour to take on the Komizars. The nation is the key; if they are to rekindle the passion of the good old 20th century Republic. This is why he feels good about the decision to collaborate with Helgi. They have already had discussions with some Nation's leaders.

And young Júlía Ingólfsdóttir hasn't disappointed them. She has agreed to return and take up the Icelandic baton.

Never betray
your loyalty to your father's land,
instead drink,
drink yourself to death.

She strikes a chord in the spirit of the old national poets and plucks a string in the heart of the nation. It is already dark. They walk across Austurvöllur Square to the meeting, in the old building that lies beneath the old national telephone building once owned by the old Independents. The splendid Valkyrie between the grinning Westmann Giant and the thoughtful grey-haired professor.

Opinions are divided among the leaders of the Nation Party about this collaboration with Helgi and Krummi which has not been made public. There are many people who consider it crazy to collaborate with men who have received prison sentences; one for stirring up unrest and using violence against the Icelandic police force and the other for violence against European police squads in Brussels, not to mention clipping the nets of European fishing vessels on the Selvogur fishing ground. Others point out, it would be useless to discuss collaboration in any case, because laws prohibit those who have violated national security from running for parliamentary positions.

The leadership is particularly luke-warm on the whole idea. It is absolutely absurd to reward terrorists. Helgi and Krummi are controversial in Iceland to say the least. Collaboration with such men can undermine political credibility and frighten off the Crats and Unionists, not to mention spoil relations with Berlin.

Júlía, however, is a different story. There is excitement about the nationally renowned poet; her elegant, sparkling eloquence

As soon as it was rumoured that Júlía was planning to take to the stage of the political struggle at home in Iceland, many people felt that a splendid leader and worthy successor to the aged chairman of the Nation Party had emerged. The time of a new generation has arrived, said the younger Nationist activists; a generation that turns defence into offence, recovers political control and restores it to the country; reawakens national pride for new advancements. However, some of the older Nationists are not too sure, but that was to be expected.

Júlía, Helgi, and Krummi enter the old building on Austurvöllur.

The assembly-room is packed, despite little information about the meeting or invitations to it having been given out. Páll Bjarnfreðsson, the chairman of the Nation Party, easygoing, well-liked, yet advanced in age, stands up and walks over to the trio.

"It's our special pleasure to welcome you here to this place," says Páll with a smile, shaking their hands.

"Though varying degrees of pleasure," says Krummi, grinning.

Júlía and Helgi smile wryly.

"The crux of the matter is to tune the strings in order to waken the nation from its Cinderella sleep," says Páll, looking at Júlía.

Júlía is scheduled to address the party members, but has insisted that she have her companions by her side. She has actually made that one of the conditions of her speech. The appearance of Helgi and Krummi is quite a surprise. Júlía knows that they are extremely controversial, but she has no doubts that they will be needed. They touch the soul of the Icelandic people, if they aren't simply the soul of the Icelandic nation itself. She looks over the leadership of the Nation Party and finds the group little apt for great deeds. She senses that some of them regard her as a threat to their positions. However, she will not let that bother her.

Páll steps up to the lectern and introduces Júlía to the attendees. The crowd burst into applause: the atmosphere is heavy with expectation although there are a few sceptical faces out there. Júlía looks over the crowded room and takes a deep breath.

She starts with a poem by Hannes Hafstein, the great poet and Iceland's first minister back in 1904 when the nation acquired home-rule:

Oh, how it pains me to see
birds so innocent, small,
removed from the danger of being free,
their flight cut short whose life is all
far out in the clear blue sky.
For those who are able to fly,
prison's a sad place to live and die.

She pauses and looks calmly and deliberately over the room. She senses the attendees' expectation. "The nation is a prisoner in a cage where it is sad to live. It has been so ever since the European net was cast over the nation. That was an unhealthy step that we must unravel and expose. The Icelandic nation is not highly populated, but it yearns for freedom, like our eagle, which flies highest of all birds. The nation deserves something better than European pity and alms; its people crossed the sea with freedom as their guiding light; they created literature that will dwell among mankind throughout the ages. The nation lost its freedom but survived tragedies that shaped its desire for freedom. It fought for sovereignty, independence and prosperity to drag itself up from the dregs of poverty and hardship, only to misstep once more at the dawn of the Current Age. A nation with such a legacy will never accept the role of the slave. It is our job to awaken the nation and lead it to freedom once again.

"Icelandic people!

"It is time to straighten your backs, step forth and seek the freedom of the Icelandic nation."

Júlía pauses as the room celebrates; people applaud and stamp their feet.

*I wish that there were a proper rain
and Icelandic wind on Kaldidalur.*

Júlía exerts all of her powers of eloquence and personal charm.

"Freedom is like a storm on the desolate mountain slopes of Kaldidalur. We need to know how to appreciate freedom in order to enjoy freedom. We need to embrace freedom as we embrace Iceland in all of its forms; with all of its greatness and flaws. Iceland is a strict master, and so is freedom. Many people find it tempting to use evil against the defects of society; they feel that evil can be driven out with evil, but lurking in this is the danger that freedom will be suppressed and suffocated. The Icelandic nation gave away its freedom, and in doing so the people's initiative was suppressed and suffocated. "Therefore it is imperative that freedom of action be the basis for our advance toward the freedom of the Icelandic nation; the recovery of our political authority. We must move away from our isolated mentality toward the creation of our own destiny. Freedom was Jón Sigurðsson's guiding light; freedom is our guiding light when we take hands and unravel the hard-tangled knot that appears made for eternity." Every word of Júlía's carries weight.

"We shall untangle the knot. Together we shall untangle that seemingly unentangleable knot like our great leaders Jón Sigurðsson and Hannes Hafstein: the men who enkindled the fires for Iceland's glorious march to freedom and prosperity in the 20th century," she says in conclusion.

The people's reaction is amazing.

The audience applaud rhythmically, rhythmically, and cries, "Freedom... freedom... we shall fly... fly to meet freedom!"

The Nationists sense that the leadership of a new generation has stepped forth to grapple with the tasks of new times that soon will arise at the outermost horizon of the sea.

26

A click is heard, a door is opened, a beam of light illuminates a wall. Tape is put over a lock. Three dark-clad beings slide silently into a large room. Seiferdal, Smiley, and Díella are breaking into the large, bow-shaped house at Höfðabakki – Head Street. They are in the lobby, and walk quietly up the stairs to the top storey, where the Nation Party has its headquarters. Seiferdal strides purposefully to the doorway to the corridor; another click is heard, a door opens, tape is put over the lock. He goes in, a beam of light illuminates a wall.

Seiferdal puts a finger to his lips as he turns to his assistants.

"Careful," he whispers.

They walk briskly down the long corridor straight toward the office of the party chairman, since Seiferdal knows what they are looking for. They are surprised to find the internal doors locked; Seiferdal had been informed that they were never so. "Bummer," he says out loud as he pauses to carefully ease open the door lock. He does such a great professional job that hardly any evidence is visible unless inspected closely. He takes pride in his work. The door glides silently wide open. Seiferdal goes directly to a painting on the wall and takes it down, revealing a safe. He takes a slip of paper from his pocket, shines his torch on it and asks Díella to read the numbers off it. Seiferdal enters them one by one.

Seiferdal smiles contentedly when the safe opens. Facing him are various documents and an envelope. He leafs through the documents one by one and lays them on a table. He then takes out a very thin scanner and starts copying the documents. One of them in particular draws his attention.

"Discussions on the next steps," is written on the front page, and the document is stamped "Confidential."

Seiferdal scans a five-page report on discussions with Júlía and the other two ruffians.

"This should put Júlía on cold ice in Berlin," he says in a low voice, and laughs out loud.

He asks Smiley and Díella to go out and keep watch on the corridor. He puts the documents back in their place and picks up the envelope. Seiferdal is flabbergasted when he sees the contents. There are six photographs of the Nationist chairman in rather convoluted poses with a pair of attractive young women, all naked. Tucked in with the photos is a huge wad of cash.

He puts the photos and money back into the envelope and sticks it in his pocket. "This shouldn't be lying around," he mutters, but is startled upon seeing Smiley at the door. The man should have been standing watch in the corridor. Seiferdal stays calm and goes over to Smiley and shows him a photograph.

"Dirty old man," says Smiley, smugly before whispering a joke about a husband who holds up a condom, sternly asking his wife: "I found this in bed ... are you having sex with somebody?" to which the wife replies innocently: "No, I just lay there."

They both laugh but Seiferdal remains silent about the money.

Smiley goes to the window and carefully pushes the curtain back. He smiles; there is no one to be seen in the vicinity of Höfðabakki.

Down on the ground floor the caretaker Guðmundur Magnússon is surprised to find tape placed over the front door lock. What idiot has taped over the lock, he thinks, tearing the tape off.

"That's odd," he mutters.

The caretaker walks slowly out into the car park. Guðmundur is a calm man by nature and doesn't get worked up over small things. Still, he finds it strange that tape had been placed over the lock. "I mustn't imagine some nonsense," he thinks. His eyes wander upward and he sees a beam of light shine from the top storey for a moment.

Then everything goes dark again on that storey. "This isn't normal," he says out loud, and calls the night staff at Sectas to report suspicious activity. After some deliberation he decides to let the police know as well; one can't be sure.

Custodian Guðmundur goes into the lobby and waits for what comes next, since he is under strict orders not to do anything without backup.

The two walk down the corridor to the door, where Díella is waiting. They're on the top storey and decide that their safest bet is to go down the stairs. "It's better to display the utmost caution and professionalism," whispers Seiferdal. Everything seems calm, and there is no one to be seen. When they reach the lobby a man steps out of the darkness and asks in a sharp, loud voice nervously pointing a club at them: "Who goes there? Stop!"

They are quite startled, and just then blue lights begin flashing in the parking lot outside. Seiferdal tears open the door and orders Smiley and Díella to follow him. Three Sectas vehicles are arriving one the scene and security guards jump out of the cars. Seiferdal and the two run out onto the lot but are soon surrounded by six security guards, who order them to stop. Smiley and Díella stop but Seiferdal keeps running, with two guards at his heels. Seiferdal hears them shout that they are security officers. "Idiots, bloody fools," he mutters to himself. It's vital that they don't discover his identity, he thinks. Seiferdal runs northward from the house, toward the intersection. The distance between them increases rapidly. He will have no trouble shaking these wretches. Then a flashing light appears, and suddenly another guard is at his heels. Seiferdal runs north of Höfðabakki and is at the old printing house when he slips on a patch of ice and falls flat. He curses, as he feels the excruciating pain in his bad knee.

The security guard pounces on him like a tiger.

"God bloody dammit," growls Seiferdal. "I'm a policeman," he shouts in old Norwegian.

"Why are you running?" asks the bulky Sectas guard as he handcuffs Seiferdal unceremoniously and leads the ill-tempered foreigner away. In recent months foreigners have been involved in ever-increasing numbers of burglaries.

"I'm a European security officer of the Secret Service," reiterates

Seiferdal angrily but the fellow is strong as an ox.

"I'm Donald Duck," replies the Sectas guard laughing.

Seiferdal is bundled into the back of a van with what he considers unnecessary roughness. He lands on the floor to find Smiley and Díella already sitting with their backs against the sides of the van.

"Bollocks", snarls Seiferdal.

The security guard is surprised that the police haven't shown up, but he climbs into the front of the red-white Sectas van and sets off for the police station. The other Sectas vehicles have already left the scene. He thinks it is odd that the intruders have all claimed that they are undercover police officers, but he has heard all sorts of stories in his time and shrugs it off with a laugh since they don't have any identification.

A young guard accompanies Caretaker Guðmundur up the stairs to investigate the situation. Everything appears to be normal, until they come to the top storey. There the guard spots a small piece of tape lying by the door of the Nation's Party office, just like the tape found on the front door.

"What the hell! They've been in here, but must have been disappointed, since there's no money here," says Guðmundur.

"We'll take a closer look," says the Sectas guard. They enter the corridor, but everything appears normal.

"This is bizarre," says the guard. "No one's been here."

They turn back and start shutting off the lights. Then Guðmundur notices that the door to the Chairman's office is ajar and there are one or two tiny scratches by the lock.

"That door is kept locked," Guðmundur says. He walks to the door and pushes it open, the scratches can hardly been seen. It doesn't look to them as if anything has been moved, until Guðmundur sees the painting hanging crooked on the wall. They lift the painting. The safe appears. "There's been a burglary here. I smell a rat. Can they have tampered with the safe?" asks Caretaker Guðmundur. They go downstair again to meet with the police.

"Finally they show up," says Guðmundur annoyedly as he sees the police arrive on scene. "It's no wonder, actually, it being the police — they're always lazy and late."

They accompany two young police officers up to the top storey and show them the scene. The young officers take statements, but in fact there is little to do other than to photograph the damage at the scene. A reporter from *The Post* then arrives, short-winded, but they tell him that there's really nothing to see. He curses animatedly but takes photos of the building and the scratches at the door.

Soon everyone is gone, leaving Caretaker Guðmundur alone in the lobby.

27

In Berlin the screen of an e-notebook springs into life. The owner calls up the front page of the *The Reykjavík Post*. There is nothing there. He had been alerted last night to clean up some mess in Iceland. Now he's checking results. He scans quickly and finds what he is looking for on page five. There is a little article concerning the arrest of three men claiming to be police officers at Höfðabakki for breaking and entering. The story is short and contains no details. The man smiles. He flicks off the e-notebook and drops it into the pocket of his black jacket. Excellent.

In Reykjavík another screen calls up the self same report. "That's rubbish," shouts the reporter Geir Thórisson: "How could Thóra give such a small space to the story?"

He had received a phone call the previous evening about breaking news at Höfðabakki, but little was happening when he arrived on the scene. The breaking news turned out to be just a trivial burglary coupled with a misunderstanding, the duty officer at the police station had said, laughing wildly. Geir is forced to admit that Thóra Hringsdóttir, the news director, had been right to a certain degree. He didn't even get a good photograph of the scene. His only photograph was of the door of Chairman Páll, with the bit of tape, although it is suspected that the thieves had gotten into the chairman's safe. What did they want? Geir had pointed out that a burglary at the offices of a political party must always be considered suspicious.

He had written the story and demanded that it be printed in the paper because naturally a burglary at the offices of a political party ought to be considered news, no matter how inconsequential. He projects the paper in holograph, coffee cup in hand, and flips through the news.

"What a damn shame not to have gotten a photo of the suspects," he mutters frustratedly as he turns to page five and clicks on the story; the reading voice of Valdi Pop always gets on his nerves. Valdi Pop supposedly appeals to young folk. Of course he can choose to read the news, which isn't fashionable among young people. He turns off Valdi Pop and reads his article. Geir is incensed. The story has been gutted, cut down to a quarter of what he had written.

"Something is wrong here", Geir mutters. "I can smell it." He has been a reporter for thirty years now and has come to trust his instincts. He flips the holograph off with a snap. "This stinks as bad as one of Krummi's pollacks," he scowls.

He goes back to Höfðabakki and finds the old caretaker, who had informed him that a foreigner had been among the suspects and was apprehended after a sensational chase. Now Geir wants more details.

Caretaker Guðmundur shrugs. "The Sectas guards handcuffed the foreigner after he ran off, but slipped on some ice. They had broken into the Nation's offices. There were three of them; they broke open the door, but it was a clever job. I would never have seen anything wrong if I had not seen the light in the window and them coming down the stairs. Very professional break in if you ask me. Mind you the police seem to have strangely little interest in it. Actually, the case seems to be one big misunderstanding, with everything in it all mixed up."

Geir moves on to the police station and talks to the duty officer. Who is the foreigner and who are his accomplices? The duty officer consults the night book. No names are recorded.

"Isn't that odd?" ask Geir.

The duty officer looks back at the night book. "It says here that they were released immediately without charge. All some sort of a mix up, apparently. No crime recorded, so no need to detain anyone. Sorry, old boy," the duty officer smiles at Geir. "You will have to fill your column inches with some other story."

Geir finds the behaviour of the police peculiar. He is annoyed, sullen, and shamefaced as he walks into the office of the news director, his harvest having been scanty.

"No news. Have you been chasing nothing at all the entire day?" shouts News Director Thóra, doing nothing to conceal her disappointment.

"I can write a story on how all the suspects have been released, among them a foreigner," replies Geir embarrassedly.

"Oh great! Are we going to be accused of fuelling xenophobia? No, thanks!" replies Thóra. She looks at the man in front of her. When she had been a university graduate looking for her first job in journalism, Geir had been the star reporter for *The Post*, breaking one big story after another. Now she sees only an overweight, middle-aged man in a scruffy suit who has let himself go. His divorce six years ago was fairly unpleasant, she heard, and since then he had picked up with one floozy after another. She knows he drinks more than he should. It may be time to replace him. She wonders if she can arrange one of those Special Lifetime Achievement Awards from the Euro News Agency. Then she can pension him off quietly. She smiles. "Never mind," she says brightly. "You can't win them all. Better luck next time."

Geir frowns and marches brusquely out of the news director's office. It has been a strange day in which nothing has worked. He stomps downstairs to his office, and spends an hour or two flicking through notes and news that has come in over the past hour or two. The usual cases at the courts, a vote at the town hall about litter bins. He yawns and glances at the clock. He suddenly fancies a beer, maybe two.

Geir is putting on his overcoat when the holph rings. He picks up it up distractedly, not wanting anything to get between him and that beer down at the Harbour Bar.

"Are you the reporter who wrote the article about Höfðabakki?" someone asks in a deep voice. The speaker has disabled his camera, so there is nothing to see on the holph.

"What does that matter to you?" asks Geir curtly.

"Would you like some information?" The voice does not let the reporter's harsh voice put it off.

"Information?" asks Geir, standing up instinctively.

"Yes, information," replies the deep voice.

"What information?" asks Geir, but the voice interrupts him.

"Meet me at midnight at the multi-storey car park on Vesturgata Street."

"That's too late...," replies Geir, but the person on the other end has hung up. "Hello... hello... hello!" he yells, before hanging up.

"It's just some lunatic," he mutters sullenly.

Is he supposed to meet some nutter in a dark car park at midnight? Admittedly, he has little interest in strolling in the cold through some car park, besides the fact that he feels it likely that this is just some hoax.

The man has hung up on him, not the usual behaviour for an informant.

Geir walks out of the editorial offices over to the Harbour Bar on Tryggvagata Street. There are few people there, it being a Thursday and getting too late for most after-work drinkers. He orders a beer and takes a seat in a comfortably shadowy spot. He feels best in his own company. Two women are in close conversation nearby. They pay him no attention, being probably fifteen or twenty years younger.

He looks over at them but they pretend not to notice the old geezer.

He flips through *The Post* with a grumpy look on his face. He is dissatisfied with his job at the paper. Little has gone his way in recent years and it has been a long time since he's had a good, truly good scoop. His story today is an insignificant one-column piece, hardly noticeable. Damn shame that he didn't get any real photos. In retrospect, he's surprised at how little interest the police showed.

That's right. He'd arrived twenty minutes after the call came in. Only then had the police straggled to the scene.

"There's something odd about this," he says out loud.

The women look up, whisper and giggle: it's kinky to see a middle-aged man talking to himself.

"Strange guy," he hears them say as they move away from him.

But it's true. There's something odd about this whole thing.

No investigation seems to have taken place. "Three people handcuffed. People tear off from the scene as if the Devil were at their heels," mutters Geir as he finishes his beer. He shakes his head and orders another but then decides to skip it. Geir has made up his mind. He is going to go to Vesturgata Street, hoping to meet the man and delve thoroughly into this case. And then tomorrow he is going to go back to Höfðabakki to have a better talk with the custodian. He is going to speak to the delicate little chairman of the Nationists. Why is he so tight-lipped about the break-in into his own office? All rather peculiar. His good old nose for news tells him that there is something behind all this. He feels better.

Geir leaves the bar and goes over to Vesturgata, where the car park is on the two lowest levels. He curses as he realizes that the fellow hadn't mentioned on which storey they should meet.

He walks up to the upper level.

He is startled when a young couple appears from behind a column. "Bloody hell, are you sneaking up on us?" shouts the man, who has fiery red, obviously dyed hair. They run out of the car park. A two-wheeler is started on the lower level, the low whine carries up to the top level, while the sound of the grainy tyres is quite clear. Geir turns back and is on his way down the stairs when a man steps out from behind a column and motions for him to approach.

His heart skips a beat. This is no hoax. He walks briskly over to the column, but is disappointed when a commanding voice says: "Don't come any closer." He feels as if he recognizes the voice, but can't figure out from where.

He stops, slightly annoyed, but the voice is deep and commanding, causing him to obey instinctively.

"This morning at ten-thirty a private jet flew to Europe. On board was one of the burglars. Follow his tracks. Do not try to reach me. I'll be in touch if necessary."

He watches a figure walk away beneath a drawn umbrella, making it impossible to see who it is. However, he is completely unworried, because the voice has awakened his confidence. He knows that something major is in the works.

A private jet to Europe. No common burglar could afford one of those. If a private jet had left that morning, he would soon find out about it.

Geir grins.

28

Sólman stares out of the window of his new office in the European Parliament. His campaign to get a special Komizar for Iceland has been gathering pace. So much so that he has managed to form a political party in Iceland and get himself elected to the Althingi. And then it was a simple matter to get himself made one of the three MEPs sent to Brussels by the Althingi. Those yokel Icelanders had been so simple to hoodwink.

He is waiting for John Bjornson, Managing Editor of the *The Reykjavík Post*, to arrive. He's is late and Sólman fidgets. He is eager to get out of the office. It has been a busy few months since he took his decision in the rain in Berlin. He had taken his friends and work colleagues by surprise, but he regrets nothing. Standing there in the rain he had suddenly remembered Valtýr Guðmundsson.

Valtýr had been a scholar in Denmark when Iceland was ruled by the Danish crown in the late 19th century. He had worked within the Danish establishment to pave the way forward for Icelandic patriotism, campaigning for a minister for Icelandic affairs based in Copenhagen and a member of the Danish government. Valtýr Guðmundsson had achieved much for his fellow citizens. Sólman feels a strong connection to Valtýr and has copied his tactics by seeking to work within the Great European State slowly, step by step to restore some political authority to the Icelandic nation. He believes it will have to be won in stages, and in cooperation with the European government. The first step must be the appointment of a special Komizar for Icelandic affairs, ideally based in Berlin. That will put Iceland on the bureaucratic agenda of the committees in Berlin. Then he can start to think about moving forward to the next stage.

He is fully aware that Júlía has formed an alliance with Helgi and

Krummi, but he sees them as dreamers who will bring further disasters to the nation. "Violence is not the way forward," he says out loud, to himself. "Fighting Berlin will just lead to trouble and disaster. No, working with Berlin is the way to go."

Sólman had composed a poem that attracted some attention at home in Iceland:

We are a nation, let the world know,
our language, flag let us boldy show.
The banner of freedom let us raise.
Iceland's cod let us praise!

Sólman wants to make the Icelandic cod the symbol of the nation. The old Icelandic flag with its bold red and white cross would only antagonise Berlin and the bureaucrats, as it would be seen a sign of backwardness and a desire for independence. Much better to adopt the cod as a symbol and work for limited self-government within the Great European State. Sólman dreams of seeing a new cod flag waving throughout the country, along with the blue European flag with its forty-one golden stars. After all, the cod is the basis of Iceland's economy. The seeds of his struggle have fallen onto fruitful soil in Iceland, but onto rocky ground in Berlin.

He had begun his campaign to be elected to Parliament with a speech in which he declared: "Europe says that we have a European flag, but the Icelanders have never recognized it as their only one. The flag was foisted on us arbitrarily." His words spread like wildfire across Iceland. Back in Brussels, his bosses had been enraged and told him that he could abandon all hope of further promotion within the bureaucracy. Fellow workers have gone out of their way to avoid him in the corridors of Brussels. It had been quite a shock, but he knows he is right.

He had won his seat in parliament by a landslide.

With his new-found position and popularity he had founded a movement among the people of Iceland: it is called Sólýska —

always written with a "ý", likely because of its connection to the old Valtýska Party from 1900. Sólman had become involved in a whirlpool of events that led him to America. He had flown to Boston when some rich Americans wanted his opinion on old Nordic remains in Massachusetts. They thought they'd found the settlement of Thorfinnur Karlsefni, one of the first Viking explorers of the New World, but it had unfortunately turned out to be a later settlement.

His tactics have moved many people, who consider his politics practical. They are called "real politics" in Iceland. Back in the days of Valtýr, the poet Thorsteinn Erlingsson had written:

Our journey is so tragically late,
sluggishness we've tried,
our tricks all conspire –
yet the future-land seems only to retire.

As the movement had gathered strength, Sólman had grown in confidence. He is seen as the man to take on the sluggishness that is blocking the path to the future-land. He had arranged a meeting with First Komizar Rikard Trinxon in Berlin, and before discussed tactics with some of his allies in Reykjavík. "It may well be that Trinxon ruins everything for me," Sólman had said with perfect realism.

Editor John Bjornson had agreed in all respects. "We're certainly taking risks," the Editor had said but the general mood had been optimistic.

The meeting in Berlin did not go well. Trinxon had looked completely different than in the portrait hanging in the Berlaymont. His large black moustache had turned grey; his hair shorter and a great deal thinner, all of his wrinkles deeper. It was obvious that the daily toil of caring for the people of Europe have carved its mark on Trinxon. Sólman had stood firm despite the First Komizar's cold reception. He had pleaded his case with the resolve and determination of one who stands on the rock of principles and certainty that he is doing right. After the usual opening pleasantries, he had told the Komizar what he wanted.

"It is my opinion that Berlin should appoint a special Komizar for Icelandic affairs, independent of the Supreme Council and responsible to the Icelandic Althingi for every governmental act. The Komizar has to be an Icelander, holding a seat on the Althingi, replacing the one-sided Berlin directives that currently control things. The Komizar should be based in Berlin."

"Is that so?" Trinxon had asked in astonishment.

"I will now rest my case with the wish that you, Komizar Trinxon, be flexible and respond well to this humble and peaceful request. The way that things are organized now is harmful to both Europe and Iceland. Instead of holding things together, the existing structure is tearing us apart. I am convinced that the cold and discordant spirit, that has up until now undeniably prevailed between Europe and Iceland, will disappear and in its place will be kindled a spirit of friendship and brotherhood that will be the most powerful bond connecting us; many times more powerful than any jurisprudence. Fortune grant that this may happen as swiftly as possible."

There had been complete silence in the room, Trinxon had stared at Sólman who bowed graciously.

After a while, Trinxon had said: "Leave your request here, in writing. I cannot state anything definitive now." Then he had sneered and shouted: "Truth be told, I think this is bullshit. The reply will be one big Danish Nej. You understand; nej, nej, nej." Trinxon's face had turned totally red.

Sólman had been taken aback by Trinxon's sudden foul mood, which had come from nowhere, but had tried to stay calm. "I trust that you can see Iceland's point of view, even if you do not agree with it," Sólman had said trying to calm things down.

"This is just like you Icelanders," Trinxon had snapped back. "You grabbed your independence by conspiring with America when Denmark was occupied by the Nazi's and unable to react. Stabbing your friends in the back when they needed you most."

Sólman had tried to hold things together, but felt that he had caught the Euro-Dane on a bad day. Looking back he is even more convinced that something else was bothering Trinxon that day. Given time, Sólman hopes that Trinxon will come around. He knows the Euro-Dane has his own sources of information and must know what is going on in Iceland. The fanatics – like Krummi and Helgi – want independence at once. Even some of Sólman's own followers want the Althingi to act independently and pass a motion demanding a Komizar for Iceland, even having the new official based in Iceland instead of in Berlin. It's as if they don't know that Althingi has no powers. Everything back in Iceland is in a deadlock.

Sólman sighs and checks his watch again. He wants to pull Iceland out of the rut it has got into over the past few decades. The nation is slowly bleeding to death, due to the departure of thousands of Icelanders for other countries. Something has to be done. It would be better if Berlin acted fast to appoint a Komizar without the initiative of Reykjavík getting in the way. Of course, Sólman would take up the position himself. But right now he feels trapped between a rock and a hard place. On the one hand his nation, and on the other the European authorities. Both have their fanatics, both have their moderates.

Sólman looks at his watch. Editor John is only fifteen minutes late. Was that all? It feels like hours.

There is a knock at the door, the Editor at last.

"So how did it go?" asks Editor John Bjornson.

Sólman grimaces. "Could have been better," he admits. "The Komizar was in a foul mood but will hopefully make some sort of offer. I'll likely not be in the most comfortable of positions, because if I'm perceived as supporting the First Komizar, I'll naturally be called a traitor back home, but if I turn against the Komizar, all of my plans here will likely go to pot and nothing will be won. But I have heard informally that it is most likely that Iceland will get its own Komizar based in Berlin with a seat on the Supreme Council; like any other Komizar of the Supreme Council."

"Hmmmm," muses John. "I don't know how well that will go down back home. I think most people will see getting our own Komizar as a step forward, but you know how unpopular the Supreme Council is right now. Having our Komizar kowtowing to the Council might smack of treason. Krummi and his mates will see it as acknowledging that the Supreme Council is Iceland's principal governing body. And I'm not sure how many people will agree with him. That Júlía can be a persuasive speaker."

Sólman nods. "Maybe I should not go any further in this matter without talking to my supporters in Iceland. This really would be a substantial achievement, a real step forward. I don't agree that it undermines Iceland, having the Icelandic Komizar sitting on the Supreme European Council in accordance with European law, but I suppose it is something of a compromise. But Berlin is making big compromises as well. Iceland will have to make some sacrifices in order to take a step forward. Surely people can see that?"

John Bjornson shrugs. "Maybe. I'm not saying they won't, just that you shouldn't take it for granted. Then there is the question of residence. Where the Icelandic Komizar has his main office and his home could be a tricky issue," he says.

"Well it is out of the question for the Icelandic Komizar to have to settle in Brussels, like any other pauper," declares Sólman. "I can assure you that the idea is being advocated behind closed doors, so as to send out a signal of the insignificance of the new Komizar's position. That would be typical. No, Berlin is the place. The new Komizar will have to be at the heart of things to get anything done."

"Others think he should be based in Reykjavík," says Editor John. "That way he will know what is going on in Iceland. Give him a plush office in Berlin and he might go native."

"Not if you get the right man," counters Sólman. What he does not tell Editor John is that he wants to become the first Komizar for Icelandic affairs, and is already taking steps to make that happen. He knows he will face rivals, probably Júlía and Governor Steffensen. Now is his chance to put the boot into his rivals. "Steffensen would go native straight away. He'd be Berlin's poodle in a week. But Júlía would make the opposite mistake. She would pick fights when she does not need to and put everyone's back up. She would achieve nothing for Iceland. We need somebody sensible, but trustworthy: a man to do deals to Iceland's advantage."

"I can't imagine who you have in mind," smiles Editor John Bjornson. He gets up to leave. "Let me know how you get on," he says. "You know you can rely on *The Post*."

Sólman watches him go. "If only I could rely on everyone else," he mutters. His trusted deputy, Múli Thordarsen, has been sounding out other MPs and some business high-fliers about the idea of Sólman being Komizar for Iceland. The results were grim. Only three fellow Solýta MPs promised unequivocally to support him for the office of Komizar. The business leaders were better, but unwilling to go public.

Sólman would ideally like to enter personally into negotiations with Berlin and bring the case to a successful conclusion; then take the matter up back home in Iceland. "If I know that I'm trusted to make agreements I can accomplish a great deal," he believes.

Yet there are other problems to deal with. Growing political turmoil prevails in Berlin; recalcitrance can be noticed in Trinxon. Again Sólman wonders what is going on behind the scenes.

★ 29 ★

Geir has arrived at work early; in fact he's the first in. He gets a surprised look from the journalists as they arrive one after another, since such a thing has not happened in years. Geir is well-known for sleeping off his evening drinks. At 9am he knocks on the door of News Director Thóra, who looks up in surprise.

"You... you're here?" she says with a sarcastic expression, glancing at the clock.

Geir's only reaction is to smile wryly. "I've got some news for you," he says with an excited look. He describes to her the events of the previous evening and his meeting with the deep-voiced man beneath the umbrella.

Thóra listens to Geir's narrative. "What ... an informant with a deep voice. We'll call him Deep Throat, naturally," she says. "Take the case, follow the trail," adds Thóra enthusiastically, unable to conceal her interest. "But keep it quiet for now. Editor John got me to spike that last story of yours. I don't want this to go the same way."

Geir starts making phone calls to his connections at the police commissioner's office, but is disappointed when he has terrible trouble reaching them. "Bizarre; clearly something fishy's going on," he mutters. It appears as if people's lips are zipped tight.

He calls Stefán, an old acquaintance at Air Traffic Control, and asks him to check on the flight of a private jet to Europe yesterday morning. It is past noon when Stefán calls him back. "Yes," he says. "There was a private jet out of here yesterday. One owned by the European State Security Bureau.

"State Security Bureau. What?" yells Geir, overwhelmed.

"What's so remarkable about that?" replies Stefán, clearly surprised at his friend's dramatic reaction. "We get one or two a month."

Geir does not answer, and instead asks: "Do you have a passenger list?"

"There was just one passenger," replies Stefán. "Olav Seiferdal, European of Norwegian origin."

Geir has become very agitated, he thanks Stefán for the information and marches to Thóra's office.

"Why the devil is the European security apparatus sending someone to spy on the Nationists?" he asks, puzzled.

"The European Security Bureau," replies Thóra in a quiet voice.

"Yes, an Olav Seiferdal," says Geir.

"We need more information about this Seiferdal," says Thóra. "Do you want help?"

Geir is quick to reply. "It's my story," he says. "I will deal with it."

The Post breaks the story the following day. It receives a great deal of attention in Iceland. The figures show a large number of viewers reading the story in Berlin.

One of them wears a black suit – and this time he is not so pleased.

Rudolf Kessler walks nervously into the office of the First Komizar at Beethoven Hall in Berlin. He is not looking forward to this meeting. Rikard Trinxon looks anything but pleased; in fact storm clouds seem to hang over the Komizar. He hammers his fist on the table as he turns to face Kessler.

"What sort of idiots do you have working for you?" shouts Trinxon, still pounding the table. "That Norwegian idiot has let himself be arrested like some petty thief. And now the Icelandic press have printed the story."

"This is a cock-up, that's for sure, but we've got complete control of the situation, Kessler hurriedly explains. "They've got nothing concrete on us." Kessler waits for the response. He knows from experience that Trinxon in such a mood is no lamb to play with. Kessler is in charge of the First Komizars' Security Division. Over the years the job has become increasingly comprehensive, the security of the state being at stake. Experience has shown that it is better to know than not to know. And recently, Trinxon has had Kessler monitoring the First Komizar's political opponents closely; in general, the political movements within the federation.

"The bastard was arrested," shouts Trinxon.

"That's certainly true, but it's a matter of state security. The operation in Reykjavík is a step in the struggle against terrorism. The secrecy laws apply, and the police are bound to confidentiality, and they are being very co-operative. The public will understand that we're preventing terrorism," replies Kessler. "I am on top of it. And anyway, we needed to know what was going on in Iceland."

"You've got to put a stop to this nonsense," demands Trinxon.

"Don't forget that you authorized the operation," counters Kessler.

"Alright, alright. So, what the bloody hell is going on up there in the goddamn north?" asks Trinxon, a bit more calmly.

"Seiferdal is investigating two Icelandic independence activists who have repeatedly used violent tactics. One of them wreaked havoc in Brussels recently – you remember all those rotten fish in the Berlaymont. He has a colourful history; among other things wrecked the equipment of European fishermen in Icelandic waters and did major damage to a Spanish frigate. The other instigated riots on Austurvöllur Square years ago that resulted in the deaths of two students," replies Kessler.

"Of course these are deadly serious issues," says Trinxon. "Did your Norwegian dolt find any evidence?"

"We have hints that the Icelandic Nationists are planning to commence an illegal struggle against the European state and do damage at the Olympic Games. That's why we went in. Don't forget that you authorized me to conduct the operation, since the security of the state is at stake," says Kessler.

"Yes, goddamn it; I don't need to know everything. What did you find out about this political scoundrel, Chairman Páll? I've heard that he's a loose canon," replies Trinxon.

"Seiferdal found six photos of the chairman's secret sex orgies." Kessler pulls the photos of Páll and the naked women from his brief case and puts them on Trinxon's desk. "The old fool could be their father."

"You'll leak this information about this lowlife," says Trinxon laughing, rubbing his hands together.

"Of course," smiles Kessler. "We have a loyal journalist in Reykjavík who can get this story printed without our fingerprints on it. It should be enough to discredit Páll to his supporters, especially after his speeches about traditional family values. And not before time. Seiferdal found confidential documents about Chairman Páll's discussions with those two activists. They show plans are being drawn up for the opposition against the true government and unity of the European state. And wait for this." He pauses.

"Well?" asks Trinxon. Kessler grins.

"One of Erich Devereaux's closest associates is in league with them – plotting against the European state. Her name is Júlía Ingólfsdóttir. This is a serious matter," says Kessler, laying on the table a copy of the documents that Seiferdal had gotten hold of in Reykjavík. Trinxon grins and snatches up the documents.

"Good, good. Excellent in fact. I've been waiting for Devereaux to make a slip. We can use this against him. These Icelanders are a peculiar bunch. I've had some petty MEP called Sólman Smithson who claims to be a political leader in Iceland in here demanding an Icelandic Komizar in Berlin. He is under the illusion that it will grant Iceland some kind of freedom. What an idiot! I've had to leak stories that I'm considering the plan. As if! And now this Júlía. I know her, of course. She's pretty and popular, but we've got to stop this damned nonsense. This independence virus could spread to other states," says Trinxon grouchily, before asking abruptly: "Are these bastards planning terrorist acts?"

"We're investigating the matter but I think that the main thing is to stop those troublemakers Helgi and Krummi in time. You don't want putrid pollock on Berlin tables. Erich's got to put a stop to Júlía's nonsense. Can't you get him to rein her in? Then we'd only have a fisherman and a saga scholar to deal with," says Kessler.

"That could prove difficult. Everyone round here seems to love

Erich. I'll have a word, start a few rumours. But if that does not work you'll have to put a stop to the whole thing," says Trinxon.

He feels better, much better; Kessler seems to have control of the situation, despite the mess made by that Norwegian idiot.

"You can rest assured; I'll put an unbreakable knot with a fourfold bow on it. And we'll start by leaking the photos of the chairman's orgies. That'll put an end to the little bugger," said Kessler cheerfully.

"That's an order," says Trinxon. They laugh loudly.

It hasn't proven to be an easy task for Geir to gather information on Olav Seiferdal. The man is from Oslo, around forty-five years old. He had been in the intelligence agency in Oslo for over a decade but had gone to work in Berlin six years ago. It seems as if the man evaporated after going to Berlin. Geir finds this particularly peculiar, even security men leave a paper trail somewhere – credit card bills, travel tickets and the like. And it is just as odd that the Reykjavík police cannot give the names of the arrested men. He has been on the phone all day, with little result.

Geir hasn't made much progress on the follow up to his story. He is seething, resentful, and annoyed. Yet another day has passed; now it is evening. It is nearly ten and his press deadline is approaching, when the phone light flashes.

He picks up the phone with a grumpy expression, which disappears as if a hand were waved.

"Meet me in the same place in ten minutes," says Deep Throat, before hanging up.

Geir jumps up from his chair.

He wants to try to get there ahead of Deep Throat, so he rushes to the car park, arriving there five minutes later. He goes to the column, from behind which Deep Throat now silently steps out. Geir is startled but recognizes the man immediately. It is the head of State Security himself, Jón H. Matthíasson, the one and only Highpoint.

"We must proceed carefully," says Highpoint, raising a finger to his lips. "Olav Seiferdal used to work in the Surveillance Section in

Brussels but he is now in the Security Division of the First Komizar, no less. When he was arrested he had with him two Icelandic police officers working under his direction. They were men from my office, Díella Stensen and Thord Thorson called Smiley, but neither I nor my office has authority over them any more. Seiferdal has his own office here now, obeying his orders and answering to nobody in Iceland – not even me. The Security Division of the First Komizar now has a branch office in Iceland."

"Since when?" asks Geir in surprise.

"Last week," replies Highpoint gruffly. "They are on my payroll and spend my expenses, but they are working for Seiferdal now, and Seiferdal works for Trinxon." A noise makes him look round nervously. "This meeting is finished. I will never call you again or you me. It's too risky. If I need to get information to you, there will be a vase in my kitchen window at eight in the evening. We will then meet at midnight at this column," he says, and is gone.

Geir remains behind, stunned. He rushes back to the offices of *The Post* and writes up the greatest scoop in his career.

What a story!

The column in *The Post* attracts huge attention. In fact, all society is abuzz. "European Cop Flees the Country after Arrest." Thóra is a genius at headlines and this was of course correct, strictly speaking. The man had swiftly left the country after mysteriously breaking into the offices of the Nation Party.

Isn't that fleeing?

All of the media outlets have picked up the story and even the *Euro-News* adds a special bulletin on it to the evening newscast. A holo-tv journalist springs the news on Governor Mangi Steffensen during an interview about care for the elderly, and Steffensen is completely at a loss. The same goes for Jón H. Matthíasson, State Security Director, when he is asked about the matter. He states that he can neither confirm nor deny anything since he never comments on security matters. Police sources confirm that the previous week a new security bureau had been established under direct control of

Berlin, responsible to State Security. Two Icelandic police officers belong to the division. The police in Reykjavík verify the call-out to Höfðabakki and the burglary at the offices of the Nation Party, where a door was damaged. However, the investigation has been dropped "due to a lack of evidence". The case is closed and there was nothing more to say about it.

Geir laughs loudly. "There's nothing more to say about it. There'll be a lot more to say about this matter, and pretty damn soon too!" he shouts, slapping his knee.

Nationist Chairman Páll Bjarnfreðsson gets to his feet at the Althingi next morning to demand a public investigation. "This is not good enough," he thunders. "All we know is that three people have been arrested after having broken into the offices of my party, but have been released. We haven't received any formal information, but the newspapers know more than we do. Why is the European government rummaging in our drawers? They broke open my office door. We don't know whether they took anything with them. If they wanted something, they should have paid us a daytime visit, because we have nothing to hide," says Páll, shaking his fist.

His fellow MPs are surprised by this outburst from such a normally mild man, but they applaud in support.

"Why did the man flee the country?" shouts Páll who is outraged. People have never seen the Chairman in such a mood.

Governor Mangi Steffensen steps up to the lectern with an oily smile and promises he will send a query to Berlin. It appears as if Mangi has little interest in making excuses for the European Komizars. "This is a European affair," he declares. "A special European Security Bureau was established here in Reykjavík under Berlin's direction. The case is subject to European federal law. It concerns the security of the European nation. We have nothing to do with the work of the Security Bureau. Yet everything happened so quickly. The European Division Chief came to this country with orders and the matter is out of our hands. We will, however, send a query to Berlin," says Mangi calmly and deliberately on the rostrum.

Shouts are directed at the Governor but he merely smiles.

Most MPs for the Nation Party take to the lectern and demand a public investigation.

Steffensen steps back up to the lectern and waves for silence. "I would love to help," he smiles, "but it is not in the power of the Icelandic authorities to investigate cases that concern the security of the European state. If people want an investigation, they will have to gain the approval of the European Parliament. And I am sure our European MPs will take the matter up," he concludes with obvious irony. He glances toward Guðlaugur Hauksson, who is one of the three members of the Althingi currently sitting in the European Parliament.

Hauksson jumps to his feet as all eyes fall on him. "Well, of course I am going to take up the matter in Brussels," he blusters. "I can and will demand a public investigation. But there will have to be a vote in the European Parliament and the majority will have to approve, you see, the matter is complicated. The Security Bureau answers to the Supreme Council in Berlin. Special secrecy laws apply to it. A closed commission of Parliament oversees the European Security Bureau, and we have no representative on the committee. In fact there is only one Nordic representative on the committee, the Swede Gunnar Segerström." Hauksson feels his audience turning against him and hurriedly waves his fist in the air. "I will talk to him at once and demand that he take this matter up in the committee. Anyway, what do my two colleagues in the European Parliament have to say?" He glares around, eager to shift the blame for inaction on to somebody else.

Chairman Páll is back on his feet, shouting from his chair without bothering to go to the lectern. "I demand to know your position, Europe lovers!" shouts Páll, extremely upset. "Are you going to keep your bloody mouths shut over this case, you traitors, you scum?"

The president of the assembly repeatedly rings a bell interrupting Páll. "I reprimand the MP for indecent language," says Thor Bjarnsen.

But Páll does not seem to hear. "Those pro-Europe MPs are traitors. They keep their bloody mouths shut," he says in a loud voice.

The president strikes the bell again and again.

"If the MP continues with his wording he will be shown out of the assembly chamber," threatens the president.

Páll's face is fiery red with anger. "They keep their bloody mouths shut. They are keeping their bloody mouths bloody shut! They are traitors to Iceland. Bloody traitors," he shouts. The assembly is in an uproar; the president rings the bell violently as the Nationists shout and scream.

"I've presented my case but the nation has witnessed the cowardice of blockheads who act as the lapdogs of the federal government," cries Chairman Páll, stalking to his seat.

Geir watches the broadcast from the Althingi with his feet up on his desk. He has never witnessed anything like it and enjoys himself immensely. Reaction to his scoop has gone far beyond even his wildest dreams.

Thóra appears in the doorway. "Good man," she says, hands over a paper and is gone.

Geir picks up the paper to find it is a statement from Berlin. He reads it, then laughs. The response pitiful; just nothing, in fact.

"The European Security Bureau is conducting an investigation based on suspicions and indications of terrorist acts in Iceland. Recent terrorist acts have confirmed the need to be extremely vigilant. It is impossible to make the evidence public, since it would be in violation of laws on national security."

He throws the paper into the bin and smiles. He does not fancy a beer.

30

It is some months since Sólman had his first meeting with Trinxon about a Komizar for Iceland. The news from Iceland is horrid. Everything is crazy; there is growing support for the Nationists while his own Sólýta Party is on the defence.

And then there was that bizarre business with the sex scandal involving Chairman Páll Bjarnfreðsson. The newspapers somehow got hold of photos of Bjarnfreðsson's in a naked orgy with two teenage prostitutes. Not only that, but it turned out he had paid the girls with money taken from the campaign funds of the Nationist Party, even state funds. The news had shaken Icelandic politics to the core. People were shocked, but Sólman had been delighted. He had anticipated the collapse of the Nationists and the triumph of his own Sólýta Party.

Next day at the Althingi, Chairman Páll had come under immense pressure to hand back the money, then he had become the butt of a series of lewd jokes. Finally he had resigned his seat. The next day he tragically committed suicide, hanging himself with a belt in his office. The death of Chairman Páll came like thunder out of a clear blue sky and made Icelandic politics more complicated – and more deadly.

But to Sólman's horror and surprise the scandal had not undermined the Nationist Party in any way. All that happened was that the damned Julía woman had taken over as Chairman, promised reforms to the way the Party's finances worked and had gone from strength to strength. Sólman was on the ropes and he knew it. If he could not pull off some sudden success his dreams of power and popularity would be ruined.

So he has redoubled his efforts to gain an Icelandic Komizar. He has met with Trinxon on several occasions and is very pleased with progress. Finally, finally Sólman feels he has achieved a result.

He is extremely pleased, especially satisfied, as an Icelandic Komizar with offices in Berlin is now within his grasp. He has had to make concessions, of course, but both parties have had to curb their idealism, and making compromises is what negotiations are all about. Sólman conceded the point concerning the Supreme Council; the Icelandic Komizar will have to hold a seat on the Supreme Council in Berlin. Personally, he is in favour of holding a seat on the council, since it comes with a great deal of power and dignity, but the matter is extremely sensitive in Iceland. In Reykjavík membership in the council is regarded as a transfer of power to Berlin and eternal incorporation into the Great European State. Sólman feels this to be narrow-minded but the fundamental laws of the Great European State cannot be changed. Iceland will have to abide by the European constitution if it is going to get anywhere. This cannot be avoided. Naturally, some view it as a relinquishment of power and a submission, but this is just one step in a long process. People will have to understand that the question of Iceland's status can only be settled after lengthy talks and a constitutional process that might take decades. It isn't possible to gain everything at once.

Rome was not built in a day.

The most annoying thing about it all was that due to civil unrest across Europe Trinxon had decided to keep the talks with Sólman confidential. Sólman recalled one particularly awkward holph conversation with Editor John Bjornson just a week ago.

"I've had constructive conferences with the First Komizar," Sólman had reported. "And not always at his convenience either. Sometimes I have gone on my own initiative. And finally we've reached a firm agreement on the matter, but what it is I cannot tell, not even you. Yesterday we concluded the matter, the First Komizar and I, in full agreement in the end."

"You can tell me in confidence," said John annoyed, his expression sharp; he had stood up from his chair and leant over his desk in his office in Reykjavík. They looked each other in the eye for moment.

"Sorry, my friend. Trinxon made me promise," replied Sólman, ending the call. The editor's angry face vanished into thin air, as if it had never appeared to Sólman as he sat in his hotel room in Berlin.

And now that very morning Trinxon had invited Sólman to his office. The First Komizar had been extremely irritated at the news from Iceland. He had waved a copy of an article at Sólman.

"Can't you exert your influence to curb this web of lies in *The Post*?" Trinxon had asked. "I thought you knew the Editor. Have a word with him."

"I'll do my best, very best but few believe *The Post's* sensational rubbish," Sólman had replied. "But it would help if we had good news to announce from Berlin. If I could tell him about the new Komizar for Iceland that would help calm things down." Trinxon had scowled, but then agreed. Not only that, but he had agreed that Sólman will be Komizar for Icelandic affairs based in Berlin.

It is time to break the great news to the Icelandic public. Sólman gazes out of the window and imagines the positive headlines he is going to get. Time to talk to the press. He has organised a joint call to Editor John Bjornson and Múli Thordarsen. The holph on his desk buzzes. The call has come through. Sólman pushes the button to call up the images of Editor John Bjornson and Múli Thordarsen. His relationships with these men, his closest colleagues in Iceland, have been rather rocky recently. They have been dissatisfied with what they call Sólman's secrecy and servility.

Sólman puts on his best and brightest smile, then tells them about his deal with Trinxon. He waits for their congratulations, but instead they look at each other. "The new Komizar should not sit on the Council," growls Editor John.

Sólman scowls back: "The main thing is that we've gained a permanent Icelandic Komizar. No other nation has been accorded such an honour. The Constitution neither allows nor forbids a Komizar from holding a seat on the Supreme Council, but a seat there is praxis. This praxis is based on the fundamental laws of

196

Europe. No Komizar is recognized unless he sits on the council. A special Icelandic Komizar must sit at the table with his European counterparts at least sometimes. I find that an honour. They say that the fundamental European laws apply to Iceland as they do any other member state within the Great European State. We have to get on with Europe if we are to achieve our ends."

The others try to interrupt Sólman, but he waves his hand and continues: "This is a question of real politics."

"But taking the seat means Iceland will be incorporated forever...," begins Editor John, before Sólman interrupts him again.

"It is of course our legitimate demand that an Icelandic Komizar is not to sit with the other Komizars, but we can't go against the constitution of Europe. It is a fantasy, based on obsolete nationalism of the past to expect that Iceland will ever stand again on its two feet. It is unrealistic jabber, plain and simple rubbish to speak of independence."

Sólman will not be moved.

His colleagues are now furious as they sit there in the office of Editor John. They have jumped up from their seats and point their fingers at him. Sólman is quite alarmed as they tower over him, sitting in his office in Brussels, so he reduces them to one-tenth size.

"People here in Iceland will never accept fundamental European laws as the basis for the Icelandic constitution!" thunders Editor John furiously.

"This is crazy!" shouts Múli.

They stare each other down. The atmosphere is tense.

Sólman sees that he cannot keep them under control in their state, so he ends the conversation. The colleagues vanish into thin air. "They'll get over it," he mutters annoyed at their vulgarity. "Icelanders never know how to behave," he adds.

In irritation Sólman flicks on the holo-tv, but it does not help his mood. The screen shows a mass demonstration in London where protestors are waving placards insulting Berlin – one of them shows a Lancaster bomber dropping bombs on the Brandenburg Gate. Many of the protestors are waving the old fashioned Union Jack flags. A reporter stops a demonstrator and asks him a question.

"When we finish here we are going down to Devon," the man declares angrily. "We've arranged to play Drake's Drum down by the shore on Plymouth Hoe. That will bloody show them." The crowd cheers.

"The British are mad," mutters Sólman. "How can playing a musical instrument owned by a duck do them any good?"

Then the holo-tv news report shifts to Paris where a riot has broken out after some meeting of students at the Sorbonne had discussed something called the "democratic deficit". One placard demands that the Komizar system wiped out. A scruffy student appears on screen and demands that the Komizars be replaced by elected representatives, accountable to the citizens of Europe.

"Away with the Kom'zars," shout crowds in the background. The signs are quite graphic.

Sólman has read the confidential reports, of course. Cars are set on fire on the streets of Paris, London, Madrid and Rome, a stench drifts from the rubbish piles of Naples over the entire continent and there are fights on the borders of Ukraine, when the Russians fuel hatred toward Europe. The situation on both sides of the Caspian Sea grows steadily worse and in Kazikistnam government troops, supported by European military advisers, find themselves hard-pressed by guerrillas who are thought to be financed by the Kremlin. Relations with foreign states are extremely delicate, especially Russia, which has shut off the supply of gas and demands changes to the countries' borders. And there is growing unrest in Reykjavík, like the rest of Europe.

The deskcom flashes. Trinxon is summoning Sólman to his office. Sólman hurries along the corridor, enters the ante chamber and is waved in by one of Trinxon's glamorous aides. He finds Trinxon at his desk holding a report.

"You won't have seen this," glares Trinxon. "I don't show you everything." He throws the report to Sólman. It is titled "Current Political Situation in Iceland", the words "Most Secret" are stamped underneath and it is signed "Kessler".

"Turn to page 4," says Trinxon. Sólman does so and reads in horror that the analysis concludes that his party is losing support rapidly to the Nationists. It includes some unfortunate cartoons from local newspapers and concludes that Sólman is now a joke in Iceland.

"An increasing number of Icelanders echo the demands for authority to be returned home," continues the report. "There is growing support for the extremists led by Júlía Ingólfsdóttir. The Icelanders demand a Komizar based in Iceland; for the nation to gain full authority over the fish in the sea. Support for the terrorist Krummi is spreading beyond fishing communities and is now heard in Reykjavík. The Althingi is to vote on a resolution for a Komizar based in Reykjavík."

Sólman shakes his head. "Damned nonsense," he says loudly.

"Kessler is never wrong," counters Trinxman.

"The corruption in Reykjavík is horrendous," says Sólman. "This motion in the Althingi is a put up job. They would never dare do it if I were there. It is only natural that the office of Komizar be based in Berlin. I can deal with it. I know these people. I know my opponents as well as my allies and a majority of the Althingi will support me in this matter, despite what this Kessler writes."

"Then get your lazy arse back to Iceland and take care of things," growls Trinxon. "Otherwise, and most unfortunately, we must suspend all talks. The situation is flammable, politically". Trinxon turns his chair toward the window overlooking the Speer. "Berlin must hold back due to the political uncertainty and unrest on the continent." He does not even deign to turn his chair back toward Sólman. The Komizar then waves his hand and concludes the meeting.

Sólman slouches out, humiliated. His hopes for a Komizar's office in Berlin appear to have evaporated; collapsed like any other house of cards. What a pile of rubbish.

Sólman decides to broadcast an address from Brussels to the Icelandic nation. He quickly fixes up a prime-time holo-tv slot for that evening. Speaking from his impressive office he reads out his carefully prepared statement.

"Fellow Icelanders! This case now comes under the verdict of the nation. The appointment of the first Icelandic Komizar in Berlin would be a major step in a long process, but fantasies about returning authority to Iceland fix us on the same old path." He talks on for several minutes, but the live blog of viewers' comments that scrolls across the bottom of the screen makes for uncomfortable reading. His ideas are called disgraceful and the most preposterous incorporation into the Great European State.

After the broadcast, Sólman wonders if he really is having difficulty interpreting the wishes of his nation. Perhaps it is his long stay abroad, he ponders. Then he shakes his head. "I'll bet it was that damned Krummi or Júlía behind it all," he thinks. "They got their supporters to blog on screen. Sensible people will listen to me."

Later that evening, Editor John and Múli publish a statement in support of him, despite still being furious at him: "What loss can we expect by accepting the offer for a Komizar in Berlin with a seat on the Supreme Council? Absolutely none! We won't yield in the slightest in our demands for self-rule. We'll accept what we've been offered. And we reserve the right to go after the remainder; whenever we wish; whenever we feel that we have the opportunity."

But the vote at the Althingi goes against Sólman. By just one vote the Althingi votes to demand a Komizar based in Iceland. But the vote is only advisory. It has no real force.

Sólman continues to divide his time between Berlin and Brussels. Meanwhile, Editor John manages things in Iceland and the public mood quietens down. True, the summer passes by without any positive response from the authorities in Berlin, but then neither has Berlin definitely turned down any proposals either. Sólman feels in a state of limbo. Eager to push events forward he writes an article in which he quotes private statements made by his political allies in Iceland word-for-word.

The article promps an immediate holph call from Editor John.

"How the bloody hell could you do this without showing me the draft first," thunders Editor John. "People are furious that long passages in your article on the constitutional issue are published either word-for-word or nearly word-for-word from drafts and manuscripts that we sent you. The arrangement and treatment of the material is generally the same or very similar; the order of sections changed maybe, but they are basically the same. We sent this stuff to you in confidence, you fool. People feel betrayed. And so do I."

Sólman is alarmed to see the editor's vehemence and anger, which continues to thunder over him.

"We had and still have the idea that this piece would be completely objective; would be presented as a contribution from a neutral observer, who by his own reflections came to the conclusion that your policy was the most proper and just. But now the piece appears to the public to be just a piece of propaganda. We are almost completely at a loss about what should be done. Either revise the entire article or just simply do not publish it, because as a plagiarized document it completely loses its raison d'étre and misses its intended effect. It's like each in its own direction; this unfortunate incident could scarcely have occurred if you had been in Reykjavík."

Sólman goes on the offensive. He is furious, his authority having been undermined. "Why may my name not be seen? My name has been so blackened in Iceland that you colleagues of mine want to keep me out of the loop entirely," he shouts, standing up. He finds the editor's attitude dreary, and witness to a despicable nature. "Its absurd to argue that I'm domineering and that the propaganda value of the article is higher if I have nothing to do with it," he shouts.

He is terribly irritated, and when the editor disappears from view he almost has a fit. Editor John has hung up on him. "How bloody rude is that?" shouts Sólman, in an horrendously foul mood as he kicks at the desk.

Sólman soon has other things to think about. The debate over the Iceland Komizar is coming to a head. Trinxon will not be budged.

The Althingi will have to agree to an Icelandic Komizar based in Berlin with a seat on the Supreme Council, under fundamental European law, or they won't get a Komizar at all. But Sólman sees little chance of getting such a policy agreed back in Iceland. There is no budging anything, because the Nationists have grown stronger. If Sólman is to achieve anything, he will have to present a bill at the Althingi in person, get it passed and then have it ratified in Berlin. But with neither side wanting to make concessions the feat seems politically impossible. He cannot think how to word a bill so that it would pass both in Iceland and in Berlin.

Sólman wants to try to get more MPs to support his cause, but it is likely an uphill battle, since a division has arisen in the ranks of the Sólýta Party. The division has arisen not least because of the conduct of Sólman himself. Even people who agree with him are getting fed up with the way events are shaping up.

On the eve of his return to Iceland to attend the Althingi, Sólman tells *Euro-News* that Icelanders will have to place emphasis on three things: his theory of the Status Act, the constitution, and fundamental European law.

"The Status Act stipulates that Iceland is an inseparable part of Europe and Icelandic legislation in all common matters is entrusted to the general legislative powers of the European State. Iceland is under the authority of federal law. Thus those laws apply to Iceland. We cannot change that. We must work within the European Constitution to gain self-rule for Iceland." Sólman is confident that this is the heart of what he calls his real politics – co-operate with Berlin to get what Iceland wants.

But when he arrives in Reykjavík and meets his party colleagues in an office at the Althingi he gets a rude shock. His theory on the Status Act is taken poorly by his legally trained colleagues. They consider the theory to be a victory for the enemy. The nation will never agree to the European Constitution forming the basis for Iceland's constitution. Every single concession rings badly in their ears and represents a boon for his political opponents.

"Enemy victory! What rubbish!" snorts Sólman. "There is no

enemy here, only friends that we need to get on with. Is this is all you make of my attempts to conjure increased autonomy for the Icelanders. Dammit, I sometimes wish that I had never lit the flame that has turned into such a bonfire of hope. We are on the brink of getting our own Komizar and now you lot are losing your minds and demanding ever more freedom before we have got anything in the first place."

Editor John bristles and takes him angrily to task. "People are quite angry with your Status Act theory. We must take a determined position against it; it is your personal opinion, not ours. The Party must emphasize that this theory of yours is completely irrelevant for our program of getting a Komizar for Iceland. Our future depends on holding fast to our reasonable demands and dispelling all doubt about them. We must push our demands, not get dragged into constitutional theory. I expect that you will defend your view, but do so in your own name — not the party's. Otherwise it will become a dangerous incendiary torch. We need everyone's help to extinguish the flames."

The meeting rumbles on for some time, with party members taking sides and arguing fruitlessly. When it ends in bad-tempered deadlock, Sólman walks off to his hotel. He wonders if he is growing distant from his supporters and colleagues. He is forced to admit to himself that his theory on the Status Act was formulated in haste. He isn't trained in law. Yet Sólman feels it important to remain firm; not to give way. He decides to continue in the same vein in an interview with *Euro-News* next day.

"The theory is impossible to test except by denying the validity of the Status Act," he says. "But is there any sense in denying the validity of a law that we have recognized in practice and lived with for years? The legislation was ratified, issued and approved by Europe. We have lived with it. It's de facto. We are by law a nation within the European State."

As soon as the broadcast is over, Sólman rushes off to attend the opening of the Althingi. As usual, the session is formally opened by

Governor Mangi Steffensen. Unusually, his speech has been written for him by bureaucrats in Berlin. Steffensen resents having the words foisted on him. He is accustomed to sending his speeches to Berlin for approval and has got used to seeing passages crossed out, but this time his entire speech had been crossed out and a new speech sent to him instead. The Berlin Speech, as he calls it is deadset against any concessions to autonomy in his address, which was written and ratified in Berlin. "We have unfortunately seen that the same misunderstanding prevails regarding Iceland's political position within the Great European State. This misunderstanding is standing in the way of progress. Iceland is an integral part of Europe. The assembly must understand this."

Even as he reads it out, Steffensen sees it is going down badly. The Nationists at once raise a point of order. They state that the opening speech is supposed to be written by the Governor, but they denounce the "Mangi Speech" as having been written by Komizar Trinxon himself. Steffensen wriggles back into his chair and keeps silent. They are right, he knows. But Berlin is not going to give way or give in. He had tried explaining the speech would go down badly, but Trinxon had not wanted to hear it. Berlin's stance appears as unbreakable as the steel in a German panzer.

The Althingi meeting degenerates into a rude slanging match as the MPs refuse to debate politely. Steel meets steel. No majority can be gained on anything. Sólman stands up to move his motion about the Komizar in Berlin, but cannot make himself heard. Concord between political parties in Iceland appear impossible. In the end Steffensen declares the meeting adjourned for 48 hours. He tells everyone to calm down and come back when they are willing to talk sensibly.

Next day *The Post* prints an editorial that grabs the nation's attention.

"The Sólýska Party is falling".

"Political opponents want to kill Sólman's agenda and demand a Komizar seated in Reykjavík. The sooner the better, they say. They doubtless think it an advantage to be able to humiliate Sólman. But, the Icelandic nation has to admit that much has been achieved through Sólýska. With the help of Sólman Smithson, the nation has managed to break out of its lethargy. The nation is able to gain a Komizar in Berlin who will attend to no other matters. The Icelandic Komizar is to hold a seat on the Supreme Council, attend the Althingi, and bear political responsibility, even though all control is to be in Berlin in accordance with fundamental European law. Iceland has not had a Komizar for decades, ever since Rútur Finnlaugsson was in charge of matters pertaining to Europe's peripheries.

"A Komizar in Berlin would mark a political watershed. This does not go as far as many people want, but it is a start.

"Sólman states that he has the support of a majority of MPs, but his opponents brought him down with all sorts of tricky points of order and obsolete rules. He claims to be optimistic despite it all, saying he was unable to win the vote this time, but that he claims a moral victory. And he promises to win the vote next time.

"This newspaper thinks he is wrong. Indications show that he will lose the vote, whenever it comes. But he is right about one thing. There is suddenly more at stake than ever in Icelandic politics, which continues to debate the office of an Icelandic Komizar in Berlin, said to be Iceland's greatest position of honour in the Great European State. No other nation has its own Komizar."

31

Geir Thórisson has driven down the same street every evening
for eight months now. Summer turned to winter, then back to
spring, but on no occasion has Deep Throat put a flowerpot in the
window. Geir has made little progress in his investigation of the
scandal at Höfðabakki. Everything is stuck beneath a mysterious
veil of secrecy laws. It is more out of habit than hope that Geir turns
down the side street on his way home once again. But on this bright
spring day he notices the flowerpot in the window. Deep Throat
wants to talk to him.

"Finally, finally!" he shouts, banging the wheel with both hands.

Geir and Deep Throat meet at the column in the car park at
midnight.

"What's up?" asks Geir.

"Seiferdal stole confidential political documents that have nothing
to do with terrorism," says Deep Throat, without waiting for a
response from Geir. "The man who directed the operation is named
Rudolf Kessler. He is the First Komizar's errand-boy; directs
Trinxon's secret police. Here is a photo of Kessler, so far as I can
discover it is the only photo that has ever been taken of the man
since he left kindergarten. Seiferdal is a kind of floor-wiper for
Kessler. Here are the documents that they stole. It was political
espionage, pure and simple," says Deep Throat.

"Illegal secret police, political espionage. This story is going to be
crazy," says Geir excitedly.

"And just one other thing. Those photos from Chairman Páll's
orgies were leaked from the First Komizar's office," says Deep
Throat.

"How do you know that?" asks Geir in surprise.

"You can rest assured that I know and have proof of Trinxon's complicity, which will come out at the right place and time, but not quite yet," says Highpoint, who walks away without waiting for an answer. Geir remains behind, half done-in after the effects of the adrenaline that has coursed through his body. He decides to go straight to the editorial offices and before he realizes it, he's running.

The Post's story next day is like a bomb going off within Icelandic society, and for the first time ever all of the major European media outlets in Europe run with the story at full steam, and start putting the screws on Trinxon.

The photograph of Trinxon's personal spy is like the icing on the most delicious-looking cake. The news of Kessler's relationship with the First Komizar and the existence of the secret service comes like thunder in the clear Berlin sky. The political manoeuvring against Chairman Páll is considered deplorable.

"This is an Icelandic lie. The residents of Europe know better," the German paper *Bild* quotes Trinxon.

But *Bild* does not buy the First Komizar's explanations. It puts its own investigative reporters on the case and a week later splashes the headline "Trinxon's Secret Police" across the front page. Photos of all eight members of the secret police department, along with its organizational chart, are published. "They do Trinxon's dirty work," states *Bild*. *Sky News* calls the scandal 'Headgate'.

Headgate is like lint on Trinxon's white collar.

Geir is highly amused watching *Sky's* news report on the Komizar's pitiful evasions. "You're in a free fall, you fool," he shouts, and his colleagues at the office give him bewildered looks. He is extremely pleased with *Sky's* name of the scandal, although he curses himself for missing it. However, the story keeps getting bigger which of course is the main thing. Afterward it's always Headgate; the name gets stuck to the building. Geir loves it. "Trinxon is going down the drain," he comments to his colleagues.

"Watch your words," Thóra admonishes him quietly. "That man has many friends."

The First Komizar has his back against the wall. The names of

Kessler and Seiferdal are on everyone's lips across the continent. Headgate is the most talked-about scandal in Europe. For the first time an Icelandic member of the European Parliament gets universal attention across the continent. Guðlaugur Hauksson is making front-page coverage. His proposal calling for an investigation into Trinxon's secret police is approved. Trinxon comes under fire from all directions and decides to deliver a speech to the European Parliament in order to calm things down.

The day after Hauksson's motion is carried, Trinxon attends a full plenary session of the Parliament. At a prearranged moment he gets to his feet and humbly asks the Parliament President for permission to speak. "I address you from the bottom of my heart regarding an issue that weighs heavily on the citizens of Europe," says Trinxon knowing that he has arranged for his speech to be broadcast live across the continent — in fact across the world.

"Serious allegations have emerged concerning my close associates. I have investigated these allegations. It is sadly true that three employees have unfortunately acted without orders and have broken the law. They did so in good faith, because evidence of terrorist activities had emerged. This is not the first time that the residents of Europe have had to endure violence on the part of Icelandic fanatics.

"I, like all good European citizens, was shocked at the burglary in Iceland. It was illegal, even though it had been for a good purpose. I neither had before nor had after any knowledge of the burglary until it appeared in the media. However, although these employees acted without my knowledge, they were working for me, so I accept responsibility and must now work to put things straight. In order to win back the confidence of the citizens of Europe, I explain here and now that Seiferdal and Kessler have proffered his resignations, and the two Icelandic individuals have been removed from their posts. None of them works for the government any longer. My investigative team will be disbanded; employees of the Security Bureau of the First Komizar will be transferred to the offices of the Komizar of Justice.

"When I wrote this speech, I noticed that 1,361 days are left in my term of office. I would like these days to be the best in the history of Europe. May fortune follow Europe and all the inhabitants of our great continent."

The majority of the Members of the European Parliament break into applause as Trinxon sits down. A small minority remain seated in silence. Hauksson hurries outside to speak to reporters. "Trinxon's speech leaves many questions unanswered," he says. "It was a great piece of eloquent rhetoric. Trinxon has bought himself some precious time to try to get things sorted out. However, a political storm is on its way."

Over the next few weeks, numerous demands are made for the resignation of Trinxon, over Headgate. He rejects them all, but the European Parliament holds hearings on the Icelandic burglary and Trinxon's secret police. The Komizar is experiencing difficult political days, but he states that resignation is out of the question. The government has shouldered political responsibility; good men have misstepped in the service of good causes in the eternal war against terrorism. They have resigned their positions. The secret police now reports to the Komizar of Justice.

"I already have accepted political responsibility," announces Trinxon at a press conference.

Meanwhile, Geir Thórisson is enjoying himself. Numerous articles are written about him and television programs are made about his career. In interviews, News Director Thóra praises Geir's journalism. "He is and always has been our star reporter; a model for young journalists," she states in an interview with the British *BBC*. Geir receives the Icelandic Journalists Award and the European Journalists Award for his story on Headgate. His star shines brightly.

And yet, he feels extremely frustrated; he is particularly annoyed at Deep Throat, who has not been in touch for months. Still, Geir has heeded Highpoint's orders. He has made no attempt to contact the State Security Director even though he has often been tempted to do so.

He has often discussed this with Thóra and they are in perfect agreement. They will respect the confidentiality of their source. This is the most sacred obligation for a journalist. They know that Trinxon has made an extensive search for the source of the information that has been causing such trouble. In fact stories leak out of Berlin and Brussels that a witch hunt is under way. Bureaucrats are being given the third degree by the secret service in an effort to find out who knew what, and who leaked the facts. Geir curses the fact that no signal is to be seen in Highpoint's house, the continued absence of the flowerpot in the kitchen window annoy him immensely and makes him wonder if something is wrong – if Trinxon has got to Deep Throat.

The political fall out of the affair reaches Iceland later that summer. Elections to the Althing sees Júlía Ingólfsdóttir resign her Berlin post and stand as the Nation Party candidate. She wins her seat on the Althingi by a landslide. The Nation Party gains a strong, fresh wind in its sails due to a new leader who has emerged on the scene. "A brilliant leader," say the media, who adore the splendid young cosmopolitan.

"Political Power Back Home — No Compromise," reads the lead article of *The Press*, a new paper that campaigns for the Nationists and home rule.

New times are ahead.

The same elections see the Sólýska Party suffer a heavy blow and there are increasing demands for home rule to be restored to Iceland. With her eloquence and bright persona Júlía lights the nation's flame. She goes further, speaking of making a bid for Icelandic independence. She brings a new, fresh voice to Iceland.

This dreamy girl wants the old tattered króna, shout her critics.

Júlía replies energetically. She accuses the major statists of subservience to the Berlin government. They have lost their daring and courage. There is a need to light the spark of freedom, which was extinguished at the dissolution of the Republic and the violence on Austurvöllur Square. It is stated that as long as the Komizars are in charge in Berlin, nothing will be changed. A raggedy hardline agenda prevails there.

"Trinxon can bully us and spy on us, but freedom will prevail," predicts a leading article in *The Press*.

In the wake of the elections the general mood is one of optimism for better times in Iceland.

And then, on a blustery autumn evening as wind brings salt spray lashing over Reykjavík from the harbour, the flowerpot finally appears in Highpoint's window.

32

Geir beats Deep Throat to the column. Highpoint smiles wryly, the reporter's impatience being clear. "A recording exists of Trinxon's conversation with Kessler after the burglary. Kessler discusses the entire matter thoroughly. It's clear that Trinxon has been lying the whole time. Kessler was authorized to engage in illegal operations," says Deep Throat.

"What's that?" says Geir, hardly believing what he is hearing.

"Here's a transcript of part of the rascals' conversation," says Deep Throat, before walking briskly out of the car park. Geir remains behind alone and reads the text. "Now I've got you by the balls, you bastard Trinxon," he says triumphantly.

There is an uproar in the European Parliament when Guðlaugur Hauksson projects *The Post's* front page in double size from the rostrum. He demands that recordings from the office of the First Komizar be made public. "Trinxon knows much more than he has admitted. He has abused his authority. He has authorized illegal activities. He organized a campaign of slander against his political opponents in Iceland, which ended in personal tragedy. He has encouraged political espionage," thunders Guðlaugur, who is beside himself.

Yet reactions are mixed. A large number of MEPs address the assembly and urge self-control. "We cannot let ourselves be startled by sensationalistic news from Iceland," says a Ukrainian MEP. "This is only a newspaper report. We have not heard the tapes. We must not leap to conclusions." But others call it a serious matter for the First Komizar to have abused his authority for political purposes.

The office of the First Komizar publishes a brief declaration: "The accusations of the Icelandic tabloid are fabrications. Rikard Trinxon is personally considering suing *The Post*."

Despite the Komizar's harsh declaration, the European Parliament agrees by an overwhelming majority to refer the case to a subcommittee of the Justice Committee, the powerful closed commission. The committee meets to investigate Headgate. It has summoned the Icelandic journalist Geir Thórisson.

Geir has never experienced such a thing.

All of the major media outlets in Europe are in attendance and the hearing is broadcast across the continent. Eleven MPs sit on the committee. The chairman opens the discussion, stating that serious allegations have been published in an Icelandic newspaper, allegations that must be taken into careful consideration.

"Journalist Thórisson. What evidence do you have for these serious allegations?" asks the chairman, Irishman Peter Donaldson.

Geir is perfectly calm as he looks at the committee members one by one. He then opens his briefcase and among other things takes out the piece of paper that Deep Throat had handed him. He starts reading word-for-word the transcript of Trinxon's conversation with Kessler.

Geir slowly and deliberately reads sentences from the transcript:

Trinxon: That Norwegian idiot has let himself be arrested like some petty thief. And now the Icelandic press have printed the story.

Kessler: This is a cock-up, that's for sure, but we've got complete control of the situation. They've got nothing concrete on us.

Trinxon: You've got to put a stop to this nonsense.

Kessler: Don't forget that you authorized the operation.

Trinxon: Yes, goddamn it; I don't need to know everything. What did you find out about this Chairman Páll.

Kessler: Seiferdal found six photos of the chairman's secret sex orgies.

Trinxon: You'll leak this information about this lowlife. That will put an end to the little bugger.

Laughter.

A murmur runs through the room and the committee members

exchange curious glances. Nothing like this has ever happened in the entire history of Europe. Geir is extremely calm and confident, in fact very pleased with his performance. "These are word-for-word quotations taken from recordings made in the office of the First Komizar. These recordings and others have been preserved. All that Parliament needs to do is ask for them," he states coldly.

"We thank you for your informative statement. The committee owes you special gratitude, Journalist Thórisson," says Chairman Donaldson.

Numerous journalists run from the room to get the story out.

The government of Europe is in an uproar.

Demands for Trinxon's resignation come from all corners of the continent. The revelations of special tapes of the First Komizar's conversations send shock waves throughout Europe. The committee demands that the office of First Komizar hand over the tapes. The media is filled with stories about Headgate and the crisis in Berlin. People say that this is the first time that the European Parliament has grabbed its weapons in its fight with a corrupt Komizar system. Trinxon is under heavy assault. *The Times* in London runs a story claiming that Trinxon had been convicted of embezzlement before he became Komizar, but had been granted amnesty the following day. The matter is extremely delicate, because according to European legislation it is against the law to give details of a criminal case involving a Komizar without permission. The British paper is threatened with lawsuits for its revelations.

It never rains but it pours.

In Hamburg, *Bild* reveals that Trinxon had been a passenger on board a luxury yacht owned by a Greek shipping magnate several weeks before the Euro-Hellenic shipping company received hefty payments from Berlin's coffers of euros. Then the *Athenian Hermes* prints copies of travel tickets showing Trinxon had accepted a trip to Jamaica from some unknown business magnates. Trinxon's stamp of corruption becomes ever more colourful.

This is democracy in action against Komizerian Demcowill.

European newspaper headlines are quite colourful. Trinxon is aggressively criticized throughout the European state. Not only are demands made that his head be presented on a platter to the people, but also that the Komizar system be abolished. A direct representative democracy has to be established. A President of Europe has to be directly elected by the people for the people; by the citizens of Europe for the citizens of Europe.

The offices of the First Komizar in Beethoven Hall are besieged, but Trinxon rarely shows himself. Trinxon tries to focus media attention on foreign affairs. State visits to Washington and then to Peking and Moscow are announced. There is talk of a thaw in relations between Europe and Russia.

A week later Trinxon addresses the European nation directly on holo-tv.

He dresses in a sombre, formal suit and gazes steadily into the camera as he states: "For several months, reports on Headgate have overwhelmed news media coverage. All the major television stations of Europe have spent over twenty hours per week covering the case. An investigation should have revealed the truth, but in recent weeks a tasteless attempt has been made to implicate the First Komizar in the matter. An attempt has been made to suggest that the First Komizar was involved in the matter illegally.

"That is a lie; quite simply. That is a lie.

"Now people demand copies of all the conversations recorded at the Komizar's office. Such a thing is of course absurd, and would compromise European national security. Therefore, I categorically reject such demands, since on top of everything else they would undermine the dignity of the office of Komizar. I will not discuss particular details since that will only please Devil´s advocates. I say this to you: I had no prior knowledge of the burglary at Höfðabakki. I did not participate in or know of attempts to cover up the case. I ordered my subordinates not to participate in illegal or unbecoming activity.

"This is the crux of the matter.

"This is the simple truth of the matter: I did not know about the burglary at Headgate until the media reported it, nor have I participated in covering up the case.

"Now I ask you to grant me leave to do my job taking on the important issue of the day, which is to improve the lives of the citizens of the great Europe. With your help we will succeed in fulfilling the sublime objectives of Europe."

Guðlaugur Hauksson has become the most famous member of the European Parliament, which has never received similar coverage. In a parliamentary resolution he presses hard for the release of the copies of the Komizar's conversations. The closed commission seems to be hesitating. But the media picks up the scent and Parliament is put under a great deal of pressure to persist against Trinxon, who for years has dominated the political stage of Europe.

Committee Chairman Donaldson proposes that Trinxon be ordered to hand over recordings that have anything to do with Icelandic affairs. "This is certainly a compromise, because naturally we have an understanding of national security. Therefore, it is sufficient that Trinxon hands over only recordings concerning Icelandic affairs," says Chairman Donaldson.

Various MEPs are suspicious of the proposal and feel that it grants Trinxon leeway to dispense with uncomfortable recordings. Who is going to monitor the choice of material? It's impossible to let the bureaucrats do so. That would be opening the door to a cover up. Who is to monitor the European bureaucrats monitoring of themselves? No internal auditors would be acceptable.

"I propose that three MEPs be chosen to look over the shoulders of nine bureaucrats," says Donaldson, who is known for speaking to the point. "The MEPs can demand access to all the recordings of Trinxon's conversations, but they are bound by an oath to silence when it comes to anything but Headgate," he adds.

The committee approves the chairman's proposal five votes to two. Attention is drawn to the fact that many MEPs abstain or are absent during the vote.

The First Komizar's reaction is somewhat unexpected; people feel that Parliament is waffling, since the proposal is a compromise. Trinxon, on the other hand, dismisses what he calls the "attack of Parliament against the European Government". "One year of Headgate is enough. It compromises European national security for recordings of such sensitive material to be lying around," declares Trinxon in a statement.

Difficult negotiations are undertaken. Trinxon stands firm. He argues that it is out of the question for a parliamentary committee to demand his private recordings.

The obstinacy is taken badly by many people.

"What is the man hiding?" asks Guðlaugur in a speech to Parliament, right to the point. The case is referred to the European Court, which decides in favour of Parliament. "The parliamentary committee, which is bound to confidentiality, can demand all of the recordings if it has reasonable cause to do so," reads the decision.

The media take the court's decision very badly.

Who is to judge "reasonable cause," asks *Bild* in a strongly worded leading article. But the verdict of the European Court puts an end to all debate. The Komizar's office hands over the recordings dealing with Icelandic issues. Damage to the recordings gives rise to suspicions of tampering but nothing can be done about it. Bureaucrats under the supervision of a three-man parliamentary subcommittee commence the immense project of listening to the tapes.

It is time-consuming and tedious.

Trinxon's coarse language, obscene curses and paranoid suspicions on the tapes come as a surprise to many.

Geir Thórisson had submitted to the parliamentary committee a list of recordings that are related to Headgate and asks that they be made public. This was consistent with his reading in parliament, as well as with the conversations that had been printed in *The Post*.

The investigative committee discovers a conversation that receives the nickname, "The Redhanded Tape"; in the conversation between Trinxon and Kessler, the Norwegian Seiferdal is the gun in Iceland, smoke still coming from it.

"Find ways to stop those bloodhounds on the basis of national security," Trinxon orders Kessler.

"It has become difficult to justify using the excuse of national security in the matter," Kessler objects.

"I don't ****ing care," Trinxon shouts, and adds: "Make the issue one of national security."

"Seiferdal was caught redhanded," Kessler concludes.

The MEPs get wind of more recordings concerning Icelandic matters.

"Widespread Espionage" is a front-page headline of *The Post*. Geir feels that he has really hit the jackpot, since political conspiracies are part of the media's daily bread and butter.

The investigative committee publishes recordings of Trinxon and Kessler's conversations about Mangi Steffensen, Páll Bjarnfreðsson, Júlía Ingólfsdóttir and Inga Laxdal, the Chairman of the Unionist Party. *The Post* reveals character investigations of Páll that cause shock and bewilderment in Iceland, but the fact that Mangi and Inga had been on the Komizar's hitlist comes like as bolt from the blue.

"Seiferdal spies on everyone and everything," says Geir, sitting opposite Thóra in the news director's office. "This is absolutely unbelievable. It isn't enough to know their politics; they need to know everything — including the secrets of the bedroom," he says laughing.

"Petty little men have an outlet for their dirty thoughts," replies Thóra, scandalized. "You men are all alike," she says in a sharp voice.

"Absolutely right. Men are generally lowlifes," says Geir, laughing raucously.

They both laugh.

33

In Iceland Governor Mangi Steffensen issues a statement in the wake of the disclosures of the closed parliamentary commission. "A breach of confidentiality has occurred. It is completely unacceptable for people's characters to be investigated. We have seen the tragic consequences. No need to say more about that. The European Security Bureau in Iceland is to be abolished. Its employees will be transferred to positions monitoring parking meters."

Steffensen is furious with Trinxon.

He has always found the man unpleasant, his arrogance and overbearing behaviour has shocked many people. Now Trinxon has brought himself trouble. Steffensen's greatest hope is that the bastard will be driven out of office. He has been frustrated at not having any evidence of Seiferdal's work in Iceland. As far as that is concerned, Mangi is totally at a loss.

"Bloody fool," he says quietly, striking the table angrily and then turns to slam the punching bag as hard as he can. "I had no knowledge of the spies. It is absolutely intolerable." Steffensen grins sullenly, his punches carried more weight back in the old days.

Inga Laxdal issues a statement in which she regrets the European character investigations but warns against drawing conclusions that are too sweeping, since the espionage did nothing to change Iceland's position in the Great European State.

"What an idiot, this Laxdal. The woman is a worthless brown-noser," says Geir to Thóra in bewilderment when her statement is received by *The Post*.

"Watch what you say, Geir. I don't know what you're capable of, that I can vouch," says Thóra as she walks out her office.

Geir grins.

In Berlin it's clear to everyone that Trinxon's position is quickly becoming indefensible. Even political allies avoid meeting with the First Komizar, who has become isolated and despised. Rumour spreads that Trinxon is depressed and spends long hours alone in a darkened room with a whiskey glass in hand and Prozac on his desk. He is defiant; will not resign his office. In fact the man's stubbornness shocks everyone; literally everyone.

Finally a resolution is made in the European Parliament by the leaders of all the political parties. "Trinxon is being charged with malfeasance in office and being in violation of the European constitution," states the joint resolution of the party chairmen, which is approved almost unanimously in the European Parliament. The MEPs are soon in the bars congratulating themselves on what they call "the most brilliant hour of the European democratic forces in the 21st century."

Kessler walks hesitantly to the second hand record shop in Brunnhauster Strasse in a seedy suburb of Berlin. He opens the door, ignores the old man who pretends to be there to serve non-existent customers and pushes his way through the curtain that leads to the stairs. Kessler knows that the Vulture has an obsession with secrecy, but this is ridiculous. He reaches the door to the first floor office and knocks.

"Come in, Kessler," calls a cold voice.

Kessler pushes the door open and finds the Vulture wearing his trademark black suit sitting behind a desk and fiddling with an e-notebook. Kessler waits. The Vulture places the e-notebook silently down on the desk.

"Well," come the icy tones. "You are head of Trinxon's Security Bureau. How is our dear First Komizar coping with the crisis?"

"He isn't," replies Kessler. "He is falling to pieces. He always was a weak man behind that angry facade."

"Of course," hisses the Vulture. "That is what made him such an ideal First Komizar. A weak man is always so much easier to control. But his usefulness is over. The fool can't cope. He has to go."

"Agreed," replies Kessler. "But he is a stubborn fool. He wants to fight on to keep his position. Arrogant man."

"Weak, stubborn, arrogant and foolish," says the Vulture smiling. "And what else is he? He is greedy." He looks at Kessler expectantly.

"Yes, greedy," repeats Kessler. There is a short silence, then a look of sudden realisation sweeps over his face. "Greedy. Of course, the pension."

"Yes, the pension," sighs the Vulture quietly. "If he is convicted of a crime in office he loses his pension. But if he resigns first he keeps his pension. And it is a fat pension, is it not? Will he resign?"

"If he thinks he will lose his pension if he stays, he will resign tomorrow," responds Kessler.

"Then," says the Vulture. "Somebody really should bring that clause in the laws of the Great European State to his attention. For his own good, of course."

Kessler grins and nods.

"Off you go," says the Vulture picking up his e-notebook again. "And don't waste too much time. We need that fool out by lunchtime tomorrow."

Kessler slips out the room and closes the door behind him. No wonder the Vulture has got where he is, he thinks. Evil, ruthless, unscrupulous bastard. But what a brain.

First Komizar Rickhard Ditlev Trinxon resigns at 10am the following morning. Headgate has brought him down.

Trinxon delivers his final address to the European nation: "Good evening, dear citizens of Europe. It is clear that I no longer have the political backing to continue my work as First Komizar of Europe. I have tried to protect the dignity of the office and defend it on all levels, because otherwise I would have failed my duty and the office of Komizar.

"But now my political support is at an end.

"Legal disagreements have been resolved. I deliver my final address to the European nation. I, Rikard Ditlev Trinxon, resign my office as First Komizar. With this decision I hope that we can begin the healing process that Europe so desperately needs.

"I am not known for giving up, but as Komizar I place the interests of the continent above all other interests.

"I have made a mistake. That is quite apparent, but I did so when acting in good faith, with the interests of Europe as my guiding light and the security of Europe as my goal. Your security, dear citizens of the great state of Europe.

"The media no longer have Trinxon to kick like some dog. Farewell."

Trinxon stands up from his desk and sweeps out of the room without looking right or left. He walks out into the grand garden to the heli-thruster that awaits him. He bids farewell to his chief of staff and people who have been with him for most of his political career. As he boards the thruster he turns and waves with both hands, making victory signs.

A week later the whole of the Supreme Council resigns. Europe is without a government.

"This is the biggest moment in the history of Icelandic and for that matter European journalism," says Thóra after Trinxon has made his final farewell. *The Post's* reporters seem paralysed, but then a great cheer breaks out. A young rookie reporter produces a champagne bottle. The cork pops. Geir turns to his colleagues and says: "Remember that this is also a human tragedy." Then the *Post's* star reporter adds: "But notice one thing. No one has mentioned the names of Helgi Thorláksson and Hrafn Illugason. Yet they were also spied upon. Is it because they are said to be a threat to the Great European State and the fine and beautiful Olympic Games? So was it alright to spy on them? Alright to violate their human rights? How many others have been subject to personal surveillance?"

The Post's journalists applaud him heartily and Geir feels deeply proud of his work. He has accomplished something of significance for the Icelandic people, in fact the whole of Europe. It is a good feeling.

"You know what," says Geir as he grabs a glass of champagne. "I think I'm going to write up the story of the resignation of Rikard Trinxon. It should make for a great book."

Thora glances sideways. "That is going to provoke a great deal of political uncertainty in Berlin."

34

Europe is without Komizars. The bureaucrats dig out the rule books and find that an obscure old law states that if all Komizars die or resign, it is the European Parliament meeting in Strasbourg that has the right and the duty to appoint new Komizars. The old Parliament Building in Strasbourg has long been handed over to government officials to use as offices, so they are hurriedly moved out and the MEPs crowd into a chamber built for the days when the old European Union was much smaller than the Great European State and had fewer MEPs. But instead of appointing a new set of Komizars, the historic meeting the European Parliament agrees to hold an election among the citizens of Europe for the first democratically elected President of Europe.

Direct, unmediated elections will take place in the spring.

It quickly becomes clear that there are two front runners in the election, though others declare themselves. The young former Komizar Erich Devereaux is one, the other is another former Komizar the experienced Scot Anthony Browne. Browne has a reputation as a fixer who can work quietly behind the scenes to get deals done. He had been promoted rapidly under Trinxon, but he is still seen as his own man and portrays himself as a fresh start for Europe.

The electoral system chosen by the MEPs is based on a form of weighted voting in an electoral college. Each of the 41 states has a number of votes in the college based on its population. Once the population of a state have cast their votes, the candidate with most votes secures all the college votes of that state. For instance, the State of Germany has 324 college votes so whichever candidate wins there will gain 324 in the electoral college. The State of Iceland has one college vote because its population is so low. Whoever wins in Iceland will get only 1 college vote. That is why the presidential candidates spend most of their time in big countries such as France, Britain or Germany and none come to Iceland. The system means that, in theory at least, a candidate could win the election even though he has fewer popular votes than an opponent.

At the start of the race Browne has a clear lead on Devereaux, but the week before Christmas, Browne's campaign is damaged when a reporter broadcasting live asks the Scot's campaign manager for a list of his accomplishments.

"Give me a week; then I'll probably have an answer to your question," he replies with a grin.

The Press swoop and interpret the comment as meaning that nothing good and constructive has ever come from Browne. The hapless campaign manager tries to explain he was only joking, but it is too late. The case has been extremely embarrassing for Browne. Devereaux's supporters publicise the manager's blunder in all the states of Europe and the opinion polls quickly show the gap between the two candidates narrowing.

The race is thought to bear a flavour of American presidential elections, with vast amounts of money being spent on the candidates' campaigns. It soon becomes obvious, however, that Iceland is being left out of the campaigning. It is far away and the population is low out on that cold island upon the farthest sea. The candidates travel throughout the major European cities; from Kiev in the east to London and Dublin in the west; from Istanbul, Naples, and Madrid in the south to Copenhagen, Oslo and Stockholm in the north. But by February neither of them has been to Iceland.

"So who are we going to support?" asks Krummi one February day as the snow lies deep in Reykavík's streets. "Polling day is only a few weeks away. We've got to come up with a firm stance sooner rather than later.'

"I don't know," mutters Helgi. "They both seem as bad as each other. No interest in history or culture, either of them."

"You used to work with Devereaux," Krummi turns to Júlía. "What do you say?"

"I think he is our best bet," says Júlía. "He is a true European and sees Europe as the answer to most problems. But when I knew him he was at least sympathetic to calls for home rule. We are leading our national fight for 'Authority Home'. We are doing well, the cry sounds from mountain to seashore across the length and breadth of Iceland. But we all know that Iceland's demands are badly received by the European bureaucracy. At least Devereaux takes a respectful and diplomatic stance toward the Icelandic problem."

"True," replies Krummi. "But he is hardly enthusiastic is he. I haven't heard him mention Iceland once in a speech."

Júlía smiles to herself. "I still think that the key to the resurrection of the Icelandic nation will be Devereaux's presidency; the victory of public over private interests. The victory of the new over the old."

Helgi sniffs. "But let's proceed cautiously, just in case it all goes wrong."

Three days later in Dresden, Devereaux delivers what his press officers announces will be the key speech of the campaign. He calls it "The New Standards Speech".

"We shall set new standards; they will not depend on what I bring to the citizens of Europe, but rather what I demand from the citizens of Europe. We shall rebuild broken hopes; grapple with the unsolved mysteries of science; the unsolved mysteries of war and peace; the uncrossed threshold of ignorance, prejudice, poverty, and copiousness. We will go where we failed before but this time our journey will be a total victory."

The location for the speech was deliberately chosen. Dresden — the beautiful and splendid city that had been blasted back to the Stone Age in the madness of the 20th century. The speech ends to the tremendous cheers of hundreds of thousands of residents of Dresden.

And the press like it too. *Bild* prints a lead column that declares: "Devereaux preaches a new era, a new Europe. He takes on special interests, monopolies and corporate hegemony; proclaims the promotion of human rights and improved benefits to the poor. Devereaux proposes a Peace Corps for poor nations; for the advancement of education, health care, and free trade. He preaches peace with all faiths, close relationships with Russia, China, and the United States. He proclaims 'With Devereaux come fresh winds to a continent in desperate need for new ideas, new politics – new approach.' On the basis of his New Standards Speech in Dresden, Devereaux is the man."

In March Browne still has a slight lead over Devereaux. The first European elections are exciting and uncertain. The citizens of the continent take an active part in the election race although in Iceland uncertainty prevails concerning the course of events. What place does little Iceland see for itself within the New Europe? Although Júlía has raised the Nationists' hopes, the Solýta Party is still a force in the Althingi though polls show declining faith in its policies.

Sólman has expressed his support for the Scottish Browne. He binds his hopes to the office of Minister for Icelandic Affairs in the government of the first democratically elected President of Europe. Sólman meets influential individuals in Berlin and works tirelessly behind the scenes to promote important issues, as he calls them in an address to his allies. He is optimistic, since a rumour is going around that the "Icelandic Problem" will be resolved on his terms. Sólýta cannot be underestimated.

When he returns to Reykjavík to address an election rally supporting Browne, Sólman reports on his meetings with highly-placed bureaucrats.

"When I left, a high ranking office manager said to me: 'Now you will finally get your own Minister for Iceland here in Berlin.' 'It's possible,' I replied to which he commented: 'Yes, it will certainly happen. They've already budgeted the salary.'" The bureaucrats know what's being proposed and plotted behind the scenes in Berlin."

It is no wonder that Sólman is optimistic.

Júlía's responds to the Browne rally with an odd tranquillity. She has composed a verse that provokes a great deal of attention and in fact debate, because many people try to mangle her words, making them sound as bad as can be; accuse her of lack of ambition on behalf of her nation.

Time to cross out big words,
and stick instead to smaller.
The rabble's flaws we need not praise.
We attend to each word and phrase.

She is accused of speaking in riddles but the young, elegant woman is full of self-confidence. All of her deeds shine brightly; they are a light that hasn't shone from a politician since the Icelanders took their horses and saddles and rode to greet their hero, Hannes Hafstein, almost two centuries earlier. Júlía has no trouble striking the weapons from the hands of her opponents. The nation is inspired by her poetical eloquence:

You, our continent's youngest land,
our own land, our fathers land!
Like an ambitious youth, head held high
your waves whet your peaks to stretch to the sky.
Though cruel misfortune bring you woe
onward and onward through it all you go.

Many, however, are dissatisfied with Júlía's rhetoric. She composes a poem about the sun that loves everything so much that it is heavenly to live. This is called irresponsible gibberish, because people feel there is nothing heavenly about the situation at home in Iceland; thousands without work, the poor growing in number; subsidies low and scanty, causing the people to buy one-way tickets to Europe.

"The national ship is sinking and the wretched girl is writing poems about Heaven," comments a disgruntled man in the radio program "Spirit of the Nation" on *Euro-News*. However soon afterwards on the program there is a strong, fierce criticism of the Great European State. This is considered reprobate, and the program is cancelled.

"It's as though the girl lives in an ivory tower," Sólman tells Editor John.

It is reported that Júlía has met with Devereaux in Berlin, just a few weeks before the election. "What the hell is she doing in Berlin? The meeting is a tasteless attempt to get the Icelanders to elect the French-German bastard who is best kept on a hook with the rest of the overcoats," says Editor John, in a frustrated tone.

35

Media around the world follows the first European presidential election with great interest. It is said that if Europe sneezes the world will catch cold. It means a great deal for the inhabited world for Europe to resolve its constitutional crisis and strengthen the foundations of democracy.

The candidates meet in the most talked about political debate of the century when a watershed is reached in the campaign for the presidency. The debate comes at the worst possible time for Browne who has been forced to take a break from the campaign for a fortnight, after injuring a knee on the campaign trail in Romania. A car door slammed into it, snapping a tendon. The wound became infected and Browne was admitted to a hospital, where he was given large doses of antibiotics. Browne has lost weight and looks extremely bad, with dark circles under his eyes. He had vowed to visit all the member states of Europe but has been forced to abandon his plans.

The debate is the day after Browne's release from hospital. Approximately 48% of Europeans watch the candidates' debate. Browne, emaciated and haggard, comes directly from a strenuous campaign meeting to the debates, whereas Devereaux is relaxed and tanned. To top it all off Browne has refused cosmetics and the stubble on his lower jaw stands out; his five o'clock shadow makes him resemble the most shadowy Mafiosi.

Devereaux is the first to take the stage.

"A great 19th century American president said that America could not exist half enslaved, half free. He was prepared to go to war to abolish slavery though it ultimately cost him his life. In the 20th century another American president defied the infamous Wall that split the great Berlin. On one side freedom presided, on the other side a whole nation was locked inside a colossal prison. 'Ich bin ein Berliner,' the president proclaimed. A quarter of a century later his counterpart urged the Kremlin to tear down the Wall. A couple of years later the Wall collapsed.

"I say to you:

"Europe can not exist half this, half that; half democratic, half bureaucratic with no-one looking over the shoulders of a ruling Komizariat, the Nomenklatura in shady basements. That's why we are having these elections. The kind of country we have here in Europe, the kind of society we build, the strength of our society, will be based on freedom. If we fail, freedom fails and we have failed generations to come. I think it is time for Europe to start moving again."

Devereaux is relaxed and eloquent.

Browne looks uneasy; he is hesitant and sweating as he takes the stage.

"I know the way to progress. I have the programs to move Europe forward, that I promise you. Erich Devereaux implies that Europe has been standing still, that we've had stagnation and retreated into a shelter. I beg to disagree. We have been moving forward, though more can always be done. We have the Great European State. It is essential to keep the state together and united. There can be no room for the secession of member states. Disunity will lead to disaster. There is competition that must be faced; America, Russia, China and India. I ask of you that you do the right thing and vote for me."

People are baffled by Browne's performance. No one understands why he feels compelled to come to the defence of the establishment; of the former Komizariat. His performance is so poor that his mother calls immediately following the debate and asks her son: "Are you ill, Tony?"

In the wake of the debate, Devereaux grabs the initiative in the fight for the presidency. Polls show that he has edged ahead, though just barely.

The election is held on Sunday, 8 May. Turnout is just over 50%, which exceeds the brightest expectations of all the news commentators. Erich Devereaux receives 49.7% of the votes and Anthony Browne 49.6%. The victory is close, but Devereaux is duly elected president. Both candidates receive approximately 172 million votes, but in the end Devereaux has the edge. Devereaux's victory is decided by a close and unexpected victory in the State of Italy. Browne is the narrow victor in most constituencies, but the figures from the ballot boxes in Naples result in a landslide for Devereaux that give him the edge across the nation as a whole. So he gains all 277 electoral college votes from Italy.

Browne's supporters in Italy claim that the result was rigged. They say that the controversial mayor of Naples, Silvistino Del Tronto, is said to have his way no matter what. Browne declines to submit an appeal, which could cause a constitutional crisis that critics say may bring down the Great European State completely.

"We must protect the unity of the European state," says Browne, addressing an army of reporters. If Browne had won in the State of Italy, he would have received more electors even if he had had fewer votes in the popular vote. Such is the voting system.

Devereaux is in Berlin for the announcement of the count. On his first day in his new office he receives a visit from Slobodan Paśiĉevic, the head of the EIA, the European Intelligence Agency.

"May I be among the first to congratulate you on your assumption of office," says Paśiĉevic though his face remains inscrutable. "I know you will be very busy over the coming days, but I am afraid that I have the duty of bringing the incoming President up to date on the security threats to the Great European State."

"Of course," replies Devereaux. "I was hoping that there would not be many threats. We seek peace, do we not?"

"Indeed, Mr President, but there are always threats and I have no intention of discussing military matters," Paśiĉevic comments.

"I will withdraw the military from the Caspian Sea area, you know that," Devereaux interrupts.

Paśiĉevic face is as inscrutable as before as he avoids looking the

President in the eye. "I have no intention of meddling with politics. However, there is a Russian spy active in our navy at a fairly senior level. A team of Americans claiming to be monitoring polar bear populations have landed on the disputed islands off Greenland – and they seem to have some highly sophisticated equipment with them that is somewhat unusual for polar bear monitoring. And an English group calling itself "The Spitfires" seems to be planning some unnecessarily provocative political demonstrations. Nothing very serious, Mr President. Nothing at all. But I do need to tell you all about it."

Devereaux nods. He guesses, rightly, that he is in for a long meeting.

At his inauguration Devereaux holds a speech that is said to mark a turning point for Europe. After swearing an oath to the constitution, Devereaux states: "Today we do not celebrate a party victory, but rather are gathered in celebration of freedom; the freedom that signifies both a limit and an origin; the freedom that marks both renewal and transition. Because I have sworn to you and to Almighty God the same solemn oath that our forefathers adopted in Rome more than a century ago.

"The world is entirely different today, because in his mortal hand man has the power to do away with every kind of human poverty; the power to do away with every kind of human life. Yet still on everyone's lips throughout the world are the same beliefs for which our ancestors fought; the belief that human rights are not granted by the generosity of the state but are rather received from the hand of God.

"We do not dare to be unmindful today of the fact that we are the inheritors of a revolution. Let the news be spread from this place and at this moment, that the torch has been passed into the hands of a new generation of Europeans who are proud of their ancient heritage and who will neither witness nor permit that slowly but surely there will be cast aside the human rights to which we are still bound today, at home and throughout the world.

"Let all nations know, that we will sacrifice everything, bear any burden, endure every kind of trial, support every friend and resist every enemy in order to ensure the continuation and development of freedom.

"All of this is included in our vow — and more.

"To our old allies, with whom we share a common origin, we pledge our most faithfully devoted friendship. If we stand together, there is little that we cannot accomplish through concerted effort. Divided, we are capable of little, because we lack the courage to stand against powerful opposition if we are disagreed and divided. The threats that are imminent are unlike those in past times; now amoral terrorists can blast Paris back to the Stone Age. We pledge a struggle against such madness; wherever on Earth the conflict needs to take place.

"We pledge to the nations that they shall not be free of old European colonial rulers only to be replaced by other, much more stringent despots. We cannot expect that they will always follow our lead. But we trust that they will always stand guard over their own freedom; mindful that those who ignorantly thought to gain power by taking the tiger from behind, have up until now become its prey.

"To the people who in the hovels and villages of half the world attempt to break free from the claws of neediness, we pledge our utmost support for self-sufficiency as long as it is needed; not because we are angling for the votes of these people, but only because it is right. If a free society is incapable of helping the many who are poor, it cannot save the few who are rich.

"To the societies in the South we make a specific pledge: to transform friendly gestures into charitable deeds within a new alliance of progress; to support free men and free governments in breaking the chains of poverty. But this peaceful revolution in the direction of hope may fall prey to hostile powers. Let all of our neighbours know that we will join hands with them in resisting attacks and national betrayals in all places in Africa. May all other states be certain that Africa intends to manage its own household.

"And finally, to those who choose to oppose us. We do not direct a vow, but rather a determined recommendation that both parties join in the quest for peace before the dark powers of destruction, which the sciences have unleashed, plunge all of mankind into self-destruction knowingly or by accident.

"Let us remember that courtesy is not a weakness, but that honesty requires positive proof. We will never make deals out of fear.

"But let us never fear to negotiate.

"Let us unite everywhere on Earth to fulfil the command of Isaiah to 'undo the heavy burdens and let the oppressed go free.'

"And if it proves possible through a unified assault to make a clearing in the dark forest of suspicion, let us unite throughout the new world law and justice, whereby the strong are just, the weak are secure, and the peace is preserved.

"This will not be completed in the first hundred days. Nor the first thousand days nor during the days of this government, nor even while we who are here still live on this Earth.

"But let us begin.

"It is up to you, dear fellow citizens, rather than me, whether our plan succeeds or fails. European generations have been called to arms. The trumpet still sounds; not to bear arms though we require arms; not to battle though we are armed; but rather to carry the weight of a long, dismal battle year after year; 'rejoicing in hope, patient in tribulation'; a struggle against the common enemies of mankind: tyranny, poverty, disease, and war.

"Can we create a universal global alliance from north to south, east to west, against these enemies, to secure for all humanity a more fertile life? Will you participate in this historic effort?

"In the long history of the world only a few generations have been granted the task of defending freedom at crucial moments. I do not shirk from that responsibility; I celebrate it. I do not think that any of us would wish to trade places with any other nation or with any other generation. The laboriousness, faith, and devotion that we put into this effort will illuminate our land and any person who assists it. The brilliance of that fire can truly light up the entire world.

"Therefore, my fellow countrymen, ask not what Europe can do for you but what you can do for Europe.

"My fellow citizens throughout the world: ask not what Europe can do for you but what we together can do for the freedom of mankind. And finally, whether you are citizens of Europe or the world; demand of us here strength and sacrifices in equally sublime measure as of yourselves. With good consciences as our only certain reward and with history as the final judge of our works we turn to the governance of this country that we love at the same time as we ask God for his blessing and help, ever mindful that here on Earth each work of God must become our own true work."

The young president gives his speech at Paris Square, before the magnificent Beethoven Hall in Berlin. Around two hundred thousand people celebrate the first elected President of Europe, Erich Devereaux; the Franco-German humanist from the territory that for centuries has been the bone of contention between the superpowers of mainland Europe. This is thought to be a symbolic reconciliation. Again and again people applaud, celebrating the certainty that the speech will live in the history books for all time. Beside Devereaux stands the defeated candidate Browne. Devereaux has made him Vice-President in a gesture of unity and reconciliation to his opponents. The move has gone down well.

36

Sólman is surprised to bump into Júlía as he boards his flight out of Keflavík to Berlin to meet with the newly elected president of Europe. The executive class area is not too big on the aircraft, so Sólman sits next to Júlía; they share many interests. They toast each other with white wine and have a good long chat about poetry. After arriving in Berlin they go to meet with the new president.

Sólman feels it important to hold a meeting with the new president at least as soon as that girl. As soon as they land, Sólman leaps into an official car and is whisked off to the Presidential Residence. While in the waiting room Júlía arrives, along with her staff. She gives her name to the presidential aide and states, powerfully and authoritatively, that she had an appointment right then and there. The aide goes off, but when he comes back it is Sólman who he calls for and ushers into the Presidential Office. Sólman cannot help smirking at Júlía's discomfort.

Sólman's meeting with Devereaux is short. He makes a bid for the special office of Minister for Icelandic Affairs, based in Berlin. Devereaux listens to Sólman's case with courtesy and understanding.

"Now let's get down to brass tacks," says Devereaux, before adding in a soft voice: "I agree with you, dear Sólman Smithson. Iceland has been cheated of its rightful share. We have to find a solution to Iceland's special circumstances."

Sólman is extremely pleased with the response of the new European President. There is no arrogance, no coarseness. On the contrary, he is modest and moderate. Sólman likes Erich Devereaux immediately and feels that the president will repay the friendship. However, he must admit that the president's position is unclear in many ways. Does he want an Icelander in his government, or would he go even further?

As Sólman gets back into the official car that is to take him to his hotel, an aide hands him a memory stick with that day's copy of that day's Icelandic *The Post*. "Very efficient", thinks Sólman. He switches on his reader. Editor John has written a strong-worded article about the rubbish and nonsense that he feels has taken over the politicians. Sólman smiles and settles back into the plush unholstery to read it. Of course, he knows what it will say as he had discussed the article with Editor John the night before.

John feels it absurd to think that the new president would wish to go further than his predecessor, Komizar Trinxon. "Yet things are getting out of hand when 'an important Icelander in Berlin' is quoted as saying that we should have a minister, based in Reykjavík. More pitiful nonsense is certainly hardly possible to imagine." The editor is of course referring to Júlía.

He writes: "There is a woman whom everyone knows has very little understanding of politics. Her knowledge and intelligence go in a completely different direction. She is incapable of explaining matters correctly or sensibly from an Icelandic point of view. There are also people who shoulder no responsibility. They prattle ignorantly about how the new president in Berlin will take a different approach to the case; somehow different! Besides that, there are fully knowledgeable and diverse witnesses to the fact that the new president views the ministry seat and residence of the Minister for Iceland in Berlin with the same eyes as has been done for a long time. That's how out of touch the reactionaries are."

Sólman switches off the reader as he arrives at his luxury hotel. "That'll put that jumped up poet girl in her place," he thinks. And yet a feeling of irritation slowly comes over Sólman. None of the people he expected to contact him in Berlin have been in touch. He checks his holph. Nothing. It appears to him as if the office is slipping from his grasp. He seems to have no allies to consult and the bureaucrats in the Icelandic division are scarcely well-disposed to him.

Next day he manages to buttonhole Devereaux at a reception and gives him a piece of his mind. "It surprises me how people have managed to mislead you. It's absurd for your government to chase after the minority in Iceland; a minority that in addition is mostly composed of Nationists," says Sólman gravely, in terse European.

"We will never support reactionary zealots," replies Devereaux slowly and deliberately. "Now I must go. You know how these events are. If I don't smile at the right people they will get fed up with me."

Sólman is extremely dissatisfied. He feels as if he is losing control of the situation. There is more to it than meets the eye. He slips out and makes a call on his holph to Editor John and Múli Thordarsen. "It seems that it would be best and most sensible to get fully on board with the president's program, which is in fact our program. It doesn't matter whether the power is based in Reykjavík or Berlin," says Sólman. The colleagues are in John's office at *The Post*. They look in amazement at Sólman's half-size image as he sits, holding a cognac glass. They look at each other and shake their heads. It seems that their colleague is losing his grasp of events. Sólman is actually claiming that the proposal for home rule comes from him.

Sólman does not notice their reactions, since he looks constantly into his glass. "The new president says that he is eager to accept my proposals and fulfil our wishes for authority home. I take this with gratitude. There is thus no disagreement between me and Devereaux, but rather the most excellent concord. That poet girl pretends to have been victorious but her proposals are considered impossible here in Berlin," says Sólman, in his own world.

Editor John quickly finds an excuse to end the call, being very alarmed at the way that things have turned upside down. Sólman's mental fluctuations are increasing; at one moment he has a tailwind, at another an Icelandic winter storm in his face. To Sólman it appears clear that behind the curtain Júlía is enjoying the support of Devereaux and back home Governor Mangi Steffensen has put himself on the same level as the poet girl. Then he feels that Devereaux is letting him down. Sólman slips back into the reception and eyes the idiot president with dislike. Everything is going against

239

him. Sólman's isolation increases day by day.

Júlía personally finds it comical to meet Sólman again and again in the waiting rooms of the European administration. She has made giant strides in her talks in Berlin, unsparingly employing her charm and contacts. She would have preferred for Sólman to give up his fight for the ministerial position in Berlin, and instead focus his energies on the independence of the Icelandic nation. She is, however, blissfully ignorant of most of what Sólman is getting up to and the meetings that he has.

The day of the drinks reception Helgi Thorláksson is out west at his family's old farm in Hrafnseyri. Helgi has moved to the Westfjords. He has settled at his old birthplace in Hrafnseyri, since he lost his job in Copenhagen there was nowhere else to go. However, he regrets nothing and is ecstatic to have returned. He stands out in front of the old farm, gazing at the magnificent mountain scenery. "Iceland's fortune becomes its greatest weapon with a good captain on the bridge," he says loudly, looking over the mirror-smooth fjord from the farm, which is located quite high in the dell. Overhead towers Ánarmúli Peak, erect and impressive.

What a sight!

Helgi has bought a little boat and gone out fishing from the boathouse down below Svartseyrarbakki, but the European bloodhounds from the Fisheries Agency had chased him down, so he can expect charges and fines for his actions. The small, white wooden church with it's red roof is 200 years old now. Twice it had been blown off its foundation, but the Creator had made it so that the church came down in one piece both times. The locals simply heaved it back onto its foundation as if nothing were more natural. Hrafnseyri is associated with its namesake from the 12th century; Hrafn, the widely travelled chieftain who studied medicine in Salerno down south in Italy and won the respect of chieftains throughout the continent.

"Icelanders are and have always been grandiose," says Helgi out loud, smiling to himself.

On the homefield are outlines of the church from the 12th century and the old churchyard. It is heavenly to stroll from the homefield down Afglapastígur to the seaside and collect shells, conches, and crabs for a delicious fish soup. He also enjoys walking to the Grélutóttir remains where Rauðfeldur Grímsson and his wife Grélöð settled during the Age of Settlements. They had claimed land in Dufan Valley, but Grélöð thought the ground there smelled bad, so they bought all the land between Langanes and Stapi and set up house at Eyri. There Grélöð had closed her eyes and breathed in the "honey fragrance from the grass."

The honey fragrance from the grass can still be smelt as the grass undulates in the warm southerly wind. Suddenly Helgi's holph comes to live. It is Júlía.

"Iceland's freedom is the right political cause," she tells him, "while a ministerial position in Berlin would be misfortunate. But perhaps this will all turn out for the better. What program we can present will soon come clear. I've been pestering Devereaux's closest advisors far too much. In fact I sensed that from the president today. He made light of it and called me an extremely diligent woman, whatever that means. That's how things go here in Berlin," Júlía says, laughing her tender voice.

Helgi looks at her full-size hologram and finds it peculiar to see the Westfjord mountains in the background. It is as if she is there, not in Berlin. She is truly Icelandic, through and through.

"Oh, must go. Devereaux is on the line," says Júlía with a smile.

Helgi has been extremely satisfied with the vigorous conduct of this magnificent woman. "I see that you are in their good books and you achieve everything you set your mind on," he says cheerfully, smiling at Júlía as her image vanishes.

The comrades Krummi and Helgi are happy with their decision to have brought in Júlía to join the new Icelandic cause. Júlía has the trust of her nation and of the highest authorities in Europe.

Over the following days, Júlía works frenziedly, without allowing herself any rest. Despite her short political career there is no denying that she works quickly and efficiently on difficult political solutions. She has no trouble getting people on her side; she achieves results. She has Devereaux's confidence. Júlía is invited to address a meeting of the State Council, presided over by the President.

No Icelander has ever been granted such an honour.

However, all is not as it seems.

In Berlin men in thick overcoats, their wide-brimmed hats shadowing their faces, are seen more and more often, hurrying about some business of their own. On a dull Tuesday evening a black-clad woman with a lace veil covering her face slinks down into a dark, smoke-filled basement. She pushes the door open and steps into the gloomy room.

"Well?" asks a cold voice. She smiles at the man in the black suit. Unlike most she is not frightened of him.

"All is going well. Our tame MEPs and the journalists in our pay are coming round to see our point of view. It is whispered in the wind that the freedom prattle of the young president is intolerable, putting the unity of the European state at risk. There is a growing consensus that Icelandic withdrawal from the Great European State is completely unacceptable, absolutely unacceptable."

"I see no sign of it yet," states the voice.

"My people are growing restless, but we've agreed to follow your lead. You instructed me to keep opposition quiet, to work behind the scenes. That is what I have been doing. If you want me to start placing stories in the media or getting MEPs to make speeches I can do so easily. We're ready at the word go."

"No," whispers the Vulture. "Not yet." He kisses her hand and the woman in black retreats back up the stairs.

The Vulture watches her with an unblinking stare.

The dark forces gnaw and gnaw.

37

The young European nation rallies behind its president; his humanity and eloquence – its new-found freedom. The southerly breeze in Berlin puts a wind in the sails of Iceland. The Icelanders in Berlin gradually side with Júlía and the sovereignty of the Icelandic nation. They send Devereaux a declaration in support of Júlía. Among those who have joined with the Nationists are old unbending Unionists and Crats. A grand dinner is held for Júlía in Berlin. The extensive and comprehensive support for sovereign Iceland does not escape the notice of the new president, to whom so many hopes are pinned.

"Júlía is killing me with her elegance," says a disappointed Sólman to Editor John. He perceives that the match is being lost. Sólman is no longer invited to meet with President Devereaux; his time appears past. At home in Iceland, members of the Sólýta Party are aware that they are fighting a losing battle.

Even the great men of Europe support the Icelandic cause of freedom. "Icelanders will never be happy unless they achieve independence; unless authority comes home to the hands of its own government, which owes a debt of responsibility for its deeds to the oldest democratic parliament in the world as well as the Icelandic voters," the world renowned critic Georg Brandes writes in a key article for the *Politiken* in Copenhagen. "Better to let them have it now, than see Europe get bogged down in endless disputes and arguments. I would rather have Iceland as a good neighbour than as a bad lodger."

Three months after arriving in Berlin for her first meeting with President Devereaux, Júlía has a holph conversation with Krummi.

"Better to have set out than to have stayed at home," she says about her trip to Berlin. There is a touch of satisfaction in her statement.

Krummi nods in agreement. "Sólman would have misinterpreted and reversed matters if he had acted alone in negotiating with the European authorities."

"Indeed," agrees Júlía. "The European media have sided with us. I feel that that's half the battle won. I can be a bit too intense at times but I hope that my failings don't do any harm. In the opinion of wiser men there is nothing preventing the Icelandic nation from achieving sovereignty with dignity. Although I don't see any positive result clearly, we have come so far in the matter that it is in fact up to us — to us Icelanders, whether we achieve independence," says Júlía with an earnest expression.

Krummi smiles as he looks at Júlía's hologram. It always puts him in a good mood when he chats with this magnificent woman. "Your destiny is to lead your people. You put everyone out there in Berlin into check; check and mate," he says with a laugh as they say goodbye.

Bríet smiles up her giant husband. "She is doing a good job for us," she says. "Not bad for a mere 'poet girl'."

Krummi and Bríet are walking barefooted in Bjarnarey with their three grandchildren: Hjálmur, Kristján, and Bryndís. Bjarnarey Island reaches quite high and precipitous cliffs enclose the island on all sides except the northeast. There they have gone with the children, although Hvannhilla is quite a difficult hike. At its peak Bjarnarey rises 161 meters above sea level, a short distance south of Elliðaey. Puffins fly in and out of their holes on Bjarnarey this sunny day. Sheep step lightly around the steep pasture. In the middle of the island is a grassy mountain peak with a depression. Within this is the spatter cone Bunki. It feels good walking barefooted, connecting to mother Earth.

Krummi feels good about life, feels reinvigorated.

So does Bríet. "It was crucial getting Júlía to join the cause. She doesn't have too high of an opinion of herself. You would have had to answer to the past in Berlin. It would have gotten in the way, since Berlin's policy is not to make deals with terrorists," she says with a smile.

Krummi gives her a big smile. He knows that Bríet is right. They have discussed this often. "I would have brought them putrid pollock," he says with a grin, his white teeth flashing in his black beard.

"Who's Júlía?" Bryndís asks his grandmother.

"She is a model woman: independent, intellectual, educated, elegant, and is returning our freedom to us," replies the girl's grandmother.

"What's freedom?" ask Hjálmur and Kristján.

Bríet smiles; she is stuck for an answer. How do you define freedom to a four-year-old child? "A puffin is free when he flies off after fry for his nestlings in their hole under Bunki. We are free when we are granted the freedom to take responsibility for our lives," says Grandma Bríet, smiling at her young.

"Freedom has its home here in Bjarnarey," says Grandpa Krummi, with a blissful expression.

In order to reiterate and underline his good intentions, President Devereaux invites all of the Althingi MPs to Berlin for a state visit. The MP-trip is conceived as a precursor to negotiations on Iceland's status within the United States of Europe. Devereaux will personally chair the European negotiations delegation and Júlía the Icelandic one. Júlía has a mind of her own regarding the negotiations and Devereaux is fully aware of the delicacy of the matter in Europe. It is by no means easy to find a solution satisfactory to both parties. The European president's initiative is very much appreciated in Reykjavík where the MP-trip is interpreted as "...Europe's earnest desire to satisfy Iceland."

The arrival of the Icelandic MPs in Berlin is described by the influential newspaper *Die Welt* in a leading article: "It is our hope that the Icelanders' Althingi might gain living proof that all freethinking people in Europe wish wholeheartedly for Iceland to feel that it is as free as the rest of us. The time should be past, and will never again return, when the wishes of the Icelanders are buried in harsh and arrogant government offices."

Die Welt's leading article is considered a sign of European friendliness toward the Icelanders, but especially German friendliness, Iceland and Germany having always been bound by strong ties of friendship and culture.

The MPs are invited to breakfast in the presidential palace, which is bedecked with flags at their arrival. A crowd cheers them. Devereaux recalls the debt of gratitude that European culture owes to old Icelandic literature: "the most dynamic art in the Nordic countries." He praises the Icelanders for "not being lukewarm; for the obstinacy that does not melt any more than the snow on Iceland's mountains; for passions that do not cool any more than the hot springs in the land of the midnight sun. Your perseverance leads to victory."

Júlía asks to be heard and expresses her gratitude for the invitation and the evident European hospitality: "When we arrived the country smiled at us, summer-fair and sparkling with sunshine. We were not sure what warmed the roots of our hearts more: the loveliness of the country or the gentle amity that greeted us from the crowd who came to cheer us. Those who know the history of Iceland in centuries past know that what has best kept Iceland alive and protected the nation from all tragedy is the memory of our former freedom and independence and a firm grip on our nationality and national rights, small and large. Freedom is even today the most sensitive and delicate feeling in the hearts of the Icelanders."

The MP-trip inspires great celebration throughout Iceland, since the MPs do not beat around the bush about the magnificent and pleasant receptions. It is more joy than anything else that inspires unanimity regarding Iceland's special European status; the new harmony after the controversies of recent decades wakens undivided attention in Europe. *Die Welt* discusses the Icelanders' concord in a leading story: "Toward us they were all Icelanders and everyone content. This strengthened their demands and gained them respect. In addition, it witnessed to a high political maturity."

The MP-trip is a resounding success.

In its wake Devereaux makes an official visit to Iceland. There is a great deal of preparation for the president's visit, the nation having become increasingly optimistic. The entire nation greets Devereaux with respect. The main streets are adorned with flower arrangements and heather bouquets. The city centre is one huge crowd of people. For the first time since the abolition of the Republic, Icelandic women are dressed in traditional dresses and mantles. The nation is bedecked in its finest as it welcomes the arrival of the president. Even the sun shines clearly and brightly over the mountains. Júlía herself is wearing traditional dress as she walks onto Austurvöllur through the ancient doors of the Althingi and welcomes her old colleague. They ride to Thingvellir on Icelandic horses, and thence to Gullfoss and Geysir.

Devereaux and Júlía lead. The president, who is an experienced horseman, had expressed a special wish for a riding tour. He has never before ridden the native Icelandic breed with its great bushy mane and swift step. The entire nation knows of Júlía's love for horses from her poetry. The major newspaper *Bild* states in a news report from Iceland that there is no doubt that a great deal of amity prevails there regarding Devereaux. But then it goes on to say that "There is no doubt that the independence movement in Iceland is small and has little significance."

Many people are surprised at the article.

The Vulture is not surprised.

Devereaux and Júlía ride side-by-side the steep slopes of Kambar, east of Reykjavík. They have been in constant conversation about everything under the sun and all the sights around them. The President scarcely has strong enough words to express his admiration for the Icelandic scenery.

A banquet has been arranged at Kolviðarhóll.

There the President holds a speech that raises a considerable uproar in Europe. "Let this journey of ours create a trustworthy bond between the European nation and our Icelandic siblings. My goal is truth and justice for both nations. There are few things as majestic as the free Icelandic eagle."

All of the major European media reprint or rebroadcast Devereaux's remarks: television and radio as the lead story, while newspapers devote their front pages to his statements. It appears clear where the president is heading. He wishes to grant the Icelanders freedom to choose or reject full sovereignty. This goes completely counter to the policy of every European Komizar this century.

Frankfurter Algemeine Zeitung quotes European parliamentarians as saying the president must have misspoken. Devereaux, however, shakes his head and does not let the uproar and dissatisfaction affect him. "This is no misstatement; it is exactly what I said," reiterates President Devereaux.

Many people think it clear where Júlía is headed. Her influence on the president is more powerful than those who have resolutely urged him to reject Icelandic demands for sovereignty; even to threaten the Icelanders.

A tall, dark-clad woman on high-heel shoes wearing a stylish cloche hat with a black lace veil covering her face and men in overcoats with stand-up collars and wide-brimmed hats, hurry down murky basement stairs and disappear into the darkness. The clock strikes ten in the evening. The rain comes down in Berlin as if poured from a bucket; flashes of lightnings light up the overcast night sky and thunderclaps cause passers-by to shudder, people run for shelter. A dim light gleams in the basement room, hanging in the grey air over an oval table. A man invisible to everyone waits in the dark shadows in the corner.

"He is uncontrollable, this fool of a president is completely out of control!" roars a chubby frustrated man. He sits at the end of the table; is likely in his fifties. "This nonsense must be stopped," he shouts, beating his clenched fist on the table so that his enormous double chin flaps and beads of sweat pop out on his forehead. Pedro Angel Mortianŏs cannot hide his frustration. He owns one of Europe's biggest weaponry corporations, with operations across Europe.

"Precisely. Devereaux is putting the unity of the state in danger," says Edyta Zarębianka. She pushes the black veil away from her face to reveal an elegant, short-haired woman in her thirties. Edyta Zarębianka has been a lobbyist in Berlin for twelve years. Her clients hold the main strings of European industry and business. "I have tried lobbying him to send European troops to the Caspian Sea to ensure the flow of oil to the West. The fool thinks the war there is only minor and wants to pull out. I have tried everything."

Mortianŏs raises an eyebrow. He knows that Zarębianka is said to achieve the goals of her clients without much regard to the means she employs. She is clearly a tough customer with whom you wouldn't want to tangle, dressed according to the latest fashion. She turns boldly to a man sitting at the middle of the table. "The stage is yours," says Zarębianka sharply.

A wry smile plays on Rudolf Kessler's face. He gives Zarębianka and then Mortianŏs a meaningful look for a few moments, but then turns to a sturdy man with salt-and-pepper hair opposite him. "What do we do for these honourable people, Senor Buscetti?" he asks in a confidential voice.

Salvatore Buscetti is wearing a pin-striped suit, a light blue shirt with a white collar and a colourful tie in a style that had once been popular. He holds a large Cuban cigar. "A man does what needs doing and what has always been done on my island," says Buscetti, standing up and looking over the group. The Sicilian inhales, but then stubs out the cigar on the hardwood table, leaving a large burn-spot. He exhales the smoke. "The job will be done with utmost professionalism," Buscetti adds as he bends over the table. Mortianŏs and Zarębianka nod in agreement.

The room is dead silent.

"Good, then we don't need to say anything more about it," says

Buscetti, walking to the door with his constant escort, Benedetto Benso, who has had his eyes on the sexy Zaręþianka. Buscetti looks at those present, puts on his thick bright purple overcoat and then leaves along with Benso.

The cigar stands on end.

Kessler looks at his table mate. Olav Seiferdal rocks in his seat.

Mortianŏs breaks the silence. "Good! It's decided."

Zaręþianka smiles at Kessler, obviously pleased with the outcome of the meeting.

From out of the shadows walks a man in a black suit. The Vulture nods in agreement as he kisses Zaręþianka's hand and nods approvingly to Mortianŏs. Seiferdal feels a cold shiver down his spine as the Vulture looks him sharply into the eye. The Euro-Norwegian blinks and looks away as those squinting eyes seem to tear into him. He has never met the Vulture before, although he's been working for the man through Kessler.

Seiferdal is quite annoyed at the obvious rejection so he clears his throat, points to the cigar and laughs nervously. "The Mafia knows how to make a point," he comments but it all comes out rather awkwardly.

The Vulture bends quickly and grabs Seiferdal by the collar in order to draw the Norwegian close to his face. "The Mafia were never here, idiot," he whispers in a threatening voice. Seiferdal feels everything freeze within him, he's literally paralysed with sheer terror. The Vulture throws the Norseman back into the chair and gives Kessler an irritated look. "Can't you do better than this?" he hurls insultingly at the German.

Kessler gives Seiferdal an annoyed look. The Norwegian is drenched in sweat.

Mortianŏs is quite taken aback by all this but Zaręþianka is calm and relaxed. The Vulture certainly knows how to make an entry and strike fear into people, keeping them on their toes. She smiles and nods approvingly at the scowling man in the black suit. This spectacular performance is good news. The Vulture walks out of the room.

The Sicilian has been approved.

38

The goddess Victoria raises an iron cross beneath her raised eagle wings in a war chariot drawn by four horses at the top of the Brandenburg Gate in Berlin. The sun's rays glitter on the chariot this fine June day. Through the windows of Beethoven Hall, Erich Devereaux and Júlía Ingólfsdóttir look silently at the gate, which, along with what is now the presidential palace, forms the chief symbol of Europe. Formerly the gate was enwrapped by the history of mighty Germany. The great hall, dedicated to the immortal composer, stands at the edge of Paris Square, opposite the splendid Brandenburg Gate. The whirling life under the linden trees converses with time's eternal stream.

Ever since the Brandenburg Gate was raised in honour of ancient Athens, history has gone round and round and round in circles. Napoleon Bonaparte marched through Brandenburg, snatched the war chariot and brought it back with him to Paris. The chariot, however, was returned to its former seat after the fall of the great war emperor, but the goddess of victory with her iron cross replaced the goddess with olive leaf.

That did not bode well.

The Nazis made the gate a symbol of the Third Reich. Brandenburg withstood WWII's rain of bombs but became a link in the notorious Berlin Wall of Soviet Germany. "Ich bin ein Berliner," said John F. Kennedy, waving the torch of freedom, but a quarter of a century later the Wall was still standing. "General Secretary Gorbachev, if you seek peace, if you seek prosperity for the Soviet Union and Eastern Europe, if you seek liberalization: Come here to this gate! Mr. Gorbachev, open this gate! Mr. Gorbachev, tear down this wall," said Ronald Reagan. Two years later the Wall tumbled down like a house of cards. The grey wall — a symbol of the largest prison in the history of man — crumbled to dust before mankind's desire for freedom.

Berlin can look back to different days.

"I always keep a suitcase in Berlin," says Júlía with a smile as she quotes Marlene Dietrich, Berlin's most famous daughter. Júlía had always liked visiting the metropolis on the banks of the Spree. She is very happy with the discussions of recent weeks, which have exceeded expectations.

"On its eternal journey around the world humanity keeps its suitcase in Berlin," replies Devereaux with a wry smile.

"Exactly," says Júlía.

"We have reached an historic consensus that Europe and Iceland can be proud of. A consensus that will hopefully heal the wounds of the past, once and for all; wounds of colonial oppression and the mistakes of Europe. With this agreement, the second restoration of the Icelandic Republic begins," says Devereaux.

"At the signing of the agreement in Rome after the elections in Iceland," suggests Júlía and adds: "The second Icelandic Republic will be rebuilt, and will hopefully stand for centuries upon centuries to come," she adds.

"In the eternal city, appropriately. The European train set out from there on a blank piece of paper. We have corrected the mistakes and Europe shows its determination that all of its states enjoy the benefits of the Union," replies Devereaux.

They take hands; Júlía feels clearly that the nation will welcome the agreement, which will hopefully be a driving force for progress and optimism, as had happened almost 200 years earlier.

Iceland's special position within Europe is recognized; the Icelandic people as inhabitants of the westernmost country in Europe, on the farthest reaches of the sea at the junction of tectonic plates between the continents of Europe and America. The Second Icelandic Republic will be founded at the Althingi at Thingvellir. The office of the President of the Republic will be reinstated, the Althingi restored to its former status and a prime minister will lead the government. Iceland will have complete and unchallenged control of its fishing grounds. The Icelandic government regains complete and unchallenged authority to make international agreements with countries outside of Europe. Icelandic MPs will no longer have seats on the European Parliament. Iceland has achieved all of the goals that its MPs had agreed to during their Berlin Trip the previous year. The MPs' solidarity in Berlin was considered a sign of Icelanders' political maturity.

The settlement is called the Berlin Draft.

39

The Icelanders receive the news of the Berlin Draft with great joy when it is first reported. People run out onto the streets, blow horns eagerly and wave the old Icelandic flag. Soon, however, a new note is struck as elections loom around the corner.

Júlía scans the newspapers with a grim expression on her face. "If it didn't make me sound paranoid," she mutters to herself, "I'd tell Helgi that there is a great conspiracy working against us." It seems as if her opponents are set on destroying her political reputation. Dark forces behind closed doors have formed an alliance against Júlía's leadership.

There are those who proclaim it crazy to leave Europe at a time of crisis when all European nations should unite in defending the great United States of Europe and its newly established democracy. Under no circumstances should it be accepted that a gash be cut in the Great European State. There must be no betrayal of our European brothers and sisters. The Berlin Draft is said to be like sailing a tiny dinghy into a brutal Atlantic storm. The nation won't stand a chance all alone in the Atlantic without the steadying support of Europe. The króna will throw the nation down the gaping mouth of Eyjafjallajökull.

Other eyes are scanning the same newspapers, but with a gleam of triumph. The former policeman Thord Thorson called Smiley smiles with delight when he spots first one then another of planted stories. Comments made by Júlía are taken out of context, twisted and unsparingly used as evidence of a "senseless woman with an obsolete and rotten cause". One columnist even goes so far as to call her "the Little Poet Girl". He tucks the papers under his arm along with his report and hurries to a basement beneath a grand house in Reykjavík.

"Now it is imperative to defeat Júlía in the elections," runs his report. "I have the greatest hope that 'Her Highness' ends up in a political dungeon. It's imperative that Professor Helgi and Croaking Krummi do not gain supporters. They are her rocks of support despite being inveterate imbeciles, as their violent past confirms. Already we have received assurances of support from old Crats and Unionists. We have joined forces with Nationist groups that are unhappy with this upstart woman. We are winning over more Nationists by claiming that not enough is being done and that Iceland is being betrayed in its quest for independence. The Berlin Draft is being portrayed by us as a cunning attempt to incorporate Iceland eternally into Europe. It is like writing a blank cheque, where nothing can be changed. We have begun a whispering campaign that on her trip to Berlin, Júlía made a secret agreement with Devereaux; the traitor is planning to sell the nation's freedom for promotion in the downy beds of Berlin. It's whispered that something is fishy in her relationship with the European president."

Smiley pauses before entering the basement. He'd been hired by Olav Seiferdal, who is OK but truth be told, he does not like his employers much, he's especially wary of that man in the black suit. Smiley has no idea who the man is, but the way the others behave toward him, he must be important. Smiley is unsure of the man's origin. He has been present at only a few of the meetings. And Smiley has heard him speak only once, at the very first meeting where Smiley was hired. Smiley had asked to whom he should submit invoices for his work.

"You will submit no invoices," said the man in the black suit. "You will be paid in cash. There must be no trail. But if you want to call us something, then call us the Vulture's Brood." He had smiled then, and Smiley still remembered that smile with horror.

Smiley had entered the basement room knowing that earlier that day, just as before all such meetings, the room had been swept for bugs. The man in the black suit was there. Smiley felt a shudder go up his spine. He did not like this work, but what was an unemployed secret policeman supposed to do for a living?

"Reject the Berlin Draft" screams the leading article for *The Post* two days later. It finds great faults with the Draft. It is claimed that it smacks of an inexperienced, untried little girl who has let a charming, handsome man outwit her. It does not quite use the word "seduce" but it is written between the lines. The Berlin Draft is said to deprive the nation of future prosperity. Iceland will be an inferior satellite to Europe; a puppet state. Nothing can be changed in the text of the Draft. Iceland will bleed; slowly and surely bleed to economic death.

Geir, absolutely flabbergasted by the paper's complete turnaround, goes to Thóra to protest this madness but she just shrugs her shoulders. "I don't write the editorials," she says and claims to have a meeting to attend.

Sólman is shocked at the libel of Júlía and goes to see Editor John, ostensibly to discuss the Draft but really to find out what is going on. He personally feels that the girl has defended Iceland's claims well against Europe; as did Hannes Hafstein almost 200 years earlier. She might be misguided as to her aims, but her motives cannot be in doubt.

The Editor takes the opposite view. "If the bill is approved, Júlía Ingólfsdóttir will be the first prime minister of this lame Icelandic Republic," says John brusquely, obviously in a foul mood.

"That's clear," replies Sólman. "The political fight is concluded. Victory is within reach. For her conduct, Júlía deserves the office," he adds.

Editor John springs from his seat and shouts: "That shall never be!" Sólman is surprised at the editor's zealotry; this is political mudslinging.

Sólman walks silently out of the editor's office, clearly shocked by his old colleague. Yet he turns around in the doorway and says: "You are less of a man if you become a maligner of the Draft and if you put the nation's freedom at risk." Then Sólman is gone.

Editor John turns back to his desk. He issues a memo to news director Thóra. Sólman's name is not to be mentioned again. Ever. He is being erased from the panels of history. Sólman is neatly being pushed aside.

Into the editor's office walks a rather stocky, medium height man in a black suit and dark shirt, probably in his early forties. Editor John looks up from his work and puts away some files as he realises who has entered his office. The man sits down on a couch. Editor John hastily stands up to take a seat beside him. The man has just recently injected much needed cash into the running of *The Reykjavík Post* to become its secret owner.

Editor John is now the indisputable leader and common denominator for the opponents of the Nationists.

Some time later, there is an open meeting on the Draft where Editor John delivers the keynote address. "We must tell the truth; what we believe to be the truth. They've thrown Iceland to the wolves," exclaims the Editor in a loud voice. He's celebrated as a hero. People's attitudes have clearly changed. People aim their spears at the Berlin Draft. "The nation has nothing to say on this issue but one big 'Nay'. The nation is supposed to put its stamp of approval on a document that an inexperienced little hussy brings from Berlin. It is plain silly that the Althingi has no choice but to accept or reject the Draft. It's absolutely unacceptable. Can't oppose, can't amend, they say. Such things are said by people with bad consciences. I suggest that all parties sit down and work on improving this blood-document. I suggest a national consensus on amendments. I suggest national peace," says the Editor.

He is celebrated as a true friend and hero; people call out his name. Editor John is the man toward whom the nation leans. "National consensus… national unity… anything is better than the Berlin Draft!" shouts Editor John.

The people rejoice, clap, stamp their feet and call out: "The Berlin Draft is a betrayal of the nation... away with traitors to their country!"

40

The political climate in Iceland has changed as if a hand has been waved, just like the capricious Icelandic winter weather. *The Post* leads the fight against the Draft. "We must not tie the hands of future generations," says a critical leading article, which, however, does not condemn the agreement entirely. "However what is needed is a fresh team of negotiators to ensure freedom with dignity. Men who can stand up to Europe's cunning president. Powerful Icelandic negotiators should be sent to Berlin against the crafty heir of the notorious Komizariat."

The media follow the lead, not least *Euro-News* and soon business leaders and workers' representatives join in. Agitation amplifies; the call for national unity is long forgotten. Frenzied youths flock throughout the country. Anything is better than the Berlin Draft. Are you going to vote for Iceland or Europe? Do you want us to become European slaves? Are you a spy for the European authorities? No bungled deals from Berlin. The propaganda onslaught is relentless.

There are widespread fights, punch ups and beatings. Groups march through the streets chanting:

But those bastards who our freedom betray
to join with dastards rush straight-away,
and promotions they from foreigners beg,
to our land they are a shame and a plague!

Then there are demonstrations by groups that grumble about the breaking of the alliance with Europe and the founding of the second Republic. They march through the streets zealously where everything has turned upside down. "Anything is better than the Berlin Draft," shout the youngsters. "We stand with our European brothers and sisters. We are European citizens. No bungled deals. Never again the tattered old króna."

Júlía gives a speech, but the press denounce it as weak. Commentators say that she is tired, troubled, and distracted; there is little sign of the joy and passion that previously characterized all her conduct. The poetess is distant and it appears as if her hopes of victory are fading.

"There goes a woman who has lost a battle," commentators say.

Smiley is delighted. He has no doubt that Júlía is breaking down and his tactics are working perfectly; tactics that create disorder, confusion, and chaos.

"Júlía was in unusually bad form and had a hoarse voice. She moved her hands frequently and raised them to her chest and was so choked-up that sometimes you could hear nothing but a whisper. And because of that, her speech had little effect," writes Smiley in a report. "The bigger the lie the better," Smiley writes, then adding: "It is most imperative that we manage to divert Júlía's attention away from the election, due to her bottomless insolence. She is without a doubt her party's chief liar and maligner."

Smiley hasn't been idle; he has been working hard to isolate Júlía. He is in contact with powers inside the Nation Party that publicly and privately state their differences of opinion. Júlía can hardly move or speak, so that her words will not be mangled and used against her. One of the most important links in Smiley's plan is to keep Krummi and Helgi away from the political stage. He knows that in their very different ways the two men are hugely popular. Smiley spreads the seductive tale that it's beneath the Nationists to be in league with terrorists. In addition, Smiley has hired gossip-mongers to spread rumours that the two men are denigrating the integrity of the party. Day after day the media covers the disagreements and disputes among the Nationists. "The Nation Party is Engulfed in Disputes," is the headline of *Euro-News*.

Within only a few weeks, Júlía has been forced to agree that Helgi and Krummi will keep away from the political battlefield.

How she misses her two colleagues!

The elections draw nearer.

In Berlin, Trinxon begins serving his prison sentence for dereliction of office. In Iceland, the Nation Party is on the defensive. People recall the sad fate of Chairman Páll Bjarnfreðsson. The party is said to be a synonym for corruption. Smiley has bribed local Nationist officials into handing over party documents. He leaks some questionable financial activities of one of the branch officials that imply that funds had disappeared from its treasury. Smiley is ecstatic with the resulting newspaper stories that the meagre facts produce. He subsequently recruits several party members to demand a public investigation into the entire Nationists' financial affairs. He knows that the scandal affected only a local fund raising drive, but if he throws enough mud some of it will stick. The day after the story breaks a newspaper prints a cartoon showing Júlía in a prison cell alongside Trinxon who is serving his sentence. The caption runs:

Trinxon Iceland freedom enchained
with the closed fist of a knave,
toppled from his seat to dwell
within a lowly prison cell.

"One breaker after another pours over the sieve-like ship of Nationist corruption" — proclaim the media. "Captain Júlía has no control over the ship."

The press hammers relentlessly against Júlía and her character, making demands that she resign from politics, being an unsuitable little girl who has washed up into a position that she cannot handle. She is a threat to the nation. "Júlía is like the sky child hanging on to the apron strings of her old mother in Berlin," writes Editor John, the unchallenged leader of the political opponents of the Nation Party. He nicknames Júlía "Euro-toady" and uses the term relentlessly in his speeches and press releases.

It does not help her position when a respected German scholar on international law confirms in an interview with the *Euro-News*, broadcast again and again in Iceland, that the Berlin Draft is a cunning incorporation of Iceland into the Great European State for all eternity.

It starts to look as if the Nation Party will be defeated soundly in the coming elections. Júlía senses that the game will be lost unless something spectacular happens. She makes a decision contrary to the wishes of senior members of the party leadership. She calls Helgi and Krummi out of political exile for consultation.

She has listened too long to detractors in her own party.

Geir Thórisson hears that the two old warhorses are coming, and drives out to Keflavík when their planes from the Westmann Islands and Westfjords land. He manages to grab the two in the arrivals lounge and asks for an interview. Helgi and Krummi admit that they are absolutely out of their element when it comes to kicking the ball on the field of Icelandic politics, in which hypocrisy, pretence, and buffoonery seems to be the chief virtues. They emphasise that all they want is for Iceland to be independent and proud once again and say that they have come for a private chat with their old friend Júlía. Geir takes a photo of the two men outside the front of the terminal with the old Icelandic flag behind them, then writes up the story. "Nice photo and a decent story," he tells Thóra when he hands in his copy on his return to the office.

Next morning he is amazed to see photo splashed across the front page under the headline "Júlía Hires Terrorists". The story is unrecognisable, starting "In their desperation, the Nationists turn to old terrorists. Is the country to be blown up? This is the final nail in Júlía's coffin." Geir calls Thóra on the holph to protest, but she just shrugs her shoulders.

"Direct orders from Editor John," she says. "I objected, but he threatened to sack me. I would keep your head down for a while if I were you."

Geir switches off the holph and wanders across Austurvöllur Square. He feels suddenly alone. Almost without thinking he slips into a bar and orders a beer.

Two streets away Helgi, Krummi and Júlía are meeting in an anonymous office lent by a Nation Party member.

"Well, you have got to know about the Europhiles political lying rubbish, which stops at nothing," says Helgi. "Just like Krummi and I learnt years ago."

"People get away with spinning webs, without any consequences. The media has no interest in the truth. It's as if they hold a daily auction on the biggest lie," adds Krummi with a sneer.

The two men feel guilty, having persuaded Júlía to go into politics. "I am sorry that we tricked you into climbing the greasy pole," says Krummi. "It has turned into an expensive joke." Helgi nods his agreement.

"You must never think that way," replies Júlía determinedly.

"Which reminds me of an event scheduled for this week," says Helgi changing the subject. "I gather that a meeting will be held at the Old School Plaza and broadcast throughout the country. You will have a chance to put things right."

Júlía shakes her head. "My performance the other day, when my voice gave way, was thought so poor that the party decided to send Vice Chairman Stefán instead. They say that it's too late to make changes for the debate," replies Júlía with a sad expression.

"We'll see what we can do. We stand with you; you can't really get anywhere without the backing of friends," says Krummi, grinning, his white teeth flashing.

"You need to regain your confidence, gather energy. If I know you right, you'll kill them with your eloquence and elegance," says Helgi. "Now, for a start I have heard some very interesting news about Múli Thordarsen. Listen …"

Júlía feels her energy and optimism increasing. It is quite remarkable how well she feels in the company of these friends of hers, who are more Icelandic than everything Icelandic that she knows. They radiate energy that kindles passion in people's hearts. "The Queen is still on the chessboard. We will kill them with Icelandic mystic power," she laughs, smiling at the comrades.

Júlía looks for a way to gain access to the meeting. Her request provokes some uproar in the party, but she gets what she wants. Surprisingly, the organizers reject the party's request to switch speakers. It is stated that the schedule has been decided and will not be changed. The decision is debated and highly criticised. People take to the street to protest so the rejection is withdrawn. Júlía looks forward to grappling with her opponents over the Berlin Draft — with Helgi and Krummi at her side.

41

The Old School Plaza is tightly packed quite some time before the meeting commences; there are cameras at every corner and over the plaza entrance. News of Júlía's participation has inspired a great deal of discussion and debate, even excitement since the attempt to exclude her had been highly controversial. It has been whispered that Helgi and Krummi will not be far away. Editor John begins the meeting with a barnstorming speech. He accuses Júlía of having employed the most disgraceful tricks to cram the Draft down the nation's throat. He declares that it has been a long time since a politician has stooped so low and run roughshod over everything we hold dear in order to get the Draft agreed.

Editor John does not hold back, turning to a fishing metaphor his audience will know well: "Júlía can never steer the national ship. She is an impossible captain. The catch is meagre and on top of that, the trawler has run aground. A captain who does not catch fish must give way.

"Leave, leave the bridge, Captain Júlía.

"You are no sailor; so hopeless that the trawler is stranded on a skerry while other ships scoop the entire sea empty of fish. Your ship's catch is so scanty and poor that the crew's pay is below the bare minimum: Cutter Júlía will be forced to declare bankruptcy. The Cutter will be pawned because there is not enough to pay the debts. The nation spits out this Draft; this vermin that recklessness wants it to swallow whole."

The crowd applauds the editor's speech raucously, considering his delivery excellent. People shout: "Spit out the Draft... spit out the Draft... Júlía off the bridge!"

Múli Thordarsen is next to speak after the editor. He claims that Júlía has at times been more full of herself than now, since her conduct suggests highly that she is ashamed of herself for the Draft. "Spit out the Draft. Your secret plans with Devereaux threaten the freedom of the nation. Everything that Júlía says is a big fat lie," shouts Múli loudly, pointing a finger at Júlía.

The crowd cheers the speeches of the Draft's opponents, although some there keep silent. Speakers step up to the podium and revile Júlía; she has lived luxuriously in Berlin in the most comfortable villa while the populace back in Iceland has to settle for subsidies that do not suffice for living expenses or debts. No peace can prevail in Iceland with such a leader. It would be best to make a reckoning with Júlía's political bankruptcy and send her back to Berlin.

On and on it goes before Júlía finally steps up to the lectern. She looks out over the crowd and then glances back at Helgi and Krummi, who stand just behind her.

Júlía's face is calm as she begins her speech.

"They say that I do not fish. I am reviled for the fact that the Cutter Júlía is stranded on a skerry while other boats haul in huge catches of fish. They say that the crew's take from the Cutter is scant, that the Cutter operates on a deficit and is in need of loans at present. This is what is being said by those who've driven away to other countries thousands upon thousands of hard working Icelanders. This is being said by those who've brought shame and poverty to this nation. The best and brightest have been forced to move abroad as opportunities in this wonderful country are so limited. I will turn things around. I will bring back our nation's freedom; individual freedom for each and every Icelander as we are all created equal to Life, Liberty and the pursuit of Happiness. I will restore the Althingi, the worlds oldest parliament, to its former status. I will bring back pride to this once proud nation.

"They are scandalized by what they call my over-indulgence and luxury. The words "pot", "kettle" and "black" spring to mind. Have you seen Editor John's house? If I wanted to stoop to their sort of level I would point to that gleaming limousine over there." She points off to the right where a gleaming black six door Bentley is parked. "Then I would ask where Múli Thordarsen got the money to buy it from. Last month he was clattering around Reykjavík in a battered old Skoda. Now look. But that is not my style. Múli is an honourable man. I am sure he suddenly found the money from some honourable source.

"Now remember. Remember the Komizars. Remember when they came to Reykjavík we had to close the streets to local cars so that the great and the good would not be late for their meetings. Remember the leaders of the indolent Nomenklatura who lied and slandered from their luxury homes while ordinary people were on the verge of starvation on minimum wages. They've taken away people's dignity by putting them on European subsidies. I am going to give people back their dignity.

"I have no qualms about shaking these gentlemen to their roots. I do not enjoy punishing people, but when the indolent attack one person with slander, it should surprise no one when she fights back.

"Their only subject at meetings appears to be slandering of the Draft. Their goal appears to be division, so that the Draft will be thrown into a rubbish bin. Then every ship will be stranded — as well as freedom. But remember, dear friends; when we joined with Europe, Iceland was at the top of the list of prosperous nations. These indolent are successors to those who invoked the Promised Land of Euro-Iceland. Now Icelandic standards of living are among the poorest in Europe, as it was nearly two hundred years ago under Danish rule and six hundred years of humiliation.

"It is an ugly image.

"We do not merely destroy the document if the Draft is rejected.

"We lose our freedom. We believe in new times — better times, changed times. I ask you not just to believe in my ability to change Iceland, to bring freedom to the people. I ask you to believe in your ability to change Iceland. Together, let us believe in change. Let this be the moment when we break down walls and join hands in bringing freedom home."

She looks over the sea of faces. The people gaze up at her with wide, questioning eyes. She finds it difficult to judge their response, but senses that people are listening attentively; her words are reaching people's ears. That is a start.

"Remember Hannes Hafstein, our great poet-politician:

Our words on freedom must never be rash,
until for thinking we have the guts.
Let us not say we make a dash,
if we spin our wheels in the same old ruts.

"Up from the wheel ruts," says Júlía in a loud voice, and people applaud.

She turns to Helgi and Krummi. They step forward, take hands, raise them. Júlía, between them, steps forward and addresses the crowd pointing toward Krummi and Helgi: "They have never had a huge fortune, but they have been celebrated and they have been condemned. They had their doubts and are not flawless. Why did they undertake such a controversial task that demanded so much sacrifice? It was for the nation; the freedom of the Icelandic nation. Again, Hannes Hafstein knew all about it.

On freedom a price is never laid,
by empty law it's never made.
It is the spirit's own daughter, you see if you look,
not some old picture from out of a book.

"They grappled with violence and superior forces. They blew courage into the heart of their nation. They had to endure humiliating arrests and the loneliness of prison cells. They were menaced and threatened, hounded, but did not let it stop them. They cleared a path to their nation's freedom. The nation will reap Helgi and Krummi's sowing of flowers of freedom in fertile Icelandic earth, because I sense that fortune is on Iceland's side."

Together the trio step forward and raise their hands. There is a momentary silence, but then people start applauding, clapping with ever-increasing rhythm, and then stamping their feet and chanting louder and louder. "Freedom... freedom... forward to freedom!" chant the people.

The crowd has sided with Júlía; of that there is no doubt. As Júlía delivers her speech, Editor John grows restless and shifts in his seat. Júlía ignores him, although she gives the Editor a droll smile from time to time.

As she leaves the lectern she suddenly turns and says: "Now I suggest that the accordion of *The Post* play us a song." A wave of laughter passes through the crowd; people boo the Editor and his colleagues, who sit there amazed by the turn of events.

The trio wave to the crowd, which shouts their names: "Júlía... Helgi... Krummi!"

They own the plaza.

The next day, *Sky* broadcasts on the situation in Iceland. The reporter begins: "Júlía Ingólfsdóttir, Iceland's Poet-Politician, is now highly regarded for her duel with her opponents. I heard one man in a bar last night say that she has taken a group of little boys on her knees and given them all a spanking."

Privately however, Júlía confides in her friends: "It was a great event. They thought they had us trapped, but we hung them up to dry. We've never won such a victory. We took the meeting away from them and people literally wanted to devour us from joy; also at the meeting. The day after, I couldn't walk the streets for all the congratulations and overwhelming praise. We did well, but not as well as people think. But people appreciate us for fighting alone against so many. Then it became evident how the slander about the Draft has fallen onto unfertile ground. All of this puts heavier responsibilities on our shoulders. It's not enough to be able to speak and think. The people need to see their dreams come true. This is not about us. It is about the Icelandic nation."

It is a beautiful autumn day the third week in September, the weather calm throughout the country, four degrees below zero. The leaves have paled and fallen from the trees. The autumn has arrived early and been cold, but the Icelanders are used to biting cold. The low-pressure system a week ago has been the most severe in eighteen years, with high winds blowing tiles off of roofs and pulling boats from their moorings in the southwest corner of the country. Last winter was piercingly, bitterly cold, most akin to the Great Frost of 1918. The bitter weather had even replaced politics in the headlines in the last few days before the election. Now the Icelanders go to the polling booths to take part in the most important election since the nation cast its vote for membership in the EU at the start of Current century – and before that rejected the infamous Icesave-deals.

Júlía sits in Café Europe with Helgi and Krummi watching people queing up to get into the polling station opposite. They are wrapped up against the biting cold, but even as the wind whips frozen spray up from the harbour they continue to wait, patiently.

"I am extremely pleased with this day," says Júlía with her usual gentle smile as she sits with her companions. "These last ten days of the election campaign have proven to be a complete reversal in the fight over the Draft. It seems as if the tide has ebbed out from beneath the feet of our political opponents, leaving them like fish on dry land. It is said that they now suffer fits of colic and vomiting."

Krummi nods. "The polls have been turned on their heads after the meeting at the Plaza. It is said that such a thunderous meeting has not been held at the plaza since Ólafur Thors took on the Communists during the great Depression. People hail you as a hero wherever you go."

"I don't deserve it," she says. "It was you two who turned things around. The web did not carry photos of me, but photos of all three of us, our hands raised in the air. That was the photo that dominated tv reports, newsapapers and chat rooms. And not just here, but throughout all of Europe. I tell you this, Icelanders sense freedom — new times — changed times. The nation has you two guys to thank that there is a strong likelihood of a decisive victory," concludes Júlía.

Krummi shakes his head and laughs heartily. "Us! Absolutely

absurd. You belittled the little men and exposed the lie with your clear vision and sparkling eloquence."

"We'll see how it all turns out, but no matter which way things turn your performance will go into the history books as David slaying Goliath," says Helgi.

Júlía smiles thoughtfully, and then her face brightens and she cites an old proverb once used by an American president:

You may fool all the people some of the time,
you can even fool some of the people all of the time,
but you cannot fool all of the people all the time.

By midnight it is out that the Nation Party has won a sweeping victory. Applause breaks out at the party's campaign headquarters when Júlía appears on the stairs with Helgi and Krummi by her side. She waves to the people. The trio walk slowly down the steps to thunderous applause and shouts of hurrah. The Nation Party has won a decisive victory.

Other political news has come earlier that evening when the Unionists announce their determined willingness to unify the parties. The decades of fission with the old Independence Party are at an end. Júlía Ingólfsdóttir is the unchallenged leader of the civil powers; a new Independence Party.

"The Nation's Party is the indisputable victor, thanks to you. We have no need to pray for either peace or mercy. We need to defend against Sólýska inclinations and sympathies, and then we'll stick it to them. They should pray for mercy in the struggle ahead, not we. Now we must go to Rome and sign the agreement with Devereaux," says Júlía in an address, to an ovation that seems as if it will never end. The nation once again quaffs the fragrance of freedom.

In Berlin a man in a black suit flicks off his tv: Júlía's image along with her two friends at the Plaza dissappears. The man curses angrily as he picks up his e-notebook. He dials a number in Italy on his holph.

42

It is dusk. The lights of the city form a protective cover over the eternal city on the banks of the Tiber River which like a goddess drapes her veil around the city's seven hills. Rome, which rose at the dawn of Western culture, is bedecked in all its beauty, autumn having started slowly creeping over the Mediterranean Sea. Rome smells of the bittersweet fragrance of history in which human dignity has risen highest, while the city has also drooped its head in shame at the falsehood and vanity of its children. The she-wolf pulled Romulus and Remus up from the Tiber and fostered them. In the fullness of time they raised a city-state but then turned their swords on each other. Romulus killed his brother Remus. Thus flowed the blood at the birth of the capital of the world on the banks of the Tiber.

The great poet Einar Benediktsson wrote:

The Tiber sinks
slowly, surely
into the brine
slowly, heavily
— over the course
of time.

On the terrace of a restaurant overlooking Piazza Navona in the old city, three people watch the people on the square located on the ruins of the Circus Agonali; the magnificent stadium of Emperor Domitian during the first century after Christ. In the middle of the square is the most splendid Fountain of Four Rivers with white marble columns. An Egyptian obelisk rises tens of meters into the sky, topped by a statue of the Emperor; a magnificent work of art of

Bernini from the 17th century. Standing opposite the magical work of the master, is Borromini's church of Sant'Agnese in Agone, with its two towers. The square is oblong and regularly shaped, though with one end in a semi-circle like the choir in a basilica. It was built on the ruins of a chariot racing course, and retains the ancient shape.

Edyta Zarębianka looks at the clock, obviously annoyed. "He is late," she says, exhaling smoke and tapping the ash from her cigarette.

"He'll be here; have no worries," replies Rudolf Kessler, who looks deliberately over the square before turning to Seiferdal. "Go down to the plaza, Olav, and see if you can spot Salvatore." The Euro-Norwegian stands up and walks down the stairs out onto the square.

Zarębianka directs an icy glare at the waiter who is hovering nearby. "I still don't see why we have to sit in this dump of a café for so long. There are much better places up at the Quirinale."

"Piazza Navona is a tourist trap," replies Kessler. "People come and go all the time. We will attract less attention here. And if anyone has followed us and is hanging about they will stick out like a sore thumb. The tourists have a coffee or a wine, then go. Only we stay here – or anyone watching us. Olav would spot them soon enough."

All he gets from his companion is a haughty sniff. She has a lot on her mind. "My people have gone to a lot of trouble to get everything ready," she says abruptly. She takes a puff and exhales impatiently.

Then she puts out the cigarette.

"The Vulture has given a green light. They've chosen the location here in Rome. Nothing can go wrong, absolutely nothing, or we'll call down the anger of The Vulture over our heads. Believe me, we don't want that," says Kessler, but Edyta doesn't need to hear a long discourse about the anger of The Vulture. She is not afraid of him. Few people know the man better than she. "We can get no one better than the Sicilian," adds Kessler coldly, dragging his finger across his neck. "He knows what he's doing, believe me. You don't need to worry about anything; he is a professional through and through."

At these words Buscetti appears at the top of the stairs, at his heels Seiferdal and Benedetto Benso, who immediately stare transfixed at Zarębianka. She lights another cigarette and exhales smoke. She has ways to deal with guys like him.

Buscetti sits down at the table. He waves with his left hand, motioning Benso to sit at a nearby table, his expression sour. Seiferdal sits next to Benso without either of them saying a word. Kessler hails the waiter and orders a bottle of red wine. Buscetti lights a large Cuban cigar; the smoke drifts from the table out onto the square.

Zarębianka glances sharply at Kessler and then at the Sicilian. She is impatient, since it is clear that Buscetti is making a show of his authority. Kessler looks about to make sure nobody is listening. He glances at Seiferdal who nods. Nobody has followed the new arrivals into the café.

"We have a time schedule, as well as the president's itinerary. Devereaux's escorts will drive up Via della Conciliazione. With him in the limousine will be the Icelandic Governess, Júlía, as well as the Italian Governess. They will stop at the bank of the Tiber opposite Castel Sant'Angelo, but then drive up Via della Conciliazione," says Kessler.

He hands Buscetti an envelope. "It's just over four weeks to the arrival of the president," says Kessler. The Sicilian looks at Edyta, then turns to Kessler and takes the envelope.

"Have you got the apartment?" asks Buscetti. He is obviously making it clear that he is fully aware of the master plan that was drawn up in Berlin. Kessler is a bit overawed by this Sicilian. He feels a chill pass down his spine under his cold glance. You are never safe around such people.

"Everything is ready," replies Kessler.

He had personally seen to the apartment.

An aged couple living on the old street up to St. Peter's Basilica have won a trip to New York in a lottery. They will leave a little over three weeks from now. There is a great deal of excitement in the little apartment on the Via della Conciliazione. They have never visited the United States, although their son Silvio lives in Queens, along with his wife Debra and the old couple's three grandchildren. "What luck," Marco Ratazzi had shouted while making the sign of the cross after the man from the lottery had come and notified them of their winnings. He had given them two airline tickets along with a hefty bundle of travellers cheques and a voucher for rooms at the Roosevelt Hotel in New York. "It's named after the American president," Marco had said triumphantly to his Mara.

"The apartment will be available three days before the president's arrival," says Kessler stoically. He personally oversees all operations on the ground. He is absolutely certain that nothing will go wrong with his side of things. And Buscetti is completely trustworthy, has had lots of experience in this sort of thing. He had totally agreed with the Vulture at their meeting in Berlin. The man in the black suit knows his business. There is a lot at stake. He smiles to himself and looks at the Sicilian.

"The Vulture particularly wants the Icelandic Governess to receive a greeting from the apartment," says Kessler.

Buscetti looks up abruptly, this being news to him. Zarębianka looks unfazed, she herself having made the demand.

"What has changed?" asks Buscetti, taking a deep drag of his cigar and blowing the smoke over the table, covering it.

"They are going to prevent Iceland's withdrawal from the Great European State — of course," replies Kessler hesitantly. "The goal is to create chaos and confusion, expose the President's idiocy and ensure that Iceland stays in the federation. That bastard Devereaux is out of control."

Buscetti frowns. "That will be a bigger operation. Taking care of two customers is always more than double the work of one. You cannot take chances on a job like this, you know. We are not dealing with a pair of troublesome cops in Palermo." He looks out across the square without really seeing it. His brain is working quickly. "I will need more euros, many more euros. And another false passport, maybe two. This is going to be a bigger operation. You should have given me more notice," says Buscetti extremely quietly, kneading his fingers looking to Benso who is all ears.

Zarębianka lights yet another cigarette and looks coldly at the Sicilian. "Easy matter; the money will not be a problem. Just see to it that the deed is carried out with the professionalism required. No Jihad, no bombs, just effective bullets. You are supposed to be a professional, after all."

Buscetti turns slowly to fix Zarębianka with a cold stare. He flexes his fingers slowly. "Who do you think I am?" he says, knocking the ash from his cigar. "Do you think we're Moors or something? We're not blowing up anyone."

He puts out the cigar in Zarębianka's glass of wine.

She barely reacts, merely smiling and winking at Benso. She then takes a drag, blows the smoke over the table and sticks her cigarette into the Sicilian's glass. "Let's get one thing straight," she says, putting both hands on the table, her bosom showing. "We're not in Sicily. I'm neither your wife nor your mistress. You are being paid to do a job. We are paying, you are doing."

Buscetti stares in surprise for a moment, then he laughs uproariously, strikes the table firmly and lights another large cigar. "In Sicily we say: keep your friends close but your enemies closer."

The Sicilian opens his arms to Zarębianka.

She merely smiles at him, lights a cigarette and takes a drag. "I have a lot of respect for you. We are similar in many ways. We keep our business professional. I choose to have a business relationship with you. I don't want your hands down my shirt," she says, blowing smoke toward the square.

"Nothing personal, just business," replies Buscetti, knocking the ashes off his cigar.

Kessler has been sitting silently between them, wanting to reduce the tension. "The chief customer's arrival in Rome with the Icelandic girl is drawing near. It's just a few weeks until then, and lots things need to get done. Buscetti, we need to sit down and go over the details."

The Sicilian nods. "I'll take care of setting everything up. You see to it that I get all the information, and I mean all the information, and travel plans. You make sure that the apartment will be free three days before the customer's jet lands at Ciampino Airport."

All the rage and all the agitation is gone from the voice of the Sicilian. He forces a smile at Kessler, then looks at Zarębianka and smiles his most cheerful smile.

He stands up and leans over the table. He sticks his Cuban cigar in a wine glass, this time Kessler's, who is surprised. "You need to tame your girlfriend," says Buscetti, signalling to Benso to follow him. They disappear into the crowd.

Seiferdal stands up and walks to the table.

"Are you sure that you can trust that chauvinist pig?" asks Zarębianka frustratedly. "The bastard acted like an idiot."

"You played your part. The Italians are known these days for things besides blowing people up. They're more polished than that," replies Kessler, making his displeasure clear to her. "You take care of the bill," he says, gesturing to Seiferdal to follow him.

Zarębianka remains behind alone. "You dirty, sexist pigs," she says loudly. She lights another cigarette, stands up and walks down the stairs to the storey below. She orders a waiter to bring her the bill.

This shitty job is getting on my nerves, she thinks, but smiles to herself. Her clients pay well, so it's worth it.

She walks out and also disappears into the crowd of happy tourists pottering about on Piazza Navona.

43

Highpoint looks out over the Strait. There is a cold northerly wind and sleet; cloudbanks pile up over the snow-covered slopes of Mt. Esja and the sea-spray gushes over Sæbraut Road. The biting cold has not improved his mood, most things these days being turned inside-out. Smiley Thorson seems to have disappeared from the face of the earth. They have been looking for him after a suicide note written by Chairman Páll had been found by sheer coincidence in a brown envelope shoved to the back of Smiley's old desk. It had come like a bolt from the blue. In the note the Chairman admits to embezzlement of money from Party funds to pay for his sex addiction and claims that he had been blackmailed for his relationship with prostitutes.

Suddenly Smiley is linked to the suicide of Chairman Páll. And whatever he had been up to since leaving the police was clearly odd, secretive and brought him a lot of money. Highpoint had been forced to call in Europol, but it has all come to nothing; no trail to follow, no credit card transactions, no flights, trains nor taxis, no surveillance images — nothing. The cursed man had gone to London and then disappeared without a trace. Slobodan Paśiĉevic has been notified.

"This is how they work: only those who know how to and wish to hide their trail. The bastard is up to something, or maybe he's just fled the country to get away from debts or a woman? Could he be in cahoots with Seiferdal?" Highpoint directs his words at Hrönn Halldórsdóttir, department head, sitting opposite him.

"There is nothing to suggest it. Seiferdal quit the Security Bureau long ago," says Hrönn.

There is a knock on the door and in walks Díella Stensen, who has been summoned for further questioning. Highpoint wants to interview her personally, since so many things are unclear. Díella has shown a desire to collaborate. According to the initial interview she is furious with Smiley for the way he left her in the lurch after they lost their jobs. He was working on some project and suddenly wading in money. Then he suddenly left the country without a word.

Highpoint asks Díella to describe the series of events at Höfðabakki one more time. She says that she had assisted Seiferdal in opening the safe; he had gone through the documents and photographed them. They had then gone down the stairs but were terribly startled when the guard jumped out with a shout from a dark nook.

"Describe to me precisely the events in the office. You opened the safe," says Highpoint.

"We opened the safe one, two, three; extremely simple, since the Norwegian was well prepared and had the combination numbers written on a piece of paper. Seiferdal had been very pleased and rubbed his hands together, immediately started examining the documents and photographing them one after another," says Díella.

"He had the numbers on a slip of paper and didn't mess with anything other than the safe," says Highpoint thoughtfully.

"That's right. We went straight to the chairman's office and to the painting over the safe. I have no idea where he got the information," replies Díella.

"You're certain that he took no documents," interjects Hrönn.

"Absolutely, since we weren't supposed to leave behind any trail," replies Díella with a thoughtful expression, before continuing, slightly hesitantly. "Mind you, once the safe was open Seiferdal ordered us to go out into the corridor and stand watch, so I saw pretty much nothing else. I stood by the door out on the landing, while Smiley was at the door to the office."

"Smiley may have been able to watch Seiferdal in the office," says Highpoint pensively.

"That's possible," replies Díella.

"Could Smiley have seen something that you didn't?" asks Highpoint.

"Maybe," replies Díella. "It looked as if Seiferdal was surprised when he stepped into the doorway, as far as I could see from the corridor. He jumped and stopped cold. They looked each other in the eye for a moment and Smiley said something quietly. They both laughed but I didn't hear what they said. I didn't think it important."

"You're quite sure that Seiferdal didn't take any files or documents from the safe," repeats Highpoint, rather annoyed. None of this seems to be going anywhere.

"Naturally, I can't confirm anything, but Seiferdal himself emphasized that the documents were to be left in place," replies Díella.

"Quite right, of course," replies Highpoint, waving his hand.

"How has your relationship with Smiley been since you left the force?" asks Highpoint.

"We don't have one; any contact we had, came to an end a while ago. He was rude to me. All rather strange when I think about it, because I suspect that Smiley is still in contact with Seiferdal."

"Why do you suspect that?" asks Hrönn.

"I heard him talking to Seiferdal rather secretively a couple of times. I suspect that there were other conversations," replies Díella.

Highpoint is clearly quite frustrated as nothing concrete is coming out of the interview. He stands up and walks toward the window.

"You may go," says Hrönn.

Díella stands up and walks to the door. She looks down, clearly lost in thought, but then turns to Highpoint.

"Did you see the envelope?" she asks tentatively.

"What envelope?" asks Highpoint with a look of surprise as he turns back to face her.

"There was a brown envelope in the safe next to the papers," replies Díella.

"A brown envelope," exclaims Highpoint. He turns to Hrönn, who shrugs her shoulders. "The envelope in Smiley's desk," says Highpoint thoughtfully, while waiting for a response. "Get the brown envelope, Hrönn." Highpoint is quite cross with himself of not making the connection that the envelope may have been taken from the safe. He turns to Díella and asks her to wait a moment. Hrönn hurries out and Díella takes a seat opposite the security director. He stands up again, walks slowly to the window and looks out over the Strait. There's nothing blue about the Strait in this mood, he thinks as he ponders the white-foaming waves. Hrönn appears in the doorway with the brown envelope and hands it to Highpoint. He walks over to Díella and shows it to her.

"Is this the envelope that you saw in the office?" he asks.

She inspects it closely and nods in assent. "Yes, it seems to be. It has the same fold, straight across."

Highpoint looks at Hrönn and nods his head.

"The envelope is obviously part of the burglary. Seiferdal apparently took this envelope from the safe. By the suicide note, everything suggests that Smiley blackmailed Páll. Berlin needs to have this information," says Highpoint.

Díella's face turns bright red from anger, but she doesn't respond. The bastards betrayed her, she thinks. Smiley never told her about a suicide note which he'd obviously found as the investigating officer on the death of that dirty old man. They never told her about the envelope. They had kept her in the dark and Smiley had put the suicide note into the envelope. And what an idiot forgetting the envelope like that.

"Am I free to go?" she asks curtly.

"Certainly," replies Highpoint. "Thank you for clarifying the mystery of the envelope."

★ 44 ★

The ground is white, eight degrees below, a calm and clear sky over Reykjavík as Júlía walks up the steps of the Ministry Offices to meet with Governor Mangi Steffensen. The topic is the magnificent landslide victory of the Nation Party and the appointment of a new Governor. Mangi is satisfied, deeply satisfied. He stands in the doorway and welcomes Júlía wholeheartedly.

"The greatest turnaround in the history of Icelandic politics. You crushed them at the Plaza," he says cheerfully, stepping onto the stairs.

"It doesn't look like you mind losing your job," she says amicably.

The aged hero laughs heartily. "Good riddance," he says.

"A louse between nails. Tough situation," she replies with a laugh.

"I'm unspeakably glad that it's you walking up these steps and not Editor John Bjornson. There would have been an uproar if the Sólýtas or the Alliance had won. These certainly are new and exciting times," he says, trying to shake off the bitter cold.

"I understand that Inga Laxdal is considering withdrawing from politics," says Steffensen as they enter the building.

"So I hear," says Júlía, "Laxdal had a chat with me yesterday. Editor John is the real leader of the Sólýta party, with Múli at his side. No one mentions Sólman Smithson any longer. He is said to be lost and gone in the bureaucracy in Brussels although I suppose his future prospects there must be dim. Laxdal has already heard a whispering campaign is underway to blame her for the defeat of the pro European parties. Although the Editor has defended her in public, she knows he is behind it all. She wants to get out before it all turns nasty."

They walk into the Governor's grand office.

"There are a lot of things to see to in the next weeks, and time flies. The nation has spoken and granted the Nation Party full and unchallenged authority to establish the Republic. Naturally, you'll be present in Rome for the ceremony," says Júlía.

"Of course," smiles Steffensen sitting at his desk and waving Júlía to a chair opposite. "Very good of you to ask me. You will be in this chair by then and I will just be plain old Mr Steffensen."

"It is the least I could do," smiles Júlía. "You know I'll sign the agreement in Rome as Governor of Iceland. And with that flourish of a pen I will cease to be the last Governor and soon sworn in as Iceland's Prime Minister."

"You know they are already calling the new state the Second Republic?" says Steffensen.

Júlía nods. "Very apt. Now to business. The agreement will be signed at St. Peter's Square in Rome in three weeks time and the Republic restored at Thingvellir."

Steffensen calls in a team of bureaucrats who enter laden with papers, e-books and display screens. There are numerous details to work through.

Five hours later, Steffensen calls a halt. He sends out for a tray of bread, pickles and cold meats, then waves his aides away so that he and Júlía are alone.

"There is some new information on poor old Chairman Páll Bjarnfreðsson. They've found a suicide letter from him," says Steffensen suddenly.

Júlía looks up sharply. "What letter? Nobody mentioned a letter at the inquest."

Steffensen face turns grave. "It was a suicide note that in some inexplicable way had not come forth in the investigation. A few days ago the note was found shoved to the back of the old desk that used to belong to that former police officer Thord Thorson called Smiley. In the letter, Páll describes the reasons why he decided to take his own life. He was being blackmailed over his relations with prostitutes. Páll confesses to having withdrawn money for his personal use from the treasury of the Nation Party for some time; to finance his sexual addiction. He begs his party's forgiveness for what he calls his inexcusable actions. He had betrayed the trust of his colleagues and his nation. He would have to pay the consequences of his actions. The note was never put forward by that corrupt police officer." Steffensen stands up, walks to the punch bag and slams it with his right fist.

Júlía looks at him in surprise. "It is obviously a serious issue when an Icelandic police officer is responsible for covering up evidence", she says, her voice has become quite firm. "Extremely serious, especially if he was using those photos to blackmail Páll. Were the European bureaucrats party to the case? I say they were. And yes, we now know a lot more about him siphoning off funds. The party's treasurer is working overtime on an investigation of withdrawals from the treasury. Yet the entire case is difficult, and it is suspected that as much as a million euros may have disappeared. There might be some other funds missing as well, hard to tell. But the treasurer is reviewing the data. He will get there in the end. And it is extremely peculiar that the letter should have vanished during the investigation of the case. What was behind that?" Júlía asks quite agitated.

Steffensen shrugs his shoulders. "The police have been investigating. Unfortunately it hasn't been possible to take a statement from Smiley, since it seems as if the earth has swallowed him up. He disappeared from the country a week ago. Highpoint is leading the investigation here in Iceland. It seems that Smiley has been working on something very secretive over the past few weeks. He has been asking all sorts of questions and holding meetings with a wide range of people. But nobody can make out what he was up to. All very odd. Anyway, the case is being taken seriously in Berlin. It's my understanding that Slobodan Pašičevic, head of the EIA, is to be briefed personally. I doubt that Iceland has ever received similar attention in Berlin," says Mangi, with a mischievous smile.

Júlía frowns at the news. "Pašičevic will be interested. He never does anything without a reason. And I don't trust him an inch. He is a repugnant man," she says, deeply pensive.

She knows Paśićevic; he is a slippery eel, crafty and savage as a mink. Devereaux is considering getting rid of the lout. She had urged the President to act immediately following the inauguration. "Berlin needs cleaning up," she had told the President who had smiled and made a joke about it: the most dearly loved Presidents in America were those who had been shot dead. Then Devereaux had promised her that he would act before the New Year, since he had many things on his plate.

Júlía and Mangi part on the stairs. Júlía has a lot on her mind as she goes down the stairs of the Ministry Offices.

Júlía summons Helgi and Krummi to her office on Kirkjustræti Street. She tells them about her conversation with Governor Steffensen, her suspicions about the blackmail and the disappearance of Thord "Smiley" Thorson. "These things are bound to overshadow preparations for the transfer of the governorship from Steffensen to myself that will take place tomorrow at a ceremony in the Cathedral and Althingi building," declares Júlía. "But that, however, is not why I have asked you here. I want to invite you to attend the signing of the agreement in Rome. You deserve it. The Pope will attend the signing of the agreement at St. Peter's Square. Afterward, the first democratically elected president and the prospective prime minister of the restored Icelandic Republic will begin a state visit to the Vatican."

"It would be a great honour for us," says Helgi. "I have heard that many Eurocrats feel that Devereaux has granted little Iceland far too great an honour, but he ignores such criticisms. 'By granting Iceland freedom and our friendship, we honour every single European – Iceland shall be granted the right to choose,' Devereaux had said at a press conference."

"I'll enjoy rubbing their noses in it," smiles Krummi. "Perhaps I should take some pollack with me, just in case."

Helgi laughs but Júlía gives him a hard stare. "It will be a historic moment," she says.

"Mind you," continues Júlía. "I am a bit worried about this Smiley character. He was up to something devious that not even Highpoint can work out. And now it's as if the Earth has swallowed him whole. That makes me very uneasy. Could Smiley be in cahoots with Seiferdal? President Devereaux is surrounded by powerful enemies in Berlin. I don't trust this Paśiĉevic, not at all," she says to Helgi and Krummi, her face serious.

"What are you suggesting?" asks Krummi.

"Oh, I don't know. But my female intuition is telling me to be on the alert. There is a silence, secrecy, and insincerity lurking out there," says Júlía, looking at her friends.

"That makes for a poisonous trio," says Helgi.

"Rats paddle through the Berlin sewers in search of prey. There are some nasty characters over there," says Júlía.

45

Slobodan Paśiĉevic stares disconsolately over the River Spree from his office in Berlin. Two towers rise twenty stories to the sky on the bank of the river, while a fifteen-storey building extends from the towers like a sphinx in the direction of the street behind them. Paśiĉevic's luxurious office is on the top floor of the eastern tower. He is in the middle of a conversation with the Security Director in Reykjavík. He sinks on to the sofa, leans forward and glances sharply at the quarter-size image of Jón H. Matthíasson, Highpoint.

"It appears clear that Thorson tried to blackmail the chairman with the assistance of Seiferdal. But I consider the Icelander to be a puppet on a string. There is much to indicate that the Norwegian managed to get his hands on up to a million euros along with the sex photos. Now Thorson is gone, has completely vanished from the country and we haven't been able to locate him," says Highpoint with a serious look.

"This is terribly serious news," replies Paśiĉevic slowly, emphasizing each word.

"Naturally, the obvious man behind all this is Trinxon, but I don't believe that he's involved," says Highpoint.

Paśiĉevic straightens his black tie slightly. "There's enough nonsense surrounding Trinxon. He's serving a sentence in Spandau. I agree that blackmail does not seem his style, but you never know. All right. You've done a good job on this, but it seems clear to me that the investigation should be moved entirely here to Berlin. In the unlikely event that Thorson is in Iceland, then you'll arrest the rogue, of course. But we'll find Seiferdal and Thorson somewhere. You can rest assured that the case will be solved. They'll be made to pay the consequences of their actions," says Paśiĉevic. "Thank you for your work to date. It does your office credit. But for now let's keep this confidential. You keep this within your own office, far from the politicians and thus the media."

"Certainly, Director Pašiĉevic," assents Highpoint.

They part.

Highpoint leans back on the sofa in his office and tries to relax but that's not easy. He had not been totally forthcoming to the Director. However, he feels good that the supervision of the case is out of his hands and that fool Smiley will be tracked down in Europe.

Pašiĉevic walks to the desk in deep thought, then back to the window and looks over the calm river. It feels good to look at the Spree. The serenity of the river reminds him of the Danube back home but the comparison ends there. He shakes his head as his thoughts wander back to the Balkans, his eyes seem to freeze.

His childhood in the Balkans had been one of nightmare, abuse, violence and neglect. Already as an infant he would get less of almost everything compared to the other children at the orphanage in Smederevo on the banks of the Danube. He hated everything about the orphanage, that evil place that he had closed down as police commissioner of Serbia.

A faint smirk appears on Pašiĉevic sober face.

Even the food on his plate had constantly been less than other children's and frequently mouldy. The wicked bitch would slap him if he refused his meal and the sadist swine would hit him with a stick when he wet his bed, which was all too frequent. They had ridiculed him and turned the other children against him. The memories tend to overwhelm him, but he had found ways to disguise his feelings.

He had trusted no-one and had absolutely refused to share things with other children. He had learnt to terrify them: "No, no way I share my toys with you," he'd hiss in a threatening voice. He had discovered that "no" is a powerful tool. The children would do anything to appease him. And he had, as the years passed by, discovered that he didn't need to yell, just to give them that look

288

and they would be in awe of him.

He had felt best in solitude on the bank of the Danube, watching the river run downstream, thinking of ways to get even with his tormentors: the sadist, malicious swine and his ass licking bitch who had made his childhood a nightmare at the orphanage.

They had long ago been taken care of in a proper manner.

Júlía Ingólfsdóttir swears her oath of office following mass in the Cathedral, with Helgi Thorláksson and Hrafn Illugason behind her. There is a gleam in the eyes of the proud old warriors. The old flag of the Republic is raised to its pole before the Althingi building and the star-gilded European flag is taken down. Old Mangi Steffensen resigns. It is an aged man, short and bowed at the shoulders, who had walked into the Althingi building and lays the sceptre of the office on the table before the lectern.

"I am deeply gladdened that the highest authority in the country is given into the hands of an exceptional woman at the dawn of the restored Republic," Mangi says. A choir made up of people from all parts of the country sings the old national anthem, and at its conclusion Beethoven's Ode to Joy resounds for the last time.

The full freedom of the Icelandic nation is within reach.

Rudolf Kessler contentedly hums the genius' masterpiece, Piano Concerto Number 24. The Vulture hasn't yet arrived; Kessler is early. He looks toward Königsee Lake, wedged between noble mountains. The white peaks of the Alps rise high to the heavens. In the distance can be seen the Austrian pearl Salzburg, the birthplace of Mozart; such a view, such a country, such weather. He stands on the balcony of Adolf Hitler's Eagle's Nest at a height of nearly two thousand meters; Kehlsteinhaus, which Martin Borman had presented Hitler on his fiftieth birthday all those years ago. Hitler had summoned Neville Chamberlain to Berchtesgaden. The British prime-minister had subsequently signed the notorious document that he called "peace for our time." It proved to be one of the most brutally false statement of the 20th century.

Kessler had hurried from Italy to meet with The Vulture.

He hums the concerto, leans over the handrail and admires the view. Kessler straightens up, but is quite startled when he turns and looks straight in the face of The Vulture, who is standing close by him. "Oh... you have arrived," he stutters. His hands go clammy and his mouth dry.

The man in the black suit smiles coldly. "Yes, I have arrived."

Kessler senses The Vulture's heavy mood. This does not bode well.

"Seiferdal's cock-ups never cease. He and the Icelandic sluggard are being searched for throughout Europe. The Italian police have their photos. We need to take action, because people's eyes must not be directed at Rome. This idiocy cannot go on."

Kessler is very surprised, having had no knowledge of this at all. "I had no idea," he replies, trying to stay calm.

"Your head's in the clouds, Kessler," says The Vulture sharply. "I trust you, but you betray my trust by putting unqualified people in key positions. That will not do. You've got to pull yourself together."

"What do you want me to do? Name it," says Kessler earnestly, rubbing his right hand. "The time has nearly come for the president's visit and the signing at St. Peter's Square," he adds.

"We are forced into dealing with the Nordic problem," says The Vulture, heavily emphasizing every word.

He's serious, Kessler thinks. He is surprised, but The Vulture's words are like law to him. "The Sicilian must free us from the Nordic Problem," says The Vulture sharply. "No evidence; they've got to disappear, both of them. Vanish."

"I'll see to that," replies Kessler as resolutely as he can. Kessler looks over at Salzburg in the distance. He needs to hurry to Italy.

Marco Ratazzi dodders as fast as he can down the Via della Conciliazione. With a worried expression, the old man looks up the ancient street at his apartment on the top floor. Then he looks at the great basilica of St. Peter, says a prayer and makes the sign of the cross. His beloved Mara has fallen off a chair and has a bad hip. He fears that her hip may even be fractured. Marco is fetching a doctor farther down the street to examine his Mara, to whom he has been married for over half a century. He is worried, since it seems clear that they will not be meeting their grandchildren in New York. He is very downcast but the main thing is to make sure that Mara is not seriously injured. He had laid her on the bed and hurried to seek help. "There's nothing wrong with me," she had said petulantly, but Marco knows better. Mara almost never complains about anything.

46

Highpoint sits on the couch in his office in Reykjavík. An unexpected guest has arrived. Júlía sits opposite him. She had knocked at his door at short notice. She is seeking information on the investigation of the blackmail of the late Páll, and asks about the disappearance of Smiley Thorson. Highpoint finds the conversation uncomfortable, because he has promised Pašićevic that he will not allow the case to become tangled with politics. It is complicated enough as it is. But at the end of the day, the Governess is the highest authority in the Icelandic State, and that makes things delicate.

Júlía is frustrated with the Security Director's caution, because she feels as if he's holding all the cards to himself. "You understand that there may be a political angle to this," she says a bit gruffly, looking in the Security Director's eyes. "More than first appears."

Highpoint looks out the window toward the windswept Mt. Esja, but then turns back to Júlía. "To be honest, we have made disappointingly little progress in the investigation. I've been in contact with Slobodan Pašićevic. We won't get any further here in Iceland, and the secret service has taken over the investigation. An extensive search is being made for Seiferdal and Thorson throughout Europe, indeed across the world."

"No leads?" Júlía is annoyed, feeling as if he is leaving many things unsaid.

Highpoint hesitates slightly. "Actually, no. It's as if the Earth has swallowed them, but the secret service is working hard on the investigation. Europol, however, has some leads on Thorson's movements in Spain. And Seiferdal has been seen in Italy. That's all really, a bit vague. I can let you see the reports if you like, but you must not take them from this office. I would not hide anything from you, but you must understand that this a a very delicate case."

Júlía interrupts him. "In Italy. Where in Italy?" she asks gruffly.

"He was supposedly seen in Genoa," replies Highpoint.

"I want to be honest with you," she says, leaning over the table. "I don't trust Paśićevic. He is a crafty man. Although he wasn't caught up in Trinxon's mess there was always a rumour in Berlin about their close relationship. President Devereaux has always been suspicious of Paśićevic."

Highpoint scratches his neck and looks down, frowning slightly, although his expression is thoughtful. He looks at Júlía. "Yes, well. Be that as it may, he is in charge of the investigation now. Of course, I'm making my own investigation into the matter here in Iceland."

Júlía has stood up and gone to the window, lost in her thoughts. "I don't want to get ahead of myself but it gives me a bad feeling hearing that Seiferdal is in Italy. If the Norwegian is in Italy then I suspect that Kessler is not far behind. If so, the case needs to be examined closer. You know what I mean."

"You are of course referring to your trip to Italy and the signing at St. Peter's Square," replies Highpoint. "Do you think Kessler is up to something?" he asks.

"There are strong forces that oppose the President. Behind the scenes influential parties in Berlin have applied their powers against the Icelandic agreement, without much result. The Europhiles feel that the establishment of the Icelandic Republic threatens the Great European State. And that means that Devereaux is a threat. It is nonsense, of course, but it is what they think. God knows what action they may take but I've got to watch what I say," says Júlía.

Highpoint nods thoughtfully. "I understand the gravity of the issue," he assures her, very upset at this news. "I assure you we are doing all we can, and so is the secret service."

"It's less than a week until the signing and I leave for Rome on Monday, with a stop in Berlin," says Júlía. She shakes Highpoint's hand, walks to the door, says goodbye and shuts the door behind her.

The State Security Director is left alone in his office. He feels that he has failed the trust of the new Governess. Of course he should have followed his own leads and informed Júlía of the progress of the case, as he had informed Mangi Steffensen when appropriate. The disappearance of Smiley Thorson, with respect to the corruption cases in Berlin, should have alerted him to the necessity of keeping the top levels of government informed. He is annoyed at himself. He feels it urgent to try to flush Seiferdal and Smiley from their den. He will have to do something himself. Paśićevic won't be happy, but that's the way it will have to be.

47

Geir Thórisson has returned to work at *The Post* after a three-month holiday in Spain. He had gone to the Icelanders' colony close to Torrevieja. There were thirty of them, spending their days fishing, swimming, drinking beer and watching sport. Geir finds few things more pleasant than sitting in a good bar with a good beer, watching football. The English League has long been disbanded, after the biggest European clubs formed their own European League long ago. Critics blame the European League for the decline of the national teams of the union states and call for one European team for the next World Cup.

The debate is very heated.

The Euro-Icelanders in Torrevieja number in the thousands and have taken over a whole village just outside the holiday resort. Geir is satisfied with the decisive election victory of the Nationists even though he has never been political. Politics actually bore him. This is his first day back at work after his holiday. He had been quite angry at his news director, felt that she had let him down. After hitting the bottle like never before, they had talked about it and he had gone to Spain. Now, Geir has returned.

He is sitting in the office of Thóra Hringsdóttir, listening to her rabbiting on. Apparently nothing has happened for weeks. No scandals, no bank robberies, no big business deals. She is angry and resentful, not being able to see the end of a long-term news dry spell. Suddenly she stops and points an accusing finger at Geir's beer belly.

"I see you found a barrel of beer to lie in down there," she says sarcastically.

He doesn't let Thóra's remark put him off, and instead pats his belly. "You've clearly missed me and want to touch my belly," he replies light-heartedly. He's glad to be back at work but is determined to do nothing, absolutely nothing this first day back. It has got on Thóra's nerves.

"You've killed all my story ideas," she says irritatedly.

"I do my best, like you do your very best for these shadow forces behind this paper," he replies ironically.

She points a finger angrily at him. "Are these the thanks for standing by you? You have me to thank for keeping your job," she shouts at him. It's true that she had stood by Geir. Editor John had wanted to kick him out but she had refused. "Where would *The Post* be and what would people think if Geir is sacked," she had shouted back. Yes, she had stood by that old boozer.

The receptionist appears in the doorway and complains about Geir not answering his holph, which he has left on his desk. "You've got to answer," he says dejectedly. "There's a guy who insists that you wouldn't want to miss a call. He refuses to send his image."

Geir stands up, grabbing his own belly. "You'll have to wait a little longer for this to disappear, my dear Thóra," he says with a laugh as he walks to the door.

"Drunk," mutters Thóra.

Geir walks to his cubicle and picks up his holph. He's surprised to hear a familiar voice on the line. "Meet me in fifteen minutes," says Deep Throat, before hanging up.

Adrenaline surges through Geir's body. Something big must be looming.

The doorbell is rung repeatedly in the little apartment on the Via della Conciliazione. "I'm coming, I'm coming," calls old Marco. He is feeding Mara soup as she sits up in bed. She's recovering, but they've put off their flight to America by a month on Dr. Dominic's orders.

The doorbell continues to ring.

"What goddamn ruckus is this? People have no manners," says the old woman irritably. Old Marco dodders down the hallway as quickly as he can, as the bell continues to ring.

"I'm coming," calls the old man.

The bell stops ringing. Whoever has come calling has heard old Marco, who now reaches the apartment's door, turns and releases the lock chain. The old man opens the door.

Rudolf Kessler is irritated, having heard that the old couple have postponed their flight to New York.

"I'm from El'Europa Airlines," says Kessler as calmly as possible.

Old Marco is a bit surprised, but then his face brightens. "My Mara will be back to her old self after a month, the doctor promises it. We're just going a month later," says the old man apologetically. "That's okay, isn't it?" he asks.

Kessler asks for permission to come inside.

"Of course," replies the old man.

"That's the problem," Kessler says to the old man. "It's difficult to change your ticket, because your flight is fully booked."

This comes as a surprise to Marco, since this goes against everything the girl at the El'Europa office had told him. She had said it would be easy to change the ticket. The only thing they needed was medical certification for Mara. Marco said that he had thought it would be no trouble, Dr. Dominic being a good man.

Kessler looks down the hallway but then turns again to the old man. "Of course I'm checking on the matter now. May I speak to your wife?"

Of course he could. Marco walks down the hallway to the bedroom, Kessler at his heels. "This man is from the airline," he says to his wife.

She looks at her spouse questioningly, and then at Kessler, who towers over the old man. "I fell off my chair," she says apologetically.

"There are obstacles to changing the ticket," says Kessler. "We're wondering whether you might feel up to leaving next week, after all." He smiles at the old woman and sits down on the edge of the bed.

"I have a bad hip," replies the old woman with a sigh as the pain gets to her. "I can't stand on my own two feet, but Dr. Dominic says

297

that I'll be much better in a month. My hip isn't broken, as Marco feared. Our Silvio says that it's alright for us to come a month later."

Kessler asks her to stand up; this nonsense is trying his patience.

"The doctor forbids it," Marco says hurriedly. "Dr. Dominic says that she has to stay in bed for a week, but that she can get up next week."

Kessler looks frustratedly at Marco but realizes that this is all useless. Besides that, his aggressiveness may raise some uncomfortable questions. He needs to think this over. He throws up his hands and smiles at the old man. "Of course Mara must have time," he says lightheartedly, standing up. He walks down the hallway, makes ready to leave. "We must give Mara time," he repeats, and then says goodbye to the old man.

"I knew you would understand. We'll get a medical certificate," says Marco in parting as he closes the door.

Kessler's expression turns severe as he stands alone in the corridor. He curses silently and goes down the stairs. "Bloody mess. This matter must be dealt with," he mutters. He strides out into the crowded street in the sunshine, looks at St. Peter's Basilica, and then walks off quickly in the direction of the Tiber, on his way to the old town. Kessler crosses the ancient bridge opposite Castel Sant'Angelo over the river that slowly but surely sinks to the sea over the course of time.

48

When Geir reaches the column, Deep Throat is not there. He exits the car park the way that Deep Throat always does, then circles the building to make sure that no one is monitoring his movements. Deep Throat greets him when Geir returns. "Peculiar things have happened," says Highpoint, waving his hand before Geir has a chance to speak. "Páll was blackmailed by Seiferdal and Smiley Thorson, who, on top of everything, has disappeared from the country."

"That's news to me," is all that Geir says.

"Despite an extensive search, they haven't managed to find Smiley. It's as though the Earth has swallowed the man. We've also searched for Seiferdal but without success. Yet it's thought most likely that the rascals are in southern Europe."

"What about Trinxon and Kessler?" asks Geir, since it's the first thing that comes to his mind as the old rascal has served his sentence.

"There's no evidence that they're connected to the case; quite the contrary," replies Highpoint.

"That's what Trinxon said at the start of Headgate," objects Geir.

"But this is still how it is," interjects Highpoint impatiently. "The European Security Bureau is in charge of the case, but for special reasons I want the search to be public."

"What do you mean? I smell a rat," says Geir, interrupting Highpoint.

"They're not on a wanted list anywhere," says Highpoint with an angry look. "It's as if nobody wants to find them. I can't go into further detail on it, but it's unnatural to wrap a veil of secrecy around them when you are trying to search for the two. So we need to get the blackmail out into the open," says Highpoint, and instead of waiting for a reply he walks away.

Geir rubs his hands together. His adrenaline is flowing and his old nose for news is alert, making him feel as if he's flying. It was just as well that he hadn't given in to the temptation to remain the winter in the sun and instead returned home to Iceland and what used to be his beloved *The Post*.

The news that Seiferdal and Thorson had blackmailed the deceased Páll Bjarnfreðsson is a bombshell in Iceland and is picked up by the European media, although there it is only covered as a secondary story. That's enough for most people, since there is no way connecting Trinxon to the blackmail.

The European press has stopped nipping at Trinxon's heels.

As soon as he sees the story, Pasiĉevic calls Highpoint to tear him off a strip. Highpoint puts on a sympathetic face. "I know it must be annoying," he says. "I have already ordered an investigation into who leaked the story to the press. Now I know you are interested, I will crack the whip to get some quick action." Highpoint is sitting in his chair at his desk, while Pasiĉevic walks quickly back and forth in his office in Berlin. "I find it hard to follow you when you stalk around like that," says Highpoint as calmly as possible, reducing Pasiĉevic to quarter size.

Pasiĉevic understands the gibe and stops abruptly. "This puts the investigation at risk," he says, trying to calm down. "The matter concerns state security," he adds, looking sharply into the eyes of Highpoint, who does not blink.

"You've still got no leads?" asks the Icelandic commissioner innocently.

"We haven't been able to find the men. It's as though they've been buried beneath the patio somewhere," replies Pasiĉevic. The man's sharp laughter pierces the ears of his fellow conversant in Reykjavík. Highpoint has difficulty understanding the humour.

"Wouldn't it be right to put out warrants for them across the continent?" asks Highpoint.

"No, not at this point, but we're looking into the matter. It pertains to national security, so we need to consider possible connections to Trinxon," replies Paśiĉevic before hanging up.

Highpoint is uneasy with Paśiĉevic's response. "There's something not right there," he mutters. "He should have threatened to take my head."

There are clouds on the horizon. Krummi and Helgi have a bad feeling about the situation, and ever-growing concerns about the trip to Rome, Júlía having made her point clearly. They're not familiar with Berlin manoeuvring but their friend has spoken clearly enough. What is Seiferdal up to, or Thorson? On top of everything else it appears the Security Bureau is dragging its feet. Although Júlía is worried, the President seems unconcerned.

The signing approaches rapidly.

Storm clouds have piled up in the European sky.

Devereaux is subject to tough, ever-growing criticism for setting Iceland free from the net of the Great European State. It is said that the Icelandic agreement threatens the state's future. The President had displayed an unparalleled lack of judgement in making Júlía Ingólfsdóttir his closest advisor, with her thanks for it being Iceland's withdrawal from Europe. Iceland's withdrawal ignites a spark in Greenland, with the richest oil reserves in the world. With Iceland's independence, the naval base in Hvalfjörður will no doubt be scrapped, considering the waxing opposition to the military presence in the cold country. The oil refineries in the Westfjords are in a state of confusion. The President's critics momentum seems to be increasing. The press seems to pick up on everything that makes the President look bad.

Europhiles, those zealous advocates of the Great European State throughout the continent, recall the Russian Resurgence with stars in their eyes. Vladimir Putin is elevated to a pedestal with the greatest men in Russian history. He took over Russia when it was licking its wounds and made it a superpower, suppressing rebellion absolutely mercilessly. This century Russian influence on the world has grown immensely. Putin is remembered respectfully as one of the most influential president of Russia. He is on a pedestal with Peter the Great and Joseph Stalin. No one mentions the kind-hearted Gorbachev or the drunkard Yeltsin.

Devereaux's critics say that great leaders are judged according to the growth and development of their states.

The war in Kazikistnam, and indeed around the Caspian Sea, is becoming ever more brutal. The governments in in the region are all in a difficult position, there have been fierce conflicts. Government forces have retreated from important oil fields after a wave of defeats that have paralysed battle-weary soldiers, despite the presence of the European military. During Trinxon's time, European military "advisers" had grown rapidly in number, now more than sixty thousand. European generals call for additional forces to be sent east to Kazikistnam or the war will be lost. Devereaux has refused all demands for European forces in the area. To the contrary, he will call the army home.

In an interview with one of the world's best-known journalists, Wal Chrômcite, the President speaks frankly about the war.

"Every man is born to freedom and independence and along with this comes accepting one's own responsibility. This is not our war, after all, this is their war," Devereaux says in the interview with the renowned reporter.

The President warns about the rise of European militarism and the trend toward government secrecy. "We want democracy to survive for future generations, not to become the insolvent phantom called Demcowill. In the councils of government, we must guard against the acquisition of unwarranted influence, whether sought or unsought, by the military-industrial complex. The potential for the disastrous rise of misplaced power exists and will persist.

"We must never let the weight of this combination endanger our liberties or democratic processes. We should take nothing for granted. Only an alert and knowledgeable citizenry can compel the proper meshing of the huge industrial and military machinery of defence with our peaceful methods and goals, so that security and liberty may prosper together.

"Government secrecy is despicable in a free and open society of men. Our society has fought against totalitarianism and government secrecy; against societies where oaths are sworn to dark forces. Long ago we discovered that few things are more threatening to a free society than attempts to hide and obscure facts. It is worth little to fight against totalitarianism if we turn off the road of democracy to some obscure Demcowill. There is a real danger that public security is a pretext for keeping the truth from the people."

After watching the interview, Krummi calls Helgi in the Westfjords.

"The President speaks eloquently, but he needs to watch his step in the political snake-pit of the Great European State. There are plenty of thorns to step on," says Krummi.

"He has certainly stepped on many, and more appear daily, but of course we mustn't lose our perspective in chasing shadows," replies Helgi. "We need only concentrate on Iceland now. Europe can look after itself, and so can Devereaux."

"You are being too laid back about all this," says Krummi.

"All right," counters Helgi. "So say you are right. Say Devereaux is surrounded by enemies just waiting to tear him down. What can we do about it?"

"I don't know," admits Krummi. "But just sitting here in the High North is achieving nothing. You know me. Sitting about is not the raven's style, I am a man of action. I'm going to Rome immediately," he says curtly.

Helgi looks up in surprise. "What are you thinking?" asks Helgi.

Krummi does not answer his question, and instead asks one of his own. "Are you coming with me?"

Helgi is frustrated, feeling that his friend is talking sheer nonsense. "What are you going to do in Rome besides visit the Colosseum?"

Krummi grins at his friend but does not budge an inch. "Of course I will visit the Colosseum, but I won't feel at ease unless I do something," he says, as his grin changes into the brightest smile. "If there are any plots in action, then Rome is their venue. We're in a better position in Rome than going with Júlía to Berlin and then off to Rome. Who knows, maybe Seiferdal and Thorson will turn up smiling in Rome. If they're planning and plotting there down south, there'll be a chance for us to find the needle in the haystack. All we have to do is stroll from café to café in the eternal city," he says, grinning broadly and stroking his beard.

"And have a look at the Colosseum," Helgi adds with a smile. "OK. I'll come along. There are few things more enjoyable than strolling amid Roman cafés and viewing the Colosseum — and discovering the truth. There may even be a needle to be found."

"Let's look for needles," says Krummi as he puts forward his missing thumb.

Helgi feels good about their decision to go to Rome ahead of Júlía.

He breaths deeply, and looks over Arnarfjörður to Dynjandi, Iceland's most musical waterfall. It's heavy, alluring, thunderous roar is embraced by every cliff-wall in the fjord. The waterfall's stairs up through the cliffs are like an entrance to the realm of the pagan Gods. Helgi is in good humour as he walks over the soft, mild heather. He is in a world of his own, contemplating life's wonders and the trip to Rome, when he suddenly hears flaps of wings over his head. He looks up and sees a raven lift itself to the sky. He doesn't think much about it and continues his journey to the bottom of the fjord.

He thinks of Hugi and Muni, Óðin's ravens, who each dawn fly out and over all the ancient world Miðgarð to watch over humans and report to the supreme God. At dusk they return and sit on Óðin's shoulders and croak the day's events into his ears. Thus Óðin knows everything that happens in the world of humans, the future included.

Again there is a strong flapping of wings, and this time the raven croaks powerfully as it dives towards the human. Helgi is quite startled, but smiles at his own reaction. He is in good humour; the weather being quite nice these last few days. He crosses an old wooden bridge and has almost reached the bottom of the fjord, when for the third time the raven flaps its wings, and dives toward him; this time the bird lands in front of him. The raven starts to swagger in front of Helgi, croaking as if the pitch-black bird has something important to say to the human in front of him... croak... croak... croak.

Then the raven's croaks intensifies as it attacks Helgi, who retreats in astonishment at the bird's uniquely peculiar behaviour. "What do you want from me?" he shouts, but the raven croaks still louder, attacking the human, flapping its wings until Helgi hits the bird firmly on the beak. The pitch-black raven retreats as if betrayed; strangely silent, it flies up and lands on a peak nearby.

"You're an impertinent little bastard," Helgi murmurs surly, before continuing his walk. The bird sits on the peak until the human disappears from its sight. Finally the raven takes flight and disappears into a rock-face at Dynjandi's highest point.

The sun turns black,
earth sinks in the sea,
the hot stars down
from heaven are whirled.

Rhythmically beneath Dynjandi's thunderous purl, the croaking of ravens can be heard from the rock-face: croak... croak... croak.

49

It is dawn; the medieval tower Tor Caldara at Anzio Beach is clearly visible from the luxury villa on the waterfront. Rudolf Kessler is sitting on a sofa, watching a rock opera in half-size in between flipping through a book about the ancient Roman town, Antium, or Anzio as it is called now. The powerful sounds of *The Wall*, the immortal masterwork of the British super-group Pink Floyd, crash over him. He had found the recording lying on a shelf and stuck it under the beam, projecting it in half-size in the middle of the room; although large, the room is not big enough for a full-size hologram.

Kessler walks over to a young man at a Wall, and reaches out with his hand but meets only thin air. Although the young man appears tangible, he is just an image; a tangible virtual reality. Kessler is enjoying himself immensely. He reduces the image to one-tenth size and then enlarges it to full-size, filling the whole room. He then sets it to quarter-size and finally half-size once more. "Under the beam," says Kessler out loud, looking thoughtfully at the beam of the steering glove, before adding distractedly: "Amazing how some expressions survive in the language." He smiles as he takes off the metallic glove and places it on the screen-top.

He had never heard of Pink Floyd, but their music thrills him ever more deeply. The room swirls with life. The bricks are stacked into a gigantic Wall of a nameless system, which with hammer in hand, hammers the downtrodden... hammers the downtrodden… hammers the downtrodden, powerless young man holding hands over his head, disappearing into the all-encompassing Wall. The young man in extreme anguish calls for help.

"Tear down this Wall; break the Wall," he shouts, but no one answers.

Over the relentless course of time the young man himself changes into a tyrant who with hammer in hand builds a Wall; an ever larger, ever higher Wall. His destiny is to hammer the next generation of the downtrodden.

Madness feeds more madness and everything spins in circles.

"All in all you're just another brick… in the Wall," resounds in the room.

The Wall closes in around the young man.

Kessler smiles to himself, since the idea is so familiar; in fact it is the most disputed topic in contemporary times. Europe has built a gigantic Wall around itself to keep the world at a distance and then Walls within the continent; Walls, more Walls, ever higher Walls, all of which aim is to turn the nameless into cogwheels in a gigantic system. He is a cogwheel in a gigantic system that hammers the downtrodden, the powerless, the nameless.

"People at all times have needed to go above and beyond," he mutters. He frowns and looks over at Anzio Beach.

Kessler has made the luxury villa the headquarters for the operation that will soon commence. He is expecting Olav Seiferdal and Smiley Thorson shortly. The song under the needle is by Pink Floyd's bigshot — the genius Roger Waters: "When the Tigers Broke Free." Anzio Beachhead from the dark, cold days of WWII appear in the room. The video for the song suddenly moves to Anzio Beach in 1944, mimicking the scene outside the window. It's all dark around … There's frost in the ground.

Kessler looks with empty eyes at the scenes of the battle fought there so long ago. He clearly feels the cold emanating from the snow, coloured with the blood of soldiers who were made to march into open death. Suddenly Kessler realises that the "tigers" of the song title are not big cats, but a type of German tank used in World War II.

Kessler's mind goes back to his school-days. He remembers being taught about Cicero, the great orator and philosopher of ancient Rome who had found refuge with his books in Anzio after he lost out in a political battle in Rome. Soldiers of his enemy, Mark Antony had come to kill him. When Cicero saw the men and realised why they had come to Anzio he said: "There is nothing proper about what you are doing, soldier, but do try to kill me properly."

Kessler smiles grimly. He is determined to do everything properly.

It rains and shines in the world of mankind. History goes round and round and round. The only thing that changes is life's stage.

Kessler feels the villa to be an excellent choice of location, being a short distance from Rome. He is going over the plan. There have been significant changes, far too many changes for his taste. He is annoyed, since the postponement of the old couple's trip to America has forced him switch to Plan B.

Kessler had gone to meet Buscetti. "A situation has come up," he had said as calmly as he could; the old woman was injured, meaning that the couple would not be going to America. The Sicilian had looked at him patronizingly; unforeseen occurrences during the final stages of an operation were like poison in his veins.

"You've got to clear this up," Buscetti had said sharply, taking a cigar from his breast pocket.

Kessler was growing more agitated, since he had hoped that the Italian would see to the old couple. Buscetti had been anything but pleased.

"Are you nuts? You think that we bully old people?" Buscetti had spat out, waving his hand. "What have I done to deserve this attitude from you? You ask neither out of respect nor friendship. You ask me to kill old people. With complete disrespect you ask me to kill old people. You who won't get your hands dirty; who works for the state under the protective wing of the police and courts; you who have found your wretched paradise in the service of the authorities."

Kessler was quite startled. "I beg you, Salvatore," he had stammered.

"You don't call me Salvatore. You lack the class. You're like every other common lout," Buscetti had exclaimed. "What have I done to deserve this disrespect?" he had shouted.

Kessler had bowed his head and the Sicilian lit his cigar.

Kessler had asked him to wait a moment while consulting with Berlin. He had returned in a completely calm mood after his conversation. "We'll take care of this situation," he had said as coldly as possible.

"You have twenty-four hours to fix this problem," Salvatore Buscetti had said. Kessler was anything but pleased. He had always thought Buscetti's insistence upon full control over the apartment so early before the operation absurd, but hadn't questioned it. "One doesn't argue with a man like that," he had told The Vulture.

"We'll take care of the plumbing in the little apartment, but, dear Senor Buscetti, can you see to the shipping of the package?" Kessler had asked with the utmost humility.

Buscetti had looked at him for a good long time as he considered the matter, and then nodded in approval. "We'll ship the package," he had replied.

The matter was settled.

Then there was the small matter of the clumsy colleagues whom Kessler has taken to calling "Dumb and Dumber", though never in their presence. Senor Buscetti had burst into laughter and said that of course Dumb and Dumber should be offered first class seats for the final journey. The deed is to be done tomorrow; the day before the operation on Via della Conciliazione.

"There is no problem, but my people here have their hands full with the main job. I must call in men from Sicily, but it will cost a shed-load of money," the Sicilian had said, completely calmly.

Kessler had nodded in approval, since Zarębianka had granted him full authority in making the deal.

"Good," had agreed Buscetti. "I will arrange the collection of the old couple from the flat. Tell your idiots to prepare their travel. I will arrange for their final journey to be done here. Best keep such business out of Rome. Agreed?" Kessler had nodded. Buscetti had then left.

Everything is ready, thinks Kessler.

Dumb and Dumber walk into the room. They had gone about 60 kilometres south to Latina to purchase equipment. The Vulture had insisted on this. "Don't do any business in Lazio; instead go to Latina," he had said determinedly.

"We'll be careful, of course," Kessler had replied.

Kessler nods at Dumb and Dumber and invites them to take seats on the sofa.

"A situation has come up that I need you to resolve for me," says Kessler, smiling at his colleagues. In retrospect, it had been a good idea to bring in Smiley to assist Olav, or was it Olav assisting Smiley? Kessler smiles to himself. Dumb and Dumber, indeed.

"A situation?" replies Smiley, bewildered.

"That will be no problem," Seiferdal hurriedly says.

"Unfortunately my suspicion proved right. I visited the old couple. They're not on their way to America anytime soon," says Kessler.

They look at each other in surprise. "Does this mean that we halt everything?" asks Smiley hesitantly.

"No, but you complete your assignment today," replies Kessler. "Pay a visit to the old couple and hasten their journey. No loud bangs, just chloroform, then the injections, and then pack the bodies carefully. The Sicilian will take care of the rest."

Smiley is clearly surprised, but he says nothing. Seiferdal understands and immediately nods his head. "We'll take care of this, and I expect that you have the required tools." They're used to speaking in riddles. Smiley keeps quiet and looks at his friend Olav, obviously having difficulty comprehending their conversation.

Kessler nods in return. "Everything you need is in the wardrobe. You need to finish the work by tonight. The packages will be collected in the morning."

They go to the foyer, where Kessler hands them a black handbag. "Here is everything you need," he says.

Smiley opens the door, and they make ready to leave. "While I remember it," says Kessler, who goes into the sitting room, returns and hands them a laminated piece of paper. Seiferdal glances at the text. "Gone to America. Best wishes, Marco and Mara."

"We'll hang the notice on the door," says Seiferdal with a smile.

"Sure," says Smiley lamely. He hasn't thought of this.

Kessler thinks of everything.

✦ 50 ✦

The shadow stretches its legs as the Airbus jet lands at Ciampino Airport outside of Rome. Helgi and Krummi walk out onto the airplane's staircase and quaff the warm Roman weather. The sun rests on the hills where eternity dwells. The day has grown quite long; they are quite weary, although the trip has gone better than they hoped. They have let Júlía know about the change in their travel plans. They could hear the relieved note in her voice. Now all they have to do is go to their hotel, the Dei Mellini, on the banks of the Tiber, an unassuming little hotel not far from Castel Sant'Angelo.

They want to stick close to St. Peter's Square.

"What, more visitors?" says Marco when the bell rings. The old couple don't get many visitors, with their son living in America. Relatives and friends had stopped coming to visit them long ago. Kessler had satisfied himself of this when he chose the apartment. He had been pleased with the selection.

"Hurry up and answer, man," says old Mara gruffly.

The old man hurries down the hallway, as quickly as he can. He calls to the visitor, turns the lock, releases the chain and opens the door. Before the door stand two men, smiling warmly. "Your neighbour complained about a leak in the sink," says Seiferdal in broken Italian.

Marco is surprised at this bother. He scratches his head. "Is the sink leaking?" he shouts down the hallway.

Mara doesn't think so.

"There's no leak here," says the old man as he moves to shut the door, being little given for foreigners.

Seiferdal puts his foot between the door and the stave, asks whether they might look under the sink, just to make sure that everything is okay before they leave. The old man looks at them a little suspiciously. He turns back to convey their request to Mara.

As he does so, Seiferdal covers the man's nose and mouth with a white cloth, and he sinks to the floor without a sound.

Smiley rushes down the hallway to the bedroom with a cloth beneath his lapel. "Good morning," he says in Icelandic.

"Who are you?" asks the old woman in a sharp voice.

Smiley does not reply, but instead goes straight to the old woman and puts the cloth over her nose and mouth.

Mara emits a choking sound.

The darkness has laid its heavy paw over Rome. Helgi and Krummi's taxi skims effortlessly over Vittorio Bridge. Krummi looks distractedly at the river, while Helgi scrutinizes a map of Rome. They need to make a detour and cross Conciliazione on their way to the hotel, which is just ahead. St. Peter's Basilica fills Krummi's sight as the yellow cab crosses the intersection. He is terribly surprised. Sitting there like a statue in a two-seater is Smiley Thorson, with another man. Krummi turns around quickly. "Did you see the guy?" he shouts, slapping Helgi's shoulder. Helgi looks up from the map in annoyance but says nothing.

As if a hand were waved, Smiley is gone and the red two-seater as well.

"You'll scare the life out of me if you see Smiley Thorson on every street corner," says Helgi dryly. He can scarcely believe that Krummi has found the needle in the haystack just like that, as soon as they arrive in Rome.

"Am I losing my mind? I thought I saw Smiley a moment ago," says Krummi hesitantly, scratching his beard. "Was that Seiferdal with him?" he asks himself. He clearly has his doubts, since the men had appeared for a spilt second, and then disappeared as if they never existed.

"Yes, and the Pope was sitting between them," adds Helgi with a smile.

Krummi says nothing, and turns around again. It's as if nothing has taken place, simply nothing at all.

Júlía has gone to Berlin to make preparations. She has accepted an informal dinner invitation from Devereaux. The President has expressed his congratulations to her on her magnificent election victory.

"It's my understanding that in Iceland's entire political history, there has never, simply never been such a turnabout in an election campaign," says Devereaux as they sit at dinner.

"The nation saw through the lies and falsehoods of my opponents at the eleventh hour," replies Júlía.

"I've seen footage from the meeting; have rarely seen a performance as good," says Devereaux, smiling.

"A watershed was reached at the Plaza, that's absolutely true. I may well have been effective, but I think that it were my two friends, Helgi and Krummi, who made the difference. When the nation saw them step forward by my side, celebrating and raising their hands in victory, it gained the strength necessary to stand on its own two feet. Then and only then was the spark lit that ignited the bonfire," says Júlía.

"I saw images of you three, extremely powerful images," says Devereaux.

Júlía turns to another topic that is on her mind. "Erich, I have worries about you in Rome," she says. "I've been getting a bad feeling."

He tries to interrupt her. "Júlía...," but she places her hand in his and they look each other in the eye.

"Erich, listen to my feminine intuition," she says heavily. "There are too many signs. Those two men who broke into Headgate have vanished, but most think they're in southern Europe. Have your people find them. What are they up to? I beg you to be careful."

"You can rest assured that security in St. Peter's Square will be extremely tight," replies the President with a smile.

"Find those rascals. I'm not implying anything, just asking you to be careful. You have angered a lot of people," she reiterates.

"What about you, Júlía? The same goes for you. You must be worried about your own welfare if you're worried about mine," says Devereaux curtly.

Júlía is surprised, having never seen this side of things. She feels it out of the question that the rats of the Berlin gutters would think it worth the trouble to waste their time on a female Icelandic politician, as the poet wrote:

No one mourns an Icelander
alone and dead.

Júlía is distracted, as if in another world, the remark having caught her by surprise. She is becoming ever more grateful that Krummi and Helgi have gone ahead of her to Rome.

"I'll ask Paśićevic to tighten the search for the fugitive." It is the President who breaks the silence, smiling as he fills their glasses.

"That's precisely the problem. I don't trust Paśićevic," says Júlía, who still has a lot on her mind.

The President waves off the remark. "I'm not fond of the Serb, but you mustn't forget that he is the head of the EIA; the man has a spotless career. Don't lose perspective, Júlía." The President's mood has darkened, but then he adds, much more mildly, as if to calm Júlía: "I'm donning my wellington boots to clear out he stables in the fourth week in November. There will be a clean-out, but now let us toast to the prosperity of Iceland and of Europe."

She understands without everything needing to be said, since this isn't the first time that they have difference of opinion. Their situation has changed. Previously, she was his chief advisor, but now they are the leaders of two states; the most powerful state in the world and the smallest at the farthest reaches of the sea, soon to gain full independence. They discuss the trip to Rome and the signing at St. Peter's Square; that historical moment. The restoration of the Republic at Thingvellir will be the greatest event in the history of Iceland since the establishment of the Republic in 1944. It gladdens Júlía to hear that the President is planning to attend the ceremony at

Thingvellir next summer.

They will leave Berlin with an entourage aboard the President's jet early Friday. The signing at St. Peter's Square is scheduled for noon; they have one working day before leaving, with many things to attend to.

Kessler cannot help but smile.

He had originally conceived the operation at St. Peter's Square as a "copy-cat" of the shooting of John Paul II back in 1981, but decided against it after much consideration. Such a plan involved too many uncertainties; the assassination at the Square and the escape would be risky, way too risky. It would have been tempting, since such an attack was more stylish; the Pope on the square with Devereaux and Júlía, there to grant the final sacrament.

No, it would be safer for the shooter to have a good view from a tall building, that is what a sniper needs. That attempt on the Pope back in the day had been a mess, lacking in all professionalism, feels Kessler. Utter amateurism, again Kessler can't help but smile.

No, it would be safer for the shooter to have a good view from a tall building, that is what a sniper needs. That attempt on the Pope back in the day had been a mess, lacking in all professionalism, feels Kessler. Utter amateurism, Kessler can't help but smile.

51

Salvatore Buscetti walks though the entranceway to the Colosseum, along with Benedetto Benso. The Sicilian's glamorous clothing attracts the attention of the few people out and about: his wide-brimmed hat, striped suit, colourful tie and snow-white shirt, polished shoes, loose light-brown cashmere coat. The elegant Benso in a violet coat looks almost ordinary compared to the Sicilian. They step out onto the platform and look over the ruins of the magnificent 2,000 year old arena, where sixty thousand Romans watched gladiators battle each other. Four men come walking along the walkway from the opposite direction. They had arrived on the morning flight from Sicily. It is nearly noon.

They have work to do; their sojourn in Rome will be short.

Buscetti embraces the leader of the four, his friend from childhood, Guiseppe Russo. The others greet him with Sicilian handshakes. There is friendship in the air. The four are to pick up a package in Rome, it is straightforward. Then Buscetti takes out a black folder and hands it to Russo, who flips through it and stops at photos of Seiferdal and Thorson. "You must remember that they are well trained, but unsuspecting," says Buscetti. "Do your work cleanly and quietly."

Russo nods and flips through the files. They are supposed to arrive at the villa at precisely three o'clock. By then the German Rudolf Kessler will have gone to Rome, along with Buscetti and Benso. The Scandinavians will be unsuspecting, since they are fully aware of the participation of the Mafia in the operation at St. Peter's Square and consider them allies. Russo takes out documents on Olav Seiferdal and Smiley Thorson, distributes photographs to his colleagues. Then he takes out a photo of Rudolf Kessler so that there will be no misunderstanding.

The event will take place in the sitting room. Russo will go to the window and point out at Anzio beachhead. His talk about the battle with the Tigers will confuse the victims, get their attention out of the room. That had been Kessler's idea. Russo's cohorts will then draw their guns, the targets fall, the task completed. The four are then to proceed to Naples that afternoon, with the four packages in the back of their van. From there the packages will be sent with Neapolitan rubbish for recycling in Germany. This operation of the Sicilian Mafia has never failed; never failed in decades, there being trusty men at every post. From Naples the four men will then continue south to the big toe of Italy and over the Messina Strait to Sicily.

The task will then be completed, simply and securely, in the manner of Sicilian professionals.

"No problem, no problem at all," says Russo, nodding at Buscetti. They hug and kiss each other's cheeks. Russo nods amicably at Benso. Buscetti trusts no one better to complete the job than Russo.

He is very satisfied.

Krummi and Helgi walk through the pleasantly shady entrance and out into the sun on the viewing walkway at the Colosseum. It has been nice to come into the shade, if even for a moment. They look over the ruins of the ancient stadium. "Everything here smells of history," says Helgi, drinking in the Roman fragrance of the ages. They stroll out onto the platform that runs lengthwise through the stadium. Krummi finds himself staring at a colourful Italian in a cashmere overcoat who walks past them with another man, after conversing with four men who walk off in the opposite direction. Krummi guesses that the man is Italian, since tourists would never dress like that.

"They know how to attract attention," he says, pointing out to Helgi the man in the cashmere coat. They watch the two men disappear into the shadow of the entranceway. "I should buy myself a coat like that while I am here," says Krummi.

"They won't have your size," responds Helgi, laughing.

Pink Floyd's great work plays ceaselessly this autumn day in the luxury villa a short distance from Anzio Beach. Kessler is going over the operation one final time with Dumb and Dumber. They are expecting the Sicilian at any moment. Around noon Kessler will leave with Buscetti and Benso for the venue in Rome. The four men will come shortly afterward to the villa and Dumb and Dumber will meet their fate. Better to call them by their nicknames than by their proper names.

Better to objectify the oafs, Kessler thinks. He can't help but be extremely pleased at how everything is working out.

He is going over President Devereaux's latest itinerary from Ciampino Airport to the Vatican with Seiferdal and Thorson. He is happy to include them in the plan, because it strengthens their belief that they are an integral part of the plan. Shortly before noon a special envoy had come with the President's plan signed and sealed. There are no significant changes; the jet will land at ten. Admittedly, they will change vehicles at Bainsizza Square and not at Castel Sant'Angelo. This will be done in order to fulfil the wishes of the locals, it being considered certain that a great crowd will welcome its president. The Italian Governess will be in the limousine along with her husband, and Júlía next to the President. The entourage will stop at Castel Sant'Angelo, where the President will step out of his limousine along with the two governesses. They will spend a few minutes on a walkabout with the crowd, then get into the Italian state limousine to drive to the Vatican.

Kessler is contented. The bottom line is simple: they will be riding in an open limousine up Via della Conciliazione to St. Peter's Square.

The bell rings. Buscetti is standing cheerfully in the doorway alongside Benso. Kessler invites them into the sitting room, where Pink Floyd is under the beam at full volume, in three-quarter size. The eddying Wall and terrifying figures flash throughout the room. We don't need no education ... we don't need no thought control.

"It's just another brick in the Wall," Kessler sings quite thrilled.

But the guest is startled; the Sicilian frowns. "What the hell is this?" shouts Buscetti over the noise, while Benso snaps his fingers, obviously taken by the music.

"This was lying on the shelf; an old composition," replies Kessler, swaying in time with the music.

"Turn off that rubbish," snaps the Sicilian in a commanding voice.

Kessler is startled and hurriedly shuts off the device. Seiferdal is surprised at Kessler's nervousness; he's never seen his boss like this. Smiley takes a step backwards, a frightened expression on his face.

"I don't want any Anglo-Saxon rubbish," says Buscetti angrily. "Put on a good opera instead."

Kessler hurries to select an opera, any opera. He grabs *The Marriage of Figaro* by Mozart and places it under the beam. Figaro steps out onto the floor and sings an aria, but since the sitting room cannot accommodate the full-size image of the huge opera stage, Kessler reduces it to half-size. Buscetti relaxes and leans back on the sofa. "That's more like it," he exclaims contentedly.

Kessler takes out the notes from Berlin and they browse through maps of Rome. They go over their plans for over an hour, since they are complicated. The escape is the most difficult part, it being important not to leave behind any loose ends. This is the part that Benso is most concerned about; Benso is the shooter.

Devereaux will arrive at Castel Sant'Angelo at eleven thirty am local time. It's less than twenty-four hours until the operation. Security at the castle will be tremendous, as well as on St. Peter's Square. On the other hand, the grip will be more relaxed on Via della Conciliazione. At noon the limousine will cross the intersection at Piazza Pia near the middle of Via della Conciliazione on its way to St. Peter's Square. The University is the first building on the right as they come to Via della Conciliazione. Benso has already set up his equipment in the old couple's apartment in the apartment building to the west of the university building. Everything has gone according to plan; all the practice and necessary adjustments behind them.

The escape route has been plotted. Tomorrow after the shooting,

Benso will flee along the roof — or rather, the roof garden — about 150 meters to the northern face of the house where two of the Sicilian's men will be waiting to assist him. They will throw a cable over to the old city wall parallel to Via della Conciliazione in the Borgo neighbourhood. Benso will zip down from the house onto the wall at Pupazzi Street, where fast, white one-seaters will be waiting. Together they will go down into the Catacombs at the ancient Appian Way, where the Earth will swallow them. The mafia has used the Catacombs at the Appian Way for many ages. They have proven to be a fail-safe location and escape route, tunnels having been dug out from the Catacombs to key locations in Rome.

"We're leaving Rome this afternoon and I will be in Munich before evening," says Kessler meaningfully. He will be far away tomorrow, lessening the chance of implicating himself in the assassination. He smiles wryly. By then Dumb and Dumber will be on their way to Germany for recycling.

Kessler looks up and smiles at Buscetti. "I know that the operation is in good hands, so it will be safe for us to leave Rome." Seiferdal and Smiley nod in assent. It's just like those secret agents in the President's assassination. They were out 24 hours before the hit in Dallas.

The Sicilian looks thoughtfully at Kessler. "I'm going over to Sicily, myself," he says dryly.

Kessler turns to Benso. "The future of the European state is in your hands, Benedetto," he says. Benso could not care less, yet he nods in assent. It is necessary to dress such operations in beautiful costumes, beautiful words. That's what these guys always do. For him the temptation is a thick stack of euros. The euros that will make him a rich man. Benso smiles, feeling as if nothing can go wrong.

Benedetto Benso was an elite marksman in the leading special forces group of the European Military in Kazikistnam. Only six months have passed since he returned home to Sicily from military service. Back to his mafia friends. And they pay much better than the Army has ever done.

He is entirely accustomed to hitting targets from eight-hundred-to-thousand-meter ranges; has done it again, again, and again, giving him the nickname the Sicilian Shooter. The range to his target on Via della Conciliazione will be only approximately one hundred meters, and it is no problem to hit two targets in under five seconds; no problem even though the black limousine will be on the move, no problem. Benso's record for a single day is nineteen guerrillas in the great mountains of Kazikistnam, near the border of Iran. He had shot them one by one from a range of nine-hundred meters. Four fell before the others realized that they were under ambush. Then he had killed the other fifteen; all of them highly trained guerrillas. One by one they had fallen to the bullets of the Sicilian Shooter as they desperately sought shelter.

He had been awarded the Star of Europe for the deed. But no extra money.

52

Kessler leans back and sips from his wine glass. "Everything has gone according to plan," he says contentedly. The situation with the old couple has been solved with the utmost efficiency in Rome. Seiferdal and Smiley did their job with the utmost professionalism. Kessler says that he is grateful for it, but now he needs to make an inspection of the little apartment on the Via della Conciliazione with Buscetti and Benso.

"Final check," says Kessler apologetically.

Seiferdal and Smiley feel it natural that the location be scrutinized one more time. Kessler urges them to grant a warm welcome to four Sicilians who are coming to join the operation. They are expected at three o'clock on the dot. Buscetti calls them the Valiant Four.

"You can rest assured, Herr Kessler," says Smiley reverentially.

Smiley is extremely pleased with his lot, since the job guarantees him lifelong financial security. The job at the old couple's apartment had of course been rather unpleasant, but had been accomplished professionally. It had gone better than Smiley had imagined. He likes his new role, as it gets him away from the cold and darkness of the old country. Smiley smiles, feeling good about himself.

Kessler puts on a thick black overcoat, a wide-brimmed hat and sunglasses, making him virtually unrecognisable. Kessler feels he is nearly a match for the colourful Buscetti. They walk out to a black limousine on the driveway. The glamorous Benso in his violet coat follows them, his mood calm.

Highpoint is not at ease with the situation: no news are not good news.

He holphs a colleague in Copenhagen and an Icelandic connection at Europol in the Hague. Since Trinxon's resignation, relationships with Berlin and Brussels have frayed, he thinks. The same trust doesn't exist, as if the European security authorities have withdrawn into shells regarding Icelanders who have turned their backs on Europe. They have no news on those bastards Seiferdal and Smiley.

Highpoint puts himself in touch with Paśiĉevic in Berlin who appears on the holph, calm and composed as he stands in his office. Highpoint enlarges him, standing up at the same time. He feels more confident, being taller than Paśiĉevic. They discuss various security issues in connection with the trip to Rome, then move on to the search for Seiferdal and Thorson.

"We've got a development there," says Paśiĉevic. "One of our operatives saw them in Thailand. They might be involved in gun running for one of those Hindu terrorist groups that operate from there. Seiferdal would be up for that sort of thing."

Highpoint feels relieve. "In Asia, that's good news," he responds, although he is surprised that the Director had not informed him.

"Sorry, I've got a call coming in from our operative in Beijing. I'd better go, it might be important." Highpoint detects an irritated tone in the voice of his colleague as the holph goes blank.

Highpoint asks his secretary to contact Júlía in Berlin. The Governess had particularly stressed being allowed to monitor progress of events. Shortly afterward Júlía appears. He projects her in full-size. She is sitting comfortably on a sofa in her hotel room in Berlin, viewing Highpoint in quarter-size.

"Any news?" asks Júlía.

"Seiferdal and Thorson have been seen in Thailand. It looks to me as if you can breathe easy there in St. Peter's Square," replies Highpoint, feeling good about himself.

Júlía stands up and walks around clearly relieved. "Good work," she says and smiles before hanging up. Highpoint feels good about the conversation. She had smiled, their relationship grows constantly better.

"Maybe I'll keep my job after all," thinks Highpoint.

The clock strikes three at the villa by Anzio Beach. A sun-red four-seater glides up the driveway. Seiferdal and Smiley walk to the door to greet the Valiant Four from Sicily. Seiferdal opens the door and walks out onto the veranda. Smiley follows.

Guiseppe Russo greets them companionably. "Call me Guiseppe," he says, and then introduces his colleagues: Simone, Michele, and Gennado.

"This sure is no shack," says Guiseppe as he takes a large black handbag from the boot of the car.

They walk in.

Mozart's opera is playing in quarter size. Figaro steps forward, full of despair, feeling as if his trust has been betrayed by his beloved; the beautiful Susanna. Intense music and passionate feelings fill the room. The Sicilians are captivated and they enlarge the stage. The opera will soon come to an end; the drama reach its climax; Mozart's magical genius moves them all. Figaro walks into the middle of the room and laments female fickleness, deeply emotional. "Open your eyes, you foolish husbands!" sings Figaro mournfully.

"Open your eyes!"

The countess enters the stage along with Susanna, Figaro's betrothed. They have exchanged clothing to deceive the hero, who falls for the trick.

"Betrayer!" sings Figaro passionately, and repeats his accusation in great despair. "Betrayer!"

His dearly beloved Susanna is now alone on stage. Figaro hides behind a column, overcome with jealousy in his solitude. He has not yet seen through his beloved's web of deceit.

"Oh, come! Do not delay," sings Susanna, placing her hand on her bosom.

"Magnificent, what music, what emotions," shouts Guiseppe, moved to tears by the genius of the great master. He turns away from the drama and walks to the window. "What a view!" he shouts even louder in order to be heard over the music, pointing toward Anzio Beach.

Olav Seiferdal and Smiley Thorson look over at the beach and nod in agreement.

"Italy is fantastic," shouts Smiley.

They go to the window with the view opening up. "Lovely, but this doesn't compare to the midnight sun back in Iceland," shouts the smiling Smiley.

"Well if Iceland is so marvellous, how come you didn't stay there?" Guisseppe shouts back annoyingly.

"Well," explains Smiley in even louder voice, "They're all so clever up there, that I had to go to Berlin to have any chance of making it." He laughs heartily, as does Seiferdal.

Guisseppe smiles at them, extends his left hand, and raises it with fingers together, then turns to his Sicilian compatriots and steps aside. The two Scandinavians start walking back, smiling happily. "What a glorious day," shouts Smiley.

Guiseppe snaps his fingers.

The Three Valiants draw their pistols. The Scandinavians Olav Seiferdal and Smiley Thorson are dead before they hit the floor, their expressions stunned and their eyes glazed. The Sicilian Mafia accomplishes its tasks with impeccable professionalism. Guisseppe smiles.

The room is filled with the sounds of the final aria. "Forgive me," sings the Count full of remorse as the Countess catches him in the act. He is forgiven. Everyone embraces, the deceit is exposed. The curtain falls.

Guiseppe still sheds tears. "Wonderful music, glorious music of an immortal master," he shouts, kissing the fingertips of his left hand, which he then raises, opening his palm abruptly. "Masterpiece!"

Krummi and Helgi sit in a small restaurant above Piazza del Campo di Fiori in the old city. The busy market is humming with locals shopping for fruit, vegetables, cheese and salami.

The two Icelanders had been trying to find the Ara Pacis, the ancient Altar of Peace, but the Tiber fooled them. They are not the first tourists to get lost in the eternal city, where the Tiber squirms like a snake and nothing is level, clean, or straight; house upon house, hills and sloping, narrow winding streets that lead one astray. Still, they had found their way along the ultra-narrow Pilgrim's Way. There one finds the cloaked statue of the monk Giordano Bruno, head bowed; he claimed that the sun was the centre of the universe and the stars in the sky distant suns.

The Inquisition sentenced the monk to be burned at the stake. The bowed, cloaked Bruno met his fate in the year 1600. And there one finds a cluster of houses resembling a crescent moon in the ruins of the Pompeii Theatre, where Julius Caesar was stabbed twenty-three times. "Casca, you rogue. What is it you do?" asked Caesar, grasping the hand of the cowardly traitor, who called for help. A group of assassins stepped up, among them an old friend of Caesar. "You too, Brutus?" were the last words of the victorious emperor who had brought Gaul under the Roman Empire and made inroads into Britain.

Rome was indeed the first Great European State.

The two of them sit alone on a patio of the little restaurant.

They are not entirely alone, because they are on the holph in close conversation with Júlía. She's in the most elegant hotel room in Berlin in a Dante-chair. What a magical device, this holph, although they are a bit wary of it. She tells them about her conversation with Highpoint. "Everything is calm. Kessler is at home, Seiferdal and Thorson in Thailand," says Júlía with a smile.

Helgi bursts out laughing.

"Why are you laughing?" asks Júlía in surprise.

"He's making fun of me," replies Krummi, telling her about what he calls the mirage on Via della Conciliazione.

"Yes, and the pope was sitting between them," adds Helgi with a laugh.

"I've grown too old for such nonsense," says Krummi, grinning.

"What rubbish; you're supremely fit," says Júlía, smiling warmly. "Got to go, see you tomorrow," she adds as she vanishes.

The two friends sip coffee as they silently watch the colourful crowd on the square, each in his own world. It's Helgi who breaks the silence.

"How is it that Europe hasn't come to terms with the madness of the 20th century; what is it that causes such destruction?" he asks, referring to his conversations with Sólman in Brussels. "Back home, a 20th century philosopher, claimed that through the ages, power-struggle and wars in the world of humans have basically been between the religious and the atheists," Helgi says.

Krummi´s face turns serious. "It's an interesting thought. Is it possible that the power-struggle you mention, is between the closed mind and the open mind?"

"What do you mean?" Helgi asks.

Krummi looks at his friend, and continues. "In western democratic civilization, open minded people with good-will are the rock of society. Out on the edges are political mavericks who seek strength in the closed mind, revolving around Nay and Yea attitudes, controlled by negative emotions. It's the closed mind that dominates totalitarian and dictatorial societies where Nay reigns with terror. Authoritarianism has roots in a special kind of mind-set; compulsive Nay-behaviour that seeks strength and support among vacillating Yea-behaviour."

"A prominent gestalt-therapist and a good friend of mine used to visit us in the Westmann Islands. We worked on opening minds to live in the present with good-will toward others. He argues that dysfunction's sanctuary is the compulsive Nay and Yea reaction of the closed mind. Negative emotions are in control of behaviour before matters are thought through. The most difficult to tackle is the compulsive Nay on people's minds. Confusion and chaos is the Nay's fertile hunting ground paving the way for a takeover of power in extreme circumstances."

Krummi takes a sip of coffee. "Nay-people are constantly grumpy, sulky and irrational, putting things off and postponing them around the Nay. It's called psychological reversal; the polarity of the body's energy system is reversed. The Nay-people turn against society, as well as against people around them and eventually against themselves; brawling, breaking and bullying. The Nay is deeply rooted in western societies, exceptionally skilful in the art of hiding its trail.

"Sounds really simple," remarks Helgi. He watches an old woman dressed in black argue with a stall holder about the quality of his tomatoes. Helgi cannot hear a word over the market noises, but the body language is clear enough.

Krummi grabs a napkin and draws a circle. He marks it the closed mind. At the edges are the poles, which he marks Nay and Yea. The closed mind's first reaction to life's challenges is either Nay or Yea. There is an invisible link between the Nay and the Yea that draws them together, not unlike the magnetic field between Mother Earth's two poles: North and South.

The open mind on the other hand has view to all directions, not just Nay or Yea. Helgi's attention is drawn back to his friend. He looks thoughtfully at the drawing on the napkin and then at his friend.

Krummi grins, his white teeth flashing in his black beard. "Like North and South are the two connected opposing poles, the Yea and Nay are the connected poles of human behaviour," he says, his voice turning serious. "Toward the edge of society are people with closed minds, constantly reacting to life's challenges with either Nay or Yea; people's first reaction to life is based on negative emotions and instincts, created by negative experience, starting in childhood; rejection, abuse, violence or what have you. The Nay-people are authoritative, envious, and compulsive, craving for people to march in time to their ideas.

"Yea-people have a soft spot for Nay-people, who tend to be masters of propaganda, claiming to be guardians of right and wrong; the poor and the oppressed. The Nay sucks up the Yea like a powerful vacuum cleaner. It's well known, that flies are attracted to light. Salesmen are drawn to Yea-people, selling them everything between Heaven and Earth, ideas no less than goods. Yea-people tend to appease and bring gifts. The most radiant Yea-people with the biggest smile and widest Yea tend to have a soft spot for the Nay." Krummi leans backward in his chair.

"You mean that character, mind-set or mentality, whatever you call it, groups people the same way sheep are rounded up?" Helgi asks.

Krummi nods in assent. "Nay-persons may be few, but they can be extremely powerful in chaotic circumstances when the strongest Nay becomes the leader of the pack, seeking strength in fear and terror," he says and snaps his fingers, continuing: "The Communists coup d'état in Russia occurred as the tzar's empire fell like a house of cards. The Nazis grabbed power in Germany as the Weimar-republic collapsed. A small group of extreme Nay-persons grabbed power. Immoral, deceitful, evil men grasped societies by the neck with terror, fraud and lies. They played to the gallery, ordering people to march in time; fuelling fear, envy, hate and terror, staging political trials, shackling innocent people in Gulags, concentration camps, killing and executing people. They had special relationships with soul mates all over the world, western societies included; political comrades-in-arms were ready to shackle their own people to the madness of their isms.

"They were linked by the invisible force of the closed mind.

"Hitler, Stalin, Mao and the rest of them shared the same domicile: the Nay. Nazism and Communism shared the Nay domicile along with fear, lies, wickedness and evil. Hundreds of millions of people were victims to the madness of these evil isms. There was constantly growing authoritarianism and terror. The Nay-people are, however, masters at covering their tracks. They've convinced people that Communism is Nazism's adversary and opponent; right versus left politics. The fact is that both isms share a domicile. It's claimed that totalitarianism and dictatorship are evils of the past never to return. That is incorrect. The compulsive-Nay is still vigilant, gathering strength and abides its time." Krummi looks to the people at the square.

"Phew," Krummi sighs and adds: "The closed mind paves the way to serfdom, where Nay is Hell's estate and the Devil its landlord."

"You are saying that Evil is the adopted offspring of the compulsive-Nay," concludes Helgi, there is a mixture of shock and sadness in his voice as he goes on: "Those brutal tyrants, like Kim Il Sung, Colonel Gadaffi, Saddam Hussein, Idi Amin and the rest of them, were motivated and driven by the Nay. In the same way, Mafia gangsters like Al Capone."

Krummi nods in assent. "They created Hell. People will say that the matter is infinitely more complicated and that I'm simplifying. There is some truth in that, but the fact remains that the very root of man's evil originates in the dreadful compulsive-Nay-behaviour."

"Well, whatever truth there is in your theory, it's fair to ask: what drove Hitler and Stalin and the rest of them: what motivates the tyrant? How come that simple question is not asked in full honesty?" There is a surprise tone in Helgi's simple question.

"Here," breaks in Krummi, "do you remember that book that was in all the schools when we were kids. It was about two mice called Hem and Haw. I think it was called *Who Moved My Cheese*? As I recall it, they had a tasty bit of cheese, but somebody moved it. Hem´s reaction was total denial to life´s changes. He pointed his finger, convinced that the disappearance of his cheese was instigated by some nameless enemies. He demanded his cheese back and refused to move until it was returned. His mind was locked, closed to other options. Haw, on the other hand, came to his senses, opened his mind and started looking for and found new cheese."

Helgi nods in approval. "Hem acted upon negative emotions that controlled his life. He was his own worst enemy. He becomes dangerous given power over other people. So, you're saying that the nameless Nay-people hide in their little black holes in nameless systems. They abide their time, wait for their leader to step forward; the blokes on the box – like Hitler, Lenin, and the rest of them, who claim to know all the answers, grab power and then abuse power," he says.

"Well said, this is precisely the case." Krummi´s eyes spark as he

331

continues. "The bloke on the box shakes his fists in anger, points finger seeking enemies, constantly pessimistic. He practises on the box and bides his time, gathering Nay around him. At first people smile at his awkwardness, but he develops into a brilliant orator. As society collapses to rubble the bloke on the box grabs the seat of power. However, it turns out that he has no solutions, authoritativeness grows step by step, the situation worsens until his pitiful system collapses. His fall is to be found in the Nay which nests within him. It brought him to power, but ultimately destroys him. Slowly but surely everything he touches shrinks and declines. The question is: how much harm will the bloke inflict before he's found out." Krummi sighs as he concludes his sermon.

All this comes as quite a surprise to Helgi but he can see the logic. "Albert Einstein said that weakness of attitude becomes weakness of character. Winston Churchill said that the optimist sees opportunity in every danger; the pessimist sees danger in every opportunity," he says enthusiastically.

"There is the Nay's fall. The one who sees danger in every corner, gets infected by fear, envy, malice, cowardice, wickedness and all the rest of it," replies Krummi, looking deep into his friends eyes. There is deep urgency in his voice as he slowly emphasizes each and every word: "It's mind-boggling how the people bows to the closed mind before it gathers courage and strength to rise up against it. The Nay-person with a gun in hand is a daunting and dangerous prospect." The giant recites his poem.

Nay has gun in hand,
army to command
creates Hell in land
of the Closed mind.
The Devil is landlord.

Thunders roar,
feeding despair,

fire and terror
poisoning the air.
The Nightmare rumbles.

Nay corrodes,
haunted by ghosts,
hides in holes
with panic as host.
The Wall crumples.

"The closed mind has issues with tolerance and trust so it's impossible for it to put faith in a divine being of love without things getting turned and twisted," says Krummi as he continues his sermon. "Through the centuries the closed mind has made its nest in religion, using the Church as a tool of control, tyranny and terror. The church as seat of power is a magnet for the authoritative. The infamous Inquisition, immoral preachers and priests' abuse of children are horrifying examples of evil deeds of the twisted closed mind.

"The open minded has no problem with trust and love. Christ's mission was to open humanity´s mind, lead mankind out of the destructiveness of the closed mind. Christ said: 'You have heard that it was said: you shall love your neighbour and hate your enemy, but I say to you: love your enemies and pray for those who persecute you'." Krummi stands up and walks to the railing of the balcony and looks over the square.

There is a wry smile on Helgi's face as he recalls events in Copenhagen. Education helps to open minds, however, the closed mind easily nests in the educated. He shakes his head in anguish. "Giordano Bruno was persecuted by the 'educated' of their time. We saw his statue earlier today, remember?" Helgi says, touching fingers at the educated.

As the evening draws in, the pair set off back to their hotel. They decide to detour on their way up Via della Conciliazione. From

333

Vittorio Bridge they see the magnificent Castel Sant'Angelo, and ahead of them the dome of St. Peter's Basilica. They come to the intersection of San Pio Street and Via della Conciliazione. The University is on the other side of the street, to their right. St. Peter's Basilica in all its glory appears before them at the end of the boulevard. They walk down Via della Conciliazione toward Castel Sant'Angelo, the castle that Emperor Hadrian built in the second century and that was converted into a fortress when the Visigoths invaded the Empire in the fifth century.

Krummi's eyes wander over the boulevard and come to rest on the man in the cashmere overcoat whom he had seen in the Colosseum. Thick cigar smoke emanates from him; accompanying him is the young man in the violet coat. Krummi does not recognize the third man, who wears a wide-brimmed hat, sunglasses and a black thick overcoat.

"There's that man in cashmere," says Krummi, elbowing Helgi, who looks up the street. Helgi nods but is amazed by the exceptional vision of his friend, it being such a long distance to the men who are making their way up the boulevard toward St. Peter's Basilica. The third man turns around, takes off his sunglasses and wipes them with a handkerchief, lifts his hat, strokes back his hair and looks down the street. Krummi is startled as he recognizes Kessler.

"It's Kessler," he says curtly, elbowing Helgi, who simply cannot distinguish the man's face from this distance.

"Are you sure?" asks Helgi sceptically.

"I'm fairly certain, but it's a long way," replies Krummi, pushing Helgi. They stride up Via della Conciliazione after the trio, who turn a corner onto a narrow street. Krummi goes in hot pursuit, with Helgi at his heels. In a few moments Krummi has turned the corner, only to find a narrow alley. He peers down the alley but the trio is nowhere to be seen. Helgi is some distance behind.

Krummi runs into the alley and comes to an intersection, but it's as if the Earth has swallowed the men. He stands beneath the ancient town wall with a portal to the north, large enough for a car. He is at the intersection of Borgo San Angelo and Via Pupazzi. Krummi runs on through the opening in the wall and finds himself in a residential area.

The trio is nowhere to be seen.

Krummi curses his own lack of speed; he should have done better. He runs back with a disappointed expression. Helgi comes up huffing and puffing. Krummi runs back into the alley and looks about. There is only one other way out, a door set into a high blank wall. He tears open the door and finds himself in a yard. There he finds no one but an old man, sweeping the ground. Krummi asks whether he has seen three men enter the alley.

"No, amico," replies the old man.

Krummi curses vigorously and goes back into the alley. Helgi is standing outside it, half-bent, with both hands on his knees, so winded that he has difficulty breathing.

"You're killing me," he mutters.

"That's what one gets for playing police like an amateur," says Krummi angrily. "A seasoned man would never have lost the three of them. It's as if they vanished into thin air," he adds.

They walk out on to Via della Conciliazione, surprised and disappointed.

"Are you certain it was Kessler?" Helgi is extremely suspicious, since he could never have identified a person from the distance at which Krummi said he thought he saw Kessler.

"I think I saw Kessler but am not certain, since the man was at quite a distance. And I've never seen him except in a photo. But still," says Krummi, scratching his thick hair. "Still, I think it was Rudolf Kessler."

"At least it's clear that the pope wasn't with him," sighs Helgi, without smiling. He is troubled as they leave the scene.

Disappointed, Krummi and Helgi return to their hotel. They try to reach Júlía, but she is at a meeting, her holph switched off.

The three men open a basement door and stroll out into the yard. The Sicilian nods to the old man with the broom and hands him a banknote. Buscetti scowls as he turns to Kessler. "Who are those

∍ asks gruffly.

᠊sler shakes his head and shrugs his shoulders. "I have no idea ᠊out that, but I'd best be on my way," he answers.

Benedetto Benso looks at Kessler suspiciously. "It's clear that there's a joker in the pack," he says, turning to Buscetti. "We have to consider cancelling the operation. I need information about these men."

Buscetti nods in agreement. He turns to Kessler. "I'll put my man on the case, but we only caught a glimpse of them. You'd better inform The Vulture."

Kessler nods in agreement. He needs to get going, there is no time to lose.

53

Helgi and Krummi are eating supper and anxiously discussing the day's events when Júlía finally appears from Berlin; they project her in full size. "Anything new?" asks Júlía, who is getting dressed for a dinner at the presidential palace. They are a bit surprised, but she just laughs.

"Kessler is here in Rome; I saw him on the street that goes to St. Peter's Square," says Krummi.

Júlía, who is applying mascara, looks abruptly at the holph. "Kessler in Rome," she says anxiously.

"We went after him but we lost him in a side alley," replies Krummi apologetically. "It might not mean anything, but in itself it's something for concern."

"What do you think, Helgi?" asks Júlía firmly.

"I would never have been able to identify anyone from that distance," responds Helgi hesitantly, before adding: "On the other hand, I trust Krummi absolutely and I think that we need to check on Kessler's whereabouts. And if Kessler is in Rome, then I bet that Seiferdal and Thorson are too. Maybe it was something more tangible than phantoms that Krummi saw."

Júlía stands up and considers the situation, her expression serious. "The three of them are a poisonous mixture. I'll speak to Highpoint in Reykjavík. I'll ask him to contact you."

She then ends the call.

The colleagues glance at each other.

Helgi shrugs but Krummi calls to a waiter.

Highpoint is on his way out of the office when Júlía calls and tells him the news. "Find out what's going on," she says.

"Paśiĉevic is the only man who will know that. I'll speak to him,"

337

says Highpoint. She asks Highpoint to assist her colleagues in Rome in every way possible. Highpoint thinks Júlia is overreacting, but better safe than sorry. It is evening in Berlin, but he puts a call through to Paśiĉevic anyway.

Paśiĉevic is still in his office when the Icelander calls from Reykavík.

"Who claims he saw Kessler?" Paśiĉevic asks.

Highpoint is slightly embarrassed. "Two men in the Icelandic Governess' contingent. They think they saw Kessler but aren't sure. Wanted to check whether this could be correct. They even imagine they saw Seiferdal and Thorson in Rome."

"What are their names?" asks Paśiĉevic.

"Oh, you will know their names alright: Krummi Illugason and Helgi Thorláksson but the Governess has personally vouched for them," replies Highpoint. "We have to take what they say seriously."

Paśiĉevic looks up meaningfully, as if weighing the information. "What kind of company does that woman keep?" he mutters, rather aggrieved at not knowing that the two men were in Rome. His operatives in Rome need a kick up the backside if they missed those two arriving. However he puts on a smile. "I will look into the matter, since I can't imagine what Kessler is doing in Rome and we know that the other two are in Thailand. I'll be in touch," Paśiĉevic adds firmly.

Highpoint is very satisfied with the response. That's how district commissioners should behave, he thinks. Only five minutes pass before Paśiĉevic appears on the holph. He has stood up from his desk. "I don't understand this nonsense," says Paśiĉevic. "I've reached Kessler; he's in Munich. I've briefed him. I'll put him on the line."

Kessler appears, and now they are three. Kessler is standing next to a yellow two-seater and says with a smile: "It wouldn't be bad to bring part of Rome up here to Munich." His expression darkens and he says angrily: "What nonsense is this? This is harassment and nothing else."

Highpoint is startled; Paśiĉevic apologizes for the outburst.

Kessler calms down but turns to Highpoint. "In order to squash any doubts I'll turn the holph full circle." The view moves, then the headquarters of BMW and Allianz Stadium appear. There is no doubt that Kessler is in Munich.

Highpoint quickly grows angry; not at Kessler's outburst, but rather the Icelandic idiots in Rome. "Dear Herr Kessler, I beg you to excuse the disturbance. I hope that you understand that I did not instigate this phone call. The Governess wanted to check on the matter for her friends in Rome."

"Yes, well no harm done, I suppose. But tell those dolts in Rome to wear better glasses in future. When I was working for the Security Service, we had those two down as potential terrorists, now they are in the official entourage." Kessler rolls his eyes, then turns back to Paśiĉevic. "Is that it?" he asks.

"Thank you, Herr Kessler," replies Paśiĉevic, who turns to Highpoint as soon as Kessler's hologram disappears. "It would seem that someone has lost their perspective," says Paśiĉevic calmly, ending the call.

Highpoint feels like an idiot, terribly irritated over letting himself be led on a wild goose chase. However, he makes the effort to calm down before contacting Krummi and Helgi. They appear before him, evidently at a hotel bar. That figures, thinks Highpoint. He relates to them his conversation with Paśiĉevic in Berlin and Kessler in Munich. Highpoint speaks dryly. He wants their conversation to be as short as possible and thanks them.

Kessler stares into the dark Munich street. That was a close call. He dreads to think of Paśiĉevic reaction if he had messed up. No-one is supposed to know about his little visit to Rome. Truth to tell, he's really in a state of shock. It's a good thing that he'd arrived in time in Munich.

His mind wanders back to the days in the Balkans when he first met Paśiĉevic. Kessler was serving in a top secret mission to kill the Serb prime-minister. They had decided upon forcing the PM's limousine off the steep valley road but failed miserably. Instead of pushing the PM's car into the abyss, Kessler's driver, Pagzic had lost control of the truck which skidded down into the void. Pagzic was killed instantly and Kessler broke his left leg and was really out cold, trapped in the truck when out of nowhere a young Pašiĉevic had pulled him out of the vehicle, cursing him for sluggishness, shouting that it certainly would look bad if the dead body of a Berlin secret agent was to be found in a truck involved in an assassination attempt on Prime Minister Zoranovic Pindévic.

"What were you thinking?" Pašiĉevic had exclaimed ferociously. "How would Berlin explain?" Even then he had always been thinking the next move ahead, the move that would get him the top Security job in Berlin.

They had escaped before the local police arrived to find the wreck. Kessler had, at the time, known nothing about Slobodan Pašiĉevic except that he was a local contact. Later Kessler found out that he was the head of a clandestine cell within the infamous Red Berets. That elite unit had operated ever since the break-up of old Yugoslavia under President Slobodan Milosevic who was convicted of genocide in The Hague, or did he pass away before verdict was reached? Kessler can't quite remember.

Anyway, that was how Kessler had met Pašiĉevic and he still shudders to think of the excruciating pain as he was dragged through the forest to a safe house. Afterwards, Kessler was secretly sent back to Berlin but had to admit that Pašiĉevic was right: it was, in hindsight, plain stupid to have been in that truck but he had felt so confident about the success of the operation.

A fortnight later Pindévic was assassinated as he was standing by the entrance of the Governmental offices in Belgrade, waiting for a Scandinavian foreign minister to arrive. He had been shot from the third floor of the photogrammetry approximately 200 meters away. It was a clean hit: the bullet penetrated the PM's heart killing him instantly. Pašiĉevic had organised it, Kessler thinks.

"These Serbs are not to mess with," Kessler mutters to himself.

He's still confused that only six months later the Swedish minister was assassinated in downtown Stockholm by what was claimed to be a Serb "lunatic". He suspects the assassin to have been "programmed" for the kill. It was basically the same kind of hit as when that Swedish PM was gunned down in Stockholm back in the 20th century. There were some links to the Balkans but the assassin was never found. The Slavs know their trade.

Kessler shakes his head.

He's still in awe of Paśiĉevic and after all these years he still senses his fury over the mess in the mountains. He has ever since felt obligated to the man who had risen to become head of Serbian Secret Service. And upon arrival in Berlin, Paśiĉevic had kept in touch with Kessler – secretly and in their own special way, of course.

There is grimness in Kessler's face, a sense of brokenness within. He still feels deep within the echo of that excruciating pain: the sheer terror as the truck had crashed into the abyss. How he survived is still a mystery to him. However, the worst about this horrible Balkan experience is that ever since he has never quite felt his own master. He shakes his head and goes through his hair with his hands. He takes a sip of water and buttons his coat.

He is, however, more relaxed, even smiling as that call was like a godsend, since he hadn't been able to find out the identity of the men who had suddenly appeared in Rome. Now it has all come together.

Kessler calls up a file on Helgi and Krummi. "Troublemakers, but not professionals," he mutters to himself. "They're part of the official entourage of the President and the Governess. Still they obviously don't know anything about the plan, they just saw me and think they smell a rat." Kessler laughs wholeheartedly, now completely at ease. "Now I have an alibi," he shouts into the night. He flicks on his holph and calls the Sicilian.

In Berlin, The Vulture stands up from his seat, turns and watches over the Spree in deep thought, fiddling with his moustache. His stinging eyes are fixed on the river, which quietly listens with sadness in heart.

We have done with Hope and Honour...

We're poor little lambs who've lost our way,
Baa! Baa! Baa!
We're little black sheep who've gone astray,
Baa--aa--aa!

The River Spree flows through Berlin as it has done for centuries, if only it could pass on humanity's dirty secrets.

54

The presidential jet comes in for landing at Ciampino Airport on the outskirts of Rome. It is bright and beautiful autumn day. Júlía's heart is full of anticipation, this being such a historical day. Iceland will become a sovereign state and the Republic will be restored at Thingvellir. A large number of Icelanders are said to have made their way to Rome to attend the signing at St. Peter's Square. The Eternal City spreads out before Júlía's eyes as she sits alone with her thoughts by the window. Devereaux is in his office toward the front of the jet. In the Eternal City great preparations are being made and the visit of the President of Europe is called a symbolic event. The European government wants to improve relations with the Church, which during recent times has been struggling.

The jet touches the runway; the landing is perfect.

The Italian Governess, Giulia de'Medici, stands on a red carpet on the tarmac along with her partner as Erich Devereaux walks onto the staircase landing and waves to the crowd. He walks down the steps. Shortly afterward, Júlía Ingólfsdóttir steps out of the plane in accordance with proper protocol. As the Italian Governess greets the president; Júlía walks down the steps. The three of them walk together past an honour guard of the Third Battalion of the European Military. The President is in high spirits. He has visited other union states but the visit to the Vatican is his first to a sovereign state. The Italian trip is a special one.

Krummi walks down Via della Conciliazione from St. Peter's Square. The European flag waves everywhere but the Icelandic flag is flying in a few places; people have started gathering to welcome their president even though it is still quite a long time until his arrival at Castel Sant'Angelo, where Helgi has positioned himself.

The two Icelanders have decided to divide the work between them, because there have been rather too many coincidences, especially the incident on Via della Conciliazione. Security is extremely visible, though particularly at Castel Sant'Angelo and St. Peter's Square. Krummi feels relieved seeing armed security guards out and about. He is not going to abandon his position keeping watch on all of Via della Conciliazione. The huge crowds means that the president will be a bit late. Krummi finds it only an advantage.

The President steps into a limousine along with Júlía, de'Medici and her partner. Devereaux is thrilled by the reception to his visit to Rome and the Vatican. "It's always a delight to come to Rome," says the President cheerfully as they set out for the city.

"It has certainly been a long time since a European leader visited the Vatican," replies Júlía.

"It's quite remarkable," replies Devereaux, looking in the direction of the city. "European kings, presidents and ministers were diligent in visiting, but I am the first President since the foundation of the Great European State to visit the Pope. The Komizars never shook the Pope's hand. I hadn't considered this until my speechwriter Stephan ran across it."

"Remarkable," agrees Júlía.

They drive to Piazza Bainsizza. A large crowd has gathered at the square in order to pay homage to the President who will walk out to meet his people. He shakes hands with numerous individuals and chats to them. The guards are uneasy but everything goes as planned, although they feel that the President spends rather too much time among the crowd. They're already running behind schedule.

They then switch to the old state limousine that was considered antique long ago but is kept for ceremonial purposes. It is a venerable pitch-black open car in the spirit of the limos of the 20th century. Júlía sits next to Devereaux in the back seat, with Governess de'Medici and her spouse in front of them. She is popular in Italy, an elegant woman of around fifty, endowed with great personal charm. Júlía looks out the back of the limousine; two security guards stand behind the car. A black limo loaded with men in black uniforms and sunglasses follows at a distance.

Júlía is comforted to know this. The Italian Governess turns to the president. "Rome welcomes you, Mr. President."

Devereaux nods in acknowledgement, his expression cheerful. "Well, if anyone is ever going to shoot me, this would be the day to do it," shouts the President with a laugh.

"Touch wood when you say that," says Júlía, but there is no wood to knock on; yet she smiles to President Devereaux.

The entourage drives north up Via Timavo to a long boulevard that winds along the Tiber all the way to the Vatican.

On the fourth floor of the building next to the University on Via della Conciliazione, Benedetto Benso has set himself up. The view from the apartment over the boulevard could not be better; the weather is bright and still. There is no danger of a gust of wind changing the bullet's direction, anyway there's no danger of that since the target is really so close – within 150 meters. Benso is confident that everything will go according to plan, since he trusts Buscetti to take care of the situation that has come up. He had undeniably been surprised last night, but calmed down after receiving the information about the men. "One a middle-aged geezer who threw rotten fish in Brussels; the other an overweight saga professor," he mutters with a smile. The change of plan simplifies things. He is in agreement with Buscetti that the Icelanders' presence in Rome may be a blessing in disguise. He has slept in the apartment and everything is ready. He has carefully packed away everything he brought with him, and has made sure that he kept on his gloves, skull cap and all-in-one black latex suit. He is not going to leave behind any DNA evidence.

Benso is in good humour although he has found the delay caused by the President's speech a bit annoying. It means waiting an extra half-hour. He has put the time to good use. He has gone over the escape plan for the last time with his accomplices. He nods to his two comrades on the roofs, waiting there to protect him. Benso looks at the clock.

Everything is ready.

The Sicilian stands on the banks of the swimming pool at his luxury villa in Sicily. He is dressed like a simple Sicilian farmer with a flat cap on his head. That is how he feels most comfortable. He steps forward onto the veranda and looks out over his town: Syracuse, which the Greeks founded 2,700 years ago. The Apostle Paul stopped there briefly on his way to Rome. Cicero called Syracuse the most beautiful of all Greek cities.

The view to the harbour is magnificent; the ancient houses smell of history, although Syracuse has seen better days; everything in life is transitory. In Rome the moment of truth draws near. The Scandinavians have been taken care of. Everything has gone as planned.

Guiseppe Russo walks out onto the veranda and finds Buscetti to be on edge. "Salvatore, is everything alright?" asks Russo.

The Sicilian nods and smiles. "Yes, everything is wonderful, and now the biggest moment of my life draws near," he says, looking seriously at Russo. "And yours as well, come to think of it."

"That I doubt," replies Russo, who needs to go shopping with his wife in the afternoon.

"The President of Europe is on his way into Rome. Shortly he will receive a Sicilian greeting," says Buscetti. He knows that he can rely on Russo's silence. It is a golden rule in the mafia that people know no more than necessary, but now Guiseppe needs to know. "The European underworld will be lying at our feet by dusk. No one will be able to touch us. You have to skip today's shopping," says Buscetti.

He then picks up the holph and says extremely calmly: "But there is a trifle that I need to attend to, dear friend."

Russo looks at his friend, who does not need his words clarified further. He steps aside. The Sicilian projects a full-size image of an athletic looking man wearing the black uniform of a special forces officer. He is standing on a roof overlooking the Via della Conciliazione in Rome.

"Greeting, Paolo," says Buscetti. "What news do you have of our two intruders?"

The man dressed as an officer looks down along the boulevard, then turns back to Buscetti. "No news is good news. They obviously don't know what they're looking for. The heavy-set man is ambling back and forth by Castel Sant'Angelo. The giant has been walking up and down Via della Conciliazione. I don't think they pose any threat, since they're obviously greenhorns."

"That's good, excellent. Sheer brilliance to get scapegoats like that, out of the blue." Buscetti is in joyous mood.

"I have a few shots of him," says the officer. Buscetti is somewhat startled when the image of Krummi appears on the veranda. He hadn't realized the man's size. Krummi is walking inquisitively down the street, but from his posture it's clear that he is ambling aimlessly; he even appears to joke with a singing busker and throws some money to him.

"You know the task. However, if the giant poses any threat you end the situation, but without any commotion or noise on the street. That could put everything at risk having some dolt walking back and forth sniffing the air," says Buscetti, hanging up. He feels the tension in his body. The uncertainty is devilish, but the Icelanders are like gifts from Heaven. He laughs.

Gifts from Heaven! Trust the Vulture to be able to turn a problem into an opportunity. And now they would not even need to kill the Icelandic woman. Buscetti has had to deal with many strange people over the years. He tries not to allow personal feelings to enter into business. But he has never liked the Vulture, nor for that matter, trusted him. But what a brain!

Krummi is slightly frustrated, although to a certain extent his mind is easy. He hasn't noticed anything unusual. A huge number of people are walking along the avenue, but the majority will be down at Castel Sant'Angelo when the President arrives, as well as on St. Peter's Square. People will walk from the castle to St. Peter's Basilica. He has scrutinized the windows but noticed nothing. Maybe he and his colleague have lost their perspective in their worry and speculations.

Paśićevic is in his office in Berlin, standing over a map of Rome. The local police have suggested that the entourage abandon going up Via della Conciliazione to the Vatican. Paśićevic is surprised at this suggestion but doesn't show it.

"We simply don't have enough security on Via della Conciliazione, not for that large a crowd," says the holo-image of the Italian police commander. "No one expected this presidential mania that seems to have gripped everyone. There is a real possibility that the crowd could rush the parade in their enthusiasm, and I don't have enough men on the ground to stop them. It would be better if the cars should drive up Via Crescenzio and then entered the Vatican by way of Viale Vaticano. It is a longer way round, but less crowded and so easier to guard."

Paśićevic leans over the map and examines the route. "We'll let down the people who have turned out to see the visit, and the President," he says carefully. He might have overall charge of security, but the local police have the authority to change details if they feel the situation warrants it.

"We've got to make sure that security comes first," replies the Italian officer. "They can still have their walkabout in St Peter's Square. It is only Via della Conciliazione that is the problem."

"You're absolutely right. We've already avoided going down Via Castello because it is too narrow. I suggest that we go up under Crescenzio, down Via Adriana and Piazza Pia, where they'll turn onto Via della Conciliazione," says Paśićevic, leaning back over the map. "We can increase surveillance of the street with drones, and you'll have time to herd the people into the middle lane to make them easier to control."

The Italian looks at Paśićevic, but then looks away. It is a big decision to contradict the head of European security. He straightens his back and speaks, choosing his words carefully to shift responsibility for the decision to his superior. "We don't want to disappoint our beloved President. The black limo will go down Piazza Pia and up Via della Conciliazione. We'll make the best of a difficult situation. If that is what you want."

The black limousine stops at Adriana Square, where President Erich Devereaux stands up, waves to the crowd, and steps out of the vehicle. The original plan had been to drive up the long boulevard named after Castel Sant'Angelo and park at the castle, but this idea has been abandoned due to the size of the crowd. The Governesses follow the President. They need to walk some distance to reach the old fortified wall of the castle on the right bank. The crowd stretches as far as the eye can see. Angel Bridge over the Tiber is packed with people, making it impossible for the President to walk out onto the bridge for the planned photo opportunity. The media speak of "Devereaux mania," such is the President's popularity. Devereaux looks over the sea of humanity and waves to the people; behind him stand Júlía and de'Medici.

The reception is magnificent.

Helgi watches from a distance and cannot help but feel proud of Júlía's deportment. She is truly a splendid representative.

The President delivers a short address.

Devereaux encourages the citizens of Europe to stand united for justice; not just justice in words, but rather for every living individual; from the smallest to the largest. "From here in Rome the journey was begun, in the middle of the last century, carrying the vision of Europe. The European fathers dreamed of peace on the continent, lasting peace. For the most part, peace has prevailed in Europe for over a century. With a president elected by the people for the people, a large step has been taken toward strengthening the foundations of democracy. We've abandoned the elite's Demcowill. We need to strengthen the European Parliament and we need to ensure justice for all; freedom for all. From the smallest to the largest. The smallest, on the border of two continents, has been seized with malaise in the European State, as in the Middle Ages under Danish control. Iceland does not fly as high as it once did. We intend to give the Icelandic eagle freedom; release it from its cage in the sincere hope that the nation will take flight once more. This we shall do with the symbolic signing at St. Peter's Square," says the President, signalling Júlía to step forward.

They wave to the crowd, which waves the European and Icelandic flags. Júlía is delighted to see Icelandic flags waving in the sun among the golden European stars, which will soon be reduced in number by one.

55

Krummi stands at the edge of St. Peter's Square. He has walked up Via della Conciliazione and now faces the grand facade of St Peter's. People rapidly fill the boulevard behind him, the ceremony obviously having concluded. The President is behind schedule. Krummi takes out his holph and sees that Helgi has been trying to reach him.

Something is going on, he thinks.

Helgi sounds disconcerted. "Something is wrong," he shouts over the noise of the crowd. "The President's convoy has set out from Castel Sant'Angelo, but the President's bodyguards have been called off their positions on the limousine. I saw a man go up to them and order them off somewhere else. There were angry words and two bodyguards threw up their hands in exasperation. The President's limousine then turned up Adriana Street. I don't think either the President or Júlia notice that there are no bodyguards on the car, as is customary."

"What do you think this means?" Krummi exclaims.

"This is exactly what happened in Dallas when Kennedy was shot back in 1963. The bodyguards were ordered off the car, they objected furiously, but didn't suspect any imminent threat. They weren't able to protect the President; didn't reach him until it was too late. If the guards had been on the president's car that fateful day in Dallas, they would have had time to shield the President. It was the third shot that killed the President," shouts Helgi. "The Kennedy murder was a conspiracy at the highest levels."

Krummi understands fully, what has happened is happening. "And the conspirators were in Dallas before the assassination, only to be caught in the Watergate scandal nine years later. The mosaic is taking shape. I bet that the poisonous trio is at work here in Rome," he says grimly, hanging up.

Krummi looks over the sea of humanity down along Via della Conciliazione. He manages to push his way through the crowd toward the intersection at Pia Street. It goes slowly, too slowly, so he runs into a narrow alley out on Borgo San Spirito, which lies parallel to Via della Conciliazione. "Where... where... where can they be planning to take action — think, think," he mutters in despair. He runs as fast as he can up San Pio toward the spot on Via della Conciliazione where he and Helgi had seen the three men.

Krummi stops abruptly.

Before him is the apartment building next to the University. The three men were probably coming out of that building. Was Kessler surveying the situation with the cashmere guy? Would they try to shoot the President from one of those windows? Krummi leans against a street light. "I'm too old for this sort of thing," he moans.

Krummi looks up at the building and sees a man looking out an open window, but there are others in the windows. Most windows are filled with sightseers. He curses, but if his suspicions are correct then the shooter may be in the building — in one of the windows.

He spies a black-uniformed special forces officer with a rifle at the entrance to the building on San Pio, goes over to him in the doorway and points at the building on the other side of the street. "I think they're going to shoot the President. There's a conspiracy to shoot the President," he shouts, but the black-clad guard shoves him away. Krummi doesn't hesitate, but strikes the guard with a thunderous blow, the officer falls to the ground.

"Sorry, but it's in the service of the President," mutters Krummi.

He pulls the man into a small closet in the corridor. Krummi takes the man's rifle, slings it over his shoulder, and turns. He needs to get up to the building's upper storeys to have view of the windows in the opposite building.

Another black-uniformed special forces guard appears in the foyer as Krummi prepares to lock the door. Krummi recognizes him immediately from earlier that morning. He has a bad feeling. The man had too often been peculiarly close to him on Via della

Conciliazione. He curses under his breath. With just a touch of professionalism he would have known. What an idiot I can be, he thinks.

"So you were my babysitter this morning," says Krummi with a grin.

The black-clad man smiles and nods, knowing that the giant knows. He does not hesitate, but draws his gun. Krummi still has the rifle over his shoulder, if only he could get it into action.

"The game is over. You're not getting in anyone's way again," says the officer, aiming his gun.

"It ain't over till fat lady sings," replies Krummi with a grin, throwing himself toward the open door of the closet. He hears a muted shot and feels a heavy blow on his left shoulder; feels a stabbing pain below his collarbone, touches it and looks at his bloodied hand. He is lying on the unconscious guard. Krummi scowls as he hears the armed guard draw near.

"You stop with all your nonsense, and I'll call an ambulance," says the guard confidently, fully aware that his bullet has hit the giant.

Krummi staggers to his feet; footsteps come from outside the door so he kicks at it with all his might. There is a heavy thud. Krummi shoves his way into the corridor. The man lies stunned, but fumbles for his gun on the floor not far from him. Krummi jumps on the man and punches him hard in the face. The black-clad man rolls with the blow and responds with one of his own. The Westmann Giant is thrown back, but grins in spite of the pain. The guard reaches for the gun, manages to grab it but as he does so, Krummi throws himself on to him. They wrestle for the weapon. The cutting pain is killing Krummi. He feels his strength dwindle but fights with everything he's got. He roars as he takes a heavy blow on his wounded shoulder, another in the stomach and a thunderous blow on the jaw.

The guard is no weakling.

Krummi is bigger and more powerful, but the gunshot wound has deprived him of strength. Slowly but steadily the officer turns the gun toward Krummi. Sweat drips from them; Krummi's shirt is bloody. His strength is failing him. Then Krummi the Raven croaks with all his life and soul like in Peace Harbour of old. He manages to roll himself over the guard and push the gun away. They look each other in the eye. Slowly but surely the gun is turned to aim at the man's neck. Krummi witnesses the terror in his eyes. A muffled shot sounds, followed by a moan. The man looks in surprise in Krummi's eyes; a sheepish smile comes over his face, but then his strength is suddenly exhausted.

Krummi stares into his glazed eyes.

"Now the fat lady has sung," he mutters.

Sweat beads on his forehead and he feels dizzy, but he pulls himself together. He picks up the rifle and pistol, shoves the body into the closet and shuts the door. He tries to reach Júlía on the holph, but without success. He starts selecting Helgi's number with bloody fingers, but its easier said that done since his hand trembles feverishly.

The President and his entourage have vanished, without Helgi being able to do anything about it. He pushes his way through the crowd west of Via da Castello toward the intersection of Via della Conciliazione and Piazza Pia. He is going to attempt to get Júlía's attention. It is slow going for Helgi, but he has no other option. "If only I were in better shape," he moans. Going like this, he'll never make it in time. Along the river lie bike paths; few people are on them. He pushes his way to the stairs down to Angel Bridge, rushes down the stairs and runs to the intersection.

Finally he is getting somewhere.

Sweat drips off him and he is soon out of breath. Still, Helgi is determined to reach the President's car and warn of impending danger before the entourage turns up Via della Conciliazione. He has to attract Júlía's attention and get her to stop the car. He has come just south of the intersection; jumps up on a brick wall and sees the limo approaching the intersection. He is going to reach Júlía in time. He feels relieved, and jumps down from the wall waving both hands.

Then he feels a sharp pain in his neck, a sudden dizziness, the earth starts to spin — everything turns black as he falls to the ground.

"He's probably drunk," shouts a full-grown woman as she bends over Helgi lying on the street. A choked ringing sound can be heard under Helgi's lifeless body.

"Don't come near him," says her husband and pulls her away.

Nearby a man in a black suit tosses a needle into a rubbish bin and walks away.

Benso still hasn't pointed his rifle out the window. There is plenty of time. He will do so when the President's limousine has come a good way up Via della Conciliazione past the building, so that their backs are visible. Then the President will be in the perfect position as a target, the crowd looking in the other direction. He's quite happy only to have to deal with the President, since events are taking care of the Governess. He feels tense and impatient, as the President is behind schedule. Benso pushes the sleeve of his jacket up and looks at his watch. A smile crosses his face when the black limousine appears and turns up the boulevard. It will be some time until it passes the building. He pulls the rifle from a black box.

Benso screws the barrel to the stock.

Krummi staggers up the stairs to the fifth storey of the building on the north side. All of the doors on this storey are shut. He rings the bell of an apartment in mid-corridor. No one responds, so he throws himself at the door, shouting in pain as he does so. The door cracks loudly but holds nonetheless. The pain is killing him, yet he throws himself once more at the door, which this time gives way, though it hangs by a chain. For a third time the giant slams against the door, which flies open. He runs to the sitting-room window and opens it a crack. The President's car is on the way up Via della Conciliazione, approximately two hundred meters down the street.

The President is coming in range.

Krummi has trouble breathing; sweat beads on his face. He draws his hand across his forehead but it only makes bad worse, mixing blood with his sweat and making it more difficult for him to see. He grabs a cloth lying on the sofa, wipes his bloody, sweat-drenched forehead.

"Calm down, be calm," he mutters as he kneels next to the windowsill.

Krummi takes the safety catch off the rifle.

★ 56 ★

Júlia wonders why she still hasn't seen Krummi or Helgi. They had promised to be here somewhere. The crowd reaches as far as the eye can see, Helgi and Krummi must have merged with the crowd, she thinks. The President's visit has been one great victory. She is pleased with Devereaux's speech at Castel Sant'Angelo; to grant the eagle its freedom so that the nation may fly high yet again, is a great metaphor. The President smiles at her, then stands up in the black, polished limo and waves with both hands at the people.

"Sit down, you damned fool," mutters Benso. He wants the President to be sitting in the car. That way he is more certain of hitting his target. Yet he is pleased with one thing: because of the crowd, the President's car is moving more slowly than planned. There are no bodyguards on the limousine. Everything is as it should be. He strokes the rifle. The President's car is now just ahead of the building, and a bit off to the side. Soon the President will be straight ahead of him. Benso will not take his shooting position until the limousine has passed the building, fifty meters beyond it. Then everyone will be looking in the opposite direction — in the direction of the President's limo. At that point Benso will go to the window, take aim and fire.

"Bang," he says out loud; four minutes to go, he calculates.

Preparations have gone better than expected. No surprises, no unexpected knocks on the apartment door. Kessler has done his job well. He could not have chosen a better shooting position, a better apartment for the attempt. No one has missed the old couple. If someone had come knocking on the door, the paper on it said everything that needed to be said; flown to America. Brilliant, he thinks as he stands on alert and peers out. The car will soon be opposite the building. The bodyguards who are supposed to form the human shield for the President seem restless as they sit on the limousine following the President's black antique car.

Benso takes the safety catch off the rifle.

Krummi has scrutinized the upper storeys of the building on the opposite side of the street but has seen nothing out of the ordinary. People can be seen waving from some windows, but no one looks suspicious in any way. Yet he did see a man appear for a split second before disappearing again. A reflection from the University had blinded him for a second, there are so many distractions this sunny day. The limousine is now directly ahead; the President stands upright and waves to the people. Júlía and de'Medici smile in their seats and wave to the crowd. The European flag is prominent, but the good old Icelandic flag may be seen in many places.

"Can I have been mistaken; maybe there is no shooter?" Krummi is engaged in a heated debate with himself. He strikes himself on the forehead. "Calm down," he murmurs once more. He is plagued by doubt; is drenched with sweat and in bad condition. He feels weak, having lost blood. Krummi rubs his forehead again; the black limousine moves slowly past the building.

All eyes are on the President's car, but Krummi stares at the opposite buildings. The fearless Gunnar from Hlíðarendi, the protagonist of the medieval Njáls saga, comes to mind:

The valiant man of high renown
feared not his enemies' brutal threats...

Krummi grins, his white teeth flashing.

Benso counts down: ten, nine, eight, seven, six, five, four, three, two, one. "The time has come," he says out loud. He takes a step forward, leans out the window and starts aiming the rifle slowly but surely.

Krummi sees a black jacket and a cap appear in the window at the opposite highest floor. "So there's the shooter," he says coldly, aiming his weapon. He curses silently as a line of bloodied sweat runs down his face, breaking his concentration.

Krummi needs to wipe off the sweat once more. In the rifle's scope Krummi sees a young man draw a deep breath and take aim.

In the apartment Benso scowls again. "Hold still, damn it," he curses. The President is standing up straight yet again, waving to the crowd and then finally sits beside Júlía and leans toward her. "This is our day of victory. Our policies have triumphed. What victory for democracy!" the President shouts.

"The people of Europe have never greeted their own like this before; the only comparisons are President Kennedy and presidential candidate Obama in Berlin a long time a ago," Júlía calls back.

The European President fills the scope of Benso's rifle.

Krummi's flashing, hawk-like gaze comes to rest on the man aiming the rifle across the street. "It's you or me," he says out loud. A glare distracts him for a spilt second, so he stretches further toward the window to get a better aim.

Rifle shots echo across Via della Conciliazione.

The President grabs his chest and watches bewilderedly as his shirt turns red with blood. De'Medici jerks as if punched, she turns to look back. At first Júlía thinks that fireworks are going off, until Devereaux slumps toward her. Everything is unreal. Júlía's hand gets sullied with blood when she grabs the President; the crowd falls silent for a moment, flags are lowered.

Júlía draws the President close, but another rifle shot rings out. The President's head jerks back. Júlía's suit dress gets stained with blood; she cries out in despair. People start shouting, crying out. Complete chaos seizes the throng as people either throw themselves to the ground or run for cover in panic. Júlía starts climbing up onto the boot of the limo, the tyres squeal as the weighty vehicle tears off in haste up the street, scattering people. Júlía crawls further back over the trunk and grabs some grey material. Then she turns back to the critically wounded President. As she casts herself into her bloody seat, she catches a glimpse of a bodyguard come crawling over the car's boot.

She lays the President's head gently in her lap and wraps the material carefully in a handkerchief.

"They've shot the President!" she cries out in agony. "They've shot Erich!"

De'Medici's blue suit dress is drenched with blood. The Governess is in agony but is fully conscious. The air is filled with the wail of sirens; people wander around in horror and despair.

A Special Forces officer is suddenly startled by crash of a heavy object hitting the pavement just behind him on Via della Conciliazione. He turns to see a rifle, then stares up to see what he believes to be a reflection of a man in a window above. "There's the assassin... he's the shooter!" the officer shouts, pointing to the window. The window ledge seems to be covered with blood, people start pointing but the image vanishes. A number of police officers start rushing toward the building, the officer bends to pick up the rifle. People shake their fists toward the window, there is confusion and chaos everywhere.

In the apartment on the other side of the street, Benso hurriedly breaks down the rifle. Out of the corner of his eye he sees an array of black and white police cruisers with flashing blue lights crawl up the avenue, hampered in its progress by the throng. The black Presidential limousine is gathering speed up Via della Conciliazione. People shake fists on the other side of the street, a group of police officers march toward a building and disappear into it.

"I'd better be quick about it," he says out loud as he carefully arranges the rifle parts in the box and finally shuts it.

The Presidential limousine reaches St. Peter's Square, where the physicians of His Holiness receive the terribly wounded President, who is immediately brought to the Papal hospital room. Júlia goes to a doctor and places the bloody handkerchief gently in his hand.

The doctor flips open the handkerchief and stares in astonishment at the pieces of the President's brain.

Júlia, in shock and wrecked with grief, repeats constantly: "They've shot Erich, they've shot Erich."

Half an hour later a message comes from the Vatican: the President is dead.

The bright light pierces his eyes. Helgi is lying across a table, battered, with a killer headache and a stinging pain in his shoulder. He squints, looks up, sees hazy shadows. He rubs his eyes and finds himself staring at a man who reminds him most of murder: the long, scarred face, the gleaming, unkempt hair, narrow chin and sharp eyes give him a most unpleasant feeling. Helgi rubs his eyes and glances at his watch. It is four hours after he left Castel St Angelo. What has happened?

"Helgi Thorláksson," says the police officer, who can barely cope with pronouncing the man's name. "You are accused of being an accessory to the murder of the President of Europe. Erich Devereaux was pronounced dead from his wounds within half an hour after the shooting. We know everything about your relationship with the killer with whom you came to Rome."

Helgi is stunned. "Accessory to murder," he says in a weak voice. "The President shot, Krummi a killer." His voice fades. Helgi is numb and confused. This is like a long, terrible nightmare. He pinches himself so as to shake off his distress, but the disturbing feeling is overwhelming. The police officer sits opposite Helgi and looks sharply into the Icelander's eyes. With him in the cell is a man in black suit holding an e-notebook. Helgi is puzzled as he feels he's seen the man, or somebody who looks like him.

"Krummi hasn't shot anyone," says Helgi in a heavy, dusky voice. "We were trying to prevent the assassination. We saw men who were surely..."

The police officer interrupts Helgi gruffly. "No bullshit," he says angrily. "The evidence is there for all to see: the president's assassin killed a police officer. We've found the murder weapon. Where is his hide-out," he adds harshly.

Helgi realises that they haven't captured his friend. "There is no hide-out, Krummi is no killer," he emphasizes.

The man in the black suit leans in close to Helgi's face. "What is the Icelandic Governess' part in this? What is your connection to her?"

Helgi straightens his back; bewilderment and anger radiate from his face. "Júlía, where is Júlía?" he asks, completely at a loss.

"She is unharmed, the only one who wasn't injured in the attack. Lucky coincidence, right?" The man in black leans back and his face breaks into a cold smile. "We'll root out this terrorist group of yours. You can be sure of that. We'll capture the killer."

"You must believe me," says Helgi slowly but the mosaic image has started to arrange itself. The scenario is familiar. He and Krummi had seen the warning signs, had agreed on them, but walked straight into a trap: all that can happen, happens.

"We'll move him to the prison," the man in black says plainly. "We need to focus on gathering evidence."

"No one mourns an Icelander," Helgi says sadly.

Europe is in shock at the tragic events in Rome. "Conspiracy," declare the media, who report that an investigation is being undertaken on the connections of the Icelandic Governess to her countrymen, the assassins. Demands are made that the separation of the two states be halted; it is demanded that Iceland remain an inseparable part of the young European nation. "Now it is vital that Europe stands united," declare the chief media outlets in Europe.

In Berlin, Vice President Browne is hurriedly sworn into office as President. He is led to his office in Berlin where a group of senior civil servants are crowded into the room. Each of them holds a bundle of papers and tries to push forward to the new President Browne.

Suddenly the room goes quiet and still. A man in a black suit has entered the room, an e-notebook in his hand.

"May I be among the first to congratulate you on your assumption of office," says Slobodan Paśiĉevic, the head of the EIA, the European Intelligence Agency, though his face remains inscrutable. "I know you will be very busy over the coming days, but I am afraid that I have the duty of bringing the incoming President up to date on the investigation of the assassination in Rome and security threats to the Great European State."

"Of course, we need to clear this terrible mess in Rome" replies Browne and continues: "Then there is the war in Kazikistnam that needs to be looked into."

"Indeed, Herr President, there are always threats. It's good to hear that you are well prepared for the task ahead." Paśiĉevic glares round at the civil servants. "I need to discuss matters with you of the very highest security grade. We need to be alone."

There is a sudden rush as the civil servants hurry to leave the room, making excuses for their sudden absence.

"That is better," says Paśiĉevic as the door closes. "Now, the most urgent things are the murder investigation and the Iceland crisis. Our beloved President Deveraux has been foully murdered by Icelandic terrorists travelling as part of the entourage of the Governor of Iceland, the woman Ingólfsdóttir. We have evidence that she is involved in the assassination plot."

"Good God," gasps Browne.

"Shocking," agrees Paśiĉevic quietly. "I was aghast when I heard. But we have to move fast. The terrorists must not be allowed to win."

"No, no. Of course not," stutters Browne.

"Good." Paśiĉevic places a pile of files in front of President Browne. "You need to declare a temporary State of Emergency in Iceland. The third division of the European Army is alert and ready to move once you've given the order," he states firmly as he puts the files in front of the President.

President Browne looks at Paśiĉevic in surprise, but then nods. "Yes, of course." He scans the papers as he signs them one by one.

"I've just signed these Special European Arrest Warrants for the

Icelanders," continues Pašičevic in a serious tone. "We believe they are implicated in the outrage, my operatives will be able to round them all up. We are hunting down the assassin, they call him Krummi, the Raven; a violent man. We've already arrested a man in Rome, his involvement will come to light; evidence is compelling and we've found the murder weapon. The Governor will soon be arrested, I myself will attend to that. My men are already on their way to Iceland. You will notice that most of the conspirators are leading members of the Icelandic independence movement, plus the head of state security in Iceland and a journalist from *The Reykjavík Post.*"

Browne looks up. "We will have to stop this move to Icelandic independence at once," he declares.

"If you say so," replies Pašičevic. "Of course, the Secret Service does not get involved in politics. We at EIA are mere humble servants of the Great European State."

"A State that must be preserved intact," declares Browne. "We'll deal later with Kazikistnam." Pašičevic gathers up the arrest warrants and turns to go.

"By the way," says Browne, Pašičevic turns to face him. "Now that I am President there is one question that I have always wanted to ask you."

"What is the question, Herr President?" Pašičevic asks.

"What's this whisper of you being 'The Vulture'?" the President whispers in a low voice.

"Am I?" replies Pašičevic with a thin smile. "I did not know. Some private joke, I suppose. Was that all?" Browne nods.

Then Browne suddenly gets very startled and turns to look as if there is something behind him. "What was that?" he shouts despairingly but there is nothing to see.

Somewhere a door slams.

Pašičevic can't help but find the President's frightened expression bit comical. "I'm sorry Herr President, but I've got to be on the move to attend to urgent matters in Rome," he says cynically. There is a grin on Pašičevic's face as he prepares to leave. A weak man is always so much easier to control.

Júlía is in a hotel suite, glued to the news broadcast, following the day's events. A newswoman is in the basement of the headquarters of the European Intelligence Agency, Júlía projects her in quarter size. "We are expecting an announcement very soon," says the reporter. "There are all sorts of rumours here today. Certainly some big development, some news is expected to break. Wait." She talks to somebody out of shot. "I am told that the murderer's accomplice will soon be led out. He is to be moved to Rome's top security prison."

There is a knock on the door. Júlía is standing but is in no hurry whatsoever.

The knocking on the door continues, now more aggressively and impatiently. Júlía goes to the door, opens it and finds herself facing six men. She immediately recognizes Paśiĉevic, who steps forward with a document in his hand.

"Júlía Ingólfsdóttir, you are under arrest in connection with the murder of Erich Devereaux. You are suspected of participation in a conspiracy to murder the President of Europe," she hears a distant voice rattling off something. "You have the right to remain silent concerning the accusation. Everything that you say, may be used against you in court. You have the right to an attorney."

The men walk uninvited into the suite, driving Júlía ahead of them. Two close in on her. Handcuffs clank.

Everyone's attention is then directed to the corner, where the news reporter gives a sudden start and says in a slightly excited voice that something is expected to occur in the basement of the European Intelligence Agency. Paśiĉevic grabs the remote and switches the image to full-size.

All eyes are locked on the newswoman. "The police have been hard at it. We expect the conspirator to be moved from here to prison in the next few minutes. His involvement in the assassination is still a mystery," says the newswoman, brushing her hair from her cheek.

Two police officers escort Helgi, who is unsteady on his feet, out of the tunnel. He is evidently in bad shape, obviously blinded by the bright media spotlights. All of the world's main newsgroups are on the scene. They head toward a police vehicle.

Cries of "killer, scoundrel!" are heard.

The reporter's voice cuts in. "People are in a fiery mood, some are shaking their fists. Their anger and anguish are understandable, of course," says the newswoman before continuing. "However there is confusion and disarray concerning the President's assassination. There is such chaos. And now it is suspected that the conspiracy reaches the highest ranks in Reykjavík."

Suddenly a man steps determinedly out of the crowd in the direction of Helgi. There is a flash of steel. A shot rings out. Helgi feels a cutting pain, grabs his abdomen and looks bewilderedly into the expressionless face of a man with a gun in hand, wearing a wide-brimmed hat. Terror and desperation mark the scene; shouts, cries, and the continuous flashing of cameras.

"All lies, all of it lies. These are dark times. God bless Iceland..." Helgi is heard to say as he falls to the grey pavement.

Júlía cries out in confusion and despair, runs to Helgi as he lies there on the floor. She drops to her knees as to embrace her friend, but grabs only the illusion of holo-tv. Júlía feels herself engulfed in darkness.

Paśiĉevic turns off the holo-tv, but then like a shot turns to see if there is something behind him. "What was that!" he shouts.

Somewhere a door slams.

Authors of poems or part of poems referred to:

Page 4: Númi Thorbergsson. Originally, the cod was none to fond of the British.

Page 14: Jón Sigurðsson.

Page 15: An old folk ditty from Westmann Islands.

Page 18: Tómas Guðmundsson.

Page 48: Brihadaranyaka Upanishad IV.4.5.

Page 55: Steingrímur Thorsteinsson.

Page 55: Matthías Johannessen.

Page 57: Thórarinn Eldjárn.

Page 57: Tómas Guðmundsson.

Page 61: Steinn Steinarr.

Page 62: Aldous Huxley.

Page 65: Hallur Hallsson.

Page 36: Matthías Jochumsson.

Page 75-76: Völuspá, Eddic poems.

Page 80: Jóhann Gunnar Sigurðsson. Originally, it was Danish-sound instead of Euro-sound.

Page 83: A 19th century ditty about Danish soldiers in Reykjavik.

Page 115: Gylfi Ægisson.

Page 122: Númi Thorbergsson. Composed during the Cod Wars with Britain. Originally it were British warships that were firm in their might, and the small Icelandic gunboats gave them a fright.

Page 130: Einar Benediktsson.

About Bretwalda Books

Bretwalda Books is an exciting new publishing company devoted to exploring the lesser known areas of British and European history. We aim to produce books targetted at the general market embracing popular writing styles and attractive design formats while upholding the highest standards of accuracy and reliability. Our books will deal with unusual topics in an open and engaging manner.

All our books are available as ebooks on Kindle, Kobo, Apple and other major ebook shops.

Why Bretwalda?

The term "Bretwalda" is one of the more mysterious titles in Dark Age British History. It has been translated in various ways and although entire nations were plunged into war and thousands of men were killed fighting for the right to use the title, nobody is entirely certain what it meant. We thought it summed up our mission to uncover the little known nooks and crannies of history. In fact, that gives us an idea for a book ...

Finding Bretwalda

Bretwalda has a constantly growing range of innovative books.

We have a website on
www.BretwaldaBooks.com

We have a blog on
http://bretwaldabooks.blogspot.com/

We have a Facebook Page as
Bretwalda Books

We have a Twitter account as
@Bretwaldabooks

You can email us on
info@bretwaldabooks.com

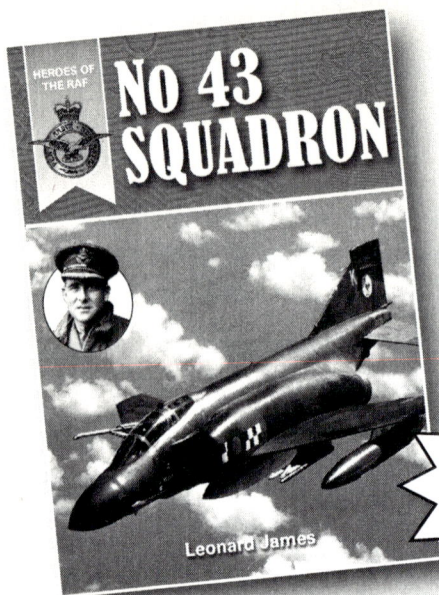

No 43 Squadron:

By

Leonard James

64 pages

£6.99

Known as the Fighting Cocks from its squadron badge, No.43 Squadron has always been one of the premier fighter squadrons in the RAF. It was formed in 1916 and went out to fly in the war torn skies over the Western Front. Returning to war in 1939, No.43 Squadron fought throughout the Battle of Britain once taking on 80 German aircraft unaided. The squadron again saw action in the 1990s over Iraq and Bosnia, then returned to Iraq for the Gulf War of 2003.

About the Author

LEONARD JAMES is the son of an RAF veteran who fought in the Battle of Britain until wounded. Leonard grew up in a household dominated the RAF, and later married the daughter of an RAF squadron leader.

Bretwalda Books Ltd

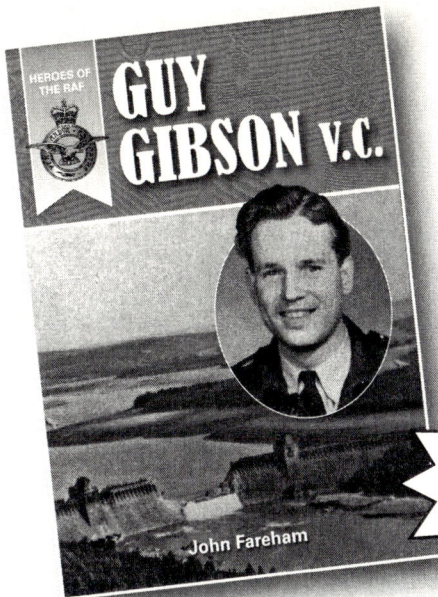

Guy Gibson VC:

By
John Fareham

128 pages

£8.99

Thrilling biography of the man who led the Dambusters Raid. Having joined the RAF in 1936, Gibson was a bomber pilot when war broke out. He won a DFC in July 1940 then volunteered for Fighter Command and flew nightfighters on 99 sorites before returning to Bomber Command to fly 46 more missions before the Dambusters Raid. This book looks at the life and career of the man who led the most famous bombing raid of World War II. It is a gripping account of his life and exploits, revealing new and little known facts about Guy Gibson for the first time.

About the Author

JOHN FAREHAM is the son of an RAF veteran who grew up on RAF bases around the world. He now lives only a short drive from RAF Scampton from which Gibson flew his famous Dambuster Raid.

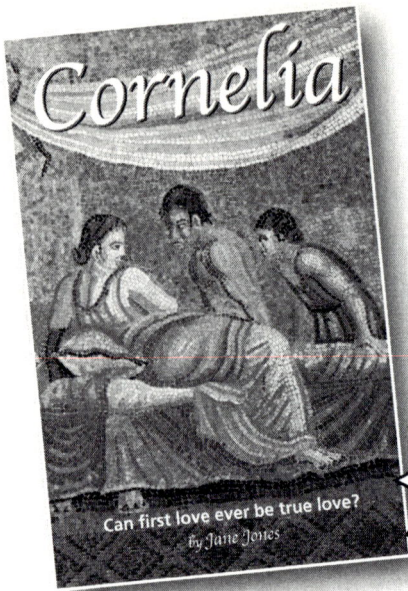

Can first love ever be true love?
by Jane Jones

Cornelia:

By
Jane Jones

152 pages

£6.99

Can First Love ever be True Love? Born the daughter of a wealthy farmer in Roman Britain, Cornelia has everything that a girl could want. But on her 16th birthday, Cornelia learns that her parents have arranged for her to marry the son of a local landowner. And when handsome army officer Marcus appears in her life, Cornelia finds her world turned upside down.

The book has been carefully researched to provide an accurate and convincing portrayal of Britain as it was in the mid-2nd century when the Roman Empire was at its most powerful, prosperous and secure.

About the Author

JANE JONES lives in a rural village in Surrey, near to where the novel opens - but some 1800 years later.

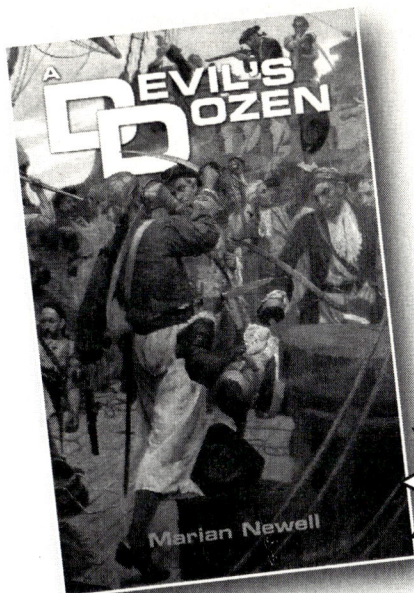

A Devil's Dozen:

By
Marian Newell

504 pages

£12.99

Violence, love, loyalty and betrayal among the smugglers who terrorise the coasts of southern England. For years the Aldington Blues and the Burmarsh Gang have fought each other over the lucrative smuggling trade in Kent. But the spectre of the gallows hangs over them all when a popular naval officer is killed by a smuggler. As the government men close in, the gangs join forces. But will it be enough to stave off defeat, capture and death? Meticulously researched, "A Devil's Dozen" recreates the vanished world of the smugglers who were once the kings of the British underworld.

About the Author
MARIAN NEWELL has lived all her life in the land where the smugglers once held sway. She grew up hearing the tales of those days and now has written them up in fictionalised form as her first published book.

Bretwalda Books Ltd

Bretwalda Books Ltd